To: Melanie
With Love

Play On

NED HOPKINS

Play On is Ned's debut novel.

Ned was born in Edinburgh but has spent much of his life in London. He worked in the BBC's News Information department before going on to train as a teacher specialising in Dramatic Art. For many years he divided his time between administering vocational qualifications for a national awarding body and working with non-commercial theatre companies in the London area.

He now concentrates on playwriting and, as Raymond Langford Jones, also contributes reviews and occasional articles to **Sardines** theatre magazine.

Ned's numerous works for the theatre include: *Darling Hypocrite*, the musical *Cliché*, an adaptation of Henry James's *The Portrait of a Lady*, the award-winning *Earnest Endeavours* and *A Lot of it About* for Organised Chaos (in 2013) at the Lowry Studio, Salford.

With its quick and witty script, A Lot of it About is a thoughtful piece of theatre.
(Whatsonstage)

<u>www.nedhopkins.com</u>

Play On

NED HOPKINS

GARDENCOURT PLAYS

First published November 2018

Cover design, typesetting and layout by Patrick Armstrong
Cover painting Sheltie in the Gardens by John Oakenfull

Gardencourt Plays
15 Rutland Gate
Bromley, Kent BR2 0TG
0208 290 0266

For

John,
Alex, Malcolm, Jonathan and David K.
And in special memory of
Peter and Cecil

'You have learnt something.
That always feels at first as if you have lost something.'
George Bernard Shaw, *Major Barbara*

Characters

The Italians
Dino Manzoni – *a shoe designer*
Stefania – *his girlfriend*
Marcello – *his friend (in Milan)*
Paolo – *his friend (in Scotland)*

The Scots
Maggy's Family and Relations
Maggy Galbraith – *née Wallis*
Don – *her husband*
Archie – *Don's father*
Doris – *his mother*
Grace – *their daughter*
Ewan – *their son*

Lachlan Wallis – *Maggy's father*
Bessie – *her mother*
Hugh – *her elder brother*
Lorna – *Hugh's daughter*
Fraser – *Maggy's younger brother*

Duncan – *Grace's husband*
Lyndsay and Kara – *Grace and Duncan's twin daughters*
Fiona – *Don's cousin*
Josh – *Fiona's husband*

Friends and Associates
Ally McKenzie – *an aspiring children's novelist*
Jean – *her mother*
Phil – *her father*
Jo – *her friend*

Paige – *Ewan's partner*
Jamie – *Ewan's friend*
Gus – *Ewan's college friend*
Jan – *Gus's wife*

Senga Robertson – *manager of the Balfour café-bar*
Cal – *her husband*
Nora – *her mother*
Aileen – *Cal's mother*

Drummond Braithwaite ('Banger') – *a BBC employee, Maggy's friend*
Casey Melville – *a counsellor*

Cameo roles
Una – *Maggy's friend*
Vicky – *Grace's friend*
Jennie McPherson – *Don's secretary*
Sam – *Duncan's boss*
Katie – *a student*
Gerda – a young Swedish woman

Prologue

⚘ ⚘

HIS car stalled.

Dino angrily slapped his hand on the wheel before coaxing the engine back to life. It was starting to purr again when, through the rear mirror, he could see the lights far ahead turning red.

He knew these lights. They let traffic from the junctions ahead take priority. Added to which it was rush hour in Zone 9. Never a good plan to travel around Milan any work evening, especially not a Friday.

He could be stuck for ages.

'Mannaggia!'

He looked at his watch. He was due to meet Stefania in the Via Ugo Bassi at eight. They were trying out a new restaurant. It was her birthday. He couldn't afford to be late and risk her fiery looks and sullenness. Not tonight of all nights.

The vehicles in front hadn't moved for several minutes. The driver closest to him seemed to have both his hands on a map and must have switched off his engine. Dino did likewise, sat back and looked around.

Between the gaps in the cars to his left he could see a newly redeveloped terrace of smallish shops with small apartments above. A large sign in red, white and black informed the world:

AFFITTASI
Spazi
per piccole imprese
(To Let - Spaces for Small Businesses)

There was also a telephone number.

Would it be large enough, Dino wondered? He was looking for a front office-cum-showroom with a separate workshop area behind.

He looked again at his watch. Barring further delays, he'd reach the restaurant by seven forty-five but would then need somewhere to park. That could prolong things. There was no time to manoeuvre the car into the side lane and stop off to investigate tonight.

Leaning across to the glove compartment, Dino drew out the pad and pencil he always kept handy and scribbled down the telephone number.

At that moment, the car ahead sprang into action.

Dino turned the ignition key.

The evening was a success. The staff at the restaurant rose to the occasion and made a fuss of Stefania who looked magnificent in her black dress with the shoes he had designed and made for her – discreetly decorated with black 'lace' and tiny gold spangles. They were much admired by a smart middle-aged woman at the adjacent table, which flattered both but reminded Dino of the urgency to set up his own business.

If only he could find the right place his work might really take off. No more kow-towing to other people's demands.

The next morning, Dino rang the number.

'Afraid there's only the one left,' the man said. 'Several people are very interested. You need to hurry. By tomorrow it will have gone.'

The roads were quieter on the Saturday morning. Dino met the man at ten. The property was perfect. A small front area with a considerably larger space at the back incorporating a tiny kitchenette, shower and toilet. Ideal for a hairdresser, podiatrist – even a fledgling shoe designer.

The flatlet on the floor above that went with the property clinched it.

There was just one small problem.

Dino was heir to Milan's renowned Piedi Bei dynasty, but his parents had always believed the next generation should make its own way in the world.

The company's on-going wealth owed a lot to in-bred parsimony. That was partly why the firm continued to be successful. Also, Dino's father and uncles, now in their sixties and early seventies, showed no signs of slowing down and releasing the reins to Dino's care – or anyone else's for that matter. Piedi Bei was their life. They intended to cling to it until they were carried out of their factory, in boxes, themselves. The shadow of Berlusconi stretched a long way. They had good reason to protect their assets.

After seeing Dino through college, partially paid for by part-time work in the family factory, Dino had been set loose, virtually empty-handed, to develop his product knowledge and commercial skills in Milan's smarter shops. He honed his creative talent in his spare time.

Dino accepted his father's lack of confidence in the country's economy but reasoned there was always a market for fine shoes in bad times as well as good – and wanted the chance to design and make them. Now twenty-eight, Dino was more than capable of running a business of his own – or so he believed. He had some savings behind him, but insufficient to capitalise his dream. Not only did he need a place to work, he required specialised materials and equipment and, sooner or later, at least one assistant.

Where would he get the rest of the money? His father had been adamant. He would only help him once he'd proved himself.

Renting property in the industrial North involved a hefty initial outlay. The agent's costs would work out at about ten percent of the annual rent, not to mention the deposit, another three months' rent and the registration fee – which was two to three percent of the yearly charge. Dino would be obliged to sign up for a minimum period of at least a year. However popular his shoes became, until he could afford to expand, it would be years before he moved into profit and finished paying off any loan.

One step at a time. Where could he find the money in the first place?

There must be a way.

The letting agent watched impatiently as Dino mulled over his predicament.

It was useless.

Or was it?

What had Marcello said about these guys he knew who might be able to help him out if ever he saw somewhere he liked?

The man squared up to him. 'I don't want to rush you,' he said, 'but I've an osteopath lined up who's interested in the place and could put a down payment on it…'

'When?

'Monday morning.'

A ruse of course. Even so, it worked. Dino had really taken to the property. It was in a decent area and convenient both for home and the city with a main road parallel. An arresting sign above the door would draw customers who'd be able to park on the side road in front of the building.

It was now or never.

'I really want it,' he said, 'but need to check something. I'll get back to you later.'

The man gave him a cynical smile. He'd heard that one before.

In the car, Dino took out his phone.

'Marcello?'
'Dino?'
'I... I need your help.'
'Glad you rang.'
They were unaware someone was listening in.

ONE
Strange Anniversary

❧ ❦

DRING-dring… dring-dring…
The cat darted beneath the card table. Arranging a vase of tulips by the bureau, Maggy froze.

Since that terrible call a year ago, the landline's ring had acquired an insistent, rasping edge. Not today, please God, of all days, Maggy thought.

How could they have forgotten?

A year to the hour.

She could see Don shaving, the door of the en-suite open, as she slipped into a T-shirt and jeans. Between mouthfuls of muesli, he'd been sounding off about the forthcoming Scottish Referendum and the unrepeatable things he'd tell Alex Salmond if they met. Grabbing his coat, he'd then roared off to work in the Audi.

She'd been thinking how healthy and energised he looked.

Two hours later, the phone rang. Don had slumped across the boardroom table in the middle of a debate on high voltage trigger transformers. By the time the ambulance had negotiated Edinburgh's wearisome traffic system, it was all over.

To begin with, Maggy couldn't absorb the implications. It was as if he'd gone away on business. Then, the men in dark suits had appeared. Her stage training helped her 'sail through' the funeral – or so everyone told her later – but then, as the stream of condolence messages dried up, she struggled to get through the bleak weeks of paperwork.

Even now, after all these months, something within her was still set to Off.

Dring-dring… dring-dring…

The queasy feeling in Maggy's stomach ratcheted up a notch. It had become a malign companion, waking her up each morning along with the radio alarm and *Today*; bullying her on and off until the closing strains of *Newsnight* and a settling mug of camomile tea. Certain things triggered it: a snatch of Stevie Wonder, a whiff of Don's Sandalwood cologne still clinging to the bathroom cupboard – and a moment ago, she'd chanced to glance at the small Fergusson

watercolour, a present from colleagues at his 60th birthday party at
The Balmoral.

Dring-dring… dring-dring…

'Damn!' Maggy stuck the parrot tulip – ragged like her nerves –
into the vase, dashed out of the living room and caught the handset
a moment before the voicemail kicked in.

'Hello?'

'It's me.'

Maggy relaxed slightly. 'Lorna, dear.'

'I'm just ringing to say…'

Maggy cut her niece short. 'Well, at least *you* remembered.'

Lorna sensed all was not well. 'I'm sorry if I rang at…'

'I'm just a wee bitty down this morning.'

It was one of Lorna's failings to go on the defensive at such
moments rather than moving swiftly on. 'Och, it's not always about
you, Maggy. He was my favourite uncle, too.'

'It came through on the phone in the hall.'

'You prefer the dulcet sounds of I Shot the Sheriff on your mobile,
I know. But mine's charging.'

'Actually, it's Hey Jude. Ewan's promised to change it back to
something cheerier.'

'I can do that for you,' Lorna said.

'But isn't that what sons are for – to provide technical support?
Besides, he's the only person who shares my retro tastes.'

'You elderly technophobes. I despair!'

'Elderly, moi? But there was now a chuckle in Maggy's voice.

'You should really consider a phone with Wi-fi,' Lorna said.

'Isn't that a dietary supplement?'

Laughter warmed things up.

'Honestly Maggy, I don't know how I ever managed without
mine.'

'I'm content with my wee wind-up, thanks.'

'I've some leave in lieu this afternoon. I hoped, maybe, you'd be
free for a wee cuppa. Say three thirty?' Lorna said.

A shorter pause, then 'That would be lovely,' Maggy said.

'Forgiven?'

'Seeing it's you.'

'And I've just finished the new Sarah Waters. Thought you might
like to think about it for your book group.'

'Ah.'

'Meet at The Rendezvous?'

'Would you not mind awfully coming here?' Maggy said. 'I don't think I could face…' She was about to list several well-meaning acquaintances, one of whom was bound to be in the café. She loathed the continued ordeal of their patronising tones and *how are things with you, Maggy dear* pleasantries. 'Sorry, I'm being such a wuss.'

'You? Never!'

'It'd be nice to have you entirely to myself.'

'I did a bake last night,' Lorna said. 'I'll bring some flapjacks.'

'That settles it!'

'Why did I think it might?'

'See you later.'

'Bye.'

Giving her tulips a final tweak, Maggy went in search of Garibaldi. Feeling foolish for over-reacting, the tabby was now washing his face on the hearthrug. Cats hate being wrong-footed. Or should that be wrong-pawed Maggy wondered, giving him a reassuring stroke? If she'd been tetchy with Lorna, she could at least be kind to her pet, who'd also remained steadfast.

Why am I being so moody? she scolded herself. I never used to be. Of course, she knew the answer to that. Also, that it was an answer, not an excuse.

Garibaldi paused in mid-lick, following Maggy with his eyes as she moved across the lounge to the bay window, resting at the spot where they'd decided to buy the house all those years ago.

Maggy's gift for vividly recalling past events wasn't always appreciated by others, especially when she thoughtlessly reminded them of things they'd conveniently edited from their personal files. The most unlikely prompt could conjure scenes from her past. She embraced everything that had happened; each thread in the tapestry of her life. Sometimes oddly coloured yarns had found their way into it.

Also, loose ends.

A couple of hours earlier, the familiar sight of their much-loved Sanderson curtains in the bedroom had triggered a silent howl from her inner depths as she'd yearned for everything that had been; things she could no longer share with the one person who'd have understood.

Out shopping together, if Don's reaction to anything that took her fancy was a polite but non-committal grunt, it meant 'I don't like it enough,' and she knew better than to pursue the matter. But, selecting the curtain fabric in Jenners not long after the wedding, it was he who'd paused over the swatch of swallows scudding across a linen sky. 'This is it!' he'd whooped enthusiastically. The other shoppers had looked up and, sensing the couple were honeymooners, smiled indulgently.

There the curtains still hung, their colours faded only where the material curved towards the sunlight; still lending taste and movement to a room that had seen important decisions made and quarrels enacted – often followed by energetic making-up. Such a good buy, that fabric. As, of course, the house had been. Remembered happiness, poignant though it was, reminded her how blessed she'd been too.

And still was.

Forty years. God, how long was that! She must learn to treasure everything that had gone. Lorna always said Maggy's glass wasn't merely half-full, that her sparkling Moët & Chandon ran exasperatingly over. Alas, all she seemed to manage nowadays was a splash of Tesco's Chardonnay. At least, with a poignant signal to her tidy brain, she could still re-run past images and sounds for as long as the playback machine remained in good working order.

THE GALBRAITH FAMILY: 1974 –
The ~~Dirty~~ Weekend in Pitlochry
Hen Party/Our Big Day
Grace's First Swim (Portobello)
Ewan's Degree Ceremony at the Usher Hall

The seeds of the future were sown in the past, Maggy told herself. Each day she waited for the cue to help her move on.

In the graveyard across the road, the most recent marble memorial stood in its shady corner beneath the cypresses. His ashes might rest there, yet Don's subtle presence continued to insinuate itself, sometimes oppressively, throughout the house and garden.

Each object or perennial recalled a shared person, place, or anniversary.

Don remained in her head too, watching her every move, informing every decision she made. Well-intended as his spirit might be, and much as she'd always love him, Maggy needed to reclaim ownership of her mind.

Forty years.

Tempus fugit indeed.

⊰⊱

TWO

Tepid Gin and Cold Turkey

∂∘ ∘∂

IN the clubroom bar, the sounds of Michel Legrand battled against the self-congratulatory babble.

Doris Galbraith stirred the dregs of the night's adrenaline. 'It didn't show, did it?' she demanded.

'What?' Don asked.

'The tear.'

'Tear?'

'In my dress.'

'What dress?'

'In Act Three.' She sighed. 'Typical male!'

'I'm sorry, I should have said how well you covered it up…' Doris looked at her son suspiciously, '… with your consummate acting,' Don said grinning.

Feigning relief, Doris hummed along with a few bars of The Windmills of Your Mind, a favourite song of hers since it topped the charts some years back. The lad hadn't turned out too badly, she thought. Taking a sip of her, by now, warm gin and vermouth she said. 'Another show ticked off.'

'You'll be auditioning for the Anouilh of course?'

'I think your father deserves my full attention now, don't you? For a while, anyway.'

'You mean, he has his own ways of filling those empty evenings?'

'Precisely!'

They exchanged knowing looks. Archie's penchant for killing time in the local bar whilst Doris was rehearsing was a family joke. He especially enjoyed engaging in conversation with younger people. Even tonight he was chatting nearby to the vivacious young woman who had been playing Major Barbara.

For different reasons, Doris and Don were mildly irritated. Archie's behaviour naturally made his wife feel her age, whilst Don had fancied Maggy Wallis for a while, but not found the right moment to home in. Archie had now got in first. Worse still, she was laughing at his corny jokes.

Doris babbled on. 'I nearly died when Jimmy left out that chunk in the last scene. Mercifully Giles ad-libbed.'

'What did you do?'

'Recalibrated in the nick of time.'

'What exactly *is* the nick of time?' Archie inquired as he strode into earshot, his new friend in tow. 'Don, you must surely have met this talented young lady?'

'I...'

'We sort of know each other, don't we?' Maggy said giving him a playful look.

Don smiled back. 'I suppose we do.'

The spotlight having drifted off her, Doris downed another slug of gin and turned away.

So far, Don and Maggy had only glimpsed each other on the evenings he picked up Doris from rehearsals. On one occasion, there had been a shared, *parents, eh?* smile as Doris scolded him for being late and a brief, frustrating connection was made. Now here she was, a hands-breadth away, his hormones once more on red alert.

Alone with Maggy at last, Don kicked himself for coming up with nothing better than, 'You gave a stunning performance.'

'You didn't think I would?' she teased.

'Stop fishing, I barely know you.'

'At least you were laughing.'

'How? I mean...'

'My eyes cautiously wandered during the other actors' long speeches.'

'Very chatty, Bernard Shaw.'

'Tell me about him!'

'And how much of Barbara was really you?'

'Zealous, robust Babs? Maybe a mite.' She grinned.

He glanced down, aching to put his hands around her neat waist. He was unsure about robust but could see she might be zealous.

'Anyway,' she said, 'I could just make out you and your Dad in Row B. Not looking *too* bored.'

'I meant it. You had your work cut out not being upstaged by my mother.'

'She's certainly in control on the boards.'

'And off!' Don said.

'I can imagine.'

They looked at each other and laughed.

Maggy glanced up at him. He could see her doing the calculations.

His six feet two to her, what, five six in high heels? She couldn't be more than nineteen… twenty at most. She wasn't conventionally pretty, but compact and with her short wavy hair and gamine features, certainly sexy. She knew how to use her deep green eyes to hold people's attention. Had she spotted the few early grey hairs in his mousey mop? Hopefully, she liked men with silver hair. It wasn't usually a stumbling block. He was irritated and flattered in equal measures by often being told by women, usually in a giggly way, that he looked like Sean Connery – who was a generation older and wore a hairpiece on screen.

'It's good to have someone intelligent to chat to,' she said. 'My lot have all gone off to catch the end of *Match of the Day*.'

'I'd normally be doing the same. Gordon Banks is a hero of mine.'

'But duty called?' Maggy said.

'I'm glad it did. Even if was the Cup Final!'

'Won't it be great when these new recording machines come in and we'll be able to watch programmes whenever we like?'

'Cannae be too soon,' Don said.

'You don't share your mother's interests?'

'I enjoy the theatre and support her totally, but can't read a menu aloud, let alone a play text. What do you do – that is, when you're not…'?

'Performing?'

He nodded.

'Getting my head around what I want to do with my life. It was certainly a nightmare, drumming all those lines into my head whilst preparing for secretarial exams. Finito, now, thank God!'

He picked her up quickly on this. 'And?'

'No flying colours. I didn't put enough into them. But at least I've enough acceptable grades to start doing something. On nights like this, it's tempting to imagine how exciting it would be to become a legit actress – or at least try.' She gave a sigh. 'First thing on Monday, I'm enrolling with a secretarial agency. At least I should soon be contributing at home. Besides,' she added with an eloquent flutter, 'what other options do I have?'

Don pondered. Who was fishing now? If she was sounding out his own territory he couldn't help her. His prospects might look good but he was still establishing himself in the engineering company he'd joined after leaving university the previous summer. Though, with her looks and strong personality, many organisations would surely jump at the chance of training Maggy up for something.

Career choices for women had improved considerably during the liberated Sixties if, admittedly, there was still a long way to go before women could compete for many of the jobs available to men – and at comparable salaries.

Then he put his foot in it big-time. 'If you don't get the stage bug out of your system while you can,' he heard himself saying, 'you'll be up to your ears in nappies before you know it' he said, 'and have lost your chance.'

On the word 'nappies', Maggy gave him a sharp look. Don saw her hackles prepare for lift-off. His heart sank. Everything had been going so well. God, you had to be so careful with women these days. Conversation was a minefield. She must think he saw her as another desperate female trying to escape a future bonded to a push-chair. Had he blown it?

A frosty silence gave him his answer.

Maggy looked around the room, presumably for an escape route. Don was furious with himself. He was really drawn to her. Not that he was short of female company, but there was something about her that deserved further investigation.

He was about to try to make amends, summoning up the courage to ask for her phone number, when the actress who'd played Barbara's fellow Salvationist, Jenny, all week, appeared at Maggy's side.

'Excuse me Mags, but you've simply got to come over and meet Banger.'

Maggy frowned. 'Banger?'

'Drummond Braithwaite?'

'Who?'

'The young radio producer I told you about.'

'Of course,' Maggy said, 'how could I have forgotten him, with a name like that – straight out of Wodehouse.'

'Presents *Nightcap* on Thursdays. Songs from the shows, drop-in guests and so on. He was greatly impressed with you.' She dropped her voice. 'I know he's wildly camp but terribly sweet. Insisted I drag you over so he can tell you himself.'

Don watched Maggy swither as her friend continued 'Not one to take no for an answer *and* he's got connections!'

On the word 'connections' Maggy's eyes lit up. She muttered apologetically to Don, and with a fleeting, dismissive smile, allowed herself to be marched her off to the other side of the room.

The music segued from Watch What Happens into I Will Wait for You.

'Shit!' Don said, none too quietly.

For the third year running, Doris won the society's Best Actress Shield for her performance as Lady Britomart, Major Barbara's bossy mother. Yet it was Maggy, on the heels of her morale-boosting tête-à-tête with 'Banger', who found herself hailed 'a young talent to watch,' in *The Scotsman*.

One night she'd caught the Stage Manager in the wings, nodding towards Doris in full throttle and big sleeves on a painted Wilton carpet. She'd overheard her whispering to her assistant 'she's just playing herself – but on amphetamines!'

Stifling a giggle, Maggy had almost missed her entrance. Yet the unkind remark endorsed what, deep down, she knew. Much as she admired Doris's powerful stage presence and characterisations, she was aware that, like many untrained actors, the older woman grafted her roles on from the outside rather than allowing them to develop from within. Also, she tended to caricature half-remembered screen performances of famous British stars of an earlier generation.

Whilst Doris's middle-aged fans lapped up these near impersonations, Maggy instinctively cringed, knowing that a booming voice and borrowed mannerisms were no substitute for the controlled projection of truthful thought and emotion, supported by well-observed body language. Having a firm belief in her own talent, she was frustrated at the thought of winding up in a dull Edinburgh office.

Thus, the following week, as well as signing on at the job agency, Maggy took a leap in the dark and applied for a place at the Royal Scottish Academy of Speech and Drama in Glasgow. To her delight, she found herself invited to audition. Not long after, a letter arrived offering her a place for the next academic year.

Much as Maggy loved her family, the need for her own life had been nagging her for a while.

'Rite of passage time,' she explained to Fraser, her younger brother.

'So long as it doesn't turn out to be a *wrong* of passage.'

She threw a cushion at him. 'Ha ha, very funny.' Then more seriously Maggy said, 'You do understand, don't you? I must stand on my own two feet. Find out who I am.'

Recently the three years between them had shrunk, adolescence having matured her brother into a thoughtful but good-humoured confidant. The pair had always got on well. Now they were good friends.

Strictly speaking, it would have made sense for her to shuttle between the two cities each day on the train. 'But all those people, all those germs,' she pleaded with her mother with histrionic pathos. Bessie wasn't totally convinced. 'And I won't be dependent on you,' Maggy continued. 'The grant will cover my basic expenses, and I can temp during vacations.' Maggy knew she'd been a drain on her parents' carefully managed finances for too long.

Her parents had no choice but to go along with Maggy's decision, knowing better than to argue with her; though her father, Lachlan, warned her of the dangers lurking for a single girl, on her own, in the rough city.

'All right, Pa,' she reassured him, 'I promise I won't stroll half-pickled down Sauchiehall Street on a Saturday night – at least not unaccompanied!'

'Maggy?'

'Why Don. Hello! '

'What are you doing in Glasgow?'

'Over for a training day.'

They were at the entrance to Princes Square in Buchanan Street.

Maggy opened her mouth to inquire further but Don, feigning a yawn, beat her to it. 'You don't want to know – a training seminar on marketing strategies. They're so intense in our office here.'

She laughed, then explained her own situation.

'I don't know a great deal about acting, except what I've picked up from Mum. Though enough to see you've got what it takes.'

'Gee, thanks,' Maggy said, good at giving but not receiving compliments.

There was a slight pause, when it seemed each was wondering if the other was in a hurry and had only stopped to talk out of courtesy.

It was almost a year since the party. On that occasion Maggy had been immediately drawn to Don, but as the conversation had progressed, concluded he was a tad too aware of his own charm. Had she misjudged him? Their lives had gone in different directions since then, but maybe she'd acquired more self-confidence – and he, more tact.

Catching sight of herself in a shop window, Maggy was grateful she'd set out looking both with-it and smart: faded blue jeans with embroidered rear pockets; a brown suede jacket over her black roll-neck jumper.

Don gave her an engaging smile which she returned with a reassuring grin. She decided to forgive his past thoughtlessness.

Soon, they were chattering away like old friends.

Ten minutes later, they were still talking.

The sky was almost dark.

Nearby, someone pulled down a creaking security grille.

A pair of office workers tore past for a bus.

A clock boomed the hour.

'Your train!' Maggy said.

Don had indeed been aiming for the five-past six, but there would be another in half an hour. He'd never stopped kicking himself for not contacting Maggy and asking her out last time they'd met. He was damned if he would let the chance slip by again.

'Look, I'm famished,' he said. 'I only had a cheese roll for lunch – how about you?'

Maggy hadn't eaten much either. 'There's a small Italian place a few minutes away. It's friendly and good value.'

'Let's go for it,' Don said.

'Great.'

'I'll get the eight fifty-three.'

Over lasagne and plenty of wine, they found they shared more in common than she'd imagined; not only mutual acquaintances but similar views – especially on the environment and architecture – but most importantly, a sense of the ridiculous.

The eight fifty-three came and went, as did the departure times for all the other trains back to Edinburgh that night. Three hours further on, by now better acquainted with each other's backstories – edited in the jokey way people trying to make a good impression on each other do – the café was about to close. The waiter pressed the bill on to Don's side plate.

Decision time.

The hours of shared laughter, wine, and proximity to each other had proved to be an aphrodisiac. Ending the evening separating on a, by now, cold, dark pavement wasn't an option. The more Maggy's eyes danced, the more insistent the strain in Don's crotch became: not something he could easily pacify on Buchanan Street.

They were soon on a bus heading for refined Bearsden.

Although she'd had several boyfriends, and her drama studies had given her at least a veneer of sophistication, Maggy had not yet fully made love with a man and sensed this evening could be the start of something important. Much as she was attracted to Don, she didn't want this to be simply a one-night stand and needed to be certain of the strength of their feelings before committing herself further. Their time together left them both happy, yet wanting more.

When the landlady discovered Don furtively slipping out of her house at six a.m. the following morning, it took all Maggy's acting skills to hold on to her rented room.

In fact, things got serious quite quickly. Words like 'commitment' kept cropping up. Maggy soon found herself struggling for breath. A forceful personality herself, she'd met her match in this persuasive man who refused to take *no* for an answer, masking stubborn determination behind his foxy sex-appeal.

No amount of intellectual rationalisation could disguise their age-old dilemma: conflicting priorities. Preparing for a serious career in tandem with a demanding love life played havoc with Maggy's energy levels.

One Saturday evening, as the jukebox churned out Tie a Yellow Ribbon Round the Old Oak Tree in a bar in the Grassmarket, Maggy begged Don to be patient. By now he'd learnt to read her better and had secreted an eternity ring in his pocket. He persuaded her to let him replace it with an engagement ring, the day she completed her course.

By the start of her second year, the pressure was even greater. Maggy became involved in more student productions – always seen by 'people who mattered' – that would progressively influence the quality of her final qualification. Whenever she skipped rehearsals and classes to tear back to Edinburgh, she short-changed herself and let down her fellow students.

The strain began to tell.

Maggy's predicament came to a head just before Christmas, when a London agent caught her performance as the gutsy heroine of Arnold Wesker's *Roots*. Would the college allow her to audition for *Cold Turkey*, a new play by an up-and-coming Northern playwright? Programmed for a short run at a well-regarded London fringe theatre, it would be in the hands of an *Evening Standard* award-winning director.

Although the production meant Maggy missing much of the summer term, and the money would barely cover her expenses, the Principal saw it could be a great opportunity for her. Given the prestigious nature of the production, if she got the part and both she and the play were a success, Bruce would expect to sign her up long-term. If not, she could always return to Glasgow and complete her studies.

Maggy was in a fever of indecision. There followed a week of soul-searching and lengthy telephone conversations with her old school-friend Una. The five-days-a-week distance from Don already made her life one of unbearable enchantment mixed with logistical discomfort. Working in London would mean three months separation from everything and everyone she cared for. A quarter of a year!

She also worried how her parents – already discussing suitable schools for their unborn grandchildren – would react.

It was still the view of many middle-class parents that girls underwent further education as a useful way of killing time prior to settling down with a nice lad with prospects. That was certainly how the Dorises of this world saw it, particularly if the studies involved the domestic sciences or were, for instance, performance-related, as opposed to 'serious' careers in law or medicine. Much as Doris enjoyed acting herself and imagined she had high standards in that department, she saw the stage as a hobby, nothing more.

Preparing for bed one night, Maggy considered the two new books on her bedside table. 'It's imperative you read *The Second Sex* and *The Female Eunuch*,' the tutor had advised Maggy's group as they began developing a docudrama on the theme *sexual inequality in contemporary society*.

Both Simone de Beauvoir's 1949 treatise and Germaine Greer's recent barnstormer immediately grabbed Maggy's attention. They made her feel that, until then, she'd been intellectually dozing. Both writers managed to convey how women ticked and what they could become if sufficiently assertive. If Maggy didn't agree with quite everything they said, it was partly because she wouldn't admit to herself that some of their reasoning went over her head.

Also, she was her own person.

Ever the practical Scot, Maggy took issue with points such as de Beauvoir's obsession with the repetitious drudgery of housework. Maggy enjoyed the therapeutic nature of domestic chores. It gave her time to think. Some of her best decisions were made whilst stripping beds – especially those concerning men, where a little tugging and pounding gave vent to any internal turbulence. Overall, however, she engaged with the writers' over-arching message.

It was her moral duty to empower herself.

Suffragists and the many bold women who succeeded them had achieved much, but a great deal of work remained. It fell to Maggy's generation to move things on. At least the theatre was a medium for spreading the word. Her time with Shaw hadn't been in vain.

One phrase of Greer's particularly caught Maggy's attention:

security is the denial of life.

Even so, supposing Don grew lukewarm during her absence? The phone numbers of erstwhile girlfriends would, no doubt, be close to hand. Most intimidating had been raven-haired Christie Blair whom they'd bumped into in John Lewis: intense in expensive spectacles and with a figure to die for. Conscious of being unfashionably proportioned, Maggy comforted herself in the knowledge that Judi Dench wasn't as classically beautiful as, say, Diana Rigg or Francesca Annis, but every bit as talented – if not more so. All the same, if not Christie, one of Don's other ex-flames like the fluttery Elspeth and a certain boyish-looking Robina – both of whom Doris had carefully drawn to her attention at a family slides evening – might race to supplant her.

After a hearty dose of Greer and another restless night, Maggy reached a decision. This would be The Big Test. If Don wasn't prepared to release her for ten weeks, how could she hand over to him the rest of her life?

Was this total selfishness? Probably, but she knew it was something she must do.

On receiving the news, her mother played the sceptical *well, it's your own life* card with its subtext of soon-to-be-relinquished emotional blackmail. Her father harrumphed and pursed his lips before grudgingly saying 'Well… if it's okay by your mother.'

At first, Don just muttered 'good luck to you,' with little feeling in his voice and avoided her gaze. His sullen moments were far scarier than the occasional heavy father rants. Still, he gave her a lingering hug before she left. 'I think I understand. I expect I'll still be here when you get back.'

But would he?

On Boxing Day in a downbeat artist's basement studio, a Liverpudlian call-girl struggles to motivate her wannabe-Hockney lover.

For over two hours Maggy mined as much comedy as she could from the earnest *Cold Turkey* dialogue, attempting to counterpoint the leading man's downbeat booze-and-drug-fuelled verbal abuse of a society that fails to appreciate him.

Despite Maggy's sexy swagger in a series of brassy costumes, nothing could brighten the play's pervading cheerlessness. She fought hard – probably too hard – to raise the dramatic temperature, throwing everything she'd learnt into the role. But even an award-winning director couldn't spin hemp into silk.

What had looked promising on the page, never took off on the stage.

'The clunky dialogue, unrelieved by wit or irony, drowns the play in a swamp of *Anger* style clichés…' ran a typical review, though the *Daily Mail* hailed Maggy for bringing 'much-needed vivacity to an undistinguished piece.'

They had to face it, the play was behind the times. Even so, a couple of trite but dramatically effective speeches in Act Two on the fragility of love and fame and how a woman's ultimate responsibility was to herself, fitted Maggy's rebellious mood.

On the night when an enthusiastic party from the Kentish Town branch of Women United graced the audience, she threw everything into her character's final lines *'Screw you Sven! I've a life to lead. I'll be fine on my own. It's not as if you've been around much recently anyway, strung out high on that cloud of yours where no one can reach you.'* She then paused to pick up her case and raincoat, delivered *'but then, who needs a bloody man anyway…?'* climbed the three steps to the symbolically open door, turned and declared: *'Not me!'*

As Maggy slammed the door in the rickety flat behind her, the small house spontaneously erupted into gratifying cheers. Simone and Germaine would have been proud.

The positive reaction was, sadly, a one-off.

Her mother and father travelled down with Fraser and Don for the second Saturday matinée and, afterwards, struggled to fake even polite enthusiasm for the play while mumbling niceties about her performance. Over omelettes and French fries in a Golden Egg, Fraser saw how disappointed Maggy was that the experience hadn't turned out to be the big break she'd hoped for.

'Take comfort, Sis, you make a great tart-with-a-heart.'

Her father had other concerns. 'I hope that young man who plays your boyfriend isn't, how can I put it… annoying you? He looked the type that might.'

'Shh Lachlan!' Bessie remonstrated 'you'll upset Don.

'Hardly,' said Maggy. 'The actor's gay.'

Her father looked puzzled. 'What?'

'Queer,' Fraser said.

'Oh.' Her father stirred his tea. Sometimes he found the way these youngsters talked confusing. 'But his hands were all over you.'

'It's called acting,' Maggy said. She was very fond of her father, even if he was a dinosaur. 'Fuddy Daddy.'

Don grunted. Maggy was uncertain whether this was because her fiancé had confused her with the role she was playing – or because her father had worried him about the kind of people she might now be mixing with. Should she be worried?

At the end of the meal, Don hailed a cab for King's Cross and opened the rear door for the other three, before turning to Maggy. She hugged him and he kissed her goodbye, although she felt, without much enthusiasm. He'd been distant all afternoon. Or was it in her imagination?

Apart from a handful of noncommittal postcards, Don made no attempt to contact Maggy during the remainder of the play's short run. She did, however, receive some reassurance from Fraser, who rang her at the flat one non-matinée afternoon and, along with the family gossip, reported that Don rang every few days to ask after her. If she expected a nightly telephone call from the man himself, however, she was deluding herself. To be fair, it would have been virtually impossible, there being only one shared phone on the landing. As usual, she was probably expecting too much.

The play staggered through five of its allotted six weeks before folding due to lack of advance bookings. No West End producers beat a path to the star dressing room. Only backstage camaraderie kept Maggy's spirits above the water line. After the last performance, everyone affected merriment in the theatre bar and wished each other well. The agent offered to keep her on his books and suggested she contact him again when she finished her training. Ouch!

It was all over.

Maggy sent Don a postcard of a German abstract tree painting she'd found in The Tate shop. 'Tie a yellow ribbon!' she scrawled, followed by *M* and 5 kisses.

Sitting on *The Flying Scotsman*, a sadder but wiser girl, it was Piaf's Je Ne Regrette Rien that defiantly buzzed around in her head. Maybe she was arriving home with a bruised ego, but she'd survived.

By the time they were chugging past Durham Cathedral, Maggy's thoughts had already moved on from what she'd left behind to what she was returning to. Would her fiancé be waiting? Was he still her fiancé or, as had happened to one of her girlfriends, would he gently take her into the nearest coffee bar and explain, sadness barely masking relief, that he'd returned to Elspeth, Robina – or someone new? Had he decided he could no longer put up with a flibbertigibbet whose ego drove her to relentlessly pursue a modest acting ability, without a thought for how it affected anyone else who cared about her?

Could she blame him if he had?

It was a huge relief to spot Don's rain-coated figure through the grimy window, patiently watching the carriages rolling along the platform, his eyes scanning each one as it passed his sightline.

He beamed when he saw her. As she let down the window to open the train door she heard him singing, off-key, *'I'm coming home'*.

Maggy blinked back tears.

Apart from courteously asking her how things had gone since he'd seen her last, Don rarely referred to the little detour in their lives again.

And, whilst the experience hadn't killed Maggy's passion for the theatre, at least she began to regard it with realistic wariness.

She thought she'd found where her priorities lay.

THREE

This is Illyria, Lady

❧ ❧

THE following weekend, Maggy told Don she had put her brilliant career on hold. 'I'll see the year out, then tell them I'm not coming back next term.'

'So, no pressure then?' he said.

'I'll make Mrs Galbraith the role of a lifetime!'

'I'll always be wondering when you're for real and when playing a part.'

He tickled her in the ribs and they scuffled happily. Then she grew earnest. 'With all I've already covered and some additional evening classes in Edinburgh, I should be able to pick up some speech training certificates and, with luck, have fall-back skills *and* letters after my name.'

Don thought for a moment. 'I imagine there's a market for junior execs wanting to develop public speaking skills?'

'And kids who need help with vocal issues,' she said.

'The extra money would come in handy – to begin with, anyway.'

'We'll need somewhere to live, incorporating, if possible, a small studio for me.'

It wouldn't be fair to ask her parents for help. Although Lachlan owned his hardware business, built up over many hard-working years, the Wallis's now – relatively – comfortable life-style relied on their customer base holding steady against the competition from retail chains. Also, Lachlan was saving to pay off the mortgage on their small terraced house before he retired. Hugh, their eldest son, was successfully establishing himself as an accountant, but Fraser wanted to be a doctor. There would be heavy demands on their income for years to come; they weren't in a good position to help Maggy and Don buy a home. On the other hand, Don was an only child and Archie, thanks to his well-established, automotive component systems business, had the means to be a generous father.

The fly in the ointment was Doris. Apart from awarding herself a generous clothes allowance, she protected the rest of Archie's substantial income with Scrooge-like zeal. Born into a strict

Presbyterian household, she'd never exploited his shrewdly earned wealth and was damned if Maggy was going to. Fortunately, Don was making good progress as a trainee manager in electronics. They'd never starve.

Maggy knew it fell to her to ensure the two families became friends and respected each other's financial status. She was grateful for the enviable security the match would bring but, at this stage, wanted to retain her own identity.

Maggy explained to her mother plans to be a speech trainer.

'Wise girl. And you could always go back on the stage as the children grow older.'

The following day, Maggy dropped Greer and de Beauvoir into a large white plastic bag, marked World Wildlife Fund. As the paperbacks thudded on top of each other, the sound jolted her conscience. They'd done their work, she argued. Or was she betraying her sex, settling for a conventional marriage financed largely by a career-husband, whilst her own talents took second place; probably to be put on indefinite hold once the children showed up?

Don and Maggy began earnestly looking for a place of their own which would provide her with somewhere to work in the short term and be large enough for a family in due course. It would also give them time to make it sufficiently presentable for moving into after their wedding which, they anticipated, might be early in the New Year.

The next Saturday, flicking through estate agents' leaflets, Maggy's attention was caught by photographs of a late nineteenth century, semi-detached house *in a valley below a quiet village*, she read, *on the southern periphery of the city… overlooking a historic and well-maintained graveyard.*

Doris would most certainly have heart failure at the price, which was well beyond the ballpark figure she'd empowered Archie to accept; but Maggy had a hunch about the place. Don was watching cricket on TV with Archie and seemed happy for her to look at it on her own. Hating the idea, whilst recognising the essential diplomacy of getting Doris on-side, she persuaded her future mother-in-law to give them a lift to a viewing.

Doris parked her car in front of a charming old church, fitted with a grass carpet peppered with buttercups and hugging lichen-encrusted tombstones. Gaudier blooms swayed in the metal containers beside monuments to once fruitful and still-remembered lives. To her left, the Water of Leith bisected an expanse of woodland. The sound of falling water underscored the overwhelming serenity of the place.

Turning around, Maggy spotted the rough-hewn walls and railings of a row of substantial houses on the other side of the road, topped with box hedges and interrupted by wrought iron gates beyond which steps led up through the gardens to the building itself.

'This one,' the young estate agent said.

Maggy had always been quick to mock people who fell in love with houses. Yet, one glance up at the façade of Illyria and her spirits rose. Worked into the black wrought iron gate, the name appealed to everything theatrical in her; the romantic subtext so delightfully at odds with the grey stonework which had long protected inhabitants from the bitter east coast winds. Generous windows exuded friendliness and stability.

Maggy's sense of destiny intensified as she tackled the steps to the delphinium front door.

Here they might be happy.

Doris made no secret of disliking the house from the off, wincing as she turned from the vast bay window and looking down the front garden to the well-maintained churchyard across the road. 'All those gravestones!' she said. 'It's not just the morbid outlook, Maggy – though heaven knows that view would never cheer me up on a frosty winter's morning – it's…' she referred to the leaflet, '… four bedrooms and three large reception rooms for heaven's sake! When we were your age, Archie and I considered ourselves lucky to start off in a wee tenement in Newhaven. How on earth would you cope once the children turn up? *And* …' pausing for effect, '… on Don's junior manager's salary?'

But the carefully positioned upward inflexion missed its target. Maggy caught the young man's downcast look and winked at him as if to say 'I'll get my way yet.'

There was a phone box on the corner of the road. She rang Don. Within fifteen minutes he had joined her.

Maggy watched Illyria cast its spell on him too.

That evening in Doris's drawing room was as bad as any First Night. Maggy improvised with child-like persuasiveness to win over her future father-in-law. 'But Archie, think of it as an investment. With inflation as it is, the worry of that alone will spur us on to pay back the deposit as soon as we can.' Maggy turned to Don. 'Isn't that right, darling?' she said, a shaving of steel in her eye.

She gambled that Don, fast learning to negotiate a hard bargain at work, knew better than to interfere when she was winning. They were well-matched. He said nothing, although Archie's amused eyes gleamed encouragingly back. A bad loser, Doris feigned disgust.

Then, a week later, Maggy lost all her remaining Brownie points.

In one of her last weeks at college, Maggy's acting group visited the Zoo, each student tasked with observing a different animal. Back in class as she was turning into a cheetah, Maggy found herself retching.

A trip to the college doctor confirmed her fears.

Fraser was the first to know. He beamed delightedly at the idea of becoming an uncle, whilst Don's initial alarm was quickly replaced by the excitement of forthcoming fatherhood. Archie found the situation hilarious but was sufficiently astute to add disappointment to his emotional mix – in front of his wife, anyway.

Doris, of course, put on her offended dowager act for the rest of the week. Then, overtaken by a terror of the social consequences of not acting quickly, she gritted her dentures and leapt into action with helpful ideas for the wedding, magnanimously offering to be Team Leader.

'Brigadier, she means,' Don joked, 'but at least her efficiency and good taste can be relied on.'

Lachlan and Bessie were relieved when Archie offered to take care of the venue hire and carriages. In the event, the Galbraiths more than fulfilled their promise and paid the lion's share of the costs, whilst giving the impression the wedding was a joint effort.

Doris abused every useful contact in her little Morocco-bound book to ensure The Big Day's success. She announced she had persuaded the rector of St John's the Evangelist in Princes Street to dislodge an existing reservation. 'We go back a long way,' she said, with affected mystery. The ceremony was set for a Monday afternoon in October.

A handsome donation to their 'favourite charity' convinced a nearby banqueting suite to reconfigure its available facilities and squeeze a hundred people in for a deluxe high tea. If Doris quietly prayed some of their older high-profile friends might still be away in the autumn, she didn't let on. In the end, the combination of Maggy's charm, and a carefully designed mediaeval-style ivory dress of lace over taffeta limited any minor, emerging damage at one of the best-attended weddings of the month.

Doris may have acquitted herself well organising the wedding and, as Mother of the Groom, pulled off a conspicuously self-deprecating performance. But it would always rankle with her that

Maggy had stolen top billing as the newer, younger Mrs Galbraith and had narrowly risked making her a laughing stock by producing a premature grandchild. Until the day Doris died, the two women contrived to be friends – but Doris vowed she would one day find a way of getting her own back.

The next six months flew by as the couple settled into their new home and way of life. Grace duly arrived, followed two years later by Ewan.

Maggy revelled in motherhood and the couple settled into a stable marriage. Inevitably, the occasional lean year alternated with, largely, optimistic times, as the young Galbraiths' lives moved forward, Don's early promotion enabling them to pay Archie back quicker than expected.

With two lively young children to manage, there was, alas, little time – or peace – available for Maggy to practise her speech-training skills until both were at secondary schools, after which she took it up again four days a week to provide herself with a degree of financial independence.

Illyria turned out to be everything they could have wished in a home. Living amongst several other young couples with youngsters provided them all with a satisfying social life.

Doris boasted to friends '… and they've this lovely big house, with a *marvellous* view…'

The graveyard became a part of their lives: privileged lives, as Maggy was the first to acknowledge. For a school assignment, Grace once researched the background of their more famous, slumbering neighbours. Ewan, Maggy and Don joined in, giving each adopted philanthropist, lawyer, and poet a lively back-story and supporting cast.

Don was a generous partner and conscientious father and, seemingly, devoted husband. Although there was one uneasy week or so in his late forties when he'd seemed to be a little too interested in a pretty, fleet-fingered secretary he'd foolishly whisked off to help run a conference in London. He'd made a joke of the matter, making her sound somewhat naïve.

'The lassie had a heavy crush,' he told Maggy sending her into gales of laughter, narrating how he'd caught her howling into a cheese plant. He'd sent her packing for dashing off to telephone her mother complaining of homesickness once too often. Or so he'd said. Maggy had dismissed the incident, but never forgot her name:

Jennie McPherson. Common enough. McPherson was the name of their butcher.

Well, if he'd given the lassie a wee hug one evening, what was the harm in that? She could write a book about married men in mid-life crisis, as the memory of a wild Burns Night party not long after her eighteenth birthday that had left her with an embarrassing mark on her neck for some weeks, reminded her.

It never occurred to Maggy and Don to swap the dated charms of their quiet village for those of the city even when, over the years, it dwindled to a handful of speciality shops, convenience store and a small café. After all, on fine days it was only a 40-minute stroll into town, accompanied by the chatter of the river.

As they grew older, Ewan and Grace turned out to be above average, if not particularly outstanding in any school subjects, in due course emerging with acceptable degrees from Heriot-Watt and Aberdeen respectively.

Grace found a job in the office of a leading Edinburgh catering company, working her way up to become Head of Human Resources. Everyone assumed staffing was Grace's total *raison d'être*, until one evening at a seminar on Aligning Organisational Strategies, a colleague introduced her to the high-flying Duncan.

For ten years the pair enjoyed busy, self-sufficient, co-joined lives until, at the age of thirty-five, Grace fell pregnant with twins. To everyone's amazement, she announced she was giving up her career to become a full-time mother, throwing herself into her new role with the same zeal she'd previously reserved for meeting recruitment targets.

Never an easy child, from early childhood Grace had been fiercely focused and self-possessed. Whilst mother and daughter had, for a long time, enjoyed a brisk, matter-of-fact relationship, she never kidded herself they were 'sisters'. As Grace became a teenager, Maggy was increasingly aware of how her own habitual breeziness grated on her daughter's more circumspect personality. She could never quite accept that Grace's inner controls were very different from her own.

Even so, Maggy never ceased hoping she might be able to share with Grace the girly things Don and Ewan found silly or boring. But Grace had her old flatmate Vicky for that. For practical advice, she had sometimes turned to Don. Now her father was no longer available to her, Grace presumably unburdened herself to her husband. Although *unburden* was hardly in her vocabulary.

Grace was a mystery to Maggy. She often felt Grace delighted in playing devil's advocate, wrong-footing her even in the most innocent small talk. Once recently, Maggy had made the mistake of remarking how nice her granddaughter Lyndsay looked in a new dress. Without waiting for the child to beam, Grace had jumped in to defend the other twin.

'What's wrong with Kara's?' she'd said.

'Kara looks lovely too,' Maggy had said quickly. 'Isn't it the same, only in lime?'

'No, it is *not*! Preserve me from mothers who make their daughters look like a singing duo. The style may be similar, but the decorative stitching is *quite* different.'

'Of course, now I look more closely I can see that...'

'And the fabric's not the same, either.'

'They're both very nice.'

'But you prefer the turquoise?'

'I like them *equally*!'

Grace's lips seemed almost permanently pursed with disgruntlement these days. Sighing, Maggy had picked up a book and offered to read the children a story. Even that was wrong. 'It's too close to their bedtime. I do that then. It's our special time. Isn't it girls?'

Maggy couldn't win.

Ewan, on the other hand, was more of a chum. With him, one never had to explain anything. Ewan and she could smilingly grunt a response to each other and know they were in harmony. With an MA in Digital Sciences he had eased his way into a mid-management niche in a national bank, where he'd grown roots and coasted. A bright, amiable lad, he'd lacked drive yet, even after the 2008 crash, was conscientious enough to keep his job.

Ewan had creative flair too, with both a pencil and a garden trowel. He'd won the school's Art prize two years running though of late appeared to have neglected his talents in that direction but helped his mother with the garden at key times during the year – when he could be released from his other duties by Paige, the obsessive-compulsive woman he'd curiously opted to live with. Despite many years of trying, for Ewan's sake, Maggy had always found it difficult to warm to Paige. One of the hardest lessons in life was to accept that not everyone liked you, however much you might wish them to. And vice versa.

Maggy felt Ewan, always something of a loner, liked to think he gave the impression he was self-sufficient as a front to hide his insecurities. He'd always lacked self-confidence and motivation, and Paige had never encouraged him to explore his potential. Don and she had sometimes wondered why he'd never managed to propose to her. She wasn't the type of person Maggy had imagined him being attracted to.

There was something in Ewan's make-up and manner that made her think sex might not have a high priority for him or, if so, some of the posters he used to put up on his bedroom wall as a teenager, of hunky tennis players and boyband vocalists, made her wonder if his inclinations really lay in another direction. Was Ewan waiting for someone quite different to liberate him? At least Duncan was dynamic, almost charismatic – if you got on with men's men. He hadn't much sense of humour of course. But then, Paige had none.

If only Ewan could break out and find someone to appreciate him as he fully deserved.

Overall, it was a good life, give or take the ups and downs experienced by every family. If Maggy occasionally entertained misgivings over her decision to abandon her professional ambitions, she carefully hid them from Don, keeping her promise to be the dependable axis on which their family's world rotated. Over and above her part-time speech training work – although this had whittled down to a handful of local clients – she sometimes directed community plays and occasionally starred in them, 'just to keep my hand in.'

If she regretted relinquishing the chance to join Diana Rigg or Francesca Annis on the list of annual Best Actress award nominations, Maggy believed she'd sublimated her creativity in other ways, and never let it show.

Now she was rattling around in a large house with nothing of importance to do.

Why then, this tiresome inertia?

∽ॐॐ

FOUR

Dents

ॐ ◌

TWO body-sized dents stared impertinently up at him.
Ewan Galbraith had arrived home early from work with a
headache and gone straight into the bedroom, intending to lie down.

But something wasn't as it should be.

They usually cut things fine in the morning. Even so, Paige
rarely dashed out of their basement flat in Great King Street before
checking everything met her strict criteria of impeccability. Bed-
wise, the under-sheet had to be taut, and the duvet cover smooth.
No dents were permitted – certainly not depressions in the mattress
– or scrunched-up pillows flung together against the headboard.
In fact, Ewan and Paige hadn't seriously scrunched-up their soft
furnishings for a long while. And certainly not during the day.

Ewan had never believed his luck being invited to move in with
Paige. They had met at a time when he felt he needed companionship,
whilst she was on the rebound from another affair and vulnerable
to any man who was nice to her. Sadly, what had begun as a fling
had dwindled, over the years, into a comfortable twosome, and then
merely a relationship of mutual convenience. Twelve years was a
large chunk of life for two people to fritter away half-heartedly in
each other's company.

Maggy once confessed that even the best-kept partnerships
slithered into a groove in time – even if, as in her case, it had been
a contented groove. And whilst Paige's feelings for Ewan may have
diminished, he still believed he needed her. At least, like most people,
he needed *someone* but couldn't accept this relationship had reached
its sell-by date. Maybe subconsciously he did, but something still
made him cling on to it out of, what, fear of the unknown maybe?
Or, was there something else holding him back, something he hadn't
yet tumbled to?

One might wonder how they had managed to jog along for so
long. Working in the Edinburgh Festival Office provided Paige with
plenty of opportunities to be chatted up by smart, eye-catching
men willing to affirm her desirability. With her well-kept swirl
of strawberry blonde hair, neat figure, and aloof manner, Ewan

increasingly feared he would lose her eventually.

Eventually looked horribly like now.

As the implications of the dents filtered into his brain, Ewan became more puzzled. Their life was so meticulously organised, how had Paige managed to embark on a full-blown affair? He'd forgotten – if he'd ever known – how lovers find stray moments in the creases of time.

Was it just possible that Paige hadn't expected him home early, intending to tidy the flat before he got back only to have been distracted?

Ewan had a tendency to give people the benefit of the doubt. Some weeks earlier, Ewan and his old friend Gus had been discussing the obscenities of the Third Reich. 'Yet, for all his faults,' Ewan said, 'Hitler wasn't a bad water-colourist.'

Came Gus's stern reply: 'Your point being?'

'She's hedging her bets,' Grace warned Ewan when he'd announced that Paige and he had decided to live together, 'quite honestly, you deserve better.' His sister's bluntness had irritated him. It was typical of her to weigh-in late in the day with an unsupportive comment.

There were times when Ewan almost summoned the courage to clarify where things stood – and might be heading. Not so long ago he'd caught Paige, sitting crisp and confident reading her Kindle, and baulked at the effect an analytical discussion might have on – whatever it was – they still had, terrified it would shatter into a thousand fragments.

Thus, they had drifted along, with only the occasional 'atmosphere' as Paige put it when one of them 'disappointed' the other in some way.

Ewan knew he needed advice. But from whom? Here, he missed his father. On the rare occasions they chatted alone, Ewan was often surprised at the common ground they shared. At least they got along fine when it came to things; people and emotions were a different matter. Maybe they'd been too much alike? But although Ewan could never have discussed his love-life with Don, whenever he appeared glum, a seventh sense could be relied on to summon up a supportive grin. Now there wasn't even that. He wished they might have grown closer. Who was it had said 'too late' was the saddest phrase in the English language?

The dents continued to mock him. How had things coasted to the point where Paige needed to demonstrate, so drastically, she had cast him off? Precisely when and why had she called time on sex?

Was it after the bad flu bug a couple of winters ago which had left her with a nasty, lingering cough and he'd been banished to the small study that doubled as a guest room? Permission for his return to the double bed was eventually granted; but things were never the same. During that time Paige had seemingly discovered how much she enjoyed her own space. A hasty attempt at re-coupling had taken place on the last night of a city break in Budapest – but that was eighteen months ago. The few inches separating their sleeping positions had, for some while, become a no-go area; any intimacy represented by ritualistic tokens of affection delivered with casual warmth: a peck on the cheek before parting; a dutiful hug before lights out.

An overwhelming sense of loss hit Ewan.

First his father had left him. Now it looked as if Paige had too.

He couldn't bear to look at the bed any longer, and certainly wasn't going to make it. That would be giving her his tacit approval. Let the dents remain as evidence of her deception.

And, of course, there might still be a perfectly good explanation, but…

Ewan had a sudden desire to brush his teeth. Maybe the scrubbing sensation and minty aftertaste would help refresh his head as well as his mouth. In the bathroom, he worked at his molars as if eliminating grime from a front doorstep.

After breaking the foil blisters around two soluble paracetamol tablets, he shuffled into the kitchen and filled the kettle. It was then that he saw two dirty mugs on the work surface. Not their everyday jokey ones, but the Royal Worcester mugs Maggy had given them that they normally saved for visitors. One was still half-full of lukewarm coffee. Probably drunk in haste. The rim of the other had a partial impression of Paige's lips – her favoured shade of Rampant Rose.

His worst fears confirmed, Ewan dissolved his tablets in a tumbler and swallowed them, screwing up his face as the bitterness kicked in.

Outside, the metal gate at the top of the area steps clanged. Through the grilled window, Paige's well-turned ankles clattered down onto the little patio, a jute bag hanging over her arm.

Maintaining the patio was one of Ewan's few joys. Paige had long tired of the novelty of plant-minding but, graciously, indulged him. She would have preferred everything to be as minimalist outside the home as in. Alas, contented flora tumbling riotously over the rims of large terracotta pots don't do minimalist. Today, the winter pansies around the statue of Persephone craned up eagerly towards the April sun, unaware of the pathetic scene about to unfold inside.

The key turned in the front door. As Ewan rinsed out his tumbler, Paige walked into the kitchen.

'Oh.' She looked surprised to see him. 'What are you doing here?'

'I live here.'

'At this time of day?'

'Could ask you the same thing.'

'I told you last night I'd got the day off in lieu. Those evening events I ran the other week. Remember?'

He didn't.

'Well?'

'I've got one of my heads,' Ewan said. 'Jim advised me to come home.'

Paige shrugged noncommittally and disgorged the contents of her bag on to the kitchen table. 'Just as well I got this wee courgette quiche at Hendersons for a late lunch. Not sure it will do two though.'

'That's ok, thanks.' Ewan had no appetite anyway.

How could she be so brazen? Even after all these years, he still forgot Paige's Embarrassment Gene Deficiency. Acting as if nothing had happened – the nerve! Not only that, but she'd perfected her body language to always suggest he was the one in the wrong. In this instance for having a headache, coming home and being an irritating presence when her own need for peace was paramount.

She'd probably planned a lazy afternoon recovering from her frenzied morning with *him* on *their* divan, washing her hair and catching up with that pretentious Arts programme she recorded.

Had he over-reacted? There was only one way to find out.

'The bed's in a mess,' he said.

Paige looked at him strangely. 'So?'

'So?' he echoed.

'Why didn't you make it?' she said.

'I thought...'

'That's a first. Tea?'

'I've just taken some tablets.'

Nonchalantly, Paige picked up the dirty mugs and rinsed them under the tap. 'I'll take that as a No, then. Actually...'

An 'actually'. An admission of guilt? A shred of hope?

'...I intended to get to the office later this morning...' she continued.

'...and give the room a dust and vacuum before I left.' Her voice sounded firm, but she was preparing her lunch and had her back to him; he couldn't see if her face was a confident as her voice. 'Then Harry rang to remind me about the targets-setting meeting, so I had to drop everything and dash.'

The Plausible Excuse. It would only make him look foolish if he persisted in making a mountain out of an unmade bed. But he had another card up his sleeve. With a nod towards the mug she was now drying, he said: 'It only takes a few seconds to rinse out two mugs.'

He knew he sounded small-minded, yet, was he imagining it, or did she falter before replying 'It wasn't my turn.'

'You know I wait till I get to the office for my first coffee of the day,' Ewan countered, still sounding more pettish than accusing.'

'Have it your own way!' she said, as if humouring a schoolboy. 'I wish you'd get off my back.'

No comment.

'Look, I'm...' her voice softened slightly, '...sorry about your head. But...'

'But?'

'Go and have a wee rest. Give the tablets a chance to kick in, eh?'

She dripped hot water on to an Intensely Tropical teabag and stirred.

Ewan left her with her hot drink and luke-warm heart.

A quarter of an hour later, as he was finally dropping off on the guest room divan, he heard ringtones. From the thudding of cupboards being opened and closed he pictured Paige, putting her washed-up dishes away with one hand whist talking quietly on the phone with the other.

'...Can't really speak now. Think I just heard him snoring, but... No, not a clue – as far as I can tell.'

There was a short pause followed by a saucy laugh Ewan hadn't heard for a long time.

'Yes... Me too...' then, in a stage whisper that was surprisingly carrying, 'Love you. too.'

Ewan felt sick.

☙❧

FIVE

Home Truths

డ్ నర్

MAGGY made a cursory inspection of her fridge. There was a limp lettuce, rubbery cucumber, half a Scotch egg, the heel of a wholemeal loaf – and a carton of something sloshed in mayonnaise three days beyond its use-by date. With careful trimming, enough for a snack supper, she hoped.

She really ought to order more rations online. Maggy was of the generation for whom mealtimes had always been opportunities for the family to get together. Now there was only Garibaldi for companionship, unless tinned tuna was on the menu when he'd brush his tail seductively against her calves for a few shreds on a saucer. Today he was out of luck and gazed at her reproachfully from his chair.

Lorna's call, earlier, had slightly alarmed Maggy about the Sarah Waters. Not for herself, of course, but her fellow bookworms, who met once a month in the James Gillespie Room off the church hall. Lorna was responsible for bullying her to join the book group as a tentative step towards getting back into circulation.

It had required a considerable struggle to summon the confidence to face this erudite band – as they considered themselves. The first novel she tackled, a Hilary Mantel, was particularly challenging. It was her turn next to suggest and lead the discussion on a book – an ordeal she approached with apprehension.

Much as she looked forward to seeing Lorna, Sarah Waters had unwittingly complicated her plans. These had been pinned on the latest Kate Mosse, poised thick and inviting on the wine table. She loved the tantalising aroma of crisp, white paper sandwiched between shiny covers.

Besides, she hadn't yet assessed how eclectic – or did she really mean broadminded? – her fellow readers were. Reformation politics were one thing; the ins and outs of Sapphic romancing – here she found herself smirking smuttily – might be a tad too much information, especially for one religiously-minded group member. She could hear the woman's emphatic voice. 'Do you not think some things are better left to the imagination?' Maybe she misjudged the woman. Maybe more wisdom on emotional discrepancies lurked behind her enigmatic countenance than she cared to admit.

One of Maggy's grandmother's favourite clichés was 'sex is what people keep coal in, in Morningside.' Although fast dying out, lingering streaks of puritanism still existed in mustier corners of the city. Maggy faintly remembered, as a toddler, how grimy-faced men in heavy boots delivered coal; huge sacks on their shoulders, stomping, through carpeted hallways to the bunker, releasing a pungent, manly odour.

Anticipating the forthcoming afternoon with her niece, divergent trains of thought chugged towards a junction in her mind.

Lorna had largely taken the place of Maggy's younger brother Fraser's role in her life. Now a doctor, he and his wife and children had emigrated to Sydney. Recently they'd tried Skyping, but she still missed their silly wrangles and easy access to his common sense.

Lorna's father, her elder brother Hugh, was a decent but bossy man, prone to tactlessness. The five years between them had made him seem intimidating when they were younger, but since his marriage to a tolerant ex-nursing sister – and one of life's saints – they'd grown closer. The appearance of Lorna, sadly destined to be an only child, had turned out to be a bonus for Maggy.

Lorna had become Maggy's friend from the moment the eager toddler had pushed *Where the Wild Things Are* into her lap. The connection strengthened when reading to her niece led to helping Lorna teach herself to read. The gap in their ages had never mattered.

Resourceful, generous, and occasionally wilful, from a young age, Lorna set Maggy chortling one moment and struggling to catch up with her the next. She recalled one sunny afternoon strolling around rural West Linton. Lorna would have been about thirteen.

'We're doing The Tudors,' she'd announced.

'Always my favourite period at school,' Maggy said.

'I've adopted Lady Jane Grey as my patron saint.'

'I think you've got that wrong, dear. She was never up for canonisation.'

'Whatever.'

'You obviously like her?'

'A political victim and a true martyr. I identify with her completely!'

Maggy wasn't clear whether Lorna saw herself as either – or both.

'I want to start a Lady Jane Grey Association,' Lorna went on.

'I think there's a Tudor Society,' Maggy said, helpfully.

'Imagine being woken up and told to prepare yourself for

execution, watching the remains of your husband being driven underneath your prison window in a cart just before you're marched off to suffer the same fate?'

That had led to a bloodthirsty exposition of sixteenth-century political life.

'Of course, things were different then. Life wasn't valued as it is today,' Maggy said.

'Only in Western society.'

She had a point.

Ever after, the mere mention of Lady Jane Grey made Lorna stare, anguished, into the middle distance.

'Poor cow,' she'd mutter.

'Language, Lorna!'

In one of the role reversals that often occur with age, the influence the aunt once exerted over the girl gradually turned about. Through Lorna, Maggy re-lived her own childhood passion for books and history but found her comfort zone increasingly challenged. After she won an exhibition to do an MA in Renaissance Studies at St Andrew's, Jean Plaidy and even Walter Scott were replaced by more Booker-ish reading material.

Maggy noted how Lorna's fixations always seemed to be with hero*ines*. Men only featured in her world as supporting goodies and baddies. Usually the latter. Strong women who changed the world were the ones who really fascinated her; and those who tried hard but narrowly failed, generally due to the overbearing arrogance and incompetence of men.

If Maggy sometimes worried that her closeness to Lorna led her to neglect her own children, she always made it clear that Grace and Ewan came first. Any qualms her children had over the special relationship between their mother and cousin, they kept to themselves.

Yet the fact remained: Maggy had more in common with Lorna than her own daughter and, on a cultural level, even with Don. Her political leanings chimed-in with Lorna's too. But then, most women of her generation thought of themselves as feminists, didn't they? You didn't have to be an activist to believe it was the responsibility of all people to accept that women were equal to men – if, sadly, many of the latter sex still saw fairness weighted in their favour.

The-way-things-are syndrome.

Maggy may never have subscribed to *Spare Rib* in its heyday, but she agreed with many of the views expressed by left-leaning women speakers on *Question Time* and, it went without saying, was hugely exercised by any discussion on the glass ceiling, even if it didn't, directly, apply to herself.

But-for-the-grace-of-God syndrome.

The word *glass* made her notice how badly the windows needed a wipe down. She was about to stir herself and fetch a damp chamois leather, when her mobile rang.

'Ewan!'

'Hi Mum.'

How are you, dear?'

Silence.

'What's up?'

'It's Paige.'

'She's not – I mean, I'm not going to be a…?'

'No. *No*! In fact, I…'

'Speak up, dear.'

'… I think she might be seeing somebody… else.'

Maggy's heart lifted.

'That relationship was dead in the water from the start,' Lorna said.

'It would seem you were correct.' Maggy raised a loyal but knowing eyebrow. 'And it's taken them so long to find out.'

Lorna whisked away a stray oat from her bottom lip with a holly napkin left over from Christmas. She wanted to say she thought Ewan never knew how to handle the little madam, but he was her son after all, and Maggy had the right to be defensive.

Before she had time to carefully phrase her next comment, Maggy saved her the trouble. 'I love him to bits, but sometimes he needs a good slap.'

'No get-up-and-go?'

Maggy sighed. 'It hurts me to admit it, but he's always afraid of upsetting people by doing the wrong thing – even when it might be right.'

'As you know, I've always been very fond of him,' Lorna said. 'Of my cousins, he's the easiest to get along with. Not that I'm dissing Grace.'

As if.

'You're quite right Lorna. Ewan's more accommodating. It's probably part of his problem. He could simply be over-reacting. Might be just a hiccup.'

'Don't be surprised if there's more to it. He plays his cards very close to his chest.'

'As indeed his father did,' Maggy sighed. 'He's a good lad, though. Warm-hearted. Totally reliable.'

'But better at designing computer systems than running his personal life?'

'Sadly. And I've always suspected that Paige's isn't… how can I put it… touchy-feely?'

'Or maybe the opposite,' Lorna added cautiously, 'too demanding?' If, she thought, not necessarily of Ewan.

Maggy gave her an old-fashioned look.

Lorna was unwilling, at this point, to pass on that, Edinburgh being a large village, she sometimes bumped into Ewan and Paige. In fact, she had recently done so at the opening of an exhibition of Victorian wood engravings. Ewan was obviously fascinated; Paige, bored. They might have been on different planets for all the interaction between them. When an attractive couple in their mid-thirties had strolled by and paused at the same picture, Lorna recalled the fleeting, but meaningful look the man had given Paige.

It had been reciprocated.

'It can be a problem,' Maggy said, 'getting the balance right… the physical side of a relationship.'

'Tell me about it.' Lorna gave a heartfelt sigh. 'I always seem to end up with emotionally dysfunctional people myself. What's the attraction: the challenge?

'A cry for help, maybe? Don't most couples go through bad patches?' Maggy stirred her Earl Grey. We'll just have to wait on developments. I suppose he could always come home for a while – if he needs time to think?'

'Wouldn't that be playing into her hands?'

'I was only considering his options.'

Lorna gave her a measured look. 'Do I detect…?'

'What?'

'You wouldn't mind a wee bit of company?'

'A very tiny wee bit,' Maggy said. 'Looking after someone else might discourage me from thinking so much about myself.'

'But a needy son?'

Maggy sighed, 'Och, you're probably right. I'm just too tired these days to be of much use to my children.'

Lorna seized her chance to say what was really on her mind, but knew she had to approach it as lightly as possible.

'Heather Honey. That's what you need, Maggy.'

Maggy looked puzzled.

'A dessertspoonful in the middle of the afternoon when you're at your lowest.'

'But honey's sugar – and sugar's the new tobacco. Or is that salt? You're usually the PC one!'

Lorna awkwardly eyed the diminishing portions of flapjacks and brownies. Nonetheless, she was determined Maggy should start facing up to life. 'Even so, we all need an occasional energy boost. Someone put me on to it when I went through a bad patch. I felt like a new woman.'

'So, we're back to Sarah Waters?'

Lorna frowned. The boot had shifted again.

Maggy said 'Incidentally, you're looking perkier than you have for ages. Don't think I hadn't noticed!'

Lorna wasn't yet ready to pursue that line of discussion. 'We were talking about you.'

'They say Mānuka's very good,' Maggy said, making an effort to be cooperative.

'And very expensive too. An antipodean product.'

'Your point being?'

'Support Scotland – go for the Heather. No air miles. There's a firm in Perthshire which specialises in it. Good for beating bacteria too.'

'I thought it was my energy you were concerned about, not my bacteria.'

'Both, if necessary. No, only Heather honey will do.'

'Okay, but…' As her aunt, Maggy still saw it as part of her role to boss Lorna about, not the other way around. She wasn't giving in without a struggle.

'I do wish you'd do as you're told, sometimes.'

Maggy gave a moue.

There was a brief pause. Lorna defiantly demolished her last mouthful of flapjack and softened her tone. 'I'm trying to help you help yourself. It would be a… symbolic gesture. You know, you can only "be marvellous" for so long, Maggy. Frankly, the brave little widow act is getting a bit wearing.' She shouldn't have said that, either.

Maggy opened her mouth as if slightly pained, but nothing emerged.

'Look,' Lorna battled on, 'when did you last have a day out, just for yourself?

'Oh, you know me, busy busy,' Maggy said, now all Ladies in

Lavender demure… 'though I haven't braved town yet.'

'Exactly.'

'Too many places. Too many… *memories.*'

'Do stop acting!' Lorna said, wearily rather than cross. 'Don would never have seen himself as Prince Albert. He'd have wanted you to start moving on as soon as a suitable gap had elapsed.'

'Define "suitable gap", Maggy said.

'It's Leap of Faith time – *now!*'

'But …'

'There you go again,' Lorna said. 'No more buts. Make a start. Confront… goddammit, celebrate them, the memories. Do things you both enjoyed together. Give that Visa card a breath of fresh air.' She bit assertively into a brownie. 'Jenners, that's where you'll get it – the honey.'

Clinging to her last shred of stubbornness, Maggy sniffed and looked away.

There was a full minute's silence before Lorna said. 'Did you see *Question Time* last night?'

'Aye.'

'Kirsty Wark really manages to make sense of the Referendum issues.'

'If you say so.' Maggy didn't sound convinced. Really, what exactly *was* the colour she was wearing?'

'I like Nicola's new hairdo.'

'You would!'

They roared.

Maggy poured them both another cup of tea.

Thoughtfully.

ஒஒ

SIX

A Touch of Tenniel

ॐ ॐ

SOME days earlier, Alison McKenzie was awakened from another bad dream.

Around five in the morning, demons still sabotaged her peace of mind, a sense of evil engulfing her in the blackness as she struggled for breath; a petrified scream straining to emerge before she woke up sweating, emitting only a whine.

Similar moments of panic also caught her out during the day, triggered by a newspaper article or radio programme. Anyone in earshot might overhear a slight strangulated sound and, to her embarrassment, show concern. Unnerving at the time, as the months passed the young woman was, mercifully, finding the attacks easier to throw off.

That morning, as on other such occasions, Ally found it helped her to leave her depressing bedsit very early and let herself into The David Balfour – generally known as the Balfour – the café-bar in Stockbridge, on the northern edge of the New Town, where she'd worked for almost a year.

After making herself a coffee, she opened her laptop at her favourite table and lost herself as she checked her emails and surfed for ideas until her bosses, Cal and Senga, arrived.

The Balfour was now Ally's second home. She'd first arrived as a customer at the suggestion of her GP back in Fife. He often used it when he visited his daughter's flat along the road in Comely Bank, and had quietly alerted Senga of Ally's possible appearance, warning them of her exceptional shyness. 'She isn't the girl she used to be,' he told them mysteriously,' but the right environment might help her considerably.'

Ally and the doctor, who had known her since she was born, sometimes swapped notes about their shared penchant for places with literary connotations. The Conan Doyle, The Abbotsford and, continuing the Waverley theme, The Kenilworth – all within walking distance. A friend had recently texted her a holiday photo of Le Hobbit Bistro in faraway Quebec.

Name-spotting was a harmless enough diversion. It only required the eyes in her head –where Ally spent much of her time these days, even when surrounded by people. Wasn't it a truism that you were most alone in a crowd? Alone, however, is not necessarily the same as abandoned. As time passed, it ceased to be a melancholy state. It was how things were.

Emailing home to her mother recently, Ally had fantasised:

When I become a famous novelist – I wish! – will someone open The Alison McKenzie – known, of course, as Ally's or the name of one of my leading characters? What d'you reckon, eh? It occurred to me recently: how many David Balfours go about their lives unaware of a bar in Edinburgh trading under their name?

Her mother had loyally mailed back:

We'll be raising half a pint to you in 'Ally's' soon enough, just you see!'

'She's very artistic,' she told friends of her only child, 'they broke the mould when they made Ally,' leaving her daughter unsure if the statements comprised a defence, an apology or both – the 'they' distancing her from any responsibility in the matter.

As a traditional pub, the Balfour had long been favoured by the friendly local community. In good Scottish tradition, residents had once taken their drinking seriously: gaggles of men enlivening the district's pavement after good-natured expulsion from the Stockbridge bars on Friday nights, their beery breath hitting the cold night air. Such behaviour occurred only occasionally nowadays. In recent years, the friendly urban village had become gentrified. The Balfour reflected the trend.

Ally replied to her mother:

Half a pint? Quelle horreur! Beer is the fare of what Cal, my boss – albeit with mock condescension – refers to as spit-and-sawdust taverns. Prosecco, please!'

The Balfour mainly attracted young professionals and better-off students, who requested artisan coffee until around 5.30 pm, and wine thereafter. How had the word *artisan* got into the urban dictionary, Ally wondered? And *craft*? Did managements imagine they gave an egalitarian ring to the product, as *heritage* – yet another tiresome 'borrowed' adjective used for marketing purposes – supposedly lent class?

Paintings by local artists with optimistic price tags covered the subtle aubergine and moss coloured walls with their Rennie Mackintosh inspired stencilled motifs. What the decorative link was with Robert Louis Stevenson was anyone's guess, but Cal and Senga liked it – and to judge by the weekly receipts, so did the customers.

Two-thirds of the space was furnished with wooden tables of different shapes and sizes, surrounded by chairs. Cosy sofas hugged either side of the fireplace, an ancient primary school table standing between them with a simple subtraction calculation still faintly etched into its patina.

Drawn by the Balfour's unthreatening atmosphere, Ally found herself spending more and more time as a customer, drinking her way through large mugs of coffee as she tapped quietly away on her laptop.

One day, when Cal and Senga were short-handed, Ally had surprised herself by silently jumping up, clearing away and washing up a pile of dishes. She wasn't to know of her doctor's initiative. He'd not betrayed her in any way, simply told them she was brighter than she might appear, and engineered a potential situation to, possibly, mutual benefit.

Having observed her as a customer for a while, Cal and Senga invited Ally to become their Girl Friday. They could only offer her pitiful wages, but she could eat as much leftover food as she liked. Along with her social benefits, Ally managed to keep fed and solvent.

With her hesitant speech, customers often supposed Ally was one of the many East Europeans who helped keep the city's catering and retail services buoyant. They'd have been surprised to learn she hailed from a small village near St Andrews.

Aware Ally could be hyper-sensitive and overreact to things other people might have brushed aside with an 'Oh, but that's life!' her friends had, in recent years, become used to her extreme reticence and inability – or was it unwillingness? – to converse. Yet those who grew closer to her saw hidden depths. As did Senga and Cal, who soon accepted Ally's reliance on a shorthand of useful words, faltering phrases and miming; and, when her vocal confidence totally deserted her, an ever-ready pad of recycled paper. For complex discussions, there was always the laptop. It wasn't that she was ever rude, just abnormally quiet, and when she did speak there was a huskiness to her voice. No one knew exactly what the matter with her was but had their own theories.

As the months passed Ally increasingly found it best to communicate by means of body language spiced with hints of her off-beat humour. An amiable grunt provided a satisfactory response to direct enquiries and a broad smile to salutations. Generally, people accepted her reserve as part of her personality – though customers rarely took advantage of it. Ally was capable of delivering a sharp response to objectionable customers and unwelcome Romeos, after which they shamefacedly backed off. Even so, there were occasionally times when a thoughtless person said something hurtful, usually late in the evening after too many glasses of wine. Then Senga and Cal stepped in and tactfully, but firmly, dealt with the matter.

Initially, Ally was terrified of working alone in the kitchen with Cal: a sturdy, dark, good-looking man with what was once termed, a 'roving eye'. He'd seen her as a challenge, attempting to flirt light-heartedly whenever Senga's back was turned; never understanding why his winks and slightly off-colour jokes provoked her to stare at him with the paralysed fear of a cobra's prey.

If he'd been more observant, Cal might have noticed how Ally initially reacted in a similar way to any male, over twelve and under eighty, who attempted to talk to her at any length. As soon as he began treating Ally in a normal, friendly manner, she became more at ease with him. By now, they had fallen into a reasonably comfortable working relationship, which was fortunate considering the time they spent tearing lettuce leaves and polishing glasses together. Even so, a slight wariness remained.

There was still some way to go but, what her friends back home would have recognised as the old Ally, was finally re-asserting itself at the Balfour, encouraged by several regulars who had befriended her and helped boost her self-confidence.

It was Ally's writing that motivated her during this period in her life. The pent-up thoughts and feelings she couldn't properly express out loud stimulated her creativity. It had begun when she was nine with the publication of *Hamish the Hamster* in a Sunday school magazine. Subsequently other pieces of fiction, along with the odd article, had appeared in local periodicals. Whilst to date Ally may have enjoyed only modest success, the feedback she'd received had encouraged her to carry on.

Like many aspiring Scottish novelists, it was inspiring to know that J.K. Rowling had drafted the first Harry Potter in The Elephant House on George IVth Bridge. When not on duty, Ally focused on the children's novel she was planning: the early life of Flora McDonald, as told through the eyes of Jock, her dog. Well, it had worked for Virginia Woolf – who'd written the autobiography of Elizabeth Barrett Browning's spaniel Flush – hadn't it? Ally's research had so far produced no documented evidence that Flora ever owned a pet. Surrounded by small farms on Benbecula, she concluded the woman must have been on friendly terms with at least one working dog. Anyway, children liked animal stories, even apocryphal ones, didn't they?

Sufficiently realistic to know her stories were unlikely to bring her fame and fortune any time soon, Ally had enough faith in herself to believe she would complete the book. If by any chance it turned out to be publishable, it might also be a way of supplementing her income. If not, at least she would have had the fun of writing and sharing it with her friends and family.

Sometimes she fretted about the extent of her dependency on the Balfour, as both her workplace and personal office. So far, the security it provided and her growing friendship with the flame-haired, statuesque Senga had discouraged her from finding another place in which to spend her days.

And sometimes a small miracle occurred.

That evening when the rush began, Ally was tidying up the tables as usual and lighting the candles in their red glass holders. As she put the leftover scraps of rolls and sandwiches into a plastic container ready to be scattered to the birds, two women she hadn't seen before, and assumed to be colleagues, wandered in chatting.

After looking around, the women settled into seats at a table by the window. One, with short dark hair, appeared to be in her late forties. The other, her greying hair pulled back into a casual bun, a few years older. Smartly but suitably dressed for the still chilly weather, their stout leather bags suggested they'd come straight from work. Each picked up a menu and began examining it.

Ally wiped her hands and was about to move towards the table when Senga beat her to it. 'One croque monsieur and one smoked mackerel toastie, Ally, please,' she called as she returned to the service area. Ally reached for the sliced sourdough bread. 'I'll do the Shiraz and Chablis if you wouldn't mind seeing to the food and serving it when it's ready.' Senga noted the orders on a slip of paper by the till and poured the wine into glasses whilst Ally organised the snacks.

When, ten minutes later, Ally hovered by the women's table with the two plates in her hand, she found them deep in discussion. After a few moments, the dark-haired one sensed her presence, looked up at her and grinned apologetically. 'I'm the mackerel,' she said. Ally placed both plates in front of the respective diners, chuckling as she visualised her as part-fish-part-human, like Tenniel's footman in *Alice*.

The woman caught on to Ally's amusement and her eyes lit up.

As Ally was about to turn and move away, the woman said 'Are you always this quiet on a Monday?' Ally nodded, instinctively making no attempt to chat any longer, although the look she was given suggested it would have been welcome.

When Ally got back to the bar, Senga leaned towards her. 'Don't look now, but the person you've just served with the short hair…' her eyes twinkled as she dropped her voice even more, '… can't keep her eyes off you!'

Entertained by the thought, several times over the next half hour Ally glanced casually back towards the table in the window. Due to some strange mutual sensitivity, the glance was usually caught and warmly returned. Ally decided the attention was well-meaning.

The following evening, the younger woman came into the Balfour again. This time alone. She returned the next night also. On each occasion, she encouraged Ally to linger a little longer at her table.

And so, a friendship developed.

Ally was accustomed to spending time with the punters when they weren't busy and Senga and Cal liked Ally to be friendly, knowing it was good for her so long as she didn't keep other people waiting. Senga watched her self-assurance blossoming with a quiet sense of pride that the Balfour may have had some hand in that.

Ally, who would initially have been reticent with a man, found her new acquaintance engaging and was flattered that anyone wanted to get to know her. She didn't read too much into the woman's motives and began to open up more than she had to anyone for some years.

At the end of the week, Ally was invited for a meal at Lorna's flat in Goldenacre.

⁓⁓

SEVEN

Monsieur Tissot

ۻ ۵

IN Great King Street, tension simmered.
During the week following the mattress incident, Ewan and
Paige's life resumed its regular routine. On the surface they behaved
as usual, but with greater coolness towards each other. During the
second week, however, Paige began acting strangely, becoming even
more distant with him, whilst looking secretly pleased with herself.

Ewan's headaches returned.

Around 4.30pm on the Sunday afternoon, Ewan took the bus to
Granton and went for a long stroll along the waterfront. Most nights
these days he slept only fitfully. Some fresh air might do him some
good.

As he gazed across the Forth, he noticed a couple of young men
unselfconsciously holding hands nearby, also sharing the view. He
envied their easy companionship.

By the time he returned to the flat, his head felt clearer than it had
for days.

Pushing open the front door, Ewan sensed something was
different. Everyone takes the unique smell of their own home for
granted, but something made his nose twitch. Into the usual mix he
detected an unaccustomed, bracing note. Someone else's aftershave,
distrust – both?

Ewan heard the shower being turned off in the bathroom. No, a
bar of new, scented soap, losing its immaculacy to hot water. He was
becoming paranoid.

Wandering into the bedroom to collect his thriller, Ewan felt a
draught from the top of the sash window. It had been opened a few
inches, though not long enough to clear the smell he'd noticed in the
hallway, mingled here with an unfamiliar, sweaty aroma.

As he looked around, the street lamp outside blinked on, throwing
bright yellow light directly through the window on to the bed. No
dents this time, yet the cushions and runner on top of the duvet
looked hastily thrown on. The room wasn't quite as he'd left it three
hours earlier. In the past he wouldn't have noticed small differences
in his surroundings. Recently, he'd become more observant.

Paige had by now emerged from the bathroom in her towelling robe and was beginning to put together a supper tray in the kitchen. 'Sorry it's a bit of a mess in there,' she called out. 'I forgot to tidy up earlier.'

She was lying. Ewan had made up the bed himself. Paige could hardly have forgotten the rebuke she'd given him earlier for not getting the stylised leaves on the duvet cover the right way round.

No Oscar this time, Ms Kidman.

Picking up the paperback from his bedside cabinet, Ewan caught sight of something shiny lying beneath the wicker chair he used for his discarded clothes. Bending down he unearthed a watch. A smart watch: a Tissot. He – Ewan assumed it was a 'he' – must have been anticipating a heavy session to have gone to all the trouble of removing it.

Placing the watch conspicuously on top of the chest of drawers, he selected sufficient clothes to see him through the rest of the week and marched into the guest room. Paige graciously accepted his lame excuse that the traffic kept him awake.

Twenty minutes later, when he returned for his slippers, the watch had gone.

Ewan pondered on his discovery and decided to bide his time.

Over the next two days, whenever he and Paige were briefly together in the flat, the silence between them was like a prolonged scream. On the third evening, Ewan could stand it no longer.

Thinking a few nights completely apart might give them both some space, he was Googling local guest houses, when he paused, as if a thought had struck him.

'I've been meaning to ask…' he said.

'Yes?' Paige said.

'About that watch…'

'What watch?'

'You know. The one left out on the chest of drawers the other day.'

'I don't remem… Oh, of course, *that* watch.'

'It appeared – then disappeared almost as quickly.'

'I… I put it away for safe-keeping.'

'A little treat to yourself?'

'Don't be silly. It's a man's watch.'

She'd noticed.

'Hardly new, either,' she went on. 'I found it… on the patio outside the window. I've been intending to hand it in at the police station or wherever.'

'How public spirited of you.'

'Well...'

Ewan put his tablet to one side. 'When?'

'Why are you making such an issue of it?' He could see she was starting to get rattled. Result!

'I'm not. But my own watch has given up the ghost,' Ewan lied. 'I wondered... if the person who dropped it hasn't called for it, and you hadn't handed it in... maybe I could borrow it until mine's mended?'

Ewan had never seen Paige look so uncomfortable. 'Sorry, but even if I still had it, that wouldn't be appropriate.'

'Why not?'

He saw her self-assurance faltering further and took a gamble. 'Think you'd better come clean, Paige, don't you?'

'Sorry?'

'You can't blame me for wondering what a man's watch, which doesn't belong to me, was doing, in *our* bedroom?'

'I've just told you... I assumed the window cleaner, or someone else had dropped it.'

Ewan snorted. 'I don't think so, do you?'

'Why ever not?'

'I'd be surprised if the window cleaner could afford expensive watches on what we pay him. Or... perhaps they can, on the very large tips *some* folk give them?'

The muscles in Paige's neck reared. Her eyes flashed. Then to Ewan's surprise, she swallowed. The moment passed. He watched the cogs turn as she weighed up her options.

'Actually...' she said.

'What?'

'It was...'

'Yes?' Ewan said.

'You know...'

He didn't.

'...just one of those things.'

'Ah. Just one of those *crazy flings*...?'

'Sorry?'

Paige's ignorance of the Cole Porter songbook gave him a moment to assimilate the harsh truth. If, until now, there had still been the remotest chance everything that had happened over the past fortnight had been a mind game – or a small attack of paranoia on his part – even she had to admit this was a turning point.

'So...' Ewan said. 'A quick tumble with the postman? Some executive from the office...?'

'No!'

'...a guy from an agency perhaps?' His tone betrayed more bitterness than satire.

Strangely, that amused Paige. Normally docile, Ewan knew it always came as a shock to her to find how articulate he could be when roused.

'Don't think I haven't considered it,' she said acidly. 'But you seem to have made up your mind. What's the point of trying to reason with you?'

'Stop stalling Paige. Put me out of my misery. Who is he?

Paige, obviously squirming inside, tightened her lips.

'WHO?'

She fidgeted with the tips of her cerise nails.

Getting no response to his question, Ewan changed tack. 'All right then. *Why*?'

'Why not? Paige snapped back. 'I thought it was tacitly assumed...'

Sorry. Why should he have assumed anything *tacitly*? At what point after a couple drifted into a more-or-less platonic relationship, was it permissible to start having sex with someone else: three months, six... a year? Was he now condemned for being naïve, for not knowing that the rules had changed, and what the new ones were? Or was that just another important message that had been delivered straight to Junk?

'You must know...' Ewan said quietly.

'What?'

His last resort was emotional honesty. He'd have to take a chance on any subsequent scorn she might heap on him. 'You're...,' Paige looked at him guardedly. '...you're still important to me,' he said.

Amazingly, his words hit their mark.

'Am I?' Paige said, her stony façade softening a little. For a few seconds Ewan glimpsed the girl he'd first met at a dance all those years ago.

'It's just...' she said.

He completed her sentence '...I'm no longer enough?'

She looked at him ruefully. If Paige's next word had been 'sorry' it might have hurt less.

It never arrived.

Ewan attempted one last desperate shot. 'I may not have been very demonstrative recently, but it doesn't mean…'

Paige rose and glanced out of the window at the stone wall beyond, then turned. 'Sorry, but all this…' she gesticulated vaguely around the the room as if it was a washing machine past its warranty date, '…hasn't been working for quite a while, has it? You must have sensed it too, yet never made any effort to…'

Ewan finally snapped. 'Force myself upon you?'

'Don't be so dramatic. That's your mother's thing.'

'*Don't* bring her into it.'

Paige then said – in a tone usually reserved for giving negative feedback to a junior colleague – 'Maybe if you'd been more… pro-active.'

So, after twelve years, Ewan's life had finally imploded. It might have been almost funny in a we'll-laugh-about-this-one-day way. Except, this wasn't a one-off row. It really was the end.

'However,' she continued, 'I'd like us to…'

What, he wondered? Stay friends, keep in touch? Go on cruises together between rejected lovers?

'…be as civilised about it all as possible.'

Condescending bitch, Ewan thought, remembering he was none the wiser about Monsieur Tissot. 'You still haven't told me who *he* is.'

'No.' Then from left field, Paige said 'And you?'

'Me?'

'Surely there must be someone else in your life?'

Did she, after all this time, understand him so little?

'Why on earth should there be someone else?' he said.

She deflected the argument back to him again. 'You're hardly Channing Tatum, but…'

'Thanks.'

'…I naturally assumed…'

Ewan chose not to dignify her remarks with a direct response, so simply asked, 'One last time, who is he?'

'It's none of your bloody…'

Ewan finally tumbled. 'Of course. He's already spoken for!'

Angry pause.

Paige left the room, slamming the door behind her.

&⤸⤵&

EIGHT

Going Under

కా సా

'IS Duncan okay?'
      'He's away,' Grace said.
'Again?'
'Yes.'
'Poor you. His work certainly carries him far and wide.'
'It pays the bills.'

Vicky had popped in for a catch-up. As she sipped her tea, Grace looked through the huge picture windows and down the landscaped garden. The house had won an award when it was built five years earlier – it was one of the reasons they had bought it. But although light and spacious, it was costly to heat in winter. Also, she had never felt it was very friendly.

'So, where's your husband off to this time. Berlin again?'
'Yes. Then Brussels… Paris. Gathering ideas for the new Edinburgh.
'Reconsidering the philistine architecture of the 'Sixties too, I hope?'
'Indeed. I'm always nagging him to ensure civic integrity conquers historical arrogance,' Grace said, sounding as if she'd read the phrase in one of Duncan's professional magazines.

Which she had.

'Like he has much say?'
'Probably not, although he participates in enough working parties.'

Grace and Vicky's generation had been reared on their parents' indignation at how the University had once torn down two sides of a handsome Georgian square, replacing them with brutalist shoeboxes. Adding to the tension of the forthcoming Referendum were concerns over plans threatening Edinburgh's status as a World Heritage site.

Vicky moved on to her main reason for dropping by. 'No chance of getting away one evening for that new musical at The Playhouse?'
'I wish.' Grace had always considered musicals mindless

entertainment, but now would welcome any opportunity to escape for an afternoon.

'Why not?'

'How can I leave the girls?'

'What about your mother?'

Grace tensed up. 'Don't go there. We're barely speaking.'

'Does she know that?'

'She knows. Mum and I never been close, as you're aware. But I've recently lost any respect I ever had for her. Things are… fraught.'

'She must be depressed after all that's happened,' Vicky said, always striving to see the other person's point of view.

'Aren't we all?' Grace said, tartly.

Vicky detected a crack in her friend's usually impenetrable armour. Grace had never come so close to admitting something was badly wrong.

'It's just so unfair!'

'I'm so sorry.'

The two women had been friends since they had rented a flat with two other girls at Aberdeen. Vicky recalled helping Grace through one of these patches before. She'd been going out with Duncan for a while and experienced a sudden confidence crisis and convinced herself he wasn't serious. He'd been very late meeting her one evening, and she'd almost made up her mind to finish with him, when he had finally appeared, very red in the face – and proposed.

'How has Ewan reacted to his father's last wishes?'

'He's too nice for his own good. Takes any crap that's thrown at him.'

'You make him sound wet.'

'Isn't nice a polite way of saying wet?'

Not wishing to embark on semantics, Vicky said, 'About the show. Doesn't Duncan let you out at all?'

'Well…'

'You're hardly Bertha Rochester.'

'Going slowly mad, though.'

'Surely he could release you for one evening? He might discover what it's like looking after kids on his own.'

'It's not that he wouldn't. He… well, he never knows from one day to the next when he can get away.'

'Then why not let me babysit?' Vicky said. 'You could go to the theatre with someone else?'

'I couldn't do that to you. You'd miss out then.'

Vicky sighed. 'Think it over and get back to me. I must dash off soon and create something tempting with mince. Try telling Duncan how you feel. I'm sure he'd understand. You'll sort something out. You're entitled to a wee bit more freedom.'

'Easier said than done.'

Grace then did something Vicky had never seen before: she burst into tears. Vicky put an arm around her. 'I'm sorry,' Grace said, 'I wouldn't have wanted you to see me like this for all the world.'

After a minute or so she stopped crying and her shoulders began to relax.

'Have you thought of seeing someone?' Vicky said carefully.

Grace looked appalled. 'Someone... professional, you mean?

Vicky nodded. 'You have a problem with that?'

'You really think I need to see a... *psychiatrist*?'

'Not necessarily a psychiatrist, but there are some very approachable, well-trained counsellors out there you could at least talk things through with, who'd be totally objective.'

'You know that's not me.'

'Not the old Grace. But then, you've not been her for some time.'

'Haven't I? Oh. All the same, I ought to be able to sort out my own problems. It's not that I'm not grateful – I mean, you're always good to talk to... In fact, you're the only person I ever could, would talk to.'

'And that's a great compliment. But maybe you need someone who could be more... objective?'

Grace stiffened. 'You really think I'd discuss my innermost thoughts with someone I didn't know?'

'Consider it, though. It might be worth trying – not just for your own sake, but the twins and Duncan.'

On cue, demanding cries issued from the next room. Vicky, who felt she'd said more than enough, was prompted to glance pointedly at her watch. Attempting to lighten the atmosphere, she slipped into the vernacular. 'And here's me blethering. It's 6.15! Must away, hen. Divorce proceedings will be initiated if I dinnae flee this minute.'

Vicky struggled into her coat and moved towards the hallway. The two friends hugged. Grace opened the front door.

'Remember what I said.'

'Thanks, Vic.'

As she went off to see to Kara, Grace reflected on her conversation with Vicky. She loved Duncan very much, was terrified of driving him away – and yet was unable to help herself behaving the way she was.

It had started not long after the twins' birth. There had been relatively stable patches, but as the girls had grown older and increasingly mobile, things had got much worse. But was it entirely her fault? Wasn't this a problem that should be shared?

Grace knew she had never given Duncan any reason to worry about her in the past. After all, he'd married someone smart and organised with a not dissimilar temperament to his own. Yet, neither of them had properly factored in the changes that occur when children turn up. Especially not two at once.

If pressed, he'd probably say he knew it was tough looking after babies, but a temporary problem that would go away. The twins would be four later in the year and starting nursery school. He'd reason that it would give her a break each day. Before they grew much older, all the hard work would start paying off and they'd soon be trotting out *we'll never have these years again* banalities.

Everything was always cut and dried with Duncan.

'Men!' as Vicky might have said.

Despite her age, Grace had sailed through pregnancy, accepting the situation with some excitement. She'd even heard herself coming out with the corny line from juvenile fiction about being a twin: *What terrific fun, having a best friend for keeps!*

It had come to haunt her.

Having waited ten years for Project Family, Grace surprised everyone when she announced 'We've both decided I'm to be a full-time mother. It's something we feel very strongly about. Duncan says it's the only way a woman can fully bond with her children and reinforce early learning and good behaviour.' Very textbookish. But then, she hadn't spent years delivering PowerPoint presentations on *Human Dynamics* for nothing.

With Duncan the *Wunderkind* of Urban Planning, money wasn't an issue. When the twins arrived they'd hired part-time assistance. Then, after a few weeks, things had grown calmer. The girls slept a lot and gave Grace time to pull herself together between feeds and nappy changes. She'd kidded herself everything was under control and dismissed the nurse.

It was when teething started that Grace's troubles really began. Kara's pain became Lyndsay's. And vice versa. Grace found she couldn't stand the continued howling, and struggled to deal with the girls' heart-rending appeals for relief.

As they began to crawl and then walk, Grace felt she was turning into a creature out of *Doctor Who*, her head maniacally swivelling in different directions. The toddlers cottoned on to her every weakness. Each time she turned to stir the soup or selfishly glance at a newspaper, there would be a piercing shriek of calamity close by. More mess and tears to be wiped away and calming down to be done, as pans boiled over and the Hotpoint bleeped for attention.

When one child howled so did the other. The contents of two stomachs, bladders and bowels contrived to empty themselves, minutes apart. Two sets of nappies needed always to be at hand with two sets of clean clothes – and two arms for reassuring two angry, wriggling bodies.

If one girl was unable to see her sister, she screeched. If another got fed first, the other howled. As soon as they could link syllables together and clutch anything that prodded or poked, they mercilessly teased each other and tormented Grace like school bullies. Kara was the leader; on her own, Lyndsay was more or less manageable. As soon as anyone came to the house, of course, the sibling rivalry ceased and they turned into Disney princesses.

Trips to the local shops reinforced Grace's self-hatred. The contented, well-behaved offspring of neighbours and other parents brought out the worst in her daughters, who showed off shamelessly. Grace translated the well-intended looks of her contemporaries and comments like *so, you get that too, do you?* into *such a pity you can't handle them.*

Only on hearing their father's footsteps on the gravel did the two faces break into angelic smiles, and a period of gurgling calm prevail.

Many young mothers revel in this anarchic, pre-school world. Grace was by now in hell. It was two against one. She came to believe she was the enemy. The twins always had each other. She was the outsider. Her sense of maternal inadequacy continued to bedevil her, implying she was also failing as a wife.

Things had built up in Grace's mind to the point where she felt trapped in a room without a door. Every way she turned, she was faced with yet another blank wall.

She'd only herself to blame she reminded herself. It had been her choice to look after the children. Even now, she could organise support if her pride would allow. Her mother, for instance, would be only too eager to get her hands on her children: spouting platitudes and feeding them unhealthy treats – though not if Grace could help it. There had been unpleasant showdowns with Maggy already.

Accustomed to a tidy office, Grace liked to have everything in its place by the time Duncan arrived home. She was also painfully conscious of how many bright women, including her less well-heeled friends, were obliged to return to work after pregnancy. Yet, when they picked up their contented kids from nursery, she doubted they were punished with the howls of retribution she got all day long.

As paranoia strengthened its grip, a part of Grace knew she should confess to Duncan the extent to which she was failing to cope, but her stubbornness wouldn't permit it. It was unfair to regale him with her problems when he arrived home tired and hungry. Besides, by the time they were having their supper, the girls were usually fast asleep. For an hour or two, everything appeared serene.

In Duncan's defence, his own parents had looked on child-rearing as an inconvenience. This was partly due to their heavy involvement with the family firm. He often talked of how, until he was seven, he'd been left in the charge of successive au pairs, and the loneliness of the latch-key years that followed, teaching himself to make toast and heat up beans to stave off hunger.

His mother, beautiful, smart and, in her distant way, well-meaning, lacked maternal instinct. Even now, she was generous and kind to Grace and the children, but remote. Duncan had eventually made friends with his father, but only after gaining a place as a boarder at a leading independent school and honing his talents on the sports field. Now, the pair never missed a major rugby event at Murrayfield during the winter months, or a local cricket club match in the summer.

Duncan didn't want his children to feel they weren't crucial to his life, as his own parents had made him, but thoughtlessly assumed his wife would take the lead, holding things together until the girls were more independent. After all, he reasoned, he worked very hard and was entitled to some relaxation.

'Some' meant disappearing to play hockey or tennis most Saturday and Sunday afternoons when not spectating. Even annual holidays on the Fife coast revolved around golfing at St Andrews.

For as long as there had been just the two of them, Duncan and Grace had adapted to each other's timetables. Grace had even learned to enjoy watching her husband on the sports field, and, in moderation, socialising with the other golf widows. Now she was left to entertain the children on the beach whilst he was off with his mates.

Having had no effective role models himself, Duncan now had no-one but his wife to gently point out to him where he was falling down. And she was too busy hiding her own inadequacies to risk doing so.

Depression, unlike some other illnesses which proclaim themselves with obvious symptoms, takes hold gradually. Its subtlety is in kidding you and the people around you, that everything is fine for too long. After all, lethargy and irritability are only to be expected in a young mother – an assumption reinforced by Grace's doctor, with his jovial *quite a handful you've got there!* whenever she took the twins for a check-up. They appeared healthy, happy, and well turned-out. Grace, if a little paler than in the past, feigned sufficient outward composure to prevent him picking up the extent to which she, herself, was falling apart inside.

The shock of her father's sudden death had made Grace susceptible to other negative emotions too. Maggy gave the impression she was the only one seriously affected as if, as Don's widow, it was her right, and Ewan's and her own feelings were secondary. Because she and Ewan were less demonstrative than Maggy, didn't mean they cared any the less. Because they had other people to consider, didn't ease their sense of loss.

Grace felt especially low in the early evening. During his final months, Don had regularly dropped by on his way home from work. He'd adored his granddaughters in whatever mood he found them and was the one person who had left her feeling better about herself. It always gave her back, if only for a while, enough self-respect to keep going.

When Grace discovered the contents of Don's will, her sadness turned to hurt, then frustration – and finally anger. He had left Maggy practically everything along with the generous pension he had organised for her. Only his most accessible savings were to be shared between his family. Most children would have accepted this arrangement as the natural order of things, but Grace's feelings towards her mother had reached a point where she sought almost any excuse to add to her list of Maggy's wrongdoings, however unreasonable.

After the deduction of expenses and some small legacies, Ewan and Grace were each left ten thousand pounds: a useful amount certainly, but hardly a fortune in the context of Don's overall worth. As in many such instances, they would receive nothing more until their mother's death – unless, of course, she re-married when things might become very different.

And that was a serious possibility.

Grace had always been appalled by Maggy's ability to connect easily to strangers: on buses, trains and in shops; chatting to people of either sex – although men, often younger than her, seemed especially entertained by her lively banter. It could sometimes be embarrassing. Now it was a threat.

Grace would have been the first to admit that they didn't need the money. What ate away at her was the knowledge that her father had left almost everything to Maggy without considering, not so much Ewan and herself, but the eventual needs of her own children – and any Ewan might yet have. The quality of private education she had in mind for her girls would certainly test their resources. She didn't want to be beholden to Duncan's parents if she could help it.

Grace couldn't admit to herself that, if anyone, it was Don she should really be angry with. But he, of course, was beyond reproach. Instead, Grace had turned all her hurt on her mother whom, she believed, had always held ultimate sway at home.

Grace wasn't to know that Don had drafted his final testament at the office one afternoon many years before, when they had still been struggling, after reading an article in *The Observer* on how *It's Never Too Early to Make Your Will*. It had been witnessed by his secretary and the final version from his solicitor filed with just a casual 'well that's out of the way' to Maggy when he got home in the evening, vaguely intending to review the situation when he retired. In your head, you're always twenty-nine. And, whatever Grace believed about her parents' relationship, Maggy, herself a prudent manager, had never been able to persuade Don into doing anything he didn't consider a priority. Dying comparatively young was not on his agenda.

When that happened, Maggy's distress was such that she barely heard the solicitor when he delicately ran past her the notion of a Deed of Variation in the children's interests. That Maggy had decided such obligations could wait until she found the emotional space to sort herself out and re-make her own will, taking it for granted Grace and Ewan could always come to her for any financial help they might need in the interim, never crossed Grace's mind. If it had, she might have tactfully raised the matter with her mother before probate.

People accept lack-of-communication contrivances in fiction and drama. Yet in life, people you might expect to be able to talk to each other often don't; either from misplaced tact, discomfort, or a fear their motives might be misinterpreted.

Sadly, Grace was now hurtling into a dark place.

She wanted to hit out in reprisal for her own imagined injuries.

At just one person.

NINE

Love, Death and Forsythia

❧ ◈

MAGGY had been mulling over what Lorna had said that afternoon a couple of weeks ago. Was guilt part of her problem?

Only the other day there had been yet another preachy Healthy Food sequence on TV. 'Everyone knows…' rebuked the emaciated young man in the Fair Isle sweater, '…that the typical Scottish diet knocks years off the average lifespan. This afternoon Sonia and I…' here he smirked at the smug blonde beside him on the sofa, '…will show you just how many saturated fats you're serving up, to…' hurriedly he changed the *him* on the tip of his tongue to '… *the family*. That must be good, mustn't it?'

'Prat!' she'd thought, sending him back into the ether. But he'd touched a nerve.

Maggy now blamed herself for the menu choices she'd made down the years. Don had never overeaten, was average in build and weight, and always received good reports after his insurance check-ups. She'd considered her meals to be varied and nutritious but had no control over the something-with-chips lunches he often enjoyed with 'the lads' – as he referred to his forty-something colleagues. He would then come home for a meat-based dinner rounded off with a sweet. Had she unknowingly, she worried, clogged his arteries?

Don's eulogy had celebrated a happy man who'd enjoyed a good marriage and accomplished everything he'd set out to. Some folk might say it was tragic for such a life to be extinguished as if by the click of a switch. At least he'd suffered little and gone out on a high.

Now Maggy was adrift without a compass. People talked about 'growing old gracefully,' She wasn't old by today's standards, yet couldn't afford to waste time still to come. Certainly, Don had left her well provided for. No problem on that score. Barring accidents, she could have at least twenty years of useful time ahead, providing she cut down on the Croft Original. Here she smiled to herself. Her one-glass-a-night tipple of sherry, or discreet finger of Scotch after a particularly tough day, had been a joke between Don and herself. She was all too aware that *discreet* had recently become *large*.

She sometimes recalled an early afternoon many years before, helping Bessie wash up after Sunday lunch. It was traditionally an activity during which confidences were exchanged, and decisions made. In her head she heard the chirpy Mozart Allegro tripping out of her mother's Roberts transistor and felt the comforting afternoon sun streaming through the window. An ordinary, relaxed Sunday.

Precious ordinariness.

Bessie would have been about the age she was now. Out of the blue, she'd said, 'You know, Maggy, I like to think we've always been good friends?'

'Of course, we have, Mum. And always will be. Why?'

'There's something I've been meaning to say. Time goes so fast. I want you to remember today. The two of us here, nice and cosy because...' here there was a significant pause, '... as people grow older, they change. Not usually for the better.'

'Not you,' Maggy said.

'Maybe me. As you know, I've inherited your grandmother's rheumatoid arthritis.'

Once pretty, her mother's knuckles were already deformed. She always kept her hands well-moisturised and nails manicured and varnished, hoping to distract attention from their deformity. 'It'll be other joints soon, probably my knees. I'll be in a lot of pain and may become quite beastly on occasions. You won't recognise the person I am today. Hopefully, only when it's bad and the medication isn't working. But I want you to remember, it won't be me, not the *real* me.'

'One of your gifts has been to prepare me for anything,' Maggy had said.

'Things never happen exactly as you expect, but it helps to have scenarios up one's sleeve. And make the most of every day.' Bessie hung her tea-towel over the radiator. 'Now, let's forget all about it.' She began sifting flour for some jam tarts. 'Did you enjoy *Blazing Saddles*?'

In time, Bessie's mobility deteriorated as she'd said it would. Slowly at first, then accelerating, until by her mid-seventies there were spells when her eyes would beseechingly scream 'help me', her voice lashing out in frustration when she found she couldn't carry out the simplest tasks. Lachlan struggled to be her second pair of hands. Then he suffered a serious stroke and died. Bessie joined him six months later.

At least Don would never endure a slow, miserable decline whilst watching the blinds roll down over her own life. How should she spend the rest of her time? More importantly, where would she find the motivation to do so?

She needed a jump-lead.

Who was she? What role should she audition for now: The Elderly Matriarch? A terrible thought struck her. Was she turning into Doris? Poor Doris, long widowed herself, with her eccentric jewellery and erratic memory, now ninety-seven and still lording it grandly over everyone in Whispering Pines. The Mad Woman of South Queensferry.

How her mother had despised a certain breed of elderly women, The Edinburgh Ladies, lampooned by comics and pantomime dames and thought to be extinct, who once upon a time, over afternoon tea in the smarter cafés, their quaint millinery bobbing, pontificated on a range of parochial topics. The more shocking the topic, the narrower their vowels became, as they scathingly dismissed last night's Shostakovich concert at the Usher Hall or condemned the latest avant-garde art exhibition. Items of Any Other Business might include the laxity of the city's retail facilities, followed, in the flash of a teaspoon, by character assassinations of friends who had fallen short of the mark.

Many of the ladies were widows or had simply missed the charabanc due to the shortage of mates after two decimating world wars. Some had even lived together as 'companions'. Maybe the frustration of secretly wanting more from such arrangements, but oppressed by convention to suppress all carnal desires, had been a factor in encouraging disapproval of anything that didn't meet their narrow definition of good taste.

If Bessie had mocked them, it was to help assuage personal terrors. Circumstances oblige us to create survival mechanisms. The ladies had once been young, hopeful, and maybe flirtatious. In contrast, Maggy's life had been spent during a sustained period of peace, taking for granted many things her grandparents could only have dreamt of.

If Don's death had isolated her and knocked out some of her former ebullience, at least Maggy now had more sympathy for old people less lucky than herself left to rearrange the chairs on the sinking deck of their self-esteem.

And what about Lorna? Dear Lorna, could she really be fifty in a couple of years? Don, rarely judgemental, had sometimes said 'It's a pity she couldn't have found a nice lad – she'd have made a good mother.'

Or would she? More to the point, *why* should she? It was so typical of a man to assume, whilst recognising they had the right to a solid career, that every woman's default setting was programmed to find a long-term heterosexual relationship and reproduce.

You accept those you love for what they are. Or try to. Maggy supposed she'd put down Lorna's lack of interest in boys to being, as her junior school teacher had once put in an Algebra report, 'a late developer in that department.'

Did it matter?

She remembered Lorna as a student, 'going out' with a couple of lads. Lorna, tomboyish by inclination and looks had, indeed, held on to them longer than most female-male relationships but, it had transpired, simply as good friends.

Then Zoë had moved in with her. For over ten years the two shared a cosy but disorganised flat off Bruntsfield Links. It was only after a friend had mentioned the set-up and said in a surprised tone, 'Did you not know? I just assumed… you being her aunt and everything…' that Maggy saw the relationship as equivalent to her own domestic arrangements, though minus the children.

She saw no need to give different types of partnerships labels, although she quite liked the term *bohemian*, an old-fashioned word but with a disarmingly romantic ring. Since her college days and experience of off-West End theatre, Maggy had always warmed to people with divergent lifestyles.

Never, out of loyalty to Lorna, had Maggy ever broached with her brother and his wife the matter of Lorna's private life. Besides, if ever anything remotely controversial crept into a conversation, their body language always said 'but it's none of our business.' Which it wasn't. Or hers. Yet there was a thin line between being gossipy and having people's best interests at heart. Nevertheless, the amount of editing that went on in family conversations, was both fascinating and exasperating in equal measures.

Then one morning, Lorna had arrived at Illyria in tears. Between sobs and over a very large G&T she'd told her how, the evening before, Zoë had moved out of their flat and into a houseboat with Gaynor. Gaynor had found God – and Zoë thought she might have done too.

Talking the matter through, Maggy had comforted Lorna as best she could and, considering her only experience of same-sex romance had been a heavy crush on her friend Una McBride at Mary Erskine's, was surprised at the extent of her empathy.

The last time they had met, for lunch at The Roxburgh, only days before Don died, a courtesy question concerning Lorna had led the old schoolfriends to recall their own adolescent intimacy.

'Remember that bitter February afternoon when we handsomely trounced St George's?' Maggy said.

'How thrilled we were!'

'How we hugged in the changing room afterwards!'

'Always thought you had a wee bit of a pash on me, Maggy!' Una said.

'*Pash*. Now there's an Angela Brazil-ism.'

'More a Miss Brodie girl, me.'

'Were we really so jolly hockey-sticks?

'Perhaps not. I always thought of myself as quite sophisticated,' Una said. 'Raring to escape school and become a dental nurse. It was the first time another girl ever kissed me.'

'The *only* time?' Maggy had queried mischievously. 'Was it such a ghastly experience?'

How they'd hooted. Yet, whilst the exchange was jokey, a wistful line had remained on their lips after her smile had faded. They both knew the more conventional lifestyles they'd opted for had worked out well, but didn't everyone have occasional *sliding doors* moments?

Maggy had sometimes envied the Lorna-Zoë setup. The bliss of not having to cater for four people, all with different food fads – or start planning in July the family clothes to be packed for a holiday a month later. And how nice to have someone on hand, who saw life from a strictly female point of view, and with whom one might sometimes share a reassuring hug without wondering if there was a subtext.

People hugged a lot nowadays. Far more than they did when she was younger. Comradely, innocent clinches. 'Group hug!' cried old friends, who'd not met up for a while.

Maggy rather liked that.

Had she herself ever been seriously attracted to another woman? That was a hard one. She certainly admired women's bodies and considered, on balance, they were aesthetically more beautiful than men's. 'A little of what you fancy…' had always been one of Bessie's pet phrases, although she'd have probably been opening a box of Black Magic at the time, not referring to à la carte sex.

Even so…

It said a lot about both women, that Maggy and Una's friendship had held together well enough for them to discuss, without awkwardness, a time when the feelings between them had been immature, yet strangely powerful.

Relationships enriched by trust and affection that looked on tempests and endured were surely the most valued.

Maggy would have liked to have kept in touch with some of her ex-boyfriends. Even now, bumping into the still-gorgeous Hugo Forsyth she'd dated several times during one blazing hot Festival in her late teens, produced a nostalgic flutter. But maddeningly, he'd dumped her – not the other way around.

Lorna had lived alone since her time with Zoë and kept a low emotional profile. Very recently though, Maggy thought she'd observed an elusive change in her: the appearance of what Mrs Henry Wood might have called *a glow*. She'd idly dropped into the conversation that she was taking on a new lodger and wasn't always at home when Maggy rang at their usual time after work. Well, much as she valued her friendship, if Lorna had found someone to care about again, that was as it should be.

There was a thump. Maggy looked up. It was Garibaldi jumping onto the kitchen window ledge. His teeth chattering, he was now gazing intently out. The forsythia bush was in bud against the outhouse wall; a blue tit hopping from twig to twig. That corner was always a suntrap, and now a hint of yellow proclaimed spring had arrived. Was that why, over the past week or so, she had finally felt restless and – if she dare admit it to herself – found a spring in her step when she'd played a Beach Boys album?

The hands on the carriage clock advised her it was two o'clock. She must vacuum downstairs, tidy up her bedroom – and ring Ewan to see if things had settled down.

Then maybe a chapter of Kate Mosse?

⋘⋙

TEN

At the Carousel

ॐ ॐ

A case trundled past.

Not his case. Dino's had a distinctively patterned strap. A giveaway. He remembered how he'd impulsively snapped it on at Milan airport. Glancing at his watch he saw three-quarters of an hour had passed since the plane landed. More lost time in Baggage Reclaim.

The oppressive atmosphere closed in.

Three-quarters of the other passengers on his flight to Edinburgh had already found their luggage and disappeared. '*Forza, svelto, svelto, svelto*,' he muttered as the same khaki duffel bag dawdled round yet again.

Various disaster scenarios ran through his mind. Dino tried to dismiss them but failed. Surely, no one could have noticed his absence so soon – not after all the messages he'd left.

Unless …

With the stop in London and all the little delays and flight-schedule adjustments, sufficient time had passed for the authorities to be on the lookout. Who could have grassed on him – and when? Dino shivered. These people were professionals. They didn't mess around when things went wrong. If anything had. In which case, he was a dead man – metaphorically speaking.

Or possibly not metaphorically...

God, how did he let himself get in this mess? Damn Marcello and his 'trust me it's fool-proof' crap.

His phone vibrated. A text from Paolo giving him directions to central Edinburgh: 'Wish I could have been there to meet you, but…'

Dino's paranoia rocketed as the unclaimed case drifted by yet again,

'*Merda!*' he groaned, furtively casting his eyes around the sides of the carousel.

'No patience you young people!' an elderly woman next to him grumbled.

The first bad moment had been at Malpensa. An official at the boarding desk had given him a strange look and walked off with his passport, leaving him red-faced and sweating in front of a queue of inquisitive passengers. A stressful ten minutes followed before it was back in his hand. No explanation. What had that been about? Only when safely in the air had he been able to relax.

It wasn't as if Dino was the sort of young man who melted in a crowd. With his striking Latin looks, he could be mistaken for one of several Italian pop stars. He mussed-up his hair. Drawing attention to himself was the last thing he needed today.

The tension was back. Everything was messing with his head. Going over the events of the past few days yet again and searching for clues as to how he'd ended up here, he didn't like what he found. Queasiness was settling in now, too. He only had himself to blame.

Accepting what people said.

Always in a hurry.

'Must slow down and keep calm at all costs,' he told himself.

As if that was going to happen. Yet, the next mistake could be fatal.

Several articles of luggage bumped up on to the conveyor belt. A trickle at first followed by more – then yet more. All shapes, sizes and shades of colour, jostling each other like workers in a rush hour queue.

More, and still more items. Gliding along. All belonging to someone else.

Finally, the unruly procession slimmed down to a dribble. Dino's case peeked up from the hatch and trundled up to him.

Grabbing it, he pulled out the handle and made for the exit.

The men in Customs appeared too busy gossiping with colleagues to scrutinise every person scurrying by.

Or was that just a ploy? Would one of them suddenly yell and beckon him over as he sneaked past?

Pulse racing, Dino blended with all other travellers coursing past the Nothing to Declare sign. Hurrying along the corridor he broke through the double doors, out into the semi-daylight. Cars and coaches streamed past in the sunshine beyond the vast building. Soon he would be back in the fresh air, lost amongst the far larger crowd.

Hastening towards the buses, Dino was unaware of a man in a beige jacket tucked in the entrance of a gift boutique.

A phone was trained on his retreating form.

∽✦✧

ELEVEN

Tumbling Off a Shelf

 handful of the line separator ornament

THE living room of Lorna's second-floor flat looked across playing fields to the silhouette of the city beyond.

Not far away was the entrance to Royal Botanic Garden with Robert Louis Stevenson's birthplace nearby. After that was the short climb to the city centre; around the corner in the other direction, a row of useful shops.

Ally immediately felt at home.

The sound of traffic drifted up as far as the windows, filtering through the double-glazing to provide a companionable hum, usually masked by the strains of Classic FM.

Between the hallway doors, a canny carpenter had sandwiched a tier of now-cluttered shelves. If jolted by someone pulling the bathroom door too hard, books fell off the upper shelves and startled the unwary passer-by.

Inside the living room, more shelves filled each side of the fireplace, the double-parked books, DVDs and CDs restrained only by stacks of old magazines wedged in the gaps. Ethnic rugs broke up the expanse of Berber carpeting. A merry assortment of squashy cushions brought life to the faded blue covers of the lumpy armchairs and sofa. On the walls, framed period Scottish prints lost the battle for attention with vivid contemporary paintings, whilst ancient theatre posters hid marks where Christmas decorations had once been fixed.

Three weeks had passed since the two women met at the Balfour. Earlier that week Lorna drove Ally to the house where she rented a room and, despite entreaties, helped her upstairs with her bags of shopping. As Ally had feared, Lorna was appalled. Not that the bedsit was particularly dirty or untidy – Ally was fastidious about her surroundings – but even her jolly patchwork quilt and collection of teddy bears couldn't disguise its inherent dreariness.

It was then that Lorna suggested Ally moved into her spare room. At the same time, they were both aware they hadn't known each other long, and that there was a considerable age difference.

Ally had taken to Lorna immediately and, by and large, was

looking forward to the arrangement. The friendly flat would provide a welcome change of scenery and reduce her concern that she was becoming too reliant on Cal and Senga.

Even so…

Ally had been aware of Lorna's preferences since that first night when she'd served her the toastie. Little tell-tale signs supported her assumptions: goodbye squeezes held a fraction too long; photos of women friends in varying degrees of – albeit social – intimacy dotted around her flat. And then there was the brilliant but startling nude oil of a young Asian girl which greeted you in the hall. More telling still, apart from one family group taken at Lorna's graduation: there were no pictures of men.

If the older woman hoped she could steer their relationship into what, for Ally, would be unwelcome waters, she must gently disabuse her. On the other hand, she didn't want to lose Lorna's friendship – and support. If she was going to move in with her, she must proceed with caution and sensitivity. How did the proverb go: *let not your foot frequent the house of your friend, lest he be weary of you and hate you*?

So far, nothing had been finalised.

And then there was her handicap. Ally hoped it wouldn't be long before she could completely stop relying on her laptop and notebook when she got involved in protracted discussions. Senga and Cal had remarked on her progress too.

One evening, sitting on the sofa enjoying mugs of coffee and listening to Michael Bublé, Ally felt the moment was right to be more open about her past. She'd been tidying up some of the files on her laptop and clicked on a folder of photographs headed Family 2013 taken that summer in Elie. One snapshot caused her to grunt nostalgically, just loud enough to catch Lorna's attention. Lorna looked up from her armchair and gave her a quizzical smile. Ally beckoned her.

Lorna put down the old colour supplement she'd finally got around to reading and joined Ally on the sofa.

'You're the dead spit of your dad,' she observed of the well-dressed group of people smiling out of the photograph. 'And that has to be your brother?' Ally nodded. 'He has the same eyes and colouring as… I presume that's your mother too?' Ally nodded again. 'I'd love to meet them some time.'

Pretending she'd clicked on another file by mistake, Ally brought up the photograph of a stocky young man with a mop of unruly auburn hair wearing a green cagoule over a red tartan shirt. Attractive, if not conventionally handsome, he had a friendly, mischievous smile.

Lorna looked at Ally questioningly. 'He's... nice,' she said at length.

Ally was at the frontier of sensitive territory. 'That's Fergus,' she said. 'We met at a summer camp. He was ...very special.' She tried not to notice Lorna trying, unsuccessfully, to take this information on the chin.

Ally had never felt the same about anyone before or since. Fergus and she had shared the same left-wing politics and outlook on life, and their personalities complemented each other perfectly. Merely being close to him was enough for her. Their happiest free daytime hours were spent snuggled up like a couple of cats on the sofa, putting the world to rights. Ally had never been so in tune with anyone before.

Until Fergus, the few men in Ally's life had all been school-boyish: selfishly over-eager or inhibited and embarrassed. Lovemaking with Fergus, however, had been amazing. He'd possessed the knack of making everything serious fun. But then, wasn't fun always improved by taking it seriously? They'd be laughing, and she'd spot a wicked gleam in his eye. Tickling would turn into merry foreplay until the moment came when, happily synchronised, they'd gently move things up a level.

This, of course, would have been far too much information for Lorna. But Ally hoped the photo would at least give her some idea of Fergus's importance in her life.

Lorna hadn't been slow to pick up the past tense in Ally's narration.

'What happened?' she said gently. Ally turned her head away and sat quietly for a few seconds. 'You don't have to tell me if you don't want to.'

Ally knew she had to explain, for both their sakes, if their friendship was to move on. If it changed things between them, so be it. It was better that happened now than later, when there could be painful misunderstandings. 'I'll take it slowly, if you don't mind,' she said.

'Eighteen months after the photo was taken, Fergus motor-cycled over to Kirkaldy to visit his grandmother. I got a text from him about six o'clock saying he was on his way home. He hoped to see me in a couple of hours. He... he didn't show up. I tried contacting him. There was... no response. At ten o'clock, I phoned his digs. No reply.

At half-past, I tried once more. Again, nothing. I rang his mother. She didn't answer. I left a message. Then I fell asleep in a chair. His mother woke me up with a call about one o'clock in the morning. She… she was in a bad way…'

At this point, Ally snuffled and, somewhat embarrassed, paused to wipe away a fugitive tear. She then grabbed her laptop, continuing the story in feverish bursts of typing:

'On his way home, on a sharp bend, Fergus collided with a speeding removal van. His bike must have swerved quickly, but the edge of the vehicle caught him and hurled him so violently on to the tarmac even his helmet couldn't save him. Someone phoned for an ambulance, but the haemorrhaging was so bad…'

Here, Ally stopped to wipe her face again.

'…he was dead on arrival at the hospital.'

Lorna gently took the laptop from Ally, processing all she had heard and trying to control her own, confused, feelings. Her immediate reaction was a desire to comfort her, but any, even tentative, approaches of that nature had, so far, been gently rebuffed. She was also aware that Ally must have spent the last few years re-telling the story to other people, so settled for briefly squeezing her hand, hoping the extent to which she'd been moved was evident in her face.

The account confirmed what Lorna already knew. Ally would only ever be a friend – though probably a good one. In the meantime, simply having her around was bringing purpose back into, what she'd confessed to herself, was a self-interested life. Her generosity wasn't really kindness; it was a bid to be needed at any level.

After a light supper, the women made plans. It was settled. Ally would give notice on her bedsit and move in with Lorna on Easter Monday. She would pay Lorna half the rent her current landlord required, but they would share household duties, shopping, and cooking.

The words Ally spoke, however hesitantly, suggested a sophisticated vocabulary. Early on, Lorna had guessed that Ally's problems were the result of a deeply traumatic experience. Whether they were long-term or comparatively temporary, and what had caused them, she could only surmise. The Fergus tragedy, she sensed, was only part of the story.

Lorna knew she was taking a risk inviting someone to live with her, whom she knew little about, and who appeared so vulnerable.

Sometimes, though, you had to back your hunch and take a gamble. If she could help Ally make progress from whatever her underlying problems were, it would be worth it.

TWELVE

Of Man and Mouse

৵ ৵

THE mouse scurried towards a small gap in the floorboards with a large crumb of pastry, a remnant of Dino's supper the previous night, clenched tightly in its jaws.

No doubt the creature was in a hurry to feed his, or was it *her*, family? Dino could picture the tiny creature behind the wainscot, its dependents snuggled up in a nest of torn newspaper and bits of rag.

He kept replaying last night's conversation with Paolo in his head. Over a bottle of very cheap wine, they'd jabbered away in their native tongue.

'Cheer up!'

'I was in a bad way when I arrived,' Dino said.

'It took ages for you to relax.'

'I felt a bit of a fraud. But wasn't sure what to expect.'

'Any progress?' Paolo said.

'No.'

'Not even security-wise?'

A note had been pushed through the letterbox the evening he arrived:

> *Sta' molto, molto attento!*
> *(Be very, very careful!)*

Dino's desire for anonymity and plans to launch himself on the city were immediately thrown into disarray. Who was on to him? What did they want? Was this a nasty game or was he seriously being warned off something?

Or somebody?

'I keep looking out of the window to check if anyone's watching the place… or an unusual car is parked nearby…' Dino said. 'And when I'm out, I glance behind me all the time.'

'Do your parents know you're staying with me?' Paolo said.

'Cesare of course, and my mother.'

'Bet they're delighted.'

Dino didn't reply, aware of his family's tendency to disparage any of his friends not building successful careers.

'How can you be sure they won't blab?' Paolo said.

'Cesare won't, and as far as my mother knows,' Dino said, 'I'm here to further my business contacts. Which is sort of true, if only I could get out there and make a start.'

'You've not heard anything from Marcello?'

'No.' Dino sighed. 'God knows what's happened to him. Frankly, I get shit-scared if I think too much about it.'

'He can look after himself. Talk himself out of anything, that guy.'

'Hopefully.'

Privately, Dino wasn't so sure. He was grateful to Paolo for the use of this temporary shelter, depressing though it was. Needing to leave Italy in haste, he hadn't had time to think his plans through too carefully. Paolo was the only person, he hoped, he could trust. Dino had once spent a weekend with Paolo before. Edinburgh was as good a place in which to hide as any. He'd contacted his friend on impulse, booked a ticket, packed his case, and made a dash for the airport.

Like a lot of Italians, Paolo's family had first come to Scotland in the 1900s and established a couple of ice cream parlours on the east coast. The cynics had laughed: 'Ice cream in freezing Scotland, are you mad?' Yet it had worked. Although, whilst there had always been a market for the genuine Italian product, the small, independent firms on the coast had lost out to the food conglomerates and by now had dwindled to a handful.

Paolo was a bright guy, but totally self-indulgent and lacking in staying power. He'd dropped out halfway through an Economics degree course, mainly from boredom and, after quarrelling with his parents, imposed himself on Edinburgh. A gifted sculptor, with considerable charm, he was frittering away his life and talents, dependent on whatever odd jobs he could get, and contributions from his lodgers. Foraging hand-to-mouth, he sold the odd sculpture he forged from old pieces of malleable material he found in skips and moved from squat to squat; illegally requisitioning them for as long as they remained standing.

Many people considered Paolo an irresponsible layabout yet, despite his vagabond lifestyle he was good-hearted and, like so many people useless at organising their own lives, a kind man who could be surprisingly sound when advising others.

'I've felt a prisoner this past week,' Dino said, 'lying low, terrified of going far except for basic food needs; sleeping, reading, and exercising. It scares me knowing someone's watching me but not who they are. I'll go mad if I stay in much longer. I really want to try and sell my designs but don't know where to start. If I pick the wrong person, they'll be on to me in no time. Since receiving that warning, I daren't go anywhere central.'

'What's the worst that could happen?' Paolo said. 'If you're spotted by someone trailing you in a crowd, they wouldn't dare try anything on. Most of the busier streets around here are reasonably safe. Stick to those and dart inside a shop the moment you sense danger. Open spaces should be all right too. It's when you turn into the quieter backstreets you really need your wits about you.'

'You're probably right,' Dino said. 'But it's not just that. My money won't last long, either.' He sighed. 'I'll have to pay Cesare back sooner or later. I've got to think of a way of earning some. What on earth can I do?'

Paolo thought for a moment. 'Have you considered…?' he said at length.

Dino looked cagey. He knew Paolo's suggestions could be creative. 'Yes?'

'How can I put this …'

Dino waited.

'Why not use your best assets?' Paolo said.

'I can hardly sell my designs here now.' Dino frowned.

'Not shoes, idiot. Your other… talents.'

'Like?'

Paolo flashed his eyes despairingly.

'Look at you. Fit… handsome… still under thirty?'

Dino caught his drift. 'You *can't* mean…?'

Paolo raised a knowing eyebrow.

'Sell *myself?*'

'Your… boyish charm, anyhow.' Paolo said, as if suggesting Dino got himself a paper round.

'Are you *serious?*' Dino said.

'You might meet some rich old biddy, or…'

Dino grimaced with disgust. 'Ugh! The thought appals me.' He was still recovering from his split from Stefania, with whom he'd been in a serious long-term relationship. Right now, the idea of making his body available to anyone else was repellent.

'Now they're on to you,' Paolo said, 'your job opportunities are limited. But it doesn't mean you can't be, well, your own boss.

Hopefully, you won't be here long. It would only be until things die down and you can go home.'

'But a good Catholic boy like me?' Dino said, forgetting he'd not been near an altar rail for years.

'Think of it as a little paid companionship. It's a burgeoning market. How do you imagine many foreign students help support themselves? You don't always have to wind up horizontally if you don't want to.'

'But old women and… worse.'

'It's up to you. Some needy people with surplus cash, happily pay attractive men and women to stave off loneliness for an hour or so.'

'And it would involve, precisely…?'

'Good conversation. An optional cuddle, maybe, to round things off.'

Dino knew Paolo was being disingenuous. More than optional cuddles would be expected, especially if he found himself desperate enough to let himself be chatted up by the wrong people. In the fashion world, he was constantly being harassed by men who begged for 'just a couple of photos' – he'd lost lucrative work opportunities turning them down.

Sure, he had a couple of friends from student days who, until they were established, had survived by hiring themselves out. Interesting guys, too, from good homes, who chose to become 'high class' escorts rather than commit to the tiring routine of serving in cafés and bars or be beholden to their families. 'Less tiring and more lucrative' they said. But then, people who thought divergently to survive often were.

'You seem to know a lot about it,' Dino said.

Paolo's face moved from indignant to mildly guilty, before settling on brazen. 'When needs must,' he said intriguingly, refusing to be drawn further. 'Anyway, you've some decent clothes with you, haven't you?' Dino nodded. 'More importantly, it would provide you with some protection. The men who have you in their sights are unlikely to pounce if you're accompanied by someone respectable-looking.'

'I wouldn't know where to begin.'

'You'll think of something.'

With that, Paolo had glanced at his watch, swallowed the last of the wine, and hauled himself across the room.

'I'm off to bed!' he said. 'Really vicious stuff, that vino.' As he turned at the door, he said, 'Consider it, anyway.'

Dino was still considering.

Despite his initial distaste of Paolo's suggestion, the seeds germinated over the long, restless night.

Dino was blessed with the ability to be innovative when it came to his craft. Yet reinventing himself in other ways, albeit for only some weeks, was easier said than done. He couldn't risk ending up in a more dangerous situation than he already was.

He pictured himself in a film montage like those in the old Hollywood musicals he'd seen. Dino the Model, the Artist, the Musician, the Actor – the *Stud*? And no, not Dino, a more glamorous name: Lorenzo, Lucio… Luca perhaps? He had a cousin called Luca.

His fantasy receded as practicalities took over. How would he market himself? It was far too dangerous to promote himself on the internet.

Dino liked what he'd seen of Edinburgh. It reminded him somewhat of Rome, despite the 'old' buildings being classical revivalist and not the magnificent, crumbling originals he was more familiar with. But he'd like to explore it – if he dared to.

Sitting astride an old bentwood chair, Dino finished off a mutton pie from a nearby takeaway, washed down the last mouthful with a bottle of sparkling water, and looked around at his surroundings: the chair salvaged from a skip, and its backless relation currently serving as a small table; the futon in the corner and crumpled heap of charity shop bedding.

The few clothes he'd brought with him were lying inside a walk-in cupboard on top of sheets of an ancient *Edinburgh News*. A spare pair of jeans and smart pair of grey slacks drooped from wire hangers on a rusty hook. His best light brown leather shoes, designed by himself – and his pride and joy – gleamed down from the one secure shelf.

A condemned property in a short terrace that had got lost in the no-man's-land of one of the city's shabbier corners, the building had been granted only a short reprieve from the wrecking ball. A previous lodger with specialist skills had provided illicit access to water and electricity. But time was running out.

A jog around the Meadows – a large, green space bordered by trees half a mile away – had left Dino's second-best T-shirt coldly damp. He must do battle with the improvised showering facilities in the malodorous bathroom and rinse it through.

The mouse had returned and was fixing him with dark beady eyes, hoping for more leftovers. Dino knew the friendship – if he could dignify their relationship as such – was based on cupboard love. He must be careful not to anthropomorphise the creature. Mice were endearing, in a children's book way, but quickly became pests if they adopted your living space as a free restaurant. Or worse, a maternity unit.

He wondered if, like humans, mice fitted into categories: drifters. foragers, predators. It was a strange planet we all shared, with its juxtaposition of compassion and brutality.

The greatest danger for mouse and man was being in the wrong place at the wrong time.

The greatest sin, not fitting in.

As he was discovering.

In thrall to Marcello's charisma, when Dino had approached his friend to see if he could help him arrange a loan for his workshop, he'd been blind to the more capricious facets of his personality, like his attraction to easy money schemes – entertaining in a friend but foolish in a business associate.

Why had it never dawned on him to investigate the trustworthiness of Marcello's connections? Why had he agreed to let Marcello 'explore the matter' for him, especially when he'd been offered such a strange, cut-price deal. And what was his friend getting out of it?

Above all, why had he been crazy enough to hand over his bank codes?

'Don't worry,' Marcello had assured him, 'these men know exactly what they're doing. It'll work out all right – you'll see.' Alas, when you've worshipped someone for as long as Dino had, one turned a deaf ear to whispers of their unreliability.

Dino's leap of faith had landed him in serious trouble.

'Didn't you make the connection between Marcello's disappearance and Stefania's reaction?' Paolo had said.

'She seemed as puzzled as I was when it all went pear-shaped. Then she turned on me as if it was all my fault.'

'Guilt, I should think. And after that?'

'There was the night when we had the terrible row and she flounced out of my room.' But not, Dino withheld from Paolo, before giving him a searing look that had broken his heart.

'I know that morally speaking, I sail close to the wind,' Paolo said, 'but I'd never recklessly help my friend borrow dodgy money for an even a dodgier project. And then, to steal his girl...'

Dino winced. Marcello's betrayal had been on two fronts.

'He was always all show and no substance,' Paolo went on. 'He knew how you regarded him. It's how he managed to manipulate you. God knows what you signed up to. Where on earth did you imagine he got the money from? They were paying him – to trap you!'

Dino defended himself. 'I know that now. But you can only judge people by the way they behave towards you, can't you? Marcello and I have been friends since childhood. Besides, he's forfeited whatever he hoped to get out of it – and may be in even more danger than I am. And at least he tried to warn me.'

The night disaster had struck, by then on the run, Marcello had managed to send Dino a hasty text: *Scappa!*

'True,' Paolo had said. 'But it wasn't soon enough. Look, Dino, haven't you realised by now that in Italy's commercial world, gladiatorial rules still apply. Marcello was probably as naïve as you. Now you must find a way of moving on. But until you do, don't let anyone see or sense your fear – and keep your antennae on alert at all times.'

Dino shuddered.

On receiving Marcello's text, Dino had panicked and blurted out as much of the story as he dared to his elder brother with whom he got on best. He had been furious, never having liked nor trusted Marcello, and had said much the same as Paolo, but more harshly. At least he'd taken pity on him and agreed to lend him some money.

The precious supply of borrowed notes, along with the meagre savings he'd held back from his reckless attempt to become a property owner, were hidden with his passport under a loose floorboard. They would need to be eked out for as long as…? He gave himself three weeks. Each week that passed increased the threat of further crises. He must find a way of turning around the impossible situation he'd created for himself.

Urgently.

Struggling to turn off the tap on the rusty shower, Dino towelled himself dry. His wash had concentrated his mind, given him a clearer idea of how he could make the next week more interesting. Above all, more lucrative.

A small furry head popped its head out of the hole and sat twitching its whiskers.

'*Mi dispiace,*' Dino murmured. He had no more food. The mouse would have to wait until the next day for another snack.

Maybe in a few days' time, they might both be heartened by something healthier than cheap pastry.

✦✦

THIRTEEN

Heather Honey

ॐ ☙

EASTER was very late.
        There would be a smaller gathering of the clans than usual that Sunday. It was Duncan's parents' turn to have the twins inflicted on them. Maggy had cried off. She couldn't afford to spend the whole holiday where she wasn't wanted. Lorna nobly made the journey to Barnton on the Saturday with the family's Easter eggs, then the following day picked up Maggy to spend the Sunday with her parents.

A fine weekend was forecast. With the daffodil and narcissi petals now withering, their leaves would need folding-down and tying in bunches: a tiresome job on her kneeler, but some stiffness later was a small price to pay for the weeks they'd lit up the garden. Summer flowers were pretty, but the spring blooms more jubilant, she thought.

Sitting in her brother's prim living room Maggy once more found herself contemplating food issues. Had any research been done on the links between the sugar consumed at Christmas and Easter and national diabetes statistics? Why did so many religious festivals oblige people to behave, gastronomically speaking, so badly? Yet another example of society's double standards, she thought. Few people seriously observed Lent, any more – although Una used it as a means of disciplining her alcohol intake; the loss of a few ounces being achieved at the cost of her normally cheerful disposition.

A closet chocoholic herself, Maggy would later set her own double standards aside and consume the box of rabbit-shaped pralines the children had given her. Hadn't Lorna said she needed a daily sugar fix? Alone, feet on the sofa and an episode of her favourite Scandi noir running, was the nearest she could get to bliss these days.

Being in her brother's home provided little opportunity to chat to Lorna alone, although her niece had made a point of nagging her as they kissed goodbye in the porch. 'And have *you* got an exciting week planned, *Auntie*?'

Chocolate… sugar – *honey*! With the good weather due to continue,

Maggy had run out of excuses. She must make that expedition into town.

It was now Tuesday. It felt strange, standing at the bus stop. Since Don's death, the Audi had hibernated in the lock-up garage around the corner. Ewan took the car for a spin every few weeks to keep the battery in good order but it was well overdue its MOT. Maggy wasn't a confident driver. Some people took to it like ducks to water; she only used the car when strictly necessary. Of late she'd been hiring cabs to avoid people and noise, but today she intended to start her new life and greet the world full on by using public transport.

Her little jaunt would at least give her a chance to look at summer coats. Even so, her all-purpose burgundy jacket had come up nicely after cleaning. It went well over the smart grey trousers. She'd put on the silver petal earrings Don had bought her that weekend in Crieff. They always gave her a lift. Maggy hoped she looked more than passably presentable – in case she ran into Una, or anyone else she hadn't seen recently. Was she even a tad over-dressed? Och awa', she chided herself. Anyway, the bus was rounding the corner. With the sun streaming in through the window and a Carole King rocking gently in her head, it purred off with her, up the hill.

Maggy began to relax and give herself up to the day. She noted one or two changes since her last journey: the little antique shop on the edge of the Meadows, now a bespoke burger café; the branch bank she'd once used in Fountainbridge, finally sold, and transformed into a chic wine bar. And the boarded-up streets: old tenements being re-developed. Poignant signs of the times.

Alighting with some trepidation, Maggy made her way along Princes Street to the handsome brick façade of Jenners department store – its second incarnation dating back to 1885. Dominating the eastern end of the street, there were statues of Greek women supporting its top three floors: a tribute to shrewd Victorian marketing in what was usually regarded as a dark male-chauvinistic age. Even then it was women who did the shopping.

Yet shopping, as she'd always known it, was going out of style. She had read somewhere that the internet was imperceptibly killing off all the great department stores. Would even Jenners be around in ten years' time?

Architectural add-ons down the years had created a clumsy labyrinth of steps and passages between departments. Catching her breath from several flights of stairs, Maggy prayed she'd given the slip to two women who had been stalking her since China & Glass. There was sufficient crockery at home to last several lifetimes, but she had a weakness for any piece of nonsense that yelled 'buy me' and might come in handy as a future gift.

A voice just behind her chimed up: 'Is it not always the case Morag, that prices keep going up whenever austerity dictates our income stays put?' Maggy caught the reflection of the speaker in a glass panel: about her own age in an expensive but unfashionable suit. She hardly looked as if ten pence on a fillet steak would make the difference between survival and penury, but appearances could be deceptive.

Her friend, a homelier body with precise Edinburgh diction, piped up, 'But cannot necessity sometimes be the mother of – well, at least inventive TV dinners, Jessie? Have I not told you about my Tuna Quickie, with pimentos, tomatoes and capers, topped with grated cheese and crumbled crisps? It's a doddle and *so* economical. You just pop it in the oven for ten minutes – and *all* the family love it!'

Maggy's stomach heaved.

No respite in the Ladies where Jessie, now making free with the courtesy moisturiser, was waxing lyrical about her Butternut and Kale Surprise. 'Ticks all the health food boxes too, Morag.' She had a point there, Maggy thought, beating a hasty retreat up the staircase to the food hall. Still the voices pursued her. Diving behind a display of bottled kumquats, she caught the words 'pesto' and 'fritter'. Then they paused – for air? After that, the chatter faded away.

Looking around, Maggy thought pessimistically it would be just her luck to find honey replaced by a *Planning Your Summer Party* display. Too often managerial initiative drove old favourites off the shelves to promote seasonal novelties.

Ah, no. There on a side table were neatly stacked pyramids of jars filled with Acacia, Orange Blossom, Mānuka – and, Maggy sighed:

SPECIAL BUY
HEATHER HONEY
Buy **TWO** get **ONE**
FREE

Just three jars left – which explained why stocks were so low.

She hastily popped the remaining jars into a basket, reflecting that the price, even with the discount, would have fed a family of ten for a week when she was a bairn – and moved across to the sour-faced woman under the *PAY HERE* sign.

The buzz of mainly women's voices echoing through the short passage linking the food hall to the restaurant grew more intimidating with each step she took. Once more hoping nobody would recognise her, she nervously patted her hair, took a few paces forward and looked around.

It was always *our* table: the one in the corner overlooking the Scott Monument. Don and she arrived as early as possible on Saturday morning to bag two chairs before selecting their treats: Millionaire's Shortbread for him; scone and jam for her. Then he'd queue for their cappuccinos while she surveyed the scene and waved to anyone she knew.

A few moments later she discovered the appetising display of fancy bread and cakes. At least some things never changed, Maggy thought, before noting with some disappointment the new restrained décor – and joining the coffee queue, alone.

Gripping the sides of her tray for dear life, Maggy was soon navigating her way through the tables, when – dammit – who was sitting in *their* seats but the two taste bud bandits, now demolishing Delia: 'So old hat, m'dear. I've been completely won over by Nigel.'

Maggy blinked back a few encroaching tears and scanned the new layout for somewhere to sit. She was about to put down her tray and rush for the nearest exit, when a pair of eyes at a table tucked away in the quieter L-shaped section drew her towards an empty seat opposite.

What eyes! She didn't know about his height, but the young man looking up at her was certainly dark and handsome, his white open-necked shirt revealing a tanned throat; one blue-jeaned leg sticking out, laundered within an inch of its life, and leading to a smart, well-shined shoe. Late twenties, maybe. A blackberry sundae of a guy.

She was caught in the headlights.

What was she like?

Dino had been nursing a cold latte for almost an hour and was starting to feel despondent when Maggy appeared.

'May… may I park here?' she said.

His new persona snapped into action. 'I am honoured.'

She sat down.

'I'm Maggy.'

'Luca', Dino said.

'Hi, Luca. On holiday or…?'

'I am here … one week or maybe… more,' he said.

'Long enough to see how you like us.'

He couldn't have given a straight answer to that, even if required, so simply grinned enigmatically.

'Och, I'm so nosey. Take no notice.'

Nosey? What did she mean? He grinned again.

Maggy tried once more. 'Could I ask where you are staying?'

This he was prepared for. 'West End,' Dino said, enunciating the two syllables separately.

'The Sheraton or The Caledonian?' Maggy said.

There, the woman was doing it again. Dino half-raised a disarming eyebrow and shrugged his shoulders. Although his English was quite good, he'd discovered the advantages of not appearing to speak, or even understand people, as well as he might. A slight language problem had its uses. Walking down to Princes Street earlier, he'd passed a couple of smart hotels – but which was which? He must investigate, although it really wasn't the woman's business to know where he was staying.

For the moment, however, Maggy was writing his script for him. Any misunderstandings could be put down to 'lost in translation'. At least the trouble he'd taken with his appearance seemed to be paying off. Dino could see she was certainly old enough to be his mother, but had good skin and was still attractive.

He had come to an understanding with his conscience over his new occupation and finally settled on a *modus operandi*, promising himself it should last only so long as strictly necessary. He'd provide company and a little light fun to the right strangers. Anything intrusive, whatever the price, was totally off limits.

That was the plan, anyway. He hadn't got as far as deciding what constituted 'light fun'. He'd have to play things by ear. Or whatever.

'You live in city?' Dino ventured.

Maggy attempted to give him some idea of the local geography but, understandably, it meant little to him.

He watched her brain retuning.

'And whereabouts do you come from, in… Italy, I presume?' she said.

If Dino's experience of life to date had taught him anything, it was that in situations where you are obliged to lie, the best approach is often to tell as much of the truth as you can, omitting or subtly changing only details the other person need not know. He could tell Maggy, truthfully, how he'd been born in Rome although his home now was just outside Milan. His parents were Italian but his grandmother was Scottish.

'And, if it's not a rude question, what do you do in Milan?' she said.

'Shoes. I design ladies' shoes.'

That had slipped out. Did Luca design shoes? He wondered. Dino hadn't given much thought to his alter ego's back-story. He had, however, picked up, from his many female clients, that they often seemed less threatened around men who were artistic, and whose romantic inclinations might initially appear ambiguous. If she felt safe with him, Maggy might more readily divulge useful information, especially about herself.

'And what do you do?' Dino said.

To his delight, the question unleashed a tidal wave of long-suppressed chatter. Maggy told Dino all about her flirtation with the stage and her family life since. She barely paused between topics, going on to share details of Don's death, and even Lorna's mission to release her from Slough of Despond.

It was amazing the information people divulged to a stranger, assuming they'll never see them again. Still, it was nice to have someone other than Paolo to chat to and it wasn't difficult to warm to the woman's outgoing personality. More importantly, he could see the image he was struggling to project was having the desired effect, lulling her into a false sense of security – though it would be dangerous to overplay his hand.

Even so, by the time Maggy had reached the dizzying, cultural heights of the book group, his eyes had begun to glaze over. He was anxious to move the conversation on. His attention wandered down to the carrier bag by the table leg.

'You spoil yourself?'

'Just some foody things,' Maggy said, making a clumsy transition from the machinations of Thomas Cromwell to the efficacious properties of honey, and concluding with 'I'm sorry, you really don't need all this. I'm being boring. I've no right to make assumptions as to what interests you. I mean, I don't even know you.'

'Not true. A person need not know someone a long time to sense a…'

'An affinity?'

He smiled, obligingly. 'I would like to know more about your late 'usband's work. Tell me, please.'

So, she did.

They continued talking for another twenty minutes, by which time the last centimetres of her coffee were undrinkable. 'Would you…?' he asked, tentatively touching the edge of her saucer.

'How kind. Another Americano would be awfully nice.'

Dino found a spare tray and took the dirty cups to the counter. He really didn't have money to waste on extra coffees, but it would be an investment if it made her beholden to him and encouraged her to suggest… what? Their conversation might have been a complete waste of time.

He returned with a tray of steaming drinks to find Maggy putting a little mirror back in her handbag. Did this mean a quick second drink and then she'd be off? *Mannaggia!* He must somehow stall her and find out where she was going next.

In the event, Maggy beat him to it. 'And what are your plans for the rest of the day?'

'I was intending to ask you also,' Dino said, handing her the cup as if it was a diamond bracelet.

'My time's my own,' she reassured him. 'I've not been shopping in town for ages and thought I might just have a wee peek at this season's fashions… and then, if the sunshine holds, a trot down to The Botanics maybe.'

'The Botanics?'

'Edinburgh's famous gardens. You've not been there yet?'

'I 'ave not.'

'Everything will be stirring right now.'

It was a window of opportunity, but he mustn't rush things. They sipped their drinks in silence for a moment, before he said. 'These… Botanics. How far?'

'No more than fifteen minutes away,' Maggy said.

'I would like to see them.'

'I'd be happy to show you,' she said.

Dino studied his watch for a moment. 'How kind.'

'But only if you have the time,' she added. Was she wondering, too late, if her impulsiveness had been an error of judgement?

'I can do other things later,' Dino said.

What other things, he couldn't have said.

In the Royal Botanic Garden the delicate foliage, highlighted by splashes of blossom, shimmered from a recent shower. Maggy recalled the contented Sunday afternoons she'd strolled along these paths with someone else. For the first time since Don's death, they were peaceful thoughts.

Her new friend seemed impressed by the ornate Victorian glasshouses. 'This is the third site,' Maggy informed him, 'going back to the 1820s. The buildings were built to house tropical palms and plants.' She indicated a path leading to the oldest and most decorative. Would you like to see inside?'

He smiled. They ventured in.

Hit by the clamminess, their voices dropped in reverence to the giant trees towering above and exotic flora exploding on either side of them.

Maggy thought how, in only a couple of hours, language had ceased to be much of a barrier. People always said she was 'a natural' when it came to getting along with people: a phrase which, for no good reason, always reminded her of Gauguin's lassies on Tahiti.

Had she ever been sensual and primitive? Sensual perhaps. Primitive, in her dreams. She had an actor's ability to fantasise but was still a sensible Edinburgh lass at heart.

Every so often as they progressed along the narrow internal path, they paused to note the information next to the exhibits. Much of the horticultural jargon confused Luca. Maggy helped him out.

One small plant caught her attention. She picked up a leaflet from a nearby stand, and read:

Dionaea muscipula
(Venus Flytrap)
In Latin, 'muscipula' means 'mousetrap'.
Sometimes known, colloquially,
as 'tippity twitchet',
an oblique reference to the plant's resemblance
to female genitalia

Maggy hoped the visitor wouldn't require a simplified version of that.

She recalled a video of *Little Shop of Horrors* she'd watched years ago. The plant looked so harmless, yet she could imagine a larger, man-eating version, its quirky but strangely threatening beauty betraying its treacherous survival mechanisms.

Like some people she'd known.

Something in the air, a minute insect or maybe simply a tiny particle of compost, hovered in the atmosphere above the plant. True to its nickname, it tentatively twitched, revealing its strange pincers. Maggy could see how easily they would quickly close over a fly or even something larger given half a chance, and…

She shivered and looked away.

The hothouse was empty, apart from themselves.

Or was it?

Hearing a rustling, Maggy peered round. A man was looking in their direction not far from the entrance. Beige coat, shades. But why were the shades trained on her?

No. They'd repositioned themselves on her companion.

Who on earth could he be?

Maggy saw him following her gaze. Abruptly, she found herself being forcibly steered towards the exit.

'What's the…'

Clutching her arm even tighter her young friend said: *'Presto!* I explain later.'

Once out of earshot, he began gabbling excitedly in Italian. Even outside, he wouldn't let go of her, finally pulling her behind a large tree.

This was pure Mills and Boon.

After a few moments, Maggy cautiously peered around the trunk. Beige Man was now striding in the direction of the Queen Mother Memorial Garden.

What was that bulging in his coat pocket?

They moved further away from the building and into a copse of trees and gulped deep breaths of fresh air. Maggy brushed down her jacket with her hand. 'I am sorry,' the fugitive said, 'it was… how you say… oppressive in there?'

What had that been about?

They found a seat and regained their equanimity. Attempting to pass off the incident as one of those things that often happened in hothouses, Maggy extricated from her jacket pocket the leaflet she'd hastily stuffed into it, with the now creased photograph of a part-ingested fly.

'Just fancy!' she said, straightening the paper. 'Apparently, the trap *doesn't close all the way at first, but stays open for a few seconds, allowing any very small insects which would not provide enough food to escape.* Fair dos, eh?'

Her companion looked puzzled.

'Did you not know that?' Maggy said.

Ignoring her question, he said 'What happened in there… was nothing. That man… he thought he recognised me, I think. Mistake, of course.' He picked up the leaflet which she'd placed between the two of them and read as much of it as he could. 'I 'ope,' he said at length, 'that I am very small insect when it is my turn.'

Maggy laughed politely, whilst wondering… 'turn?' But no explanation was forthcoming. It was then she noticed, in the scramble, the second and third buttons on his shirt had become undone to disclose a silver chain, with a small medallion dangling from it. Before Maggy could stop herself, she heard herself saying 'What a beautiful…'

'Yes,' he said, hurriedly, tucking away the necklace and doing up the buttons. But not before she'd caught the name *Dino* inscribed on it.

Curiouser and curiouser.

If, on top of everything else that had happened during the past ten minutes, that revelation hadn't rung an alarm bell, it wasn't because Maggy failed to hear it – but had chosen not to.

After exchanging mobile numbers – just as a courtesy, she told herself – Maggy waved Luca – or was it Dino? – off on the corner of George Street before sauntering on to her bus stop, reflecting on the strange but enjoyable events of the day so far. Materially, she was returning home empty-handed except for her jars of honey in a carrier bag. She had forgotten about her intention to look at summer coats in Jenners – or had she been in too much of a hurry to get to know the laddie?

He reminded her a little of Ewan, as he'd been a few years back, although she had to admit the Italian was better looking than her son, more obviously so, anyway. More aware of himself too, but not in a vain way – that would be the creative side of him, like his unselfconscious sense of style.

Ewan, always neat and tidy, had never quite made the most of his wholesome, if mousey, looks and trim figure. She blamed Paige for making him buy clothes in dreary shades of charcoal, taupe and lovat. 'Go for positive colours – especially whilst you're still young,' Maggy always urged her children. Once she'd treated Ewan to a tan suede jacket for his birthday but had never seen him wear it. No doubt Paige considered it poof-y. Huh!

Maggy's musings reminded her she must phone Ewan. He'd not contacted her again with an update on his life; she must make the effort to touch base. That would be her job for the evening; in the meantime, maybe she could think how to borrow someone else's son for company again soon.

The Italian had said he'd no plans for the rest of the week. Again, out of politeness – she told herself – Maggy had asked if he'd be interested in viewing more of the capital some other day? How his eyes had lit up! They'd agreed to meet outside the Palace of Holyroodhouse on Thursday at eleven. She'd help him follow the tour guide's spiel, and afterwards show him the Royal Mile. Maybe have a late bite in St Giles's crypt.

What was she doing?

Maybe, whoever-he-was, was only a gondola – a gondolier? – passing in the night. Maybe that was as it should be, given the gap in their ages. Still, he'd stirred her curiosity. Who was he really? Did the medallion denote the name of... what – a lover perhaps? He didn't look as if his preference would be for a Dino, although she felt it suited him better than Luca – but what did she know? Anyway, he'd probably be back off to Italy soon.

Her thoughts moved to the other mystery: Beige Man. The episode had intrigued rather than scared her. She'd been impressed at the lad's concern for her safety.

A peculiar business. What was in the man's pocket? His lunch? His hand had been clutching it as if he was terrified it might be seen – or fall out. Pockets were no place for squashy food. He'd vanished too quickly for her to take a second look.

Maybe she should have mentioned the incident to a park keeper – or would she have been accused of over-reacting? After all, the man might have simply been a park official. A detective even. It would have been galling to have reported her concern, risked being patronised as a neurotic older woman and brushed off with 'Thank you, madam. No need to worry. Our CCTV system picks up anything we need to keep an eye on.'

Och well. It had been a great morning, anyway, hadn't it?

Her bus pulled up. To the entertainment of the driver, Maggy jauntily leapt on it with the energy of a woman years younger.

A jump lead named Luca?

Or Dino?

Or...?

≈⊚≈

FOURTEEN

Learning Material

೩ ✑

O VER the past few days Ewan had withdrawn into himself.
If he'd expected further discussions with Paige on the lines
of 'Where do we go from here?' or 'What are your plans?' none were
forthcoming.

Paige considered her infidelity to be Ewan's problem, and avoided
the subject. On the surface she behaved as if nothing had happened,
treating him marginally better than she had for some time – if tinged
with the concern usually reserved for someone diagnosed with a
terminal illness. He wouldn't be around much longer, so she could
afford to be pleasant.

The former Ewan, the Ewan of a fortnight ago, might have read
into her attitude that she didn't blame him entirely for her behaviour.
But he wasn't the old Ewan. Barely welcome in his own home, and
unsure as to what the future held, he didn't know who he was.

At least Paige's involvement with the mysterious Monsieur T was
now out in the open. Not too open though. It left Ewan guessing as
to how often she required the flat to herself. Vaguely curious, in his
fragile state, he'd nevertheless no desire to risk coming across the
pair *in flagrante delicto* or cosying-up in the kitchen when he arrived
back in the evenings after one of his now, regular, pub crawls.
Although the boil was lanced, and no longer as painful as whilst
festering, the healing process would only begin when he fully took
control of his life and made a clean break.

The flat had been bought outright by Paige, largely thanks to a
handsome donation from her rich godfather, an elderly widower
with few needs who, seeing she needed help, had given Paige most
of the money he'd set aside for her in his will – with the expectation
of regular Sunday lunch invitations thereafter. Responsibility for his
sudden passing six months later could hardly be laid at her oven
door: he'd never set foot in the place.

Ewan was unsure of his rights regarding the flat. Paige's solicitor
would convince her he had few, although over the years his own
earnings had regularly contributed to the furnishing and upkeep of

the property. Paige had expensive tastes. Only last year a glistening en suite complete with jacuzzi and the finest porcelain bidet had been added to the master bedroom – the *mistress* bedroom as he now thought of it. The year before they'd installed a state-of-the-art kitchen.

The refurbishment had been undertaken to her specifications – but paid for by him with the help of a bank loan, only settled recently when he received his own inheritance. He was unwilling for Paige to take his half of everything without a struggle. Besides, who was the guilty party here? He could bear the emotional pressure no longer.

Yesterday, Ewan had done a deal with a private hotel in Leith. Luckily, it could accommodate him right away. Given his financial commitments, the additional outgoings would increase his financial burden, but at least he was free of Paige. She, of course, feigned sadness that things had come to this; probably concerned he might renege on his promise to continue sharing the utilities bills.

He'd spent the previous two evenings at the cinema, finished off with a nightcap in one of several nearby bars, half-heartedly ploughing through a Ken Follett, watching a match on the plasma screen – and staring miserably into space.

There had been a well-intentioned call from his mother. After bringing her up to date on his situation with as much flippancy as the situation would take, she had suggested he moved back into his old room in Illyria. It was typical of her to be kind and supportive. Unfortunately, since his father's death, Maggy's own growing neediness had been a matter of increasing concern. Fond though Ewan was of her, the last thing he needed right now was to find himself trapped again, if in a different way.

The skies, cheerful earlier, had darkened. Although it was the end of April, the temperature had temporarily reverted to early March. After deliberately staying late at work yet again, Ewan was wandering up Leith Walk. Splodges of rain began rhythmically striking his head and cheeks: slow beats at first, then breaking into a dance. He turned up his collar for protection.

A man came out of a bar ahead of him. Ewan couldn't recall ever having taken much notice of the place before, but with the shower by now having become a flurry of hailstones and looking for somewhere to shelter, he was already salivating at the thought of a sausage roll washed down by a decent beer. Failing to notice the rainbow sticker on the window, Ewan allowed the warm light, pop music and friendly buzz to lure him inside.

Only after settling at a table at the back of the bar and savouring his drink did he really take note of his surroundings. There were only a couple of rather loud women amongst the male clientele. Then he clocked the Pride Scotia and forthcoming Drag Night posters.

Better to stay here for a while, Ewan decided, rather than continue his aimless trudge in the wet.

He was becoming quite absorbed in yet another downbeat article in *The Banker* on the effects of a successful Referendum on the Scottish economy, when a voice said:

'Mind if I join you?'

Ewan looked up. A man around his own age smiled down at him, a glass in his hand. Not an ingratiating smile, simply a sociable grin. It was a familiar face too, although they'd never actually spoken to each other before. As he indicated the spare stool opposite, Ewan had no option but to say 'Please do.'

'Usual Edinburgh spring weather!'

'Yes,' was all Ewan could say.

Hell, he wasn't going to be chatted up, was he? He might not be obsessed with his looks but wasn't so naïve as not to be aware that he was sometimes considered attractive by members of both sexes. And in this venue, it was a given that any appeal he had was likely to be limited to one. In his tired anorak, rain-matted hair and sleep-starved face, Ewan thought the guy must be desperate.

Bars acquainted one with strange stool-fellows. Should he pull out his iphone and start checking for messages, thus effectively snubbing the man – or settle for unsolicited companionship?

Ewan looked more carefully at the neat figure next to him: tall-ish and muscular, mixed-race with smooth, café-au-lait skin and dark crinkly hair; casually but smartly attired in dress-down mode. He often saw the guy around and about, mainly during his lunch breaks. He would have passed unremarked walking down London's Piccadilly but on Leith Walk his looks were more conspicuous. Comparatively few African minorities had settled in Edinburgh, although numbers were growing,

Despite the man's conspicuous demeanour and open face, Ewan wasn't quite ready to admit to himself how striking he was. He had previously observed that he laughed a lot and interacted well with people.

He needn't have worried. The man made no attempt to prolong the conversation and pulled an evening paper out of his pocket.

They read quietly in silence for a while.

As the minutes ticked by, Ewan's initial feelings of relief segued into curiosity. By nature a friendly soul, Ewan, his glass now empty, was thinking he must make up his mind whether to go for a refill, move to another venue, or at least summon up courage to pass a pleasantry, when the man looked up and beamed.

'Top up?'

Whilst such familiarity might not be unusual in a bar, Ewan wondered, in here, was that some sort of code? He returned the grin in, what he hoped, wasn't too-matey a manner.

'Well…' Ewan said.

The man leaned forward and extended a large, nicely-kept hand. 'Jamie.'

'Ewan.'

'We sort-of know each other, don't we?'

'Erm… yes,' Ewan said.

I've seen you munching your bap in the Botanics.' Jamie said.

'Of course,' Ewan responded, as if just remembering.

'Good sandwiches at that place. You obviously think so too.'

'I've been using that shop for years. Peanut butter and jam on white?'

'Smoked salmon and cream cheese on granary?'

'You've been spying on my fillings!'

'You likewise!'

It broke the ice.

Jamie went on 'I've meant to say hello several times, but…'

'Why didn't you?'

'Why didn't *you*?'

Maybe they both knew the answer to that, though in Ewan's case only in his subconscious. Before he could answer, Jamie said 'I work in that big building just up the road.'

'I guessed you did. I'm opposite.'

'Ah. Banking too.'

'The insurance side, actually. IT support – I'm not personally stealing clients' money. You?'

'Part of a special projects team. Well, not that special. Mainly routine forward planning, developing new initiatives, that sort of thing.'

Ewan fingered his mobile. He could still finish this now without appearing too rude; make an excuse and dash off – though the odd gust of wind and rain hitting the window outside was seriously discouraging. And Jamie was already heading back to the bar with their empty glasses.

Never had Ewan considered himself boyfriend material – for another man. And a man like… Like what, precisely? Jamie seemed decent enough. Ewan always got on well enough with the two gay men on his floor at work, but one was spotty and prissy and the other fat and melancholy. Whilst Ewan laughed at some of his colleagues' outrageous banter, he'd never identified with or been physically drawn to either.

Jamie looked straightforward. And pleasant. Very pleasant. Quite attractive in fact – if you liked that sort of thing. What was prompting these comparisons? Was his current state of mind encouraging him to think outside his usual comfort zone?

How, within a few minutes of bumping into Jamie should he, for no good reason, become so curious about someone he barely knew? Was it because, after several years trapped in an emotional vacuum, his brain had shaken off its previous constraints?

Ewan remembered Paige's wounding comment about him not being 'pro-active'. He'd taken it to mean she thought he had a low sex drive. How did one know? It wasn't as if you went around asking your mates how often they 'did it' and calculated the lowest, highest, and mean levels to see where, approximately, on the graph you fitted. But then, until very recently Ewan rarely socialised in bars, and had very few friends apart from Gus – and he would have considered a conversation about their sex lives totally off limits.

Paige had also accused Ewan of being 'no Channing Tatum'. That had hurt. Why? He couldn't recall himself ever experiencing any stirrings at the sight of… He struggled to recall other contemporary male stars whose movies they'd recently seen. He recognised many who were conventionally good-looking. But, surely, it was their acting he primarily admired; much as he coveted Tatum's striking features and gym-toned physique, it was Jennifer Lawrence and Rachel McAdams who turned him on.

Wasn't it?

Then he recalled several twilit evenings in his teens, when he'd been persuaded to join a school-friend behind the cricket pavilion. He was fond of the friend, and both were into George Michael. If they were hardly Achilles and Patroclus, they'd certainly got on well and had agreed to help each other out – as schoolboys sometimes do. He hadn't fully appreciated his emotional investment in their activities until his friend met a girl one weekend at a dance. Things had never been quite the same between them. He had missed that.

As he delved further and further back into his memory, neglected – or possibly blocked – images came into focus. To Ewan's discomfort, he found himself recalling a few men who had intrigued him in a slightly erotic way over the years. Had he been dishonest with himself, not wanting to admit he was drawn to them beyond, simply, admiring their looks? And if so, was that unnatural? Was it unhealthy to be curious as to how it would feel to be affectionate with them?

He'd been ensnared by Paige into an arrangement that had outlived its usefulness but hadn't accepted it. His infatuation had become a yoke she had increasingly used for her convenience. In her thrall, he'd been blind to the wider range of opportunities for happiness that were available. Or had he simply been too scared to explore them?

Jamie strode back from the bar with their beers. Ewan was impressed by how comfortable he seemed in his own skin. He carefully deposited the refilled glasses on cork coasters and looked at Ewan quizzically. 'Penny for them – or fifty bearing in mind forty years' inflation?' he said. 'Sorry, you're the one who works for a bank.'

Ewan laughed. Jamie smiled back. Another unthreatening smile. Ewan gave up, or rather, gave in. For the moment, he was reluctant to put a name to his heightened curiosity about Jamie – or was it about himself? Either way, it was more pleasant making idle conversation here, than returning to his dreary hotel room.

He settled down to simultaneously engage in more small-talk with Jamie whilst his id and ego continued to argue. The points they raised didn't arrive tidily in one fell swoop but would tumble into his head harum-scarum over the course of the evening, to be sorted out later.

'A friendly bar, this,' Jamie said.

'Long may it continue, with the place up the road closing. The internet and all these new dating apps have ruined old-fashioned cruising, haven't they?'

Out of his depth, Ewan improvised 'You mean, people resort to using bars for drinking, chatting, and…?'

'Appalling, isn't it?'

Laughter released any residual tension, and the men fell into a more animated discussion. Ewan ducked and dived to avoid mentioning his current circumstances. He felt on safer ground chatting about career issues, discovering what they had in common and sharing grumbles about life in large corporations.

It emerged that Jamie was no slouch on the badminton court and regularly toned up at the gym, 'Although,' he confessed, 'as I approach middle age, I'm beginning to feel increasingly like granddad surrounded by all the perky wee cubs.'

Ewan, who also attended a gym, wasn't aware he'd been drawn to any 'wee cubs', until he remembered the young guy who was often there the same time after work as Ewan, and whose striking torso always compelled his eyes to wander – maybe more frequently than could be attributed to mere admiration?

Trying to brush the question aside, Ewan wondered if this was the moment to come clean about what, until half an hour ago, he'd been reasonably confident were his preferences, when the background tape switched to an old Rolling Stones number.

'Not my favourite this,' Jamie said.

'You mean you're really a Beatles fan?

'I didn't say that.'

'Stones!' Ewan chanted.

'Beatles!'

'*Stones!*'

'*Beatles!*'

As their voices grew louder, the people nearest to them overheard, and began joining in. Before long, the place was in a merry uproar. When everyone had settled down again, Jamie nodded in the direction of the loudspeaker

'As it happens,' Jamie said, 'I like them equally. How about you?'

Sixties music. Now that, Ewan could relate to.

He nodded. It was almost like being with his mother.

Or perhaps not.

Another pint on and a bond was developing.

A couple of Jamie's friends appeared and hugged him. Jamie introduced them to Ewan: Alec, dark, well-built and jolly; Ian, skin-headed, ectomorphic and profound. Jamie bought everyone a round of drinks and in a short space of time Ewan had returned the compliment, wisely moving on to sparkling water for himself.

The topic on everyone's lips – the pros and cons of an independent Scotland – dominated the discussion. Ewan, a natural middle-grounder, rarely discussed political issues with Paige, knowing he'd be made to look stupid, and tolerating rather than agreeing with her unique brand of leftism. Don had called her a 'Babycham socialist' – which would have annoyed her intensely if she'd been old enough to have understood the reference.

It appeared that Jamie had strong SNP sympathies. He was aware that many people imagined he was an outsider, but he had been born in Scotland to a Scottish mother and the country had been good to him. But he listened patiently to his friends' varying opinions and pragmatically pointed out any common ground.

By eleven o'clock, after much more quaffing and chatter, merriment had driven any heat out of the debate.

'Coffee at my place?' Jamie said.

Alec and Ian looked at each other sensing he was being polite, guessing Jamie had other plans for the night. Making excuses, they put on their coats. Ian firmly shook Ewan's hand, though the more out-going Alec kissed him warmly on both cheeks.

As they disappeared into the crowd, Ewan made as if to leave, too.

'Ewan?'

Seeing him hesitate, Jamie lightly chivvied him, 'Aw come on, I'm just down the road in Pilrig Street.'

Ewan was in two minds. On the one hand, it would be pleasant to extend the first merry evening he'd spent in a long while. On the other... No, Jamie was a decent sort, he told himself. Whatever transpired, he'd be able to handle it.

'That would be nice,' he said, 'but... Look, don't take this the wrong way. There's something I should tell you...'

Jamie interrupted him. 'You're only invited for coffee. Drop-dead gorgeous I may be – but it's obvious: you're straight.'

Why then was Ewan a little disappointed by this reply? 'Glad we got that sorted,' he said. 'How did you guess?'

'Couldn't be more obvious if it was tattooed on your forehead. And it, erm... stands out a mile,' Jamie added with a knowing look. Despite his slightly inebriated state, Ewan got the irony. There was a sudden, straining sensation below his belt.

And he wasn't thinking of Paige.

The night air was cold but fresh. The rain had paused, if not altogether ceased. Ewan was sharply reminded of the beer he'd consumed which had made him somewhat light-headed.

On the short walk to the flat, Jamie pointed out a few local landmarks of which Ewan, had been unaware. He was learning a lot of new things this evening. Jamie sounded confident and reassuring. Ewan let his sense of adventure put to the back of his mind any lingering doubts.

The flat was on the second floor of a smart terraced house a quarter of a mile away. A welcoming light spilled into the lobby and out on to the landing through fanlight above the front door.

Once inside, Ewan barely waited for an invitation to dash to the lavatory whilst Jamie disappeared into the kitchen to prepare hot drinks.

Ewan was soon sinking into one of the two capacious sofas. He took in the tasteful, masculine décor. A striking painting, by a local artist whose work he admired, instantly made him feel at ease. There was also a small table covered in stand-up framed photos of what he presumed to be family members, including several cheerful youngsters beneath some palm trees – obviously not in Scotland.

Ewan was very fond of children. He was sad not to be given the chance of seeing more of his nieces. Paige regarded babies as some people did urban foxes: cute from a safe distance. Once when her period was late, her anxiety had gone off the Richter scale. When it turned out to have been a blip, he'd felt disappointed.

Jamie came in with a cafetière, milk and mugs. Coffee late at night wasn't always a good idea but he was reassured it was decaffeinated. Putting the tray on the coffee table, Jamie joined Ewan on the sofa, poured out the drinks and handed him a mug.

'What a super bunch of kids!' Ewan said, nodding at the photos.

'My half brothers and sisters in Jamaica. It's a long story.' Jamie looked wistful. Ewan felt this wasn't the moment to pry, but for reasons he couldn't quite explain, was strangely touched by the photos – and Jamie's look of affection when he'd referred to them.

Details kept being added to what he'd so far discovered about Jamie: he was a gym-going retro-rocker about his own age, also involved in Finance, with at least a couple of interesting politically-aware friends and nice-looking relations – whose home was a beautiful Caribbean island– and who had a nice flat and collected paintings. That would do for starters. Ewan wasn't accustomed to meeting people with whom he had so much in common.

What could be the downside?

The aromatic coffee and nostalgic strains of Drive My Car throbbing gently from concealed loudspeakers lulled Ewan still further into a sense of security. Only after a few moments, when Jamie's knee nonchalantly brushed against his own, did he momentarily tense-up.

Surprisingly, the pressure was more reassuring than threatening. In fact, the longer their knees touched, the more comforting it felt. Ewan started to relax. When Jamie's hand rested along the back of the sofa and his fingers oh-so-casually touched the back of his neck, a pleasant frisson ran down his back. Neither was he too startled when Jamie's hand slipped down onto his shoulder, teasing the top of his arm, as if seeking consent to stroke it.

Why wasn't he fleeing for the door?

The sofa was now a cosy island around which the yearning waves of *Rubber Soul* ebbed and flowed. How amazing it was that he had chanced to meet someone with similar musical tastes to his own. Beatles songs had provided the soundtrack to their parents' youth. Like those of Rodgers & Hart and the Gershwins long before them, they would always be cool. How would the songs of current musicians stand the test of time?

As if by telepathy, Jamie turned his head and grinned. Ewan reciprocated. Both men strolled in harmony through Norwegian Wood.

More familiar tracks came and went. By the time the final haunting notes of Michelle faded away, Ewan felt cramp creep into his thigh. The need to change his position obliged him to carefully remove Jamie's arm, sit up and look around.

'You've got it really nice in here,' Ewan said.

'You should see the other room,' Jamie replied, rising and going over to the window.

Ewan started.

'It's pouring down again,' he said, 'you really don't want to walk all the way home, do you?'

'Well...'

Jamie walked back and stood in front of him. 'I'll behave like a gentleman.' He stretched out his hands.

Amazed that he'd allowed things to get this far, and still confused as to why he wasn't putting up more of a struggle, Ewan allowed himself to be gently hauled to his feet.

The two men were now standing face to face. Jamie placed his hand on Ewan's right arm and gave it a reassuring squeeze. Ewan knew he only needed to move abruptly away to kill the moment stone dead and extricate himself.

He could suddenly remember his early shift tomorrow – glancing at his watch he corrected himself, it was now today – necessitating him getting up at crack of dawn. But that wouldn't be true.

Besides, by now Ewan's curiosity was, on balance, outweighing his apprehension. And there were all those laws about rape, weren't there? 'No' meant 'no', didn't it? And, with his body at the point of exhaustion, it would be a nasty walk back in the cold wet streets to his own bed. His body yearned to lie down.

Ewan followed Jamie into a large, elegant bedroom dominated by a small four-poster. Two triangles of duvet were turned down on either side.

He had once attended a dinner party at his boss's home when Lobster Thermidor was the main course. They never ate such exotic dishes at home. Unsure of what to expect, Ewan had picked up his cutlery with curiosity mixed with trepidation. Rejecting the dish would have been bad manners, but fortunately, it had turned out to be strangely enjoyable.

Why had he recalled that now?

'I suggest you take that side,' Jamie said, 'after…' He indicated the bathroom off the bedroom and handed Ewan a fluffy white towel.

When it was Jamie's turn to wash, Ewan stripped down to his boxer shorts and slipped into the bed.

Returning a few minutes later in a towelling bathrobe, Jamie found Ewan lying down, facing outwards. Taking off his robe, he slid into the vacant space beside him.

The two men lay there for a minute or two before Jamie lightly touched Ewan's shoulder. Was it muscle-memory from happier days in Great King Street that caused Ewan to unthinkingly roll over into Jamie's arms – or a subconscious yearning for any affection on offer?

It felt somewhat strange to be clinging to Jamie's smooth and hairless body. Not dissimilar to his own, though more muscular. Ewan momentarily missed Paige's softer contours, pliable breasts, and delicately scented skin, whereas Jamie smelled of musk blended with shower gel.

Muzzy though he was, Ewan debated whether snuggling up to another man wasn't, overall, so *very* different from being with a woman. After all, he reasoned, we were all human, if with corporeal variations. Everyone needed physical reassurance. Other creatures curled up together for warmth and companionship.

Very lightly Jamie's lips touched Ewan's neck. Then his cheek… his mouth. One-day stubble brushed his face – that was certainly a novelty. By way of appreciation, Ewan kissed Jamie's chest. Nestled in the cotton wool of semi-consciousness, he felt the tips of Jamie's fingers gently caress the inside of his thigh.

Ewan was at the back of the cricket pavilion again, feeling both needy and needed – and Jamie was doing all the giving. That had always been his job.

Giving. Needing.

How close they were.

Clutching Jamie's hand, tighter and tighter, Ewan gave himself up to the exquisite sensations passing through his body. The moment arrived when the duvet was discreetly pulled back and two years' frustration ecstatically erupted.

Before he could return the compliment, he was blissfully unconscious.

Ewan awoke the next morning to the sound of Queen pulsating through the flat and the smell of more, this time, proper coffee. After a few moments, Jamie's head appeared around the door. 'Good, you're awake. Help yourself to the shower etcetera whilst I warm up the croissants.'

Twenty minutes later, by now both ready for work, Jamie hugged Ewan.

'Friends?'

'Defo,' Ewan said.

'The comfort of strangers, eh?'

'Thanks, Jamie, I was needing that.'

'I guessed.'

Ewan looked deep into Jamie's brown eyes. They hugged again, then kissed. Not a protracted kiss but a confirming one. He really liked the guy.

Ewan had turned a corner.

✎ぬ

FIFTEEN
The Lady from the
Wine Company

ॐ ॐ

ALLY sat back and reviewed the morning's work. Jock had arrived on Skye – with Prince Charlie disguised as a spinning maid.

He sniffed the tangy sea air and patted his paws on the warm, white sand.

Land again! But where? Jock didn't know the names of places but at least he was off the rocky boat and no longer rolling around on all that cold grey-blue water.

A frond of seaweed stirred nearby and something tiny, all legs, scrambled out sideways. Jock sniffed around it wagging his tail in a 'won't you come and play' sort of way. The crab kept very still for a few moments giving him a quizzical look before scurrying beneath a rock.

By now the men were enjoying a well-earned rest. The woman, who smelled to Jock like a man, had boarded the boat moments before they had begun the journey. Betty, they called her, laughing as they did so. What was so funny about that? Jock liked Betty. She had made a fuss of him and was now sleeping close by on a tartan rug.

Someone wide awake sat next to her, a gun by his side.

Everyone talked in hushed voices. Once or twice on the boat Jock had barked to draw attention to himself, hoping to find out what was going to happen next. Flora kept shushing him, telling him to be good and keep quiet. Not easy for a working dog used to being kept busy.

At least now he could stretch his legs again; maybe go for a walk. Jock liked walks. In the meantime, if he made a friendly noise and wagged his tail, the little creature under the rock might decide to come out and start a game of chase with him.

'What are you doing?'

Flora was smiling down at him, a bowl of fresh water in her hand.

Jock looked up at her and gave a woof of gratitude.

A stickler for facts, Ally was forever surfing to check historical details. Lorna and she agreed that young people didn't have much sense of times past and chronology. 'It's a Gradgrind world today,' Lorna said, 'contextualisation isn't as important today as it was for us.'

After the Battle of Culloden, Bonnie Prince Charlie had taken refuge on the Outer Hebridean island of Benbecula where Flora Macdonald lived. Yet there were some questions even an exhaustive online search couldn't answer, obliging Ally to rely on her imagination. Were dogs susceptible to seasickness, for instance? Were baby crabs sociable? Could they even hear? Wouldn't Jock, famished from all that time on the boat, have been more likely to eat a bite-sized crustacean than play with it and, if so, raw or only if it was cooked? Or was she seeing this from a twenty-first century health-faddy perspective?

As she continued planning the rest of her chapter in her head, Ally pottered into the kitchen and made herself a mug of tea.

It was her day off. She was enjoying having the place to herself. Until she'd moved in with Lorna, Ally's free time had been spent in the public library or other coffee shops. As Fergus might have put it, she'd really fallen with her arse in the marmalade. Ally giggled, remembering his funny turns of phrase; then groaned with sadness. She carried her drink and petticoat tail back into her room on a tray depicting McTaggart's seascape *The Storm*. Had the waves been so turbulent for Jock, Flora and Charlie, she wondered?

The room was quiet, and trapped any sun going. It had already become a sanctuary, a friend even. Ally believed that rooms, like houses, had personalities. Her meagre belongings fitted in well too. It was also a repository for what Lorna referred to as her 'overflow' pictures, for which she couldn't find spaces elsewhere. Ally liked most of them, especially a small framed pastel of a lively collie with bright, dark eyes. You could almost see his tail wagging.

Ally was getting over a spell of writer's block. She knew what she wanted to do but needed a clearer idea of what breed of dog Jock should be before she could really move on. She'd toyed with the idea of fictionalising the legend of Mary Queen of Scots' terrier, Geddon, who had accompanied his mistress to the scaffold. Mary was one of her heroines and, it turned out, along with Lady Jane Grey, also one of Lorna's. Why was the scaffold so morbidly fascinating? Did we put some sort of romantic gloss on it because of its association with several tragic but – some believed – heroic personalities?

Ally eventually rejected the story as too downbeat, whilst reflecting how we often underestimate children's capacity for being matter-of-fact about aspects of violence which make adults squeamish. It was all about how it was presented. It might have been necessary to play down Geddon clinging to Mary's bloodied clothing, refusing to part from her, only to die broken-hearted days later. Could she have contrived a happier ending for him? No, she decided, animals in fiction were too easily sentimentalised. A trap she'd sometimes fallen into herself. Jock must be more robust.

Looking at the sheepdog in Lorna's picture, Biggings had come to mind. Named after the village on the island of Papa Stour, Biggings belonged to her uncle and worked on his smallholding, some miles from Lerwick. An amiable fellow, she always found him good company whenever she visited her relatives.

Shelties were the outcome of cross-breeding between Scottish and Scandinavian sheepdogs. Maybe a Biggings-type dog would make Charles Edward feel more at home in the Hebrides? Maybe some dog had – who knew? Ally's uncle had been brought up with Shelties. He understood how highly intelligent and energetic they were and said they must always be kept active and not allowed to get bored. Well, there would be plenty of sheep on South Uist and Benbecula to keep Jock out of mischief.

After studying the picture for a while longer, Ally made up her mind. Jock would be a Sheltie.

Busily Googling for photographs of the islands and trying to imagine how different they must have looked over two hundred years ago – probably not that much – she felt her mobile vibrate in her smock pocket. A text from Senga. Ally sighed. What did she want?

Emergency! Sorry to disturb you. Mum's tumbled and hurt herself badly. Must dash over and sort her. Cal's out seeing the wine company rep. Billing problem. Any poss. of you helping out in the B?

Damn! And just as she was thinking a storm might create additional tension to Charlie's flight.

Whenever either Senga or Cal was needed away from the Balfour and Ally wasn't working, they either closed the place for a while, or arranged for Katie to mind the place. Katie was a student who lived in a flat opposite. Ally assumed she must be at college that afternoon. Usually shoppers required only coffee and cake during the quiet-ish patch between 2.30 and 5 pm. Even so, they had to be served.

Sighing, Ally texted back:

Be there soon!

Almost immediately there was a responsive jingle:

Thanks, Ally. Double time for that!!

Well, the money would come in handy, Ally thought. She next texted Lorna, who was visiting a friend later that evening. Ally had agreed to get supper started, and although she didn't expect to be out long, was aware that sessions with suppliers often dragged on.

It was twenty minutes' brisk walk from Goldenacre to Stockbridge. To her surprise, when she arrived she found the Balfour in full swing, with Katie pouring coffees behind the Gaggia.

As Ally joined her, Katie said 'Hi. It's good of you to come, but I'm managing fine.'

'Didn't know you'd be here,' Ally said.

'Well, now you are, I don't suppose you'd mind terribly if I sloped off in a wee while? There's a lecture on macrobiotics I ought to attend.'

'Course not. You mustn't miss it.'

Before they swapped over, Ally needed an update from Katie on the food situation. 'I can stay until Cal gets back,'

'*Gets back*?' Katie said.

Ally showed her Senga's text.

Katie frowned. 'But he's in the middle of a meeting with that woman in the office.'

It was now Ally's turn to look confused.

'An uppity wee madam, too,' Katie said. 'Wouldn't give me the time of day.'

Ally said 'Maybe the matter's serious?'

'On no account to disturb them, he told me.' Then Katie lowered her voice. 'But, it's a bit awkward. The girl over there wants a mango frappé. Why is it that as soon as May arrives, certain customers feel entitled to spoil themselves with summer treats? Anyway, there's no purée in the kitchen. It's stored in the refrigerator in the office. I don't suppose you…?'

'Gladly,' Ally said. Then, for no good reason, felt a sense of discomfort. 'On no account disturb them,' Cal had said. But it was a golden rule at the Balfour never to disappoint a customer if you could possibly help it. Also, Senga had been, understandably, vague about her movements and Ally wanted to be sure she could get away by five. Surely Cal wouldn't object to a quick word, if she was tactful.

The office was situated along a short passage at the rear of the building. Along with some basic items of furniture and a filing cabinet for business documents, it contained an industrial-sized refrigerator and several storage cupboards for foodstuffs.

Feeling slightly awkward, her near-silent trainers providing insufficient warning, Ally reached the heavy door. She normally used the security buttons to gain admittance but, given the situation, would knock and let Cal open it.

Only as Ally was about to raise her hand did she notice the door mechanism had prevented it from completely closing and automatically locking – but by too slight a margin for light to shine through and make it apparent until she was close to it. Glancing down, she spotted the reason: a small stone, maybe from someone's shoe, had got trapped between the lower corner of the door and its frame.

She tapped. A gentle tap, she thought. Unfortunately, Ally had underestimated her strength. With a whine, the door swung open to reveal Cal, his trousers and boxer shorts around his ankles, pumping a young woman, bound and gagged with scarves against the wall.

Ally screamed.

Frozen seconds followed before the couple hurriedly disengaged themselves and adjusted their clothing, though not in sufficient time for Cal to conceal his angry tumescence.

Ally's next cry was trapped in her throat.

She turned and ran back through the café, dementedly pushing past Katie and several anxious customers, now on their feet with concern at the commotion. Dashing out to the pavement, her sobs merging with the buzz of traffic and hollering of school-children ambling homewards, she kept on…

… running.

By now less dishevelled, Cal reached the bar. Bemused customers demanded an explanation.

'What was all that about?' one said. 'Why is she so upset?'

'She looked as if she'd had a shock' said another.

'Puir wee thing. Should you no' go after her?'

Cal thought quickly. He was the last person who could calm Ally down. 'It was entirely my fault. A big misunderstanding. She… well, she has problems. I cannae apologise enough.'

The women either tut-tutted, shook their heads, or both, as they paid Katie and quickly left. Two businessmen customers finished their drinks and shot him strange looks.

Of the woman who had been with Cal, there was no sign.

'What have you done to upset her?' Katie said, although she had a good idea. This wasn't the first time that the woman had been hanging around the Balfour when Senga wasn't there. The dining table in her flat overlooked the street. She'd spotted her on several occasions.

Cal put a finger to his lips and murmured 'I'll explain later... You get off, I'll sort things out here.'

Somewhat callously, Cal's initial impulse was to think that, as Ally tended to be uncommunicative, there might not be an immediate problem. Nonetheless, she'd find a way of telling her friend Lorna, and then Lorna would tackle Senga. Would she return to the Balfour? Cheap labour wasn't easy to find and their profit margin was finely-tuned as it was.

Hell! If only he'd checked the door, none of this would have happened, but the woman had only managed to get an hour off work. Things were far safer on the days they scrounged time at her place, but today a plumber was working all afternoon in her flat, so he'd been obliged to contrive the representative from the wine company story. Not that he was unduly worried about Katie giving him away. She relied on her odd jobs at the Balfour and it was in her best interests to keep schtum.

Part of Cal was mortified at what Ally had witnessed, whilst the other, chauvinistic part argued 'for heaven's sake, it was just a shag'; yet he knew women, generally, took sex more seriously than men.

Locating Lorna's work number, which had recently been added to the book behind the bar for emergencies, Cal decided that carefully crafted honesty would be the best policy. He'd have to trust Lorna's discretion.

'Hi. Lorna? It's Cal from the Balfour.'

'Hello,' Lorna said. 'Is something wrong?'

'Look, I'm sorry to bother you, but I'm worried about Ally. Is it okay to talk?'

'If it's important.'

'Cannae go into details now but she... well, she saw something she shouldn't, went berserk and vanished,' Cal said. 'I've looked everywhere I could think of without luck.'

'Something like... what? I need details.'

'It's very... I mean... Someone was with me.' Cal detected a slight intake of breath. 'A big mistake. It shouldn't have happened. I'm sorry.'

There was a short pause whilst Lorna took in the information.

'God. You men! Ally of all people too. You must know she overreacts to anything involving sex.'

'I know. But *why*?'

'I've yet to discover the full story. In the meantime, take my word for it. She has serious issues in that respect.'

'I'm really s...'

'I'll get there as soon as I can.'

Lorna pictured the scene. She'd seen the look on Cal's face whenever he served an attractive woman, and the way he adjusted his charm thermostat to suit. She didn't have the time to pursue the whys and wherefores of this disaster. All she knew was that Ally had been badly frightened and was out there somewhere, confused and alone. She must get moving.

First, Lorna rang the flat. Unsurprisingly, there was no answer. Making her excuses at work, she grabbed her coat and briefcase, dashed outside on to the pavement, and hailed a taxi. She remembered how, whenever Ally wanted peace and quiet, she strolled along the path by St Bernard's Well three minutes' walk from the Balfour.

Lorna asked the taxi driver to drop her off at Upper Dean Terrace. Once there she looked over the railings and scanned the view. Ally was seated, hunched and zombie-like, on a bench across the water, near the Greek folly. Lorna dashed down the slope, over the bridge and up to her.

Ally registered her presence with a confused, frightened look. Lorna longed to take her in her arms as one would a small child and reassure her everything was all right, but she knew that wasn't possible. For the time being, the shock had shut Ally down. For about twenty minutes, the two women sat in silence, Lorna's silent, but sympathetic presence, providing what comfort it could.

If you felt totally wretched, this leafy walkway by the Water of Leith was as tranquil a place as any in the city to seek solace overseen, as it was, by the gracious presence of Hygeia, Goddess of Health. How many emotional scenes had she witnessed from her plinth above the old pump room with the river trickling by? How many people over the years had ambled along this path, contemplating fraught lives?

It was easy to imagine different generations of tourists flocking to take the waters for the relief of real or imagined ills. During the late eighteenth century, the little spa had rivalled Bath. If some people had been repelled by the dubious smell and taste of the beneficial fluid, the trust they placed in its healing powers – for anything from bruises to blindness – had at least given them some peace of mind.

Lorna waited until Ally's snuffles had sufficiently quietened before the two women walked slowly back to the main road and found another cab.

Unable to make much progress with Ally that evening, whenever Lorna tried softly talking to her, she received only a perplexed look that soon turned back into a vacant stare. At some point, she must talk to Senga. The heart of the matter was Cal's bad behaviour and its ramifications. How, she wondered, would the incident affect their marriage and livelihood?

Lorna knew she was running ahead of herself. Senga and Cal's marriage might not be any of her business – but Ally's despair was. A proper explanation was needed. At least she now appreciated the extent of her friend's fragility. If Ally wasn't intending to return to the Balfour, what would she do? Whilst Lorna had no problem providing a home for her for as long as she needed, there were other matters to consider and difficult decisions to be faced.

One day at a time, Lorna told herself.

SIXTEEN

The Legacy of Goatfell

જ ઉ

SENGA arrived back at the Balfour early that evening after accompanying her mother to the hospital in the ambulance. There had been the usual hanging around waiting to see a doctor for the results of x-rays and feedback. The diagnosis was a badly bruised femur.

Given her age, and as she was still under observation, Nora couldn't go home until temporary care arrangements were in place. An only child, Senga was responsible for her mother. She was required back at the hospital later that evening after stopping off at Nora's small flat in Blackhall to pack a small case with clothes, toiletries, and some magazines. Tomorrow a dialogue would need to be established with the Social Care Officer.

Six o'clock being a popular unwinding time, the Balfour was bustling once more. Wearily, Senga pushed open the glass entrance door. The last thing she needed was to discover Ally had done a runner.

At a suitable pause in the trafficking of food and drinks, Cal gave Senga a succinctly edited account of the afternoon's events, his relief at getting things off his chest off-set by – seeming – shamefacedness.

Emphasising his concern for Ally, Cal tried hard to make it sound as if the incident was a mild flirtation that had gone horribly wrong, but his I've-been-a-bit-of-a-naughty-boy act rang even less true than usual. Senga wasn't fooled. Although she'd learnt to cope in her own way with Cal's don't-misjudge-me versions of what amounted to his inability to keep his trousers zipped, with her energy levels running on Almost Empty his appalling lack of judgement hit her hard.

Ally was special. Senga was very angry that Cal had allowed his misbehaviour to rebound on someone in whom they'd made a considerable investment, as both a colleague and friend. There was no doubt in her mind that Ally was damaged in some way. It was that which had made her so protective of her. Senga would never forgive Cal if, however indirectly, he was responsible for making her life more difficult than it already was.

What, or rather *who*, had he been up to?

Senga had never placed sexual fidelity at the top of her expectations list. Her marriage to Cal was built on a raft of more complex, shared experiences. This matter, however, needed sorting.

Brought up in a small community on the Isle of Arran, the couple had been inseparable since childhood. Two years his senior, Senga wasn't so much Cal's wife as his elder sister. She'd been delegated the task of looking after him for much of the day when they were children and their mothers working, accepting a degree of responsibility with a conscientiousness beyond her years. On that night before the final hefty dose of morphine kicked-in Senga had promised his mother, for the last time, that she would always take care of him.

However irresponsible Cal might have been, because she loved him Senga had accepted him as he was. He made her feel the grown-up. The capricious child they had learned they could never have.

It had begun the day after Senga's sixth birthday.

They were playing shops in the dining room, using spare buttons from Nora's haberdashery box as money for trading chocolate drops and jelly babies, taking it in turns to be customer and shop assistant. High and tetchy on too much sugar and E-numbers, they assumed Nora had come in to tick them off for the noise they were making. But Nora's mind was elsewhere and she hadn't noticed what they were up to.

The children fell silent. Something, they sensed, was very wrong. Beckoning them and putting her arms around them, Nora gently led them into the living room where Cal's mother, Aileen, was waiting. Aileen put out her hands to Cal, who scrambled on to her lap in the wing-backed Parker-Knoll. Tense with foreboding, Senga perched bolt upright on the edge of the sofa.

Senga remembered the greyness beyond the window; the menacing yellow chrysanthemums on the antimacassars and Nora pacing listlessly up and down.

Then stopping.

'I'm afraid…' Nora said softly to two pairs of raised, frightened eyes. 'Y… your daddies… won't be coming home.'

'Tonight?' Senga asked, fearful of the reply.

'No. Not just tonight, my darlings…' Nora, struggling ineffectively with her emotions, finally managed to whisper '…never.'

Early that afternoon the fathers, both experienced tree surgeons, had been pruning a copse with chainsaws on the lower slopes of Goatfell, when a freak storm had unexpectedly blown up. Neither man would have been prepared for the sudden force of the gale, which must have set the trees swaying beyond human control. One of the branches of the tall conifer they were working on had snapped.

From the state of their bodies afterwards, it was deduced that, possibly, Senga's father had dropped from high up in the tree. Cal's dad, it was assumed, had climbed up to help his mate when the broken branch and the wind or the kick-back of the saw had taken him down too. Their safety equipment had been no match for the elements.

No one would fully know the truth.

By the time their colleagues, realising the pair were in danger, went in search of them, it was too late. The two men were discovered motionless, yards apart on the forest floor. Although they were rushed to hospital, one died in the ambulance, the other following him an hour or so later.

A malicious, but unproven, rumour circulated concerning a dispute over a local barmaid. Cal's father, like his son later, was a law unto himself where women were concerned, whilst his colleague came across as something of a prude. Could there have been more to the struggle, some people asked themselves? Most preferred to believe the accepted version of the tragedy.

Certainly, their wives did.

It was years before Senga and Cal dragged out of their mothers more details of that afternoon, although the full horror was withheld from them. Nora and Aileen had made a pact. 'Better the bairns never know.'

Sadly, an overactive imagination needs little nourishment. With the unlikeliest provocation Senga would always be hit by bleak moods when least expected, visited by imagined sounds and images of that tragic evening. The furtive, helpless whispers; the blood and hopelessness. It underscored her continued sense of loss of a father denied to her. Perhaps it was because of her own propensity for such melancholic moods that Senga, without knowing much about her, had instinctively empathised with Ally.

The two mothers dealt with their grief in their own way, preferring to remember their husbands as quasi-romantic heroes. Senga, however, despite the emotional legacy of that day, preferred to look life in the eye – if at a price. Being younger, Cal wasn't affected by the events to the same extent as his wife and was cushioned by a more outgoing personality. Nevertheless, he was the one person who understood how she felt.

The authorities had helped persuade the insurance company to posthumously give the men the benefit of the doubt. The compensation and the women's combined resourcefulness ensured the families never suffered too much financially. They used a large part of the money to set themselves up in business: a small café-cum-art and craft shop, which became a popular attraction during the tourist season.

By the time the children reached their teens, they were helping their mothers in the shop at weekends and during their vacations. The experience provided them with transferable skills – put to good use when they ventured into business themselves. They had always been there for each other, attended the same schools and, in due course, the same college where Senga studied hotel management whilst Cal, eventually, acquired bar skills and an SVQ in Catering.

Even when they were married on her twenty-fourth birthday, Senga was aware of Cal's addiction to other women. Most wives would never have countenanced it, but not being too reliant on physical love herself, Senga believed they were, nonetheless, devoted to each other – if in different ways.

'Sex is like a pint of beer' Cal once explained, 'It doesn't mean anything. Just sorts out an immediate thirst.' More likely it was his way of dealing with his lack of confidence: for not doing well at school – or compensating for growing up in a matriarchal microclimate. Whatever the reason, Cal and Senga's lives were intertwined. A spell when Senga was away studying whilst he was still completing his school leaving exams had been intolerable for them both.

Despite her mental acceptance of the situation, Senga found it difficult keeping pace with Cal's insatiable libido and fetishes which she had only discovered after their marriage, and were unacceptable to her. Her way of coping was to try and ignore his, usually short-lived, adventures on the tacit understanding he played safe and kept them to himself. She couldn't entirely condone Cal's conduct, indeed at one level she deeply resented it, but given her long-standing feelings for him and her own limitations, she had to deal with it – or move on. So far, the latter had never been an option. Not only had they gone into business together – Senga mistakenly thought this would help her monitor him – but, despite his infidelities, Cal always worshipped her in his own way. Until now, the pact had worked. But then, he'd never flaunted his indiscretions, or become so besotted with another woman for it to unbalance the strange equilibrium of their relationship.

That was about to change.

Early in the New Year Cal had become more restless and distracted than usual. Senga observed him furtively looking at his phone whenever he wasn't working and furiously texting, even when supposedly watching television. Their sex life might be on the back burner, but they'd always been warm and affectionate with each other – that is, until the past few months. Now, Cal was rarely spontaneously demonstrative. Her wifely promptings had become self-conscious to the point of embarrassment.

Around Christmastime they'd attended a dinner party at a large, central hotel, thrown by two regular customers, Jan and Gus. The women attended the same Zumba class. Senga found herself sandwiched between an old family friend of Jan's and Gus's mate Ewan. Meanwhile, Cal was saddled with the family friend's dour wife on one side and an attractive woman – apparently Ewan's partner – on his other. To the older woman's disgust, Cal monopolised Paige for much of the evening.

Senga found it hard work dividing her attention between the courteous, but slightly deaf Hamish, and the pleasant but reticent Ewan. What with all the chatter and a pianist loudly banging out Lloyd Webber and Schönberg & Boublil ad nauseam, she was unable to hear what anyone else was saying. Whenever she looked across the table to catch her husband's eye and wink at him, he was flirting with Paige. Being par for the course, she'd put it to the back of her mind.

One chilly Tuesday evening some weeks later, towards closing time, Senga was wiping the Balfour's steamy windows, waiting for Katie to arrive so she could get ready for her class, when she noticed a woman, vaguely familiar, standing impatiently in a smart coat on the opposite pavement.

Paige caught sight of Senga watching her and hastily turned to look in the window of a gift shop.

Senga tried to think no more about it – until it happened again the following week.

This time, Senga was waiting by the door for a lift from Jan. Paige was clutching a cardboard Costa cup and had obviously come prepared. She never looked across the road but stopped to sip her hot drink by the same shop window as before.

Appearing beside her, Cal exclaimed a little too brightly 'Isn't that the woman we met some weeks ago at that do in The George? Think I should go over and invite her to come in out of the cold?'

A screech of brakes announced Jan's arrival.

'Jump in. There's someone on my tail!' she yelled.

Getting into the car, Senga caught sight of Paige moving towards the kerb and looking up and down the street prior to crossing.

That's odd, she'd thought.

SEVENTEEN

Unburdening

৶৶ ৶

'HOW long have you had negative feelings for your mother?' Grace and Casey sat opposite each other in the living room-cum-study of Casey's smart flat in Cumberland Street. Comfort came from a low-lit faux-coal gas fire set into the original early nineteenth-century fireplace. A small, polished table nudging Casey's armchair supported a few forced roses in a glass bowl and a couple of Parker biros. Another little table, next to Grace, held a bottle of sparkling water and a glass tumbler. A carriage clock sat discreetly on the mantelpiece between a pair of white china cats.

Grace considered Casey's question. 'On and off since, well, for ever, really,' she said.

Casey, resting a spiral bound notebook on her lap, raised a questioning eyebrow.

'Arithmetic was never my strongest subject,' Grace continued, 'but quite early on, I'd worked out that six was three short of nine.'

Casey looked puzzled.

'Months. A shot-gun wedding,' Grace unnecessarily added.

'Of course. And your parents never told you?'

'Mother simply said "you arrived early". As I grew older, I tumbled to the truth.'

'Why did it matter so much? After all, you were technically legitimate.'

'It was that she lied, and imagined I wasn't bright enough to work things out for myself.' Grace said. 'Even then, I had to filter the fiction to get at the shred of truth lurking beneath.'

'You never felt you could have things out with her?'

'I began to despise her too much to want to bother. The trust had gone. And then…'

'Go on.'

'I realised I didn't even come a close second. My mother already *had* a daughter.'

'You never mentioned your sister.'

'No, my cousin, Lorna. Though, being ten years older, she always seemed more like an aunt when I was growing up. They'd bonded long before I was born – and are still devoted to each other.'

Casey pondered before carefully saying, 'I can see that could be a problem.'

Grace shrugged; the gesture of someone for whom maternal disregard had become a part of her life – but there was a flash of bitterness in her eyes.

'You have a brother, though?' Casey said.

'Yes. Ewan.'

'Do you know how he feels about your mother?'

'We've never really discussed it. We get on quite well. I mean, we've no reason not to. There are two years between us. It didn't hurt badly until I was about fifteen and I could have done with another adult to talk to nearer my age. Ewan would have been... '

'Thirteen?'

'Yes. I was feeling quite grown-up when he was still at junior school. Your body's changing then, and you don't often feel comfortable confiding your thoughts and emotions in other people. Certainly not in a boy, unless you've always been extremely close. And Ewan and I weren't. As I've indicated, we rubbed along but...' Grace shrugged again.

'It didn't change as you both got older?'

'No. Probably because he gets on well with our mother.'

Casey looked at Grace intently. 'Did you feel the odd one out?'

'Yes,' Grace said.

As Casey made notes, Grace appraised her neatly-kept fair hair and crisp turquoise blouse – one she had coveted some time ago when she'd spotted it herself in the window of an expensive shop in George Street. 'God,' she thought, 'I'm paying this woman £100 an hour, and all I can do is admire what she's wearing.'

They usually went straight into the bin. Freebie newspapers were such a waste of paper, space and everyone's time. Then, as Grace bent down to pick it up, she recognised a contemporary on the front page: fussily dressed and cutting a ribbon at the entrance of a refurbished store in Linlithgow.

They'd both been members of the Scottish Dance club at college, until her friend's political interests started to consume all her extra-curricular hours and then her life. The friendship drifted, although they still exchanged Christmas cards. And here she was now, on the brink of becoming an SNP candidate. A formidable one too, of that

Grace had no doubt. Good luck to her.

Scanning the article, Grace noted things were really gearing up Referendum-wise. Not that she'd ever taken much interest in it. That's what unhappiness did to you. It turned you in on yourself, detaching you from everything that didn't impact directly on your life.

On the next page, she chanced to notice an advertisement in the bottom corner:

WORRIED ABOUT ANYTHING?
Anxious – Tense – Can't Sleep?
Maybe just want to talk to someone?
Contact: **Casey Melville**
Qualified Counsellor
caseymel@hotmail.com 0131 …

A strange coincidence. It was as if a subconscious search engine sometimes switched on in your head.

Grace's normal reaction would have been to dismiss such an advertisement out of hand, scoffing that any well-adjusted person should need to empty their mental garbage all over a stranger – surely an admission of failure and self-indulgence if ever there was. Then she remembered Vicky's suggestion some weeks ago. She'd not mentioned it since fearing, with reason, that Grace might overreact.

Was she, Grace wondered, as well-adjusted these days as she had always considered herself to be? The doubt which she'd supressed for a while now had finally matured into a proper question. Grace had only ever mentioned – and then reservedly – her problems to her father, Vicky and occasionally Duncan when he wasn't too tired; and then only as a last resort. Was it remotely feasible for anyone else to help her, provided she liked them and, as seemed the case here, they were well-qualified? Before she went any further, she must carefully scrutinise the woman's credentials.

Grace remembered watching elderly film stars on chat shows, identified by the assertive characters they had brought to life on screen yet admitting to a lifetime of psychoanalysis. Immaculately groomed and still full of enthusiasm for their work, they'd open up to Ross or Graham and six million viewers, telling them how it had helped them cope with the pressures of fame. In some cases, it had even eased them away from alcohol and drug abuse. Under the Versace they too were vulnerable.

Until very recently, Grace believed she had her own life in perspective. She took everyone very seriously, as she did herself, usually on their face value. She expected people to be who they said they were. She'd always prided herself on keeping up with global politics and the arts, conscientiously devouring articles in *The Times* and *Panorama*-type investigations and acquiring informed views about the world. She enjoyed going to concerts too – though nothing after von Weber or overly romantic – and the occasional contemporary or classic play, whilst despising people who spoke too easily about their own inner thoughts. She was wary of relating issues in fiction and drama to those in her own life. 'I can work my problems out for myself,' she told herself.

Then, the twins had arrived. Now, after a day with them, it was all Grace could do to rustle up supper before flopping in front of something mindless on TV. Anything to suppress the thought of another twenty-four hours predictably like the last. She was on a carousel whirling around ever faster. If she didn't get off now she'd be flung off, to land she knew not where.

The more she thought about it, the more Grace saw she at least owed it to Duncan to help herself. If that meant finally lifting the lid of her Pandora's box, so be it, she must summon the courage to do so. After all, she told herself, no one need know. If it failed, what had she lost? And if it helped her manage her current state of negativity and think more calmly, it might be worth it.

'Have you any idea why this has taken so long to come to a head?' Casey asked.

'I grew to accept it,' Grace said. 'I went to college, made my own friends, worked my way up into a decent job and then got married. I suppose my hurt went underground.'

'Until?'

'My father died unexpectedly, last year.'

'I'm sorry.'

'I always felt he understood my problems but couldn't share with me any reservations he had about Mum's relationship with Lorna. Presumably out of loyalty to her. Though I got the impression it irritated him too. He seemed to pay me extra attention whenever he could.'

'You miss him.'

'Dreadfully.'

Lowering her voice, Casey gently asked: 'And these feelings

manifested themselves…?'

'Almost a year after my daughters were born. I began suffering from what I now understand was a form of post-natal depression.'

Casey nodded understandingly.

Grace looked puzzled. 'You too?'

'No, but my sister went through it. So, I understand about it, although it affects women differently. I know this session is about you, but it may be helpful, if only a little, to know you aren't alone.'

'A little.'

'And, could I ask… How does your partner deal with it?'

'Duncan's one those people who is very kind and means well but doesn't really do sickness, let alone understand the way a person is feeling. How can I put it…?'

Another encouraging smile. 'Go on, you're doing well…'

'…Things like colds and flu make him very short-tempered,' Grace said. 'He sees them as a tiresome inconvenience, like bus strikes and power cuts. Says "I'm so sorry" and all the right things when it's me suffering, but you know he really expects you to grit your teeth and work through it as quickly as possible.'

Grace nodded as if she recognised the type. 'Was Duncan ever at boarding school?'

'Yes. He was sent away when he was ten. Dollar Academy.'

'Ah,' Casey said.

'When I'm particularly stressed-out,' Grace went on, 'he makes self-conscious attempts to be solicitous, then goes into the stiff-upper-lip mode, sort-of on my behalf.'

'And things have been like that for a while?'

'Yes. If Duncan finds something difficult to handle, he doesn't have an argument about it, but immerses himself even more in work and gets home late. Recently it's become later and later.'

'And you feel isolated?'

'Yes.

'Which aggravates the situation?'

'It's a vicious circle. Neither of us wants to discuss our own problems – we're both too tired. The girls monopolise our… my time.'

'And…' Casey looked at her very carefully, '…at night?'

'Bed you mean?'

Casey nodded discreetly. 'You don't have to tell me if you don't want to, but…'

There was an akward pause, then Grace said: 'It's the only time we really communicate, actually. Silently, like needy animals. A ritual that's never discussed – or explained away.'

'At least you have that.'

'Until the noises from the next room interrupt us. Kara's a very light sleeper. We're never allowed time to ourselves for long without being summoned to comfort her.'

'You feel you can't win?'

'Yes.'

Casey paused. Grace looked furtively at the clock. There were twenty minutes left. Grace took a sip of water, Casey took stock. 'Any other triggers,' she said after a minute's scribbling.

'Triggers?'

'Has anything happened recently that could have been a catalyst. Something that has hit you particularly hard?'

Grace wavered.

'You can tell me anything,' she said. 'I won't judge you.'

Grace looked uncertain.

'To misquote Blaise Pascal,' Casey said encouragingly, 'the subconscious has reasons which reason knows nothing of. A somewhat pretentious standby of mine, but it sometimes strikes a chord.'

So, Grace told her about the will. 'I don't want to sound mercenary or self-serving,' she said. 'It's just my mother's attitude. As if Ewan and I don't exist… like Dad's death doesn't affect anyone else but her. And knowing that on top of everything, she'll be sharing all her thoughts about it with *her*.'

'Your cousin?'

'Lorna. Yes.'

'If it wasn't for your mother, would you still dislike Lorna. I mean, if she was, for instance, a colleague?'

'Not really, no. Lorna's a decent enough person – although we've little in common. It's transferred resentment, I suppose – if there's such a term. It's my mother I'm angry with.'

'Is *angry* really the right word?'

Without even stopping to consider this, Grace said 'It's much closer to…' she almost spat out '… *loathing*.'

Grace could see Casey was taken aback but struggling not to let it show. At least she'd made herself clear.

'I appreciate this isn't easy for you,' Casey said after a moment or so, gently.

Grace sighed. 'If only it made me feel better.'

'At least you now seem to *understand* yourself better and may be in a stronger position to confront your...' Casey settled on lamely, '...more difficult thoughts. I've simply helped you accept ownership of them and unpack the reasoning behind any decisions you now make. But ...'

'Yes?'

'Have you thought of any way you could tell your mother exactly how you feel?'

'If I could, don't you think I'd have done so?'

'Not necessarily face-to-face but maybe another way?'

'You mean by email...?'

Looking as if she was giving the matter serious consideration before rejecting the idea, Casey said, 'Possibly not, but how about...?'

'Yes?'

'A letter?'

'Oh.'

'Something for you to consider, anyway. It works for some people and could possibly provide an overture to a more open discussion.'

'Where?'

'On neutral territory anyway. A cosy corner in a large-ish wine bar – providing you don't overdo the wine! Or a coffee shop.'

'Provided we don't overdo the coffee,' Grace said, thinking of her ill-tempered bladder.

Casey indulged Grace with a supportive look. 'Start by jotting down much of what you've told me, including the even more personal bits that would mean something to her. Be completely honest – but try to imagine how she might feel when she reads it. Couch it in straightforward language and try to use words that aren't too emotive.'

'Isn't the whole thing emotive?'

'That's the tightrope you walk. Put yourself in the other person's place if you can. Stick to the facts as you see them but edit them until you reach a version you're happy with. I always suggest drafting it on a PC but handwriting the final version. It's more personal and shows you've taken some trouble. Use notepaper if possible – avoid, for example, sheets of lined A4 student notepad and putting it in a brown envelope, which might create the wrong impression.'

Grace tensed, thinking of their spartan supply of stationery.

'Unless, of course, that's the way you always communicate and she's familiar with it,' Casey said, as if concerned she might have sounded too prescriptive. And best P5 handwriting!' she concluded jokily. 'But it's up to you. You might be surprised how much dialogue a letter generates. After all, you've not heard your mother's side of the story.'

She saw her point had sunk in. 'But it's only a thought. It's not my role to tell you what to do. Right...' Casey flicked through her desk diary, ignoring the lingering look of confusion on Grace's face.

'Same time next week?'

❧❧

EIGHTEEN

A Day Out – Morning

৵ ঌ

'WHAT say you and I pop along the coast to a nice beach?' Maggy said. 'When the weather permits?'

She thought Dino – as she'd decided he really was – was becoming more acclimatised to her English, even when her phrasing matched nothing supplied by Messrs Berlitz. She could see he didn't always understand her, usually when she most wanted him to, but always responded with a twinkly smile.

The trip to Holyrood had gone well. No stalkers. Although every so often, she observed, Dino stopped and looked warily around. There were several men about in cream jackets, but none who looked remotely threatening. Though, what did a threatening person look like until you got close enough to sense danger? Then it might be too late.

A few days later, they'd taken the coach to Traquair House in Peeblesshire. Dino's face had clouded over for a few minutes in the car park, but he never remarked on who or what he'd seen and was back to his usual self as soon as he entered the building.

A gruesome anecdote from the tour guide concerning a long-forgotten Stuart had led Maggy and Dino to share, over tea, dysfunctional aspects of their own families' behaviour. As Dino talked, Maggy couldn't help thinking one family was much like another, even if duels and daggers were no longer in vogue. The way his father treated him explained a lot about his need to prove himself, whilst his frankness gave her permission to confide in him, too.

Maggy had told him of the emotional fallout from Don's death and her increasing concern of its impact on Grace and Ewan, apologising for sounding disloyal but, after all, there were some things it was inappropriate to share with anyone else – even Lorna. She valued the reactions of a younger person, especially a stranger from a different culture. It gave her a different perspective on life. Dino was a good listener. It wasn't as if he was likely to meet Grace or Ewan. If Maggy wasn't always sure how much he was taking in, he affected interest and concern.

Today's outing to North Berwick was another first. Much as

Maggy avoided driving, she'd realised, too late, that their visit to Traquair would have been so much easier by car. This had spurred her on to brave the local roads and take the Audi for its MOT, service and a good hose-down. A spin around some local haunts afterwards had, to her surprise, invigorated her. 'Poop Poop!' she'd muttered to herself as she'd overtaken a post van.

A phone call to an elderly car-less friend, who lived in a mews off the West End, revived a long-standing arrangement for Maggy to make use of her parking space whenever she was obliged to drive into the city.

With the chance of a warm sunny day, Maggy texted Dino to suggest they meet for a coffee around ten o'clock the following morning at one of the more intimate West End hotels – a discreet, though central, sanctuary of hers.

After sending the message, Maggy remembered that Drummond Braithwaite, when not at the BBC in Glasgow, occasionally used the place as his club. Long since graduated from presenter to producer and now semi-retired, 'Banger', with his neatly trimmed pepper-and-salt hair, confident gait, and flamboyant ties, had matured into a mildly-eccentric Edinburgh treasure. As Maggy told Una, a cross between the Monarch of the Glen and an elderly Alan Cumming.

Since the *Major Barbara* party all those years ago, when Banger had beseeched Maggy to consider a stage career, they had become, culturally speaking, kindred spirits. Whilst she bowed to his considerably greater knowledge of what he referred to as 'the business', they shared a lingo no-one else in her family – since Doris's decline – enjoyed.

'You had that certain something, Maggy,' he'd say with a sigh, adding with calculated mystery, 'One of these days … eh?' before taking his leave of her and striding off into the crowd. More than a good acquaintance, if not quite an intimate friend, Banger was always affable and raised her spirits whenever they met. With him, Maggy could catch up on the enticing world she'd forsaken long ago. If the worst came to the worst, it wouldn't do him any harm to see her, finally, getting on with her life and making an interesting new friend. It might, she thought wickedly, also be amusing to see his reaction to Luca… er, Dino.

The hotel lounge was bustling with the first of the morning coffee brigade. There was a single area almost free in a corner by a window with several comfortable chairs around a small table. Sure enough, one of these was occupied by Banger, who spotted Maggy in her cheerful red blazer and indicated the empty chairs beside him.

'I thought robins were for Christmas,' he said, helping her off with her jacket.

'Och this! I know, everyone hates it. But we're off to the beach and it's nice and warm. You never know what the weather's going to do.'

He picked up on the 'we're' but only said, 'A bit nippy still, for paddling, eh?'

Before she could invent a witty riposte, Dino materialised. Maggy beckoned him to join them.

As she'd anticipated, Banger's eyes were on stalks.

'This is Luca,' Maggy said quickly as the old roué gripped Dino's hand, 'my friend Maria's son from Milan.'

'Why hello!' Banger boomed, giving Dino a smile – barely on the decent side of lascivious – which, Maggy noted with amusement, Dino awkwardly returned. Banger beamed at her as she elaborated on her story, pleased with herself at having prepared it for just such an emergency.

If Maggy thought she'd fooled Banger with her 'Maria's son' subterfuge, she was mistaken. Who was Maria for heaven's sake? Surely, he'd have remembered her link with Italy – it was a favourite country of his. Then Maggy pushed her luck too far. 'I must surely have told you about her husband, Giovanni, who left her a small castle. No?' She must have been bingeing on too many romantic novels. This masquerade wouldn't earn her five lines in Act Two. Nevertheless, Banger had always suspected Maggy of being very much her own person, not a typically sedate Edinburgh matron. The stick of eye candy beside her did nothing to modify his assessment.

A man of the world, at least the BBC world, Banger was an old hand at chatting up attractive male visitors to the city, even if at his age it was becoming an expensive hobby. This boy was unconvincing as either my-little-nephew or quality trade. Banger was experienced at sussing out auditionees going for roles outside their range. Luca fitted that category. What precisely was the real relationship between Maggy and this edible young man? Pleasant though he seemed, he wouldn't like Maggy to come to any harm physically, emotionally – or both. Did she know what she might be letting herself in for?

After a quarter of an hour's chit-chat, Maggy excused herself to visit the facilities. Banger decided to show his hand.

'Have you been working in Edinburgh long?'

'No. Mrs Galbraith explained. Is a holiday.'

The older man raised an expectant eyebrow.

'I… I like to meet new people, and…'

Banger's eyes looked expectant.

Struggling to find the right words, Dino heard himself say, crassly '…make them 'appy. No?'

'I guessed that was probably the case,' Banger said, hiding his amusement.

'And Maggy, I like … *moltissimo.*'

'It would be hard not to.'

Banger applied a quick test. 'And when she isn't busy, might you be available to…' he chose his words carefully '… make other folk… happy by, say, accompanying them to, maybe, a play or film?'

'If…' Dino started.

Banger was truly intrigued. 'Yes?'

'… it wasn't a problem. For her.'

So, he wasn't completely stupid.

'Maggy and I have known one another for over forty years,' Banger heard himself say. 'I like her *moltissimo* also.'

'Forty years is long time,' Dino said, as if unsure where all this was heading. He fished out a printed card and handed it to him.

'Is what I do in Milan,' he said.

Banger's Italian was good enough for him to make a calculated guess at the words *Designer di scare* beneath Dino's real name and his personal details. He also spotted the discrepancy in the names. Which of them was the real person: Luca or Dino? Like Maggy, he was charmed by the man. But then, one was drawn to grey squirrels: attractive, but unscrupulous and freeloading.

'So, you really belong to the fashion world?'

'Yes.'

'Does Maggy know?'

'I tell her everyt'ing about me.'

Banger didn't believe that for one moment, but gently said, 'Although I see Dino is your business name.'

'My business…?' Banger glanced knowingly at the card.

Dino blushed. 'It is…' he began.

'Complicated?' Dino nodded. 'Your secret is safe with me. But please treat her kindly.' The older man then referred to Dino's professional credentials and led the conversation towards the shoe industry, where Dino seemed on more secure territory. He was enthusiastically describing the range of his work when Banger spotted Maggy on her way back to the table. He put a finger to his lips. 'I may be in touch,' he murmured and winked conspiratorially.

'Do you drive?' Maggy had asked Dino before they'd set out.

'Yes. I miss it.'

'If I give you directions, would you like to today?'

When his eyes lit up, she knew it was settled. Now she only had the short journey to and from the West End to worry about. She'd enjoy the rest of the day, and any future excursions, much more if they shared the driving. Of course, in allowing Dino to take the wheel again, Maggy knew she would be playing fast and loose with her motor insurance policy – but what the hell! 'Madcap Maggy' Una sometimes called her. She'd be sure to take over for the last lap home.

Once out of town, Dino became daring: tootling calmly along one moment, leaving half her stomach behind when a clear stretch came into view the next. 'Someone on your tail?' she'd asked at one point. But he just gave her his cute smile. It wasn't as if he was *too* reckless. And she was seeing the familiar route with fresh eyes.

His eyes.

Soon, after they'd established themselves on the beach, Dino expressed his wish to explore. He muttered something about buying ice creams and a newspaper. 'Why the hurry?' Maggy said, 'you'll not find the *Giornali Italiani* here, and I've a *Scotsman* in my bag – so much better for your English!' But he'd simply got up, stretched and meandered off as if he hadn't heard. Terribly macho these Latins, Maggy thought.

Dino had declined the tenner she'd tried to press on him. Well, it was good occasionally to let him treat her. She could always slip him a note later, on the pretext of something else. She didn't think he was naturally mean and was prepared to go along with his excuse about a small, temporary cash-flow problem and how he was awaiting news from his accountant. He'd promised to give her a contribution towards the petrol too – as soon as the money was transferred.

Time would tell.

With her back to a rock, Maggy lounged on the Galbraith tartan rug she'd brought along and let the May sunshine melt her cares away. North Berwick was a popular seaside resort within easy reach of the capital. The family, along with many of their fellow townies, had enjoyed many a day out there. It hadn't changed significantly since her childhood and was still an ideal place to mooch around and, weather permitting, flop on the sand.

Maggy didn't really believe that Dino was staying in a five-star hotel, or had an accountant, but she hadn't yet worked out his real reason for being in Scotland or exactly where he was staying. Smart though his clothes were, he'd obviously not packed many. Most likely he was dossing down with friends on a put-u-up in some dreary studio flat but was too ashamed to admit it. And this Dino-Luca business. What was that all about?

In the months to come Maggy would accept that, at this time, a part of her was in denial. For now, however, an accomplice to her own conspiracy, she'd made an irrational pact with herself to let the charade play out. Its superficiality was part of its magic.

It was surprising to think that only two weeks ago she'd been almost a recluse, psyching herself up to catch a bus into town. Now, here she was, charging all over the place and enjoying herself immensely. What had happened to her? Could the transformation really be down to a chance encounter with a charming but dubious young man young enough to be…? Hey, she could do the maths. Ewan would have been eight when Dino was born. He wasn't entirely the reason for the change in her – but he was the catalyst. If the whole adventure ended in tears, so be it. *Carpe diem* as the life-affirming Miss Frobisher had instilled in them way back in the Fifth.

When she was with Dino, Maggy entered a parallel universe, adopting a split personality: part sober, part intoxicated. The Maggy who'd always enjoyed a sense of adventure, taken calculated risks and grabbed any chance for fun, had been reactivated – and then some. She felt as if she'd borrowed someone else's son for a week or so. If she'd been disappointed by the way Ewan, who was always good company, had currently retreated into his own crisis state – whatever it was – so be it. He needed to sort himself out in his own way.

Maggy doubted that Ewan would blame her for this restorative sabbatical even if Grace would, undoubtedly, have looked askance. Ah, Grace. The thought of her stubborn daughter made her wonder, yet again, what she had done to cause the ever-widening distance between them. Every time she saw her she wanted to say 'lighten up a little, darling, *please!*' But it would have only made matters worse.

What if her life at present was only a mirage? Whoever Dino was, his naturally courteous manner and much of what he'd told her about himself had at least given her to understand he was from a decent family. It was more what he'd *not* said that intrigued her.

She hadn't told Lorna about her 'project'. Lorna would only have given her unsolicited advice and called her Mrs Robinson – or, what was the name of that woman Vivien Leigh played in the Tennessee Williams film, *The Roman Spring of…*? Mrs Stone, was that it? Newly widowed and enjoying an affair with a gorgeous Italian gigolo. She wished! No, she was happy to give Dino rides and lunches, but whatever fantasies she might have, taking the friendship any further would be totally inappropriate. Better love a dream.

Maggy had faced up to the fact that Dino was extremely attractive. If she was being totally honest, he had awakened in her feelings she'd by now consigned to a rosemary-scented drawer in her memory. Or thought she had.

Alas, whatever the PC arguments and proselytising of women presenters on late-night Channel 4 programmes, to many provincial minds the thought of flabby, female pensioners rolling around with anyone – let alone a much younger person – was still regarded as something of a joke. Or maybe that was only by people who'd given up on love or were hung-up because either they or their partner was no longer interested – or interest*ing*? Yet, whilst one happily visualised beautiful young bodies rhythmically entwined on mattresses, social decorum permitted cougars a shelf life of what, fifty-something, whilst silver foxes had carte blanche? Another example of social hypocrisy. Mercifully, a lot of people took no notice, although Maggy had so far accepted no more than a chaste kiss on each cheek from Dino.

But who knew what observers thought?

She comforted herself with a more obtainable reason for nurturing her new friendship. Italy was a place she loved. Maria really existed: an ex-girlfriend of Fraser's whom Maggy had befriended when her brother moved on to another, less unpredictable lady. Though, if truth be told, Maria lived in Verona, not Milan and in a tiny flat, not a castle. Don had been so boring about vacations, preferring to flop all day alongside Spanish swimming pools than expand his mind exploring iconic cities. The bond had sadly fallen into disrepair.

The past few days, Maggy had imagined a visit to the homeland of Caravaggio and Modigliani, maybe taking in Milan and meeting Dino's family, before catching up with Maria and seeing an opera with her at Verona's glorious amphitheatre. Why, she might even move on to Florence as well. Maggy gave a moan of anticipation.

Coming down to earth, she was about to explore her *Scottish Field* when Maggy noticed a man standing roughly ten yards away. Not just any man, but one who looked vaguely familiar in a pale fawn jacket; his eyes, protected as before with shades, searching the beach.

What was that all about?

She was not dressed as she had been a fortnight ago and was wearing a pair of huge sunglasses, so it was unlikely he'd recognise her. As it happened, his eyes weren't trained on her anyway. Relieved when he turned away, she thought it safe to assume he was looking for someone else.

In brief moments, when short-lived shafts of reality filtered through her gauze of self-deception, Maggy vaguely wondered if Dino's occasional, but sudden, swings from vivacity to a darker mood could possibly indicate a drug habit? Although he usually wore his sleeves turned back a couple of times and she would have noticed any tell-tale marks. Now, the re-appearance of the man in the shades prompted scarier thoughts. Supposing Dino wasn't so much *using* drugs as *trading* in them?

Dearie me, she thought, her imagination was working overtime.

Maggy couldn't be bothered any more. Six months ago, she might have been seriously troubled by such thoughts; today she was merely chewing the matter over. A gull wailed above her. Nearby, the swish followed by the gravelly withdrawal of the tide washed all the beach it could reach. She rested her eyes for a few moments, basking in the apparent gentleness of the day.

Returning to an article on the recent restoration of a popular Highland hotel, Maggy failed to notice the man had stalked off in the same direction as Dino.

Meanwhile, Dino was exploring North Berwick.

He was learning to keep his options open. His new vocation hadn't yet proved very lucrative. There had been a brief skirmish with a mature contralto on her day off from a tour of *Turandot* – resulting in a hearty lunch at The Sheraton but no hard cash. He discounted a distasteful ten minutes' in a lock-up in the Gents at The Balmoral with a bearded Canadian, whose Dior Homme had failed to disguise a bad case of halitosis. That had raised a trio of ten-pound notes – but nothing else.

Noting the smartly-dressed guests in the hotel lounge earlier, Dino had momentarily considered he could always chance his luck at that hotel another day, on his own. The larger hotels had proved to be somewhat impersonal and he'd felt more at home there. Who knew what helpful, interesting people he might meet? An expectation of good conversation, good quality alcohol and a hot shower might just mitigate his distaste for any shut-your-eyes-and-think-of-Italy toil required to earn them. The coffees were expensive, but he could always chat up the receptionist and say he was waiting for someone. It vaguely crossed his mind he'd do better enquiring about temporary vacancies for ancillary staff.

With Maggy, Dino was playing the longer game. She was, of course, a useful meal ticket and helping him discover his temporary environment. He was grateful to her and enjoyed her company, whilst uncomfortably aware of using her. If he could start paying his own way a little more, his façade might appear more convincing. Speculate to accumulate as Paolo kept chivvying him.

Maggy was flirtatious, in a disarmingly innocent way that reminded him of his mother's stepsister who'd taken him under her wing as a boy, and of whom Dino was very fond. Yet, if he and Maggy grew too close, it might jeopardise his ability to take advantage of her when strictly necessary. The challenge was to win her confidence whilst holding part of himself back.

None of this came naturally to Dino, but Necessity led you to strange stepmothers.

He cynically recalled twee photos of *Amicizie Inaspettate*: the cute hamster or gosling nestling in the paws of a docile cat. Mercifully perhaps, one never knew what happened when the cameras stopped clicking. Still, he decided, the time had come for him to at least be straight with Maggy about the name business. It was important she trusted him.

Tucked away in a backstreet, an ice cream parlour with a smart white exterior came into focus, with the name Rossi painted in coffee coloured copperplate above the door. Several wrought iron tables and chairs decorated the pavement outside. The shiny windows revealed the pristine parlour within. Rossi was a familiar Italian name. Competitors could only claim the 'best ices for miles around.'

Dino wondered if the owners were related to Paolo's family. Dare he go inside and make himself known, or just stick to making a purchase? He walked over to the shop, unaware there was someone lurking in a nearby doorway.

When it came to his turn in the queue, Dino smiled at the middle-aged man behind the counter.

'How can I help you?'

'I'd like a couple of...' Dino was flummoxed by the extraordinary swirls of ice creams in the freezer, from snowy white through creamy pastels to shades of chocolate and toffee, often mixed with snippings of nuts, dried fruits and broken biscuits. He'd forgotten to ask Maggy if there was a flavour she especially liked. In the end, he settled on a scoop of lemon and zabaglione for one cone and blackberry and mocha for the other. She would have first choice.

Whilst the shopkeeper prised each squashy dollop into two large cornets, Dino enquired about the shop. The man was indeed Marco Rossi and was interested in Dino's story. He recollected someone who might have been Paolo's grandfather, coming to Scotland years ago; but his family was Neapolitan and sadly they were most likely unrelated. Handing over a ten-pound note with his back turned to the window, Dino failed to register a man's shadow fall across the glass counter.

The transaction having been completed and with no one else waiting to be served, the two men lapsed into Italian and continued chattering nostalgically for a few minutes about their homeland. Inevitably other customers joined the queue and it became necessary for Marco to excuse himself and serve them. Then he opened the shop door for Dino, whose hands were now wrestling with slowly melting ice cream oozing over the greaseproof paper wrappers.

As he sauntered back towards the beach, Dino was oblivious to Beige Man cautiously trailing him, taking care to ensure there were always several pedestrians between them. On reaching the corner of the street at the crossing for the beach, he was obliged to slow down and let a car pass in front of him. As it drove on, Dino glanced behind him to check there was no more traffic and was starting to cross over. Out of the corner of his eye, he caught sight of the man some yards away, dodging a woman with a baby in a pram.

Dino froze. Then his heart began racing. He moved off quickly, accelerating as the footsteps pattered menacingly closer behind him. Handicapped by the melting ice cream now trickling down over his wrists and seeping into his cuffs and shirt sleeves, he broke into a trot; any moment it would be impossible not to jerk it all over his clothes as well. A waste bin came into view. Dino slowed down for just a couple of moments, ditched the cornets, and turned to dash off. As he turned around, a strong hand caught his arm in an iron grip.

A few minutes later, Maggy was surprised to see Dino by her side, unkempt, with sticky ice-creamy patches on his shirt and jeans but no cornets. Far worse, there was a gash on his face. It was bleeding profusely. From what she deduced from his garbled half-English-half-Italian apology, Dino had narrowly missed being hit by a car. Brushing his thigh, he'd apparently fallen cheek down on to the unforgiving pavement. He was lucky not to have hit his head, he said.

If Maggy had her suspicions as to the truth of his story, it suited her to accept Dino's version on its face value. The real facts would emerge in due course. All she could do was look after him as best she could whilst he was, so to speak, in her care.

By now they'd been in North Berwick a couple of hours. The sky had clouded over. The young man went in search of a Gents to wash his wound and smarten himself up, whilst Maggy purchased antiseptic ointment and plasters. Of Beige Man there was no further sign.

They enjoyed a late lunch of fish and chips and delayed-gratification ice creams in another promenade café. Afterwards, Dino said he felt brighter and was more composed but, their holiday mood having faded, they decided to make their way back to the city.

Dino cruised silently for the first part of the journey. Maybe he was in more discomfort than he was letting on.

At length he said 'I t'ink I should be truthful with you.'

Maggy's heart skipped a beat. 'Truthful?' Please don't spoil things, Dino, she thought.

'My name...' he said.

At last.

'I 'ave two. It is really Dino. But sometimes, with people, I do not know...'

'Luca?'

'Yes. Is other name,' he fibbed. 'But as we 'ave become friends...'

'She interrupted him, 'I saw your necklace in the Botanics.'

Dino's face reddened. He really was gorgeous, Maggy thought, especially at moments like now, when his was manly ego was bruised. 'I'm sorry I misled you,' Dino said.

'We'll say no more about it. Dino it shall be, from now on, if you like?'

'Yes.' He gave her a smile; the sort that actors assume with insouciance – as, of course she knew.

In Maggy's mind the young man would always be two people: Dino, the likeable but slightly immature twenty-something, about whose character and motives she hadn't quite made up her mind; and his alter ego, Luca, the sophisticated, charismatic fantasy figure she'd partly invented for herself.

There was something Shakespearean about it.

Which twin was she with today?

◈

NINETEEN

A Day Out – Afternoon

ॐ ॐ

G RACE drafted umpteen letters, but none satisfied her.
Unlike the previous week, after her second session with
Casey, Grace left the flat in Cumberland Street unsure as to her next
move. Calm though she might appear outwardly, the click-thud of
the heavy door as it shut behind her intensified a gnawing anxiety.

As a schoolgirl Grace would spend a morning tidying up her study-
bedroom: putting everything away, stacking it neatly on shelves in
boxes, tins, jars, folders; arranging her books by author and height,
and making up the bed with clean bed linen. It had been satisfying,
but only up to a point. A tidy room couldn't do your homework for
you, it could only provide a calm, orderly environment in which
to study. Similarly, a counsellor could help put your thoughts in
perspective, sweep away some culpability, and guide you towards
possible strategies – but you had to select those you could use and
take them forward yourself. Whatever she'd told Casey, she wasn't
convinced about the letter idea. She had never opened up her heart to
anyone in that way – and certainly not her mother. She was at a loss.

It was a nice afternoon. Grace turned into Dundas Street and
began walking up the hill. Normally around this time of day the
area around the National Gallery was buzzing. Besides, she always
enjoyed wandering around the craft market. She might even treat
herself to coffee and a little something. One of the food stalls baked
amazing cheese and tomato croissants. Vicky had said not to hurry
back. It was still only four o'clock. A breath of air would do her good.

Reflecting on the past hour, Grace tried to analyse why the
session hadn't gone quite as well as the previous week. After an
initial recapitulation, she'd shown Casey her best attempt at a letter
for Maggy. Objective though she was supposed to be, Casey's face
failed to disguise her concern that she wasn't totally convinced by it.

After carefully considering the matter, Casey said: 'I can see
you've covered everything. You've made your points clearly and
concisely. And, of course, I don't know your mother, but…'

'But?'

'You may care to look again at the... tone.'

The word 'care' irritated Grace.

Casey carefully suggested some amendments to phrases that might possibly aggravate an already delicate situation and hinder diplomacy. 'But it's entirely up to you,' she said.

When, deep down, one is dissatisfied with a piece of work on which considerable time and thought has been spent, even constructive advice can initially be irritating if it's not what you want to hear.

The counsellor saw her comments hadn't gone down well and hastily changed the subject. 'Since our previous session, has anything else occurred to you which might shed light on why you feel the way you do?'

'Such as?'

'You mentioned your mother had always glossed over the circumstances of your birth. Can you recall why that made you feel so unsecure?'

'As a matter of fact...'

'Go on.'

Grace remembered how, as a teenager, she'd once spent a few days with Doris and Archie. Producing an old box full of old family photographs including several of Maggy and herself in various productions, Doris had light-heartedly supplied tales of the 'friendly' rivalry between them.

Doris, for whom it was second nature to turn any anecdote with dramatic potential into a Barbara Taylor Bradford storyline, had taken the opportunity to fill Grace in on some family background – from her own perspective.

'As you know, your mother was a gifted actress. I mean, I was accomplished, but even I could see Maggy had that *quelque chose de supplémentaire*. Your unexpected arrival must have been tough for her. But,' Doris said generously, 'I'm sure she never regretted her unplanned pregnancy, and anyway, I personally believe a woman's responsibility is first and foremost to her husband and family – don't you? You must never blame yourself, my dear...' Which of course, was precisely what Doris – who felt no great affection for her taciturn grandchild, preferring the more docile, manageable Ewan – wanted Grace to do.

Although Grace had lived out her early years against the backdrop of Maggy's love of the theatre, the full extent of the sacrifice her mother had made in marrying Doris's amazing son hadn't hit her until then. Maybe by the time Ewan turned up, Maggy had become more reconciled to being primarily a wife and mother? Whatever the reason, Doris successfully allowed another poisonous seed to fertilise in Grace's soul over the years, along with other perceived resentments.

What of course Doris had omitted to say was that Maggy agreed to marry Don *before* discovering she was pregnant. Nor did Grace know how Maggy had regularly fielded her mother-in-law's sugar-coated toxic remarks without complaint even to Don – except when Doris seriously overstepped the mark.

Casey, who knew better than anyone how family skeletons often rattled unnecessarily loudly, urged Grace to give Doris's story low priority. Grace, unfortunately, was not an easy person to reassure. She still mulishly clutched at any straw to justify her state of mind. It was like a fire: the embers had died down a little, but the slightest breeze would rekindle them.

A further session had still to be booked.

Feeling more settled, and carefully clutching a steaming cardboard cup of coffee and a paper bag containing her croissant, Grace found a bench in Princes Street Gardens looking up towards the castle esplanade and leading down one of the grassy slopes dotted with trees, to a little valley divided by well-maintained pathways.

Grace felt sure it was the same spot where, on many occasions during her school holidays, Maggy and she would recover from a hard morning's shopping. Not interested in trailing around stores after her mother, here she could finally get a chance to look at her comic before lunch whilst her mother perused *The Stage*. To give Maggy her due, she'd always made their excursions bearable by devising little treats. Something accompanied by chips at the end of the morning was a big deal to a peckish nine-year-old. Her mother was a different person then, Grace thought.

She forgot that she had been too.

The sight of the lawns broken up with flowerbeds, geometrically planted with assorted wallflowers, fell nostalgically on her eyes. Taking a tissue from her bag, she wiped off a few drops of rainwater from the bench, sat down and tucked into her snack.

With Maggy still on her mind, Grace was about to open her *Guardian*, when someone paused in front of her.

'May I?' A young woman, whom she guessed was still a student, indicated the space next to Grace. Grace smiled back encouragingly.

'I hope you do not mind, but it is such a beautiful day,' she said. 'And every person has had the same idea. There are no empty seats on this stretch at all.'

Not a British voice, Grace thought. 'Please do,' she said.

'I am thinking I will visit that exhibition,' the woman nodded towards the huge display of posters at the side of the gallery closest to them. It was a clear, precise voice – possibly Scandinavian.

'Then you're obviously interested in art?'

'My partner is an artist. He believes he is. No, that is unkind. He has talent. I am here on a short study break and cannot go home without evidence of visiting your museums. I like your shops too. Although a few postcards are all I can afford.'

'They're ridiculously priced too!' Grace retorted. The woman smiled regretfully. A person after her own heart, she thought.

'I'm Grace.'

'Gerda.'

'*The Snow Queen!*'

Gerda looked momentarily blank.

'Hans Andersen?' Grace said.

'Of course – Kai and Gerda! Although I am Swedish, not Danish.'

'Stockholm's nice. So clean.'

'Sometimes,' her new friend replied, 'that is the, how do you say here… received wisdom?' Grace smiled encouragingly. 'I live in a little town about thirty kilometres away from the centre of the city.'

Grace's nagging doubts about her unfortunate session earlier began to recede as she relaxed and enjoyed the sunshine and unexpectedly pleasant company.

The two women were enthusiastically sharing opinions about Matisse and Braque when, needing to clear her throat, Grace turned her head away and happened to glance diagonally down the slope ahead.

In that moment, a flash of scarlet caught her eye from another bench about fifteen yards away. It was a familiar item of clothing. She'd seen Maggy wear that jacket on many occasions and always considered it rather loud – and told her so. It was a shade of red she disliked and considered garish for a woman of her mother's age.

'I always wear it in the country to annoy the bulls,' had been Maggy's perennial joke. Even with her back turned away from her, there was no mistaking the offending item, nor her mother's wavy, greying hair and, most irritating of all, the blue scarf Grace had given her the previous Christmas. What did she think she looked like?

There were, of course, no bulls around, although her mother was in animated conversation with a strikingly good-looking Escamillo, at least thirty years her junior.

Grace noted how close together the pair sat; the young man listening intently as Maggy chatted away, a pen and small notebook in his hand. Every so often, she casually indicated the book and he solicitously jotted something down. She was stung by the warm look Maggy threw him, followed by that exasperating gesture she adopted when trying to be disarming. Irrationally blinded by rage redder than any jacket, something exploded in Grace's brain.

Maggy remembered it would soon be her cousin's birthday. After returning from North Berwick and parking the car, she'd suggested to Dino that they visit the National Gallery. Dino made a quick tour of the lower rooms for pictorial boots and buckles whilst Maggy perused the art-inspired merchandise.

After selecting an art deco dish and a birthday card for her cousin, Maggy settled on a small notebook for Dino, along with a tartan propelling pencil and a few postcards of iconic paintings from the regular collection as additional mementoes. She'd grown up with these great canvases; they were old acquaintances. Hopefully he'd been impressed by some of them, too.

The weather was brighter in town. They'd left the Gallery and wandered through The Gardens. Dino was due to meet a friend at The Sheraton later. Or so he said. She was surprised he didn't want to go home and rest after his misadventure. Well, that was his decision. Both having an hour to waste, they relaxed on a quiet bench.

Maggy produced her purchases. 'As a child, I always found this one so mysterious,' she said showing him the postcard of Gauguin's *Vision After the Sermon*, with its intense, blood-coloured background and ecstatic Breton women watching Jacob wrestle with the angel. Dino nodded. 'And this,' she next handed him *Old Woman Cooking Eggs*. 'You might well know the artist.'

'Is Velázquez?' Dino said, without hesitation. Maggy nodded. 'My sister. She is an artist. We have many books always in our home. I like him.'

'And here are Reynolds's *The Sisters Waldegrave*, engrossed in their needlework,' Maggy continued giving him the card. 'Their mother arranged for it to be painted to entice prospective suitors. Now, of course, we have social media!' She laughed at her own joke. Dino courteously smiled. Maggy moved on to the last card, the Scottish artist Joan Eardley's *Catterline in Winter*.

'Doesn't it make you shiver?'

'Is amazing,' he agreed. 'I looked at that one also. More my taste.'

Throughout the ensuing discussion, Dino dutifully made notes in his new notebook, whilst Maggy helped him with his spelling.

Really, she was turning into Auntie Mame.

All around them visitors to Edinburgh delightedly took in the handsome green spaces and majestic castle towering above them; a number with their cameras at the ready. If out of the corner of her eye Maggy spotted a young woman she didn't know hovering with a phone in her hands, she thought nothing of it.

Arriving home, a couple of hours or so later, after picking up some groceries and visiting a sick friend, Maggy was surprised to see her answerphone flickering with half a dozen recorded messages.

Unusual, she thought.

She played them back.

The first was a simple 'Sly-boots! Didn't know I was one of Grace's Facebook friends – but there you go. The full story pronto! Hugs, Una.'

Mystified, Maggy then played the second message from a reformed punk artist friend, 'Good on you gal!'

She was still baffled.

The remaining messages, two from theatre friends who'd done quite well for themselves in the business, ran on similar lines to Una's. Determined to get to the bottom of the matter, Maggy switched on the big computer in the den. As usual, it took an age to get into its stride. She really must get a new, efficient one.

Finally, her Facebook page appeared. There was a recent posting. Staring back at her she saw Dino and herself on the bench in Princes Street Gardens.

The clip was headed: Tête-à-tête.

Maggy clicked the arrow. The video stirred. Shot obliquely from behind the bench, the footage hid all but her left arm stretched along the top.

- A tiny insect, almost invisible to the camera, lands on Maggy's face.
- Dino leans across to her showing the side of his face without the plaster.
- He gently brushes it away with his fingertips.
- Their eyes meet.
- They smile at each other.

Scalding tears ran down Maggy's cheeks.

◈◈

TWENTY
Confronting Demons

֍ ֎

THE letter had fallen out of *To the Moon and Back* in a batch of books Ally had brought with her to Edinburgh. A friend had given it to her some time ago. She'd given up on it as being too chick-lit, but finding herself short of light reading matter recently, had decided to give it another go.

Coburg Street
Edinburgh
lesleyb@hotmail.com
0777…
8ᵗʰ November 2011

Dear Ms McKenzie

Forgive me for writing out of the blue like this.

Your appalling ordeal was drawn to my attention by my cousin as something similar happened to her. I therefore have an idea of what you've been though – and must still be enduring.

Let me introduce myself. I'm a playwright who has recently embarked on a piece of work in the hope it that might raise greater awareness of the issue. This is a heartfelt request to see if you'd be willing to meet me one day – when you feel up to it? It goes without saying that anything you tell me would remain in the strictest confidence until I'd something to show you. I would, of course, seek your blessing before the play, hopefully, went into production.

I attach a CV of my produced and published plays to date, along with a draft of the current work-in-progress. So far, only the Artistic Director of The Traverse Theatre has, tentatively, expressed interest in the synopsis (also enclosed).

Not having your address, I've left this at your local shop, where the lady behind the post office desk gave me her assurance you would receive it.

Hoping to hear from you.

With sincere good wishes,
Lesley Bushell

A nice letter, but…

The CV suggested Lesley was an experienced writer, her play synopsis based on the oral testimonies of a young man, an elderly woman, and an adolescent schoolgirl. Ally could see there was room for a story dealing with someone her own age. She'd written back giving Lesley her blessing to use any information about her she found in the public domain providing links to her case, but confessing she wasn't ready yet to give interviews etcetera. One day she might welcome the opportunity to meet up with her and help promote the issue. In the meantime, she wished her every success. However…

Ally had made good progress from the events, some years previously, that had shattered her life but which, until now, she'd withheld from her new friends. The incident at the Balfour was a set-back but, thanks to Lorna's support, she was once more slowly returning to the person she had been.

An explanation of her severe neurosis was long overdue, however difficult that might be. She owed it foremost to Lorna, who must seriously be questioning the wisdom of letting such a disturbed woman into her life.

Six months after Fergus's death, Ally accepted an invitation to a party at a popular pub in the centre of Dundee. Jo and she had been best friends since Infants. The party was to celebrate Jo's younger sister's twenty-first. Ally hated parties and usually avoided long boozy nights in rooms crowded with people screaming to be heard against loud music. Even Ally's most sensible women friends changed character after a couple of drinks and began vying for the attention of any unaccompanied male with a pulse.

Many of the guests would be several years younger than Jo and herself. Still, she looked forward to meeting up with the sisters and their parents – who had been hospitable to Ally on many occasions. As her mother pointed out, 'you cannae let them down. After all, you accepted the invitation, and you've bought the present.' Phil, her father, agreed: 'Go and enjoy yourself. You'll find other faces you know there. And it'll help you …' She could see him about say '…forget Fergus.' But, how could she? Nevertheless, Ally had given him an appreciative look.

It's something of a Marmite place, Scotland's fourth city on the banks of the Tay. Despite its university, employment opportunities, thriving repertory theatre and many places of historical interest,

Ally's overriding sense of Dundee, even on a sunny summer's day, was of its overall greyness. It lacked the old-fashioned charm of St Andrews, the noisy energy of Glasgow and grandeur of Auld Reekie.

After leaving St Andrews, Jo had settled on a career in Retail and was now Assistant Manager of the women's Fashion department in the Dundee store of a national chain. She shared a three-bedroomed flat with her sister, who was still a student at the university.

Despite the good bus service to and from St Andrews, it wouldn't be easy getting back home after midnight without a car – and no one drove after a booze-up. 'No argument, Jo told Ally, 'you're staying the night with us.'

The party was still in full swing at around 2 am, when Ally said her goodbyes. Only the elderly guests and those with babysitters had left earlier, but she was tired and ready to lay her head down.

After the noisy, claustrophobic pub, it was refreshing to breathe in the early morning air, clear from an earlier shower, and feel the mild breeze on her skin. The flat was about six minutes walk away and she'd been given a set of keys to let herself in. The mottled moon and stars, suspended in the cloudless night sky, were reflected in the wet asphalt. Ally walked along the pavement with a spring in her step.

There was a short-cut across a small temporary car park awaiting redevelopment leading to a short street adjacent to the flat. It was a clear, open space that Ally thought she could cross quickly and safely. By now there were only half a dozen cars parked and a small van. Only the occasional swish of vehicles moving along the neighbouring streets broke the silence.

As she began walking diagonally across the car park, Ally noticed a man get out of the van. He was about six feet tall, probably in his late forties with dark cropped hair and wearing a smart outdoor jacket, one hand casually resting in his pocket. There was nothing intimidating about his demeanour, so when he strolled towards her with a two-pound piece between his fingers and asked if she could let him have change for the parking meter, his polite, educated voice put her even more at ease.

Only as she began searching her anorak pocket for small coins did it dawn on her that most parking meters stopped operating after six.

In the precious seconds during which Ally knew she should make a dash for it, the man slipped behind her, grasped her by the neck with his arm and pulled her against his body, constricting her throat to prevent her from screaming. She heard a rasping sound before, with well-practised sleight-of-hand, a large patch of what she assumed to be Elastoplast was clasped over her mouth.

Struggling violently, Ally was manoeuvred towards the van. Before reaching it, she managed to kick the man's leg with the back of her shoe. For just a second, he loosened his grip giving her a chance to wriggle free and run. But her feet slipped on a cluster of wet leaves. She lost her balance, falling backwards and hitting her head on the tarmac.

The next thing Ally knew, she was lying on the floor in the back of the van on some foul-smelling matting, her hands tied behind her. The doors were closed. The weight of the man was on top of her. Being forced to breathe through her nose added to her claustrophobia. Her head throbbed, hitting her with strobe-like flashes, as dull stabs of pain besieged her lower body.

Eerily detached, now beyond panicking, it occurred to her that this was how the pig must feel as it queued to be stunned. Silently begging that whatever the man intended to do to her might be over quickly and allow her the dignity of oblivion, she passed out.

When Ally came to, she was lying in a small grassy area surrounded by trees with no idea of where she was, or how long she'd been there. A woman was bending over her, trying to comfort her. She was on her way to an early shift at a nearby supermarket on the outskirts of the city when she'd spotted Ally bundled-up on the ground. Every part of Ally hurt from what she soon discovered were livid marks and scratches on her face, neck, and legs. Her creased dress was covered in patches of dirt and black grease and there was dried blood on her left leg.

The woman had rung for the police and the ambulance service. They were on their way.

Only when her kindly Samaritan had carefully, but painfully, removed the adhesive-backed plaster did Ally realise she couldn't produce any sound but a strained moan. Her lips, chin and the skin where the plaster had been were burning. She was also having difficulty swallowing and her head was still aching. Not until later, when severe bruise marks appeared on her neck, did the full horror of how her life had nearly been extinguished become apparent. In dumb-show, Ally tried to explain as much as she could remember of what had happened, but the woman begged her not to exhaust herself.

One of the few images Ally retained of that night was that of the hands of the large clock in A&E, positioned shortly after five. A nurse asked if she needed to contact anyone. Ally discovered she'd lost her bag but was able to scribble down Jo's address.

Swabs of blood, urine and possible traces of semen had to be taken before she could wash. She was given a Morning After pill – it appeared the man hadn't used any protection – and put on a course of antibiotics to obviate the risk of infection. She had also sustained mild concussion from her fall.

To everyone's relief, Ally was STD free – though further examination showed she'd been torn inside. Undignified though much of this was, the hospital staff handled her with gentleness and sensitivity, and followed the official guidelines to the letter.

Ally was allocated a bed in a small room off a ward. Her vocal problems, the doctors reassured her, were hopefully due to shock and temporary trauma – although X-rays confirmed some damage had been done to her vocal cords because of the attempted strangulation. Nevertheless, everyone seemed confident that, gradually, her voice would fully return.

It didn't.

Ally was sedated for the remainder of that night. She awoke after midday, heavy-headed and queasy, to find the ward sister and two policewomen by her bedside looking at her with a mixture of relief and concern. The one sitting closest, with a somewhat masculine haircut – she guessed in her late forties – was kind but serious. The other, around her own age, kept pushing back wisps of blonde hair struggling free of its restraining grips. The sister offered Ally a cup of heavily sugared tea which, although she was thirsty, she found even harder to swallow than the water she'd been given the night before.

The women had expected to interview her, but after about five minutes it became apparent that although Ally's brain hadn't seriously been affected and she could now utter monosyllables, she'd be unable to dictate a statement.

After a polite but firm discussion between the more senior police officer and the sister, who was reluctant to move her until she was fully rested, the pair gently persuaded Ally to get out of bed. They helped her into a dressing gown provided by the hospital then led her into a small, glass-partitioned office, making her comfortable in front of a PC. A memory stick was inserted and, after a few seconds, an official template appeared.

The women urged Ally to type up everything she could remember about her ordeal of the night before. Looking at the sister, who was concerned about Ally's fragility, the older policewoman said, 'I hate asking her to do this for us – but you'll appreciate time is of the essence if we're to track down the man responsible.'

Ally started typing, slowly at first, still somewhat confused and uncoordinated. Tactfully prompted by the women, who periodically looked over her shoulder, she gained confidence as the events of the night before returned in some sort of order. The fair one, the softer and more approachable of the two, provided encouragement and guidance whenever Ally faltered. 'Take it at your own pace,' she said quietly.

When she had finished, they checked the statement and asked the sister to print off a copy of the document for her to read, initial each page and finally, sign and date.

The police were impressed by Ally's testimony, unaware she worked as a clerk in a local solicitors' practice. Later, she was amazed herself at her presence of mind, and how her professional skills had kicked in, allowing her to type, seemingly, on auto-pilot.

All Ally recalled of the days that followed was a general dislocation of flesh and spirit; her nerves barely on speaking terms with the body parts they serviced. You heard of people walking miles after breaking a leg. Similarly, the wheels of Ally's mind kept functioning, but in limbo.

At least her inability to talk allowed Ally to withhold the more repugnant aspects of her attack from friends and family. Nevertheless, the police were obliged to issue a brief statement alerting the public to the danger of her attacker whilst he was still at large. It didn't take long for the incident to be announced on local radio and TV.

Jo was very upset by what had happened and visited Ally on both the days she remained in the hospital under observation, regaining her strength and receiving psychiatric support.

On the Wednesday morning, by which time the hospital and social services had contacted Ally's own doctor and local psychiatric unit, Ally was discharged and given a follow-up appointment for the following week. Her parents collected her and took her home.

Either the man had lost his nerve or been scared off from completing the job. Certainly, the damage done to her throat, in his attempt to stifle the life out of Ally, justified her current speech difficulties. There was also some talk of aphasia – although this was usually associated with stroke victims.

Having retained her initial statement, the police pressed Ally to record, a second time, the events of that shocking night whilst they were fresh in her memory. This would enable other professionals to help her in the weeks and months ahead. A tough assignment. But the next day she managed to summon enough courage to produce a version which, thereafter, she kept in a rarely used PC file labelled, simply, Bad Stuff.

Barely three weeks later, Ally's assailant had attempted to rape another woman, in Aberdeen. This time he'd chosen an Olympic standard gymnast. The sportswoman had used a well-judged karate move to render him immobile, giving her time to notify and await the arrival of the police. It was rare for rapists to be caught so comparatively easily; but the DNA evidence against him was irrefutable.

After the verdict it transpired that the man, who was married with three children, had not long been released from a spell in HMP Glenochil for an earlier conviction. Previously, however, he'd not attempted murder. This time he'd enjoy a far longer vacation in Clackmannanshire.

Despite mention of her case in the local media, editors could only refer to her as 'a woman from St Andrews', although a pushy right-wing investigative journalist somehow discovered Ally's identity, inveigling herself into her home under the pretext of being a sympathetic researcher. Notwithstanding Phil's firm stance, the woman wasn't to be done out of good copy, overriding him and publishing a sharp piece headed *Are Dundee's Streets Dangerous at Night?* deploring such occurrences in a place usually regarded as fairly safe. At least she observed the legal requirement for personal details to be fictionalised.

After some months, Ally's body healed. The psychological wounds were to take much longer. She slowly began to produce distinct words, and sometimes join several up – although reluctant to unless pressed. A full assessment of the damage from which she might never altogether recover had yet to be determined.

Then there had been the approach from Lesley Bushell. As far as Ally knew, the play, if ever completed, had remained unproduced. She eventually regretted not cooperating with Lesley, but the timing was unfortunate. The opportunity never came again and the request had completely slipped her mind – until now. Ally wondered if she could belatedly write and apologise, or maybe even start a dialogue with the playwright to see if she was still interested. She decided it would be too upsetting to rake up the matter.

Although Ally's news value was soon superseded by more

sensational events, she was condemned to get through the years to come wondering when the man would be released, haunted by the terror of one day coming face to face with him.

Her job with the solicitors abandoned and now living at home, Ally began to share the housework with her mother. She also took over her father's responsibilities for maintaining the green areas in front of and behind the house, to Jean's exacting standards.

For the next two years, Ally's happiest moments were spent out of doors. The aroma of a fresh breeze, the smell of turned soil or, even better, newly mown grass, helped her feel a part of the world again. On sunny days, she scattered stale bread, nuts, and small fat-balls on the lawn, discreetly sipping her mug of tea and observing from the sidelines as gregarious house sparrows, great tits and chaffinches swooped greedily down.

By the third year, Ally was strong enough to extend her domestic and gardening skills to understanding, elderly acquaintances. During her time off, she attended a voluntary support group, and whilst she couldn't contribute much to the discussion, found it encouraging to hear how other rape victims had come to terms with their own experiences.

One evening during a meeting, Ally realised she might finally have regained sufficient confidence to assume a more normal life and find a role in the real world. Over recent months she'd become more independent. She'd started shopping, going to the cinema and amateur concerts or plays in St Andrews accompanied by a sympathetic friend and mingling with acquaintances. Sooner or later she must try and re-charge her life. Her confidence and independent spirit would never bounce back if she remained cosseted and contained at home.

Catching a television programme on opportunities for women in the Scottish cities and how tourism relied on the skills of immigrant workers, Ally guessed her own communication issues placed her in a similar category. She would stand a far better chance of regaining her full powers of speech standing on her feet in a more cosmopolitan city than St Andrews. But although Ally had proven skills to offer, she wanted to avoid the legal world if she could possibly help it.

Thus, the idea of moving to Edinburgh was born.

It seemed a foolish dream to begin with, but then Ally found herself believing that, although it would be a huge undertaking and test her to the limits, she was now strong enough for it become a reality. Even if she only survived a week or so before running back home, tail between her legs, then so be it. At least she'd have tried; though it was an indication of the progress she'd made that she could tell herself failure wasn't really an option. Was she being too ambitious, too heroic? On the other hand, what had she to lose?

What would Fergus have done?

Ally's parents were already middle-aged when she was born. Phil was now starting to suffer mobility problems, whilst Jean had long coped with a weak heart, aggravated all those years ago by Ally's difficult birth. It would soon be her turn to keep an eye on them rather than the other way around. At the same time, by doing too much for them, Ally was already beginning to deprive them of the chance to help themselves whilst they still could.

When she first tried to introduce the idea of leaving home, Phil and Jean were aghast. The tentative conversation had gone along the lines:

'I can't impose on you for ever. Dad will be retiring in a couple of years... and I'll be twenty-seven in May.'

'But where will you live?' Jean said.

'I'll find somewhere. Enough to put a roof over my head... feed myself.'

'You're still so fragile.'

'Maybe. But I won't get much stronger here. It's too... cosy. And if it doesn't work out... I know you'll always let me come home.'

What about a doctor?'

'The NHS knows all about me. Honestly, I'm a big lassie.'

Phil and Jean made a private appointment to see the GP which, with Ally also being his patient, raised confidentiality issues. Fortunately, he'd known the family for many years – he and Phil were both elders at the Kirk – and could be considered a friend. Ally's parents contrived to make it sound as if they were worried about themselves, and how the risk Ally was taking was giving them sleepless nights.

'If her heart's set on it, you can't stop her,' the doctor said. And she's right. She's known on the system. Yes, I'm aware she's highly sensitive but she's also a sensible lass. And it's easy to keep in touch with people these days. Not like when you and I were younger.'

'But supposing something else happens to her and she's damaged even more?' Jean protested. At which point the kindly physician shook his head and, mentally crossing his fingers, gave them a reassuring smile.

It was only after this discussion that he remembered that his daughter, who lived in Edinburgh, was friendly with the pleasant couple who ran the friendly café-bar in Stockbridge where he often enjoyed a morning coffee and lunchtime snack.

He might give them a ring.

So Ally moved to the second stage of her recuperation. Nevertheless, despite the indications that her inner strength was growing, on some days it required an enormous effort for her to stop herself dashing to the bus station and jumping on the first coach back to St Andrews.

TWENTY-ONE

Gospel Truth

☞ ☜

WEIGHED down with carrier bags and a heavy heart, Lorna arrived home from her trip to the local supermarket.

Everywhere was quiet. Ally must be asleep. That gave her some time to herself to quietly potter and prepare supper. Lorna tiptoed into the kitchen and put away the food before popping her head around Ally's bedroom door. As she guessed, Ally was curled up in a foetal position, her eyes shut, a turned-over Anne Tyler beside her on the duvet.

In the living room Ally's laptop was open on the coffee table. Stuck to it was a yellow Post-it note:

> *LORNA*
> *This tells you everything you need to know*
> *A x*

Sitting on the sofa, Lorna clicked. The front page of Ally's report of her ordeal three years earlier came into view. She read it, felt sick and then re-read it. Although Lorna had drawn her own conclusions concerning Ally – a scenario on similar lines to what now emerged as the true facts – the rawness of the narrative shocked her more than she could have imagined. She could only guess at how confident and orally eloquent Ally might have been before the brutal attack and felt ashamed of the few niggling doubts she'd recently harboured about her new house-mate – and what she'd let herself in for. The truth, in Ally's no-holds-barred prose, put everything into perspective.

Then and there, Lorna renewed her pledge to support Ally's rehabilitation, if not to the woman she had been – that would be too much to expect after such a violent experience – to at least the point where she could, more fully, reassert her independence.

Moving the cursor back up through the document, Lorna's finger slipped on the mouse to reveal a second file lying beneath. She assumed it was related information until she saw the layout was quite different from that of the report – also the style. The phrase

Jock's wet nose tickled Betty's shins compelled her to read on.

Lorna knew Ally was working on a children's story, but being of a superstitious disposition, the budding author had explained her intention to keep the details a secret until she felt it was in a fit state to share them with anyone. Lorna had therefore been unaware of the extent of Ally's creative abilities.

Ten minutes later, having scrolled back to the beginning and by now engrossed in the Sheltie's story, Lorna failed to hear the scuffle of slippered feet in the passage outside.

Lorna was suddenly aware of the door creaking and briefly froze. She then turned to see Ally, looking at her quizzically over the back of the sofa. She got up and moved round to her. 'You clever, clever girl,' she cried, 'it's… it's delightful! Engaging and utterly charming. You write beautifully. I want to adopt Jock right away!'

Ally's confused frown briefly made Lorna anxious: not only about how Ally might expect her to respond to the report, but her reaction to her discovering *Jock*. What if Ally thought she'd been snooping amongst her most personal files? That would be a violation of trust. And if Ally was offended that might, if not undermine their relationship, certainly hamper a useful discussion.

She was greatly relieved when, after only a few moments awkwardness, Ally brightened. She prayed after the oppressive atmosphere of recent days that this meant they had turned a corner. 'Spagbol in twenty minutes do you?' Lorna said as cheerily as she could. Ally smiled again. 'I'll take that as a yes. In the meantime, I think drinks are called for, pronto, eh?'

Ally's eyes opened even wider and she headed for the wine rack.

Lorna never regretted the liberty she'd taken that evening. After all, Ally had left her report open intentionally, even if she'd forgotten to close down *Jock*. It was like the postman reading your postcards – what was a confirmed nosey-parker to do? Mercifully, it turned out that Lorna's curiosity had been for the best.

Over bowls of pasta and a potent Rioja, Ally was chattier than she'd ever been, and keen to share with Lorna how Jock had come into being. When her second glass began to take effect, Lorna could hardly believe it when Ally started humming a familiar tune.

'*Loud the winds howl,*' Lorna sang.

Ally beamed.

'*Loud the waves roar,*' she continued.

'*Thunderclaps rend the air,*' they both chorused.

'Now, I promise faithfully never to be so intrusive again,' Lorna said. 'What's on your PC is your own business. We'll only discuss anything… difficult if, and when, you want to.'

'Don't worry,' Ally said. 'You know practically everything now. There isn't a lot more to say. I expect you guessed about…?'

'Yes,' Lorna said quickly but softly. And I'm so glad to know the full story. Well, not exactly *glad*. You've been to hell and… well, a large part of the way back.'

'And now,' Ally said, 'I'm on my way… to Benbecula! These past couple of weeks, I've been in a sort of coma. Writer's blockage, I suppose. I kept bringing up the *Jock* file and couldn't make any progress. But yesterday I found myself wanting to get back to it. I'm so sorry for all I've put you through. You've been an angel.'

Lorna was at peace with the world again too.

After a few moments happy forking and letting the Rioja work soothingly on them, Ally said 'I've been meaning to ask you…'

'Go on.'

'The sketch of the Sheltie in my room. Do you know who… did it?'

'Ewan. Why?'

'He's quite talented, isn't he?'

'I think so. But being the self-effacing idiot he is, he hides that light, along with his many other gifts, under a very large bushel.'

'Matthew… Mark…' Ally murmured.

'Sorry?'

'Bushel. It's in one of the parables. However…' Ally tried to move the conversation on but Lorna had gone off at a tangent.

'I've always been fond of Mark,' Lorna said, picking up the tablet she'd recently treated herself to, 'although Wikipedia says his identity is a bit of a mystery. Nowadays they think his might have been the first gospel. Ah… it says here that Matthew, Mark and Luke use *light* instead of lamp – and bushel to mean *bowl*. So, it's really *hiding your lamp under a bowl*.'

Ally stared at Lorna throughout this unsolicited lecture on biblical language, waiting for it to dawn on her friend what she really wanted to know.

'Of course!' Lorna suddenly realised. 'You're thinking of a possible illustrator for *Jock*?'

Swallowing a mouthful of wine, Ally, nodded violently.

'That's easily solved. I'll invite Ewan and Jamie over to meet you as soon as you think you're up to it?' Another huge grin. 'You'll like them both. And Ewan's the most unthreatening person I know.

Remember I told you he's finally plucked up the courage to leave his awful girlfriend?' Ally nodded. 'He could probably do with a square meal. Then, that's settled.' Lorna picked up the wine bottle. There were two inches left. Splitting the remainder of the liquid, she raised her glass.

'To *Jock*!'

They clinked.

As they were clearing away the dishes, Lorna's mobile rang. It was Senga. For a few seconds, her heart sank. She was enjoying this much-needed evening, relaxing with Ally for the first time since the Balfour incident, and didn't want it disturbed by any unfortunate vibes. This wasn't good timing for Senga, of all people, to crash into their renewed tranquillity. Lorna was strongly tempted to let the call go to voicemail.

A second thought occurred to her. It could be useful. 'I hope they don't want me to work Saturday,' Lorna improvised, 'I'll take it outside.' She tapped her phone, held it against her and called to Ally: 'Leave the washing up, I'll do it later.'

'Sorry to keep you waiting,' she said to Senga, closing the kitchen door behind her and disappearing into her bedroom.

'Is it convenient to talk?'

'Yes…'

'I wanted to find out how Ally is?'

'She's been in a very bad place for a few days,' Lorna said, 'but we've had a long chat about more positive issues and, mercifully, she's brightened up considerably this evening. Not ready to fully unpack exactly what happened the other week, though…'

'Ah.'

'…not yet anyway. Hopefully, soon.'

There was short pause, then Senga said, 'Which is partly why I wanted to see if you'd be willing to meet me for coffee next Saturday morning in the National Portrait Gallery – to seek your advice?'

'Won't you be working?'

'Not this Saturday. Besides I've… '

'Yes?'

'Moved out' Senga said.

This was tricky. Lorna didn't want to sound presumptuous. 'Left Cal you mean?'

'I'm not sure yet.'

'Sorry, it's none of my business.'

'That's quite all right. I've gone to stay with my mother. For a while, anyway. I'm working to rule. Or rather making up the rules as I go along. I'm unwilling to let the Balfour go to pot. Not after all we've put into the place. Not without a struggle. But I can't bear him around me when not at work. Right now, anyway.'

Lorna sensed heavy emotions were lurking beneath Senga's matter-of-fact tone and said, 'I totally understand. And yes, I'd be very happy to meet you.'

'I'll explain everything then. In the meantime, feel free to tell Ally you and I are in touch when you think she's ready. I'd have suggested she came with us, but as we'll be mainly speaking about her...'

'Leave Ally to me,' Lorna said, sounding more confident than she felt. Having made progress this evening, she also knew that handling Ally would require a lot of continued sensitivity. The slightest brush with too harsh a reality could easily push her back into herself.

'I'd welcome the opportunity to unpack that situation with you, too.'

'Thanks. And for being so understanding,' Lorna said.

'I'm terribly sorry about... everything.'

'You and me both.'

'Ten thirty on Saturday then. The Portrait Gallery?'

'Great. See you then.'

The revelation of Ally's attack in Dundee had raised as many questions as it answered. Lorna welcomed the chance to share her concerns about Ally with someone else who had also befriended her but knew she must proceed carefully. Though it sounded as if Senga was in a confused state of mind herself.

Lorna went back into the kitchen musing that what she had so far read of Jock's story had confirmed her intuition: there was more to Ally than met the eye, though she would probably always be a conundrum.

Ally was putting away the last of the washed-up utensils.

'Just as I thought,' Lorna said. 'Work. I'll be out on Saturday morning, I'm afraid.'

Ally shrugged. A contented shrug.

Lorna bit into a sultana scone. 'I wish I could get the texture of mine like these.'

'The secret is to handle them as little as possible and keep the mixture thick,' Senga said. One always overestimates how much they rise in the oven.' Senga prided herself on her baking and privately thought her own were every bit as nice as those in front of them. She charged her customers far less too.

They had been busy queuing for their coffees, avoiding the real reasons for meeting up until they'd found a table. Now settled, there was no excuse for holding up their discussion any longer.

'Now, about Ally,' Senga ventured.

'Yes,' Lorna said knowingly.

She saw they were on the same page and aniticipated Senga's next question:

'I think it's unlikely that she will be coming back to the Balfour.'

'That's exactly what I wanted to clarify.'

'Of course, it's ultimately her decision, whether it's temporary or not. I rather doubt it though,' Lorna added.

'I'd assumed that would be the case. It's not good news, but I need to go ahead and make some arrangements to tide us over until we're certain.'

Torn between loyalty to her cohabitee, yet feeling Senga was entitled to know more about Ally's history, Lorna swithered. Did they know each other well enough for her to share what she'd discovered? On the other hand, they were Ally's closest friends in Edinburgh and both had her best interests at heart. Lorna chose her words carefully listing the main points, until Senga's increasingly appalled looks made it easier to disclose more detailed information.

'I'd guessed as much,' Senga said at last. 'I liked Ally right away, but her reaction to Cal alerted me early on to some terrible secret of that nature. I warned him about teasing her. With hindsight, it would have been better if I'd passed on more of my suspicions – he might have conducted himself with greater sensitivity.'

Lorna wondered if 'sensitivity' was a word Cal understood.

'I mightn't have discovered his deceit so soon,' Senga went on. 'Unfortunately, Cal isn't subtle. He's not a bad man but acts first and thinks afterwards. I've often wondered if he's slightly autistic.' Here, Senga chewed her last bite of scone slowly.

Lorna waited, heartened by the way the conversation was going. She now had someone with whom she could share her concerns.

'When the two of them were getting along better,' Senga said, 'Ally seemed to be settling down. Latterly, she was very chummy – with both of us. I outlined her behaviour to a friend of mine, a psychiatric nurse. From what I told her, she said it sounded as if Ally hadn't always been the way she is now but, with the right help, might one day return to… at least much of her original self. She also felt it wouldn't be surprising if she'd been raped – as we now know she had – for her to have difficulty connecting physically with people for a very long time, if not indefinitely. Especially men.'

'Poor Ally,' Lorna said.

'Yes,' Senga continued, 'I'd expect an incident like that to cause recurring anxiety attacks and related symptoms, though rarely for as long as hers have lasted. But then we're all different. I suffer from a form of depression myself sometimes.' Senga sipped her coffee but declined to elaborate. 'But I shall miss her terribly if she leaves us for good.'

'I think she's already missing you, though not the Balfour,' Lorna said, 'even if she won't admit it. And she needed that job. She's not a taker and will be uncomfortable accepting my hospitality indefinitely.'

'You think she'll go back to St Andrews?'

'I'm not sure. She has other talents, as you know. And she's started consulting the local paper and websites for local employment opportunities. I'll try and make her see the benefits of staying in Edinburgh and might even find some part-time work for her in the library where I can keep an eye on her. I... I've not fully got my head around it all yet. You could say I've lumbered myself with this problem...'

'And, have you?'

'Only if I'm unable to help her. There's a narrow line between *blessing* and *burden*. Sometimes recently it's felt a bit like the latter, but more often I see her as something good that's happened to me. Sorry, I'm rambling on about myself, How about you? Your world must have collapsed completely.'

Lorna watched Senga consider how best to reply. She was probably unused to discussing her private life, especially with people she didn't know very well, so was flattered when Senga then confided further in her.

'Cal and I are practically joined at the hip. I'm scared to realise that may be a *were* before long. It's a complex relationship...' Here Senga summarised their lives together, including the tragedy at Goatfell. 'It isn't the first time he's... strayed. Before, it's always been a short-term, physical thing. That I could cope with, but this time, he seems totally obsessed.'

'How long has the relationship been going on?'

'A few months now. Unfortunately, he seems to think the creature is as caught up with him as he is with her.'

Neither had yet made the connection between Cal's new girlfriend and Ewan whom Senga had, of course, sat next to at the Christmas party.

'And?'

'She has a nice place somewhere locally, apparently, and has asked him to move in with her.'

'Do you think he will?'

'That's the $64,000 question. If he does, then it probably, really is… all over.' Lorna saw Senga swallow hard and gave her a concerned look.

'There's no way you could carry on simply as colleagues?' she said.

'We may have to, until things sort themselves out.' Here Senga turned her head away and closed her eyes, presumably contemplating the ugly possibility of months of uncoupling. 'Fortunately, if the worst comes to the worst, we only manage the Balfour. The owners have half a dozen places around the city. We can give them, I think, three months' notice to quit. Notice on the flat is far less. But Cal's affair might yet run its course.' Lorna thought Senga sounded more optimistic than she really felt.

'Have you had time to consider your on-going living arrangements?'

'My mother sold up and joined us in Edinburgh, but in her own wee place, not long after we came here. She's been in hospital recently and is now convalescing at home. It's been a strain running the business and finding time to see her, though there are people popping in and out all the time. Oddly, it may be a sort of blessing in disguise. At least it provides me with an excuse to move back in with her for a while. I can help get her up, showered and breakfasted first thing in the morning – and put her to bed in the evening. Saves a bit on carers and gives me time to observe how things develop before finalising any big decisions.

Senga absent-mindedly licked a finger and scooped up the remaining scone crumbs on her plate. 'I'm so glad we were able to meet up.'

'Me too,' Lorna said. 'It's been a useful chat. Give it a week or so and I'm sure Ally will be delighted to see you. Then you must pop over and have supper with us.'

'But only if Ally's really happy about it.'

'I'll put her in the picture, if that's ok?'

'Of course.'

'I'm certain it will be. Would you like another coffee?'

'If you're having one.'

Lorna rose to make her way back to the counter. It seemed neither of them was anxious to impede an emerging friendship, despite the serious issues that had caused them to meet up and the domestic chores they must get back to. She'd always felt they had liked one another from a distance. It seemed her intuition was correct.

Lorna returned to their table with freshly topped-up cups. Senga plopped two large lumps of demerara into her cup. 'I need the sugar,' she said.

Lorna laughed. Why did that sound familiar?

Now free to move on to more convivial matters, the pair exchanged biographical synopses and smiles of recognition as they explored mutual interests and experiences.

Eventually, having finished their second coffees and the café by now filling up with people requiring tables for lunch, Lorna and Senga rose and put on their jackets. Wanting to eke out the last half hour of the morning, they both moved instinctively towards Rachel McLean's topical art exhibition with its playful pictorial comments on Scottish and British national pride.

Walking back along Queen Street half an hour later, Lorna prepared to turn right down Dundas Street. Senga planted brisk kisses either side of Lorna's face.

'I hope we can do this again soon?' she said. If you'd like to.'

'I'd love to,' Lorna said with enthusiasm.

◈

TWENTY-TWO

Table Talk

ço ๙

EWAN was sketching Jamie.

The claustrophobic room at Ewan's guest-house was short on storage space. Ewan had gladly accepted Jamie's invitation to keep some of his belongings at Pilrig Street, with its unspoken agenda.

When Jamie first spotted Ewan's portfolio of sketches and watercolours, they were sitting enticingly open on the spare divan in the study. On top were some rough drawings of birds and animals, including an aloof tabby cat and a portrait of a woman he'd assumed, correctly, to be Maggy. Jamie hadn't yet been introduced to either and Ewan knew the time was fast approaching when the person who had always mattered most in his life and the one who was becoming very important to him at this juncture, must meet. He was confident Maggy would accept the development with at least an outward show of support – even though it would be a surprise. There had already been some awkward moments when he and Jamie had bumped into old family friends when out shopping. Better to out himself than be outed.

When Jamie told Ewan how much he liked his drawings, Ewan had looked embarrassed. Painting and drawing had provided an escape for him since school days and had been the outlet he enjoyed most.

'So, how about doing me?' Jamie had proposed.

'A portrait?'

'No, a blow-job. On second thoughts, both.'

Ewan had been flattered by Jamie's interest in what he considered his homely talent – but drawing Jamie would be a small way of thanking him for his kindness and hospitality. Ewan knew Jamie's pride and joy was his art collection. The guy had good taste too. A Galbraith original hanging in a corner of the flat would be a huge compliment.

Since the rainy night some weeks before, the two men had seen a lot of each other. The breakdown of Ewan's partnership with Paige had propelled him into the murky unknown: not for Ewan the challenging place it was for more adventurous souls. Being with Jamie was giving him some stability during this uncertain period: most importantly, something – or rather, some*one* – else to think about.

When Ewan arrived home from school crying because his name, yet again, had been left off the cricket team list, Maggy would glibly remind him, 'When one door closes, dear…'

It applied to friendships too, it seemed.

The collision of kindred spirits can be life-transforming. You may only meet someone once or twice yet quickly know you're on the same wavelength and make a comfortable fit. At that intoxicating stage no conscious effort is required. That comes later, when the first intensity matures into something calmer and, hopefully, sustainable. It's then that friendships, like plants, require regular attention.

Jamie's sheer niceness rather than lust had been the catalyst for Ewan, drawing him repeatedly back to his new lover. Fate had helped too, for it was difficult for them to avoid each other unless they deliberately altered their daily routine. There were numerous places in the neighbourhood of their work for buying snacks besides their regular sandwich bar, and Ewan and Jamie welcomed any excuse to meet up. On fine days, there was what quickly became their regular bench in The Botanics on which, whenever it was free, they would munch and chat. In cold, wet lunch hours they warmed themselves up with soup and a roll in the nearby café. If a work issue cropped up to prevent them meeting, Ewan hastily texted Jamie to rearrange. And vice versa.

Ewan sensed qualities in his new friend he had never enjoyed in other intimate relationships. But then, prior to Paige, his only experience of anything roughly resembling a love-life had been a couple of half-hearted affairs: one at university, the other not long after he'd started working. Both had been short-lived but had at least proved everything was in working order. If Ewan had never been a Don Juan, it didn't mean he hadn't any need to regularly give and receive affection. After Paige, Jamie was accessible and uncomplicated.

The initial outpouring of confidences and exchange of information between the men had morphed into an unforced and unspoken desire to be there for each other. Jamie had so far put no pressure on Ewan and was letting him come to terms with his self-discoveries in his own time. As Ewan learnt to trust and care about Jamie, he opened himself up to a host of new experiences, sharing more of himself than he'd ever done – or been allowed to – before.

Thus, as the weeks slipped by, Ewan was spending more and more of his spare time in Leith.

This morning the two men were angled at a corner of the pine table in the kitchen-diner. Jamie was resisting the temptation to scratch. Ewan had suggested a favourite green polo-necked jumper would work best for the drawing; the turned-down collar nicely breaking the line between his long neck and wide shoulders. Having shrunk after many washes, it suggested the gym-honed body beneath, but had accidentally been washed in a biological detergent. The wool irritated Jamie's skin. Ewan kept lowering his sketching pad and raising a remonstrative eyebrow each time Jamie squirmed.

By now they'd been sitting for about an hour. Jamie was seriously fidgeting. 'I need to get out of this. Loo break *please* – then coffee?'

'Good idea,' Ewan said. 'Let me rough-in your neck; then you can change.'

A few minutes later, Ewan held his drawing board at arm's length to assess his progress. Curiosity getting the better of his bladder and tickly skin, Jamie rose and went up to him. Ewan hastily flipped another sheet of paper over his work.

'Spoilsport!' Jamie said.

'It's not quite ready for viewing,' Ewan said. 'Later, when I've completed the eyes. They're the trickiest.

After filling the kettle, Jamie pulled his sweater over his head, threw it into the washing machine with liquid soap, clicked to Wool – and dashed out.

As he slipped into a sweatshirt, Jamie told himself to tread carefully. His feelings for Ewan weren't in dispute, but he was aware the physical aspect of their relationship might yet be temporary. Many gay, and indeed, heterosexual relationships developed from an initial, highly charged phase into a more conventional but enduring relationship; one in which physical affection took its place as an integrated part of the mix. In some instances, the heavily demonstrative part ceased to matter much, although deep affection endured. And both men still had a lot to learn about each other. They could only live in the moment and see what happened.

Although they had shared much about their likes and dislikes, work, family, politics and their daily lives, they had yet to have a discussion about more intimate things.

It was Ewan who began the conversation. As they sipped their coffee, he asked, 'When were you first aware you were attracted to another man?'

Without hesitation, Jamie replied, 'When I was about four or five.'

'That early?' said Ewan.

'One Christmas at the circus I was overawed by a hunky, fake-tanned trapeze artist in his spangled trunks and had day-dreams that he came home with me.'

'When you were five? That *is* weird.'

'Whatever. I'm sure my fascination with men can be traced to then. Maybe I should ask a psychiatrist, except that I've never felt the need. I've always been grateful for the way I am. Weren't we fortunate to have been born into a world where it's been decriminalised? As you probably know, it didn't happen here until 1980. The English had been hurling their pink caps over windmills for twelve years by then.'

'Really?' Ewan said, shocked.

'I could grow up in an age when people like myself were becoming far less exceptional.'

'And also, being…?'

'Black? Yes, that as well,' Jamie said.

'It's how you define yourself, isn't it?'

'Of course. Although I've always felt the odd one out. For a long time, I felt as someone with a physical disability must. Meeting me for the first time, many people were totally accepting, but there was always one who looked at me either awkwardly or with barely disguised sympathy.' This was the first time Jamie had mentioned the matter. He knew Ewan was completely colour-blind, but it got the topic out of the way. 'As I grew older, however, I found that looking slightly different from most people gave me empowerment and, dare I say it, a touch of glamour. A trip to London's gay bars confirmed that. For one glorious fortnight in June when I was twenty, I was the Toast of Old Compton Street.'

'Sounds like an ancient musical comedy.'

Jamie laughed. 'Something like that. Well, I'm not a singer but I've certainly danced a lot – in discos, anyway. It was then that I embraced who I was.'

He didn't mention the times he'd, unintentionally, walked up the wrong street or into the wrong bar in less cosmopolitan places, attracting racial abuse from ignorant but intimidating bullies. But everyone had issues to cope with and Jamie had learnt as a small boy to grit his teeth at threatening moments and carry on. Keeping positive helped him stay in control, making him tougher and warier, and maintain a cheerful façade. As a child, and even sometimes later, he'd experienced deep hurt and anger. He wasn't ready to reveal to Ewan the negative aspects of, in his own case, belonging to not just one, but two, minority groups. Ewan still had enough adjusting of his own to do.

'And you've never really been out with a girl?' Ewan said.

'Not in the way you mean. Although, as they say, some of my best friends are women. And, though very affectionate, the relationships are spared the agonising expectations of 'going out'. I've never objectified women and my girl *friends* – two words – know all about me. It was obviously different for you?'

'Now I think about it, I had pictures of both female and male pop and film stars taped to the lid of my locker and bedroom walls.' Here, Ewan briefly meditated. 'Oh, and I had a mancrush on Matt Damon.'

'Mancrush?'

'The local cinema let me have the poster for *The Talented Mr Ripley*. It was up for ages. I told Mum I liked the artwork. There must have been something going on there I was afraid of admitting to myself.

'So, you *were* in denial!'

'Then Paige came along and the rest, as they say is…'

'A mystery?'

'I don't, actually, think I've ever been sex obsessed,' Ewan said this as if he'd only just realised it – which, perhaps, he had. 'I took it for granted I was Mr Average who did all the regular, normal things...'

'Whatever they are.'

'Apart from some adolescent messing around, I'd never really ventured off the map I'd been given – until that night in the pub.'

'Gives me a grave sense of responsibility!' Jamie said.

'It made me recall all those sporty types who swanned around changing rooms in the buff, proudly flexing their muscles and swinging their willies. They gave me a huge…'

'Ooh, Matron!'

'… inferiority complex. Never felt one of the gang, I suppose.'

'And Paige?'

'She seemed my ideal woman: very attractive, calm, focused, an answer for everything. It tells you a lot about me, that I thought I needed someone to help manage my life better. When she first suggested we might try living together, I was so chuffed, I could hardly believe my luck. I… I placed her on too high a pedestal.'

'Hard for anyone to deal with.'

'Hey, whose side are you on? Though you're probably right. Maybe that was why she never respected me.' Ewan paused. 'In the early days, bedtime was, dare I say it, really exciting. She really knew what she wanted.'

'And what about what *you* wanted?'

'Hadn't much to compare it…her with. Looking back, I was so dull.'

'Stop putting yourself down all the time!'

Ewan looked sheepish. 'I think Paige is afraid of revealing her full self.'

'That makes true closeness difficult.'

'And maybe, so am I.'

'You've opened up to me.'

Ewan seemed embarrassed. After a few moments he said, 'to think, Jamie. All those years and I never really knew her.'

'Maybe there wasn't a lot to know.'

Ewan pondered this remark. 'Certainly, I'd never known…' Ewan searched carefully for the words 'what real… sharing is until…' Jamie caught his eyes. Ewan gave him a clumsy smile. Jamie understood. It was early days, Ewan still had a lot to sort out in his own mind. And yet… Jamie watched him pick up his pencil and begin sketching the polo-neck.

'How did you ever get together?'

Ewan sighed. He really didn't want to think about Paige but recognised this was a part of his backstory he hadn't yet covered. With the air of someone who knew it was something they must get out of the way, he began: 'Gus and I had just finished at Heriot-Watt. He was engaged to Jan who was training to be a teacher. Paige was a friend-of-a-friend who had recently split from her fiancé and lacked a partner for a Christmas dance. Jan sounded me out and I agreed to make up the foursome. With Gus and Jan totally immersed in each other on the dance floor, Paige and I sat at a table in the corner, far enough removed from the noise to be able discuss our lives and ambitions. It goes without saying, we were fuelled by a plentiful supply of subsidised plonk from the college bar. Something must have stirred within us both.'

'Even though she was on the rebound?'

'Who knows. I never really understood what she saw in me.'

Dependability, stability, Jamie thought. Someone totally unthreatening with low self-esteem whom she could mould the way she wanted him to be. Like so many bossy, blinkered people, she probably took her own strengths for granted, lacking sufficient interest in other people to think about how they felt.

'Perhaps I'm someone who's drawn to people of either sex – but have only just discovered.'

'Or accepted it?'

'I'm still working that one out.'

'There's a lot of it about.' Jamie said.

'Really?'

'Some of my best lovers have been AC/DC.'

'I'm just another notch on the post, then?'

'Watch this space!' he said with a twinkle. 'So, this… Gus person?'

'Sorry?'

'How friendly are you?'

Ewan was on the spot. Over the past few weeks he'd tried not to think too much about Gus. He must give him a call and put him in the picture, although he wasn't sure how he might react. Gus was a conventional sort, who valued stability above everything and had been disappointed on hearing Ewan and Paige had split up. Ewan really didn't know how Gus might feel about Jamie. Maybe threatened because Jamie was now his new special friend in the playground. No, if Gus was the person Ewan took him to be, it wouldn't make any difference. He'd feel more comfortable with everything out in the open. On the other hand, there was still the chance his new friendship with Jamie was simply a phase he was going through. Like teenage acne, he thought. Except, nearing forty, Ewan was too old for spots.

'Gus will always be a good chum,' Ewan said at length.

'Now there's a word that dates you.'

'You'll meet him in due course. I'm sure you'll like him…'

'Why do I feel an *only* coming on?'

'He's totally unlike me. Sporty and outgoing. Straight as a ruler of course.'

'Of course. But then you thought that about yourself until a few weeks ago.'

Ewan was beginning to realise his new persona came at a price. People might need to fine-tune, if not their opinion, the angle at which they viewed him. Gus had always been everything Ewan wanted to be.

'Go on, admit it. You've always secretly fancied him.'

Jamie came right out with it, Ewan thought. That was one of the things he found so refreshing. They could say what they liked to each other. Jamie never judged him the way he was judged at... He'd nearly thought 'home' before remembering he no longer had one.

'I'd never consciously considered it before,' Ewan said. 'I wasn't in that mind-set. Gus is defo better looking than I am. More assured. Attractive too, in a first-in-to-bat sort of way.'

'You'd gobble the Calvins off him!' Jamie grinned. 'Honestly. Have you never wanted to?'

Ewan blushed. *'No!'*

'Not even... embrace him?'

'There were times when he was very kind to me – as you've been, though not in the same way.' Whilst Ewan couldn't picture himself in an amorous situation with Gus, there had been occasions when, yes, he'd have liked to have given him, well, a warm hug.

'And, tell me truthfully,' Jamie said, 'what am I to you, Ewan?'

'What do you think you are?'

'A couple more togs on the duvet?'

'Not any old duvet. Luxury alpaca.'

'Have to make that do for now, won't I?' Jamie stretched his hand across the table and took Ewan's free one. 'Another cup?'

Ewan shook his head and turned back to the half-finished portrait. 'We must get on. You can relax whilst I sketch in your hair. I don't need your full attention for that.'

They changed tack.

Jamie said: 'I've been meaning to ask. Did you ever find out if your mother was okay after...?'

It was some days since Ewan had spotted the video of Maggy and Dino. Usually he didn't bother much with social media but checked Facebook once a week for any gossip he should be aware of.

It was indicative of his own current state of mind that he'd been uncertain how to respond. Ewan always avoided controversy with his family but had considered Grace's posting a joke in very poor taste. Jokes weren't usually Grace's forte. She gave humour a bad name and, normally, was discretion personified. It had crossed Ewan's mind that she might be having some sort of breakdown. Ewan hadn't spoken to his sister for a while and felt no urgency to bring her up to date with recent developments in his life. Also, he was aware of Grace's idiotic feelings about their father's will. He'd narrowly avoided sufficient confrontations with her on the subject to last him a lifetime.

His mother appeared to have behaved out of character, but he trusted her. There would be a good reason for her behaviour. They needed to talk, although he feared a courteous call wouldn't go down very well at the moment. Maggy could be spikey, even if she usually ended up laughing at herself. Ewan guessed she might have taken Grace's behaviour badly and be grateful if she thought he didn't know about it.

Ewan had inherited his father's tendency to bury his head in the sand. Maggy, easy-going on the surface, seemingly needed sporadic outbursts to release the toxins from her soul. The short-lived detonations helped her enormously – but scared the hell out of everyone else. Grace, however, had always been contemptuous of any lack of self-control, which made her recent behaviour all the stranger.

Hopefully, by now, the Facebook incident had blown over. One post followed another quickly and yesterday's hot news was soon lost in the scrum for attention by everyone else. Besides, Ewan told himself, the video was a matter between Grace and his mother. Still, just because he hadn't heard from Maggy didn't fully absolve him from his responsibility to check up on her. After all, he was now head of the family.

During the first year of Maggy's widowhood, he'd phoned her regularly, dropped by to see her and helped her in the garden. He hadn't wished to burden her with too much information about how his own life was moving on – until he felt more settled.

'You've prompted me,' Ewan finally said to Jamie. 'I must contact Mum again.' When he'd last tried, the landline had unaccountably been switched off and her mobile gone straight to voicemail. He hoped she was all right.

As sometimes happens when you're in a particular zone, his mobile rang.

'Ewan.'

'Hi Lorna,' Ewan tried not to sound surprised, 'how are you doing?'

'I'm fine.'

'Are you phoning about Mother?' he said.

'Why, is something wrong with her?'

'Just the Facebook thingy.'

'What thingy?'

'You've not seen it?'

'I'm not with you.'

It then dawned on Ewan. Lorna, though whizzy with digital technology in the library, was contemptuous of social media.

'Forget it.'

Lorna moved on to her reason for ringing: 'How are you both fixed for next Sunday lunchtime?'

'Are we free next Sunday, Jamie?'

Jamie mimed flapping wings. They had bumped into Lorna in M&S ten days before, and all had coffee together. Ewan could see Jamie and Lorna both thoroughly approved of each other and his cousin had handled her side of the conversation tactfully and with growing warmth.

'I'd like you both to come and meet Ally.' Lorna said.

Ewan's heart sank slightly. Whilst the thought of one of Lorna's famous Sunday roasts had got him salivating, Ally had sounded like hard work.

Lorna continued, 'You might be able to help her.'

How?'

'Wait and see.'

He was puzzled and mildly irritated. Lorna loved playing social games. But Ewan knew Jamie was intrigued to see Lorna's flat. How could he refuse? 'That would be great. Thanks, cuz!'

'Say one o'clock, *cuz*?'

'On the dot.'

⋙⋘

TWENTY-THREE

In a Glass, Darkly

ॐ ॐ

GARIBALDI snuggled in the crook of Maggy's arm, immersed in grumpled duvet.

Before Don died, the tabby had spent most afternoons on their bed, until the time came for his early evening constitutional and ritual terrorising of any tiny creature within range of his searchlight eyes. Mercifully for the touchy matter of cats' negative impact on wildlife statistics, Garibaldi observed the tiny creatures keenly, but was too lazy and well-fed to give chase.

At nights, he always dossed down in his basket in the study. Recently though, as pets – even self-engrossed moggies like Garibaldi – do, he seemed to sense Maggy's loneliness and had taken to curling up for the night in the space once occupied by Don. When she was reluctant to get up, he stretched, yawned, pulled himself together and clambered purringly over her stomach for attention.

Garbaldi might be her friend but, once again, the day was doing its own thing. A chink in the curtains revealed translucent drops on the window pane. Beyond was wet, grey, and uninviting.

The Facebook crisis was dragging Maggy's early-morning stomach southwards again. She felt as she had as a child, waking up to the heavy foreboding of a scheduled dressing-down by the headmistress; the dread of it being part of the punishment for some misdemeanour against the bastion of orderliness.

After watching the video clip, Maggy had sat cold and drained for almost an hour. Only a ring from the detested landline had jerked her into action. Without lifting the receiver, she'd hauled the plug from its socket, then disconnected every extension in the house.

A strange combination of anger against her daughter's mean act, self-loathing and confused feelings about Dino had boiled up and over. Her one-finger rule abandoned, after swallowing a triple Scotch, Maggy had gone upstairs and howled herself to sleep.

Today as on every morning, Maggy's desire to stay cocooned in the warmth was compromised by a desperate need to visit the en suite.

Disturbed, Garibaldi mewed protesting, then pawed his way to an oasis of calm on another part of the quilt, where he flopped and tucked his head under his ample tail, soon lost in another entertaining dream. What were they about she always wondered? Chasing prey, other cats – or fantasies involving chopped chicken and gravy? He could shut himself out of the world. Maggy must try and pull herself together and face it.

Once showered, Maggy tried to adjust to the day. Glancing in the mirror and running a brush through her hair, the truth of her position struck her yet again. Some Lorelei she was, she thought ruefully, now dipping her forefinger into a pot of moisturiser, smoothing blobs into the sagging crevices under and either side of her eyes. A foolish, greying woman grimaced back at her.

She had contemplated confronting Grace outright, before remembering another time, many years before, when they hadn't been getting along. As a peace offering, she'd treated her daughter to an expensive cream blouse. But Grace, recently turned thirteen, was going through a grungy phase and resented her mother buying clothes for her. After unfolding the tissue paper and picking up the exquisite pale silk, she'd spat out a sarcastic 'thanks' and stomped upstairs.

The next day, tidying Grace's bedroom, Maggy discovered the garment in shreds on the carpet, her best pair of pinking shears lying nearby, flashing derisively in the light from the window. Grace knew Maggy's sewing drawer was sacrosanct. When the girl arrived home from school Maggy, having spent the day forcing her hurt and anger into some sort of perspective, had asked to see her. She unpacked the issue as dispassionately as she could, but Grace insolently stared her out and left the room.

Then, as now, Grace always took the moral high ground, whether entitled to or not. Her mother had no business second-guessing the way she should dress. Any attempt to influence her was insulting. If she was biologically old enough to conceive, she was mature enough to select her own clothes.

There had been no budging her. Her mother was in the wrong. Whilst Maggy struggled to see how she might have handled the matter better, the destruction of such a beautiful and expensive item had devastated her. Why couldn't Grace have put it into the Cancer Research bag where all doomed clothing went? That would have been hurtful enough, but less vicious. Don had supported Maggy and there had been an atmosphere in the house for days. Yet Grace never apologised.

Confrontation, Maggy reflected, would achieve nothing.

Before Don's death and her self-inflicted purdah, Maggy always tried to see her granddaughters at least once a week. Then once a month. When the strain between Grace and herself took hold, with her loathing of cross-town journeys and the logistics of coordinating several bus rides, Maggy went by cab. As time went by and the tension between the women gained ground, monthly had turned into bi-monthly, and the duration of the visits grown shorter on each subsequent occasion.

Maggy's awareness that Grace wasn't coping came to her slowly. Sometimes, on arrival, she wondered if World War Three was imminent; but within ten minutes of her calming presence the children almost always settled down.

Another black mark.

Arriving home early during Maggy's last visit, Duncan overheard Grace banishing Maggy from the house for offering to help at bath-time. He'd run Maggy home, and they'd hidden their individual concerns beneath idle chatter – mainly about the forthcoming Referendum, increasingly everyone's standby topic of conversation. Both picked up each other's silent empathy, but Duncan's loyalty to his wife prevented any meaningful discussion. Only as he dropped her off at Illyria, had he said, 'I'm so sorry about what happened. Grace seems to get very tired these days.'

'Have you suggested she see a specialist?'

He'd given her a rueful smile. 'I want to stay alive.' She understood the subtext only too well.

For those moments they'd silently bonded. Duncan had then given her a look, as if wanting to retract his treacherous remark as Maggy waved him off with a sigh. She wasn't to know how, later that evening, he'd tried to persuade Grace to let Maggy go on seeing Lyndsay and Kara, pointing out, as lovingly as possible, that the girls might one day hold it against them both if their grandmother hadn't been more involved in their early lives – especially as Maggy was more conscientious than his own parents. By way of a reply he'd received a withering look.

He wouldn't raise the matter again.

Three months had passed. Would the girls even remember who she was? Why should they suffer? Wasn't it the role of grandmothers to assist in bringing up their grandchildren? Many working daughters' lives would be difficult to manage without parental support these days. Yet, now a full-time mother, Grace no doubt saw Maggy's appearances as a criticism of her wifely skills.

Sighing from hopelessness, Maggy turned her thoughts back to Dino. She regretted the way their budding friendship had drifted. What on earth would he be thinking? She might choose to keep her own counsel with everyone else but should put her mind at rest – and maybe his. Was he still in Edinburgh? Was he even in the country? Could he have found out about the fiasco? Had he tried to ring her? She'd not looked at her mobile or answer-phone for days. There were probably a string of unanswered calls awaiting her attention, some of which could easily be his. No, she had neglected him.

And then there was Ewan and, of course, Una. Would they not be the most understanding and sensible people with whom to, at least, talk things over? Una had once gone through a bad patch when one of her boys got into trouble for shop-lifting and they'd spent hours discussing what she should do.

Alas, Ewan, had become rather distant recently and Una seemed to have taken to retirement like a duck to water, literally, as she was away on yet another lengthy cruise. Besides, although Una had left a message after viewing the video, Maggy decided to wait until she felt more sanguine before contacting her.

Lorna would have been the obvious confidante, but was wrapped up in her own issues. It wasn't fair to dump her own problems on her.

When Maggy was a child, Orwell's vision of a world dominated by Big Brother had seemed a far-fetched fantasy. Now it was almost a reality. Each new technological development took away as much as it gave. Along with the many conveniences social media brought with it went the constant fear one's privacy was being invaded. In public, your movements were watched and recorded and personal details hijacked by faceless thieves out in the ether.

Una bore the responsibility for having introduced Maggy to Facebook. She'd emphasised, as Una tended to, all its advantages and none of the downsides. It was trendy, cool. No, 'cool' was dated: 'awesome' – even if the word didn't sound quite right tripping off the tongues of, let's face it, uncool people her age.

Through Facebook, tiresome folk from her past along with friends of acquaintances, whom she'd mentally discarded as surplus to requirements long ago, discovered she was still alive and clamoured to be befriended. To start off with, Maggy thought it might be interesting to know what they were all up to nowadays. Then she'd got bored with the trivia of their lives and considered quietly un-friending them. But then, they might discover her perfidy and be hurt. People only meant well, after all.

Or did they?

Every time she discovered a *Dierdre has updated her status* prompt, Maggy reflected that it was people meaning well who'd brought humanity to its knees. Excellent though it might be to check out old friends, it could be terribly time-wasting. She was continually appalled at people's arrogance imagining everyone else must be *so* interested in everything they and their families did. It was like getting those dreadful yuletide circulars all the year round.

Certainly, Maggy recognised that people, even those on the edges of her life, might be concerned about how she was getting along. Social media, she'd concluded, was a facility to be used with discretion. Master it or it mastered you.

The more Maggy pondered over her next move, the more it felt as if gangsters were bearing down on her with guns, forcing a decision out of her. Then she remembered how her father had always said 'Keep your own counsel. Never do anything in a hurry.'

Why should she give anyone the satisfaction of patronising her? Let them keep guessing. Keep schtum – and occupied.

Maggy grabbed her diary. As she flicked through to the past fortnight's entries she realised, to her horror: a coffee morning, hygienist appointment and a dystopian *Mother Courage* in-the-round presented by a local dramatic society, had all come and gone without her presence.

Time to make amends.

Going downstairs, with some trepidation Maggy plugged the landline back in its socket. As it kicked in, the machine gave a remonstrative chirrup. She shuddered at the thought of all the explanatory phone calls she must find the strength to embark upon, but not until she'd first been sustained by her morning cup of Darjeeling, and a round of granary toast generously topped with the heather honey she was becoming addicted to.

Minutes later, sipping the fragrant brew and somewhat mollified by her munching, she thought of the serious conversation she'd had with Lorna. Was it only a couple of months ago? Maggy felt she'd done everything her niece had urged her to – and, like Dolly in the musical, done her best to 're-join the human race.'

Alas, the human race appeared happy to declare her redundant.

Bugger it!

❧❧

TWENTY-FOUR

A Little Light Plotting

ல் ௸

DINO sat on a bench in the Meadows.

The open space made him feel reasonably safe. The tussle at North Berwick had been a wake-up call. Since then, despite a couple more threatening notes in childlike handwriting posted through the letterbox, Dino had been left alone.

The lull before the storm?

The whole business was puzzling. What had happened to his nemesis: had he given up the chase? Who was he working for: the police or his creditors? Maybe they – whoever 'they' were – were simply scaring him into going home to face the music.

Or was there a more sinister explanation? After all, the sound of gun shots ringing down a city street would cause more problems for his pursuers than it would solve.

The young man shivered. Whoever his stalker was, his surveillance methods were haphazard and amateurish. Should he be consoled by that? He couldn't afford to let his guard down. Next time they both came face to face, he might not be on his own. There might be a gang. He might not get off so lightly.

Dino touched the slowly diminishing scab on his face, hoping it was too superficial to leave a permanent scar. He was convinced the guy had been carrying a gun in The Botanics that day, and probably at North Berwick, although he'd made light of the matter so as not to frighten Maggy. He thought he'd caught sight of him once or twice when he was out and about in the city too but, if it had indeed been him, he'd vanished before he could give chase or alert the police.

Several times recently Dino had thought he'd spotted the man hovering around the end of the street where the squat was. When obliged to go out, he proceeded with extreme caution. He knew he was most vulnerable in alleyways and quieter, narrower places. Yet, nowhere was fully safe. As Paolo had advised, busy streets and open spaces provided the best protection from anyone who'd been contracted to give him another serious warning. Or worse. Who knew what enemies he'd inadvertently made and how serious was their intent to silence him?

Also, Dino's experience at North Berwick had been a salutary reminder of how unpredictable the public could be. Bystanders had watched the two men fighting in the street and, seemingly, put it down to nothing more than bad-mannered horseplay, reacting only with glares and mutterings on the lines of 'they should be ashamed of themselves!' before moving their children out of harm's way on the opposite pavement. If Beige Man could tackle him in the middle of a small seaside town and provoke only a few outraged tuts, he could be ambushed anywhere.

It all added up to the fact that Dino had been stuck in Edinburgh far longer than he'd intended. Though, precisely, *what* had he intended? Scared, he'd acted on impulse when he left Italy and never thought through future scenarios. His career as a midnight – more midday – cowboy, had failed to take off. His precarious financial situation was worsening each day.

As for Maggy, she hadn't been in touch. His calls, texts and emails had gone unanswered. When a few days had elapsed, and he still hadn't heard from her, he'd connected to Facebook in a Starbucks. A long shot. He knew she didn't use it very often, but there was a slim chance of postings on her site to indicate what was happening in her life.

There were several Magg*ie* Galbraiths, but only one Magg*y*.

The discovery of the video had shaken Dino badly and a worrying thought struck him. Supposing Maggy wasn't the person he believed she was? Could she have simply been playing a role on behalf of whom: the police or the *real* enemy? After all, she was always saying how she'd started out as an actress. Could the video have been carefully stage-managed? Had it gone viral? Dino was aware of Maggy's estrangement from her daughter. What if she'd simply told him about Grace to put him off the scent? What if the daughter was part of the charade too?

The video clip had received 35 Likes and 11 Comments. So not *too* viral. He'd also surfed YouTube to reassure himself it hadn't been posted further afield. No. Even so, the people who had seen it might still recognise him in the street.

He was being ridiculous. After all, he had been taking advantage of Maggy – and didn't altogether care for the person, through adversity, he was turning into.

One thing was clear, he had to move on as soon as possible. Staying in Edinburgh for much longer was too dangerous. But where? Paolo had a friend in a rural area south of Rome. Would that be a better place to hide? And was anywhere safe? Rome itself wasn't far. But although Rome was not Milan, its criminal world could be just as pernicious.

And how could he afford to get there and what would he use for funds when he arrived?

Searching a nearby litter bin, Dino picked out and smoothed down a clean-ish paper bag. He had a rough idea of the money still hidden in the flat. He emptied his pockets and totted up the few notes and small change he kept with him, then unclipped the biro in his shirt pocket and jotted down the figures. The calculation didn't take long.

È terribile.

Dino had to clear his mind. He got up, stretched, and started gently jogging around the edge of the vast expanse of grass. It was a fresh morning. A light breeze stroked his face. He began to feel calmer and more focused.

'Why, hello there! It's Dino, isn't it?'

'Allo, Signor… Drummond?'

Banger nodded. 'Do call me Banger, everyone does. Have you a moment? I don't want to interrupt your exercise routine.'

'No. Please…' Dino slowed down to a walk and indicated a bench a few yards away where he had left his jacket.

'I'm glad I've bumped into you, I've been wondering how Maggy is?'

'I do not know.' Dino said as they sat down. 'I 'ave not seen her since we last met. We 'ad a good time in North Berwick, but after…' he expressively displayed his hands, then suddenly added 'You use Facebook?'

'I'm one of those sad people who only uses his computer for essential emailing and purchasing tickets and books. I get too much information about other people's lives in my job as it is. Of course, my younger colleagues regard me as a relic of the Edwardian era, but I get by perfectly well without it.'

Dino glanced at Banger's thinning but well-groomed hair, open-necked blue shirt, smart fawn zip-up jacket and slacks. Maggy had told him how long she'd known him. Dino reckoned he effortlessly looked ten years younger than his real age.

'You are underestimating yourself,' he said.

'No need to flirt,' Banger reproved. 'Even if we do have unfinished business,' he added mischievously.

Dino gave him a like-that-was-ever-going-to-happen smile. His few sordid escapades to date had convinced him he wasn't cut out to be a sex worker at any level. Besides, as they were both friends of Maggy's, offering Banger anything more than companionship would be inappropriate, however strapped for cash he was.

Banger said, 'I was on my way to Tagliatelle a small but reliable Italian restaurant off Leven Street for lunch. Probably not up to your own fastidious culinary standards, but would you settle for being my guest?'

Dino agreed with alacrity. Another complimentary lunch would set him up for the day. He took a comb out of his pocket, tidied his hair and clothes and put on his jacket. He hoped he looked acceptable enough not to draw attention to himself in Leven Street.

On the short walk northwards, Dino brought Banger up to date with the park bench incident.

Once at Tagliatelle, Banger was shown the offending footage.

'Oh dear. I can see how easily that could be misconstrued. I knew Maggy and Grace had never got on, but…'

Banger had hoped Dino might have information on Maggy, whom he'd tried to contact, also without luck. At least the clip explained why she had been impossible to get hold of. Also, if he was spotted with the young man by any lurking acquaintances it would provide him with delicious social ammunition – which he'd relish deflecting.

The line, 'My friend Maria's son from Milan,' might even get recycled.

Over an excellent chicken cacciatore and chianti, chased by baked pears teamed with amaretto ice cream, Banger decided that, if his initial impression of Dino as an opportunist was correct, at least he was a charming and decorative one. He well understood how Maggy had fallen under his spell.

To his delight, he found the young shoe designer only too pleased to be taken seriously. Dino opened up about his professional hopes and fears. Indeed, the excellent food and wine worked well. Banger learned more about the real Dino in an hour than Maggy had over several days.

Finally, as Dino reached for a second and then third mint crisp, he shared his vision of a Spring-Summer collection, should he ever get the chance to contribute his work to one of Milan's *Settimana della moda*. He explained how his visit to Scotland had given him time to think laterally and fill his sketch pad with ideas.

Banger listened attentively. Enjoying the tail-end of a successful career, the old roué delighted in encouraging anyone with creative flair. From Dino's passionate sincerity, he suspected there might be real talent lurking inside him. Obviously, Luca the Gigolo had been born of desperation.

During pauses in the conversation, Banger occasionally caught the frantic flicker of desperation in the lad's eyes. What was really going on here?

Finishing his coffee, Banger said, 'I can see you really love what you do. I'd like to look at some of your designs. I can't promise anything, but in my line one gets the opportunity to meet people in the fashion and media world. If I like what I see, I'd be happy to pass them on.'

Dino's eyes lit up.

What Banger omitted to say was that his ex-partner, Quentin, still his closest friend, was a leading television designer. Quentin was obsessed with contemporary fashion and had a fetish for women's footwear. If Dino's sketches were any good, Quent would be in seventh heaven.

'That is very kind of you,' Dino said. 'I will 'ave examples of my latest ideas copied for you before I return home.'

'You intend to leave soon?'

'As soon as I am able,' Dino said enigmatically.

'But not for a week or two?' Banger hoped.

'I do not t'ink so.'

A vague plan began to coalesce in Banger's head. He was anxious to meet up with Maggy. The video had increased his concern that all might not be well with her, and he wanted to talk to her about something that might interest her. Also, he was frankly intrigued at the possibility of seeing Dino's designs.

'What are your plans for the weekend after next?' he said.

Before they parted, Banger thoughtfully slipped Dino a twenty-pound note for the photocopying.

The front doorbell rang. As they never visited each other except for the occasional pre-Christmas drinks party, Maggy was surprised to find Banger standing on her doorstep.

After saying *au revoir* to Dino, and with the afternoon at his disposal, he'd taken a bus that had dropped him off a short walk from Illyria.

'I was in the area,' he said as Maggy ushered him into the kitchen. 'I've something to run past you and hoped to catch you in.'

'You were lucky. I was just about to pop down to the shops. But it's lovely to see you, Banger. Any excuse for a cuppa and a no-reputation-left-unstoned goss, eh?'

As Maggy hunted for her best china and standby biscuits, the conversation descended into scurrilous chit-chat. Fancy Banger coming all that way from the New Town to see her, she thought.

When they were both seated and comfortably sipping, she ventured 'This *something*…?'

'Very much in the development phase,' Banger began, 'but the guys upstairs have an idea for a new twice-weekly radio soap.'

'Ah.'

'Working title: *Restless Weegies*…'

'Sorry?'

'…three generations of a Glasgow family. Set in the present. Mum and Dad, the kids now emerging from college or apprenticeships, maybe one on the dole; finding partners, struggling to get work and a place of their own etcetera. All against the perspectives of their grandparents of the… whatsit generation.'

'Never-had-it-so good-yet-still-complaining?'

Banger smiled and nodded.

'We'd originally thought of calling it *The Boom-Bangers*. You know, the whole Bank of Mum and Dad thing…'

'And Gran,' Maggy added.

'Indeedy. The tensions and conflicts those issues create.'

'Including the way we seniors feel about them?'

'You've got the picture!'

'And this might be of interest to me, because…?'

'We'll soon be casting. And call it a hunch, but I'd love to see your name on the final roll call. I know you could do the no-nonsense warmth those Glasgow matriarchs have. Think about it. There'll be two roles going: the fierce assertive gran Mrs Gordon, whose husband has not long popped his brogues – and isn't afraid to tread over people's feelings even though she's often right …'

'Tell me about it!'

'…and the other, more docile grannie, who isn't so strong, whines a lot and always wants to play devil's advocate…'

'Met those as well.'

'Although I've someone else's name to put forward for her.'

'Ah.' Maggy took in the implication of this last line and moved downstage, contemplatively.

'Look, I know it's been an awfully long time…' Banger said.

'Awfully,' Maggy said.

A couple of years back she'd played Fairy Wisteria in a local panto, but Banger didn't really do church halls. Just as well, he might have been shocked at how downmarket she'd become.

'Your Kelvinside Mrs Higgins in *Pygmalion* for The Makars was masterly,' Banger continued. You always had a Shaw touch,' he added waggishly. 'And I bet the accent's still in good working order.'

'*Havnae a Scooby,*' she volunteered.

'You see – all postcodes too! I'm not asking you to decide now. Besides, it's not in my gift. I simply wanted to let you know that auditions for the pilot will be taking place in a couple of months' time.'

'You really think I'd stand a chance – even if I wanted it?'

'A gifted young writer submitted the idea for the show. We loved it immediately. She's already drafted the first few episodes. Work produced at The Tron and up at Dundee. Lesley Bushell?'

The name didn't mean anything to Maggy.

'I think you two would get on well. She's a real person. Her scripts are truthful yet entertaining with the right balance of conflict, pathos, and humour. Character rather than plot driven, although ratings wars might make that hard to sustain if it's re-commissioned. We'll see. We've plenty of talented young actors in mind for the kids. It's finding people of the right… '

'Age?'

'Calibre. Also, we need people who could be around for the duration, who aren't likely to want to break their contract when London calls.'

A *déjà-vu* moment.

Maggy didn't say anything, but poignant memories came flooding back. It was tempting to see if she had it in her to emerge from retirement. Not that she'd ever really had a proper professional career, but she knew her acting skills were appreciated whenever she appeared in front of a local audience. It always gave her a 'what-if?' moment.

'As I said, it's not up to me, but… I'll leave the thought with you.'

'Thanks,' Maggy said, refilling Banger's cup.

They sat in silence for a few moments. 'I don't suppose you have anything planned for the Sunday after next?' he said.

'No, I don't think so. Why?'

'You know the Barkers always hold their Annual Charity Garden Party on the second Sunday in June?'

Maggy nodded. Sir John and Lady Barker were popular patrons of the arts. Their home, Primrose Bank, a beautiful eighteenth-century country house in spacious grounds twenty miles south of the city was a fashionable venue for cultural and social events.

Maggy had attended several of the Barkers' 'dos' in the past. Having been caught up with her life, she'd neglected to see this year's flyer amongst the holiday brochures and knitwear catalogues in the post, and accidentally condemned it for recycling.

'I've a couple of spare invitations,' Banger said. 'I just wondered if you, and…' here a touch of coyness crept into his voice, '…maybe a wee friend could make use of them?'

Maggy dithered. Given her current state of paranoia, her initial reaction was to say 'no'. Yet, what were the chances of bumping into anyone who knew about her Facebook ordeal? And if so, wouldn't it most likely be one of her old theatrical mates, who'd be envious rather than contemptuous – especially if Dino was available and willing to accompany her?

Providing the weather was good, the grounds at Primrose Bank could be enchanting. She must show her face in public again sooner or later. Maggy noted Banger's delight when her face finally lit up. 'Why not!' she said graciously. 'Thank you, Banger, it would be lovely! I've been trying to get hold of Dino, so far without any luck,' she dissembled. 'Did you know his name was really Dino, not Luca?'

'Really?' Banger struggled to look as if this came as a surprise. 'Anyway, try again,'

Maggy picked up her phone.

'Dino?'

'Maggy!'

'What a relief,' she said. I was afraid you'd bolted.'

'Bolted?' he said uncomprehendingly.

'Are you all right? You sound…'

'I 'ave been worried not 'earing from you for a long time.'

'Well, I'm ringing very belatedly to apologise. My phone's been…' Maggy struggled to think of an excuse and came out lamely with '… not working properly. But I'll get to the point…'

Dino was, of course, prepared for the summons that followed. When Banger had run the idea past him earlier, he'd initially doubted the wisdom of going somewhere he might easily be noticed by the wrong people, and when he'd added '… and fashion and media folk will likely be there…' Dino had become even more agitated. Then he'd said: 'but it could be an opportunity for you to bring your designs along, circulate and make some useful contacts.'

Dino considered the idea. Well, with his life in freefall, what had he to lose? He couldn't stagnate, penniless, in the squat for ever.

Maggy repeated most of the points Banger had made, before concluding 'And it's a lovely location. We could have a jolly afternoon and catch-up.'

'Yes… It would be nice.'

'Banger's sure to be there, too,' Maggy added.

Dino, of course, couldn't see Maggy winking conspiratorially at the gentleman in question, now nibbling shortbread in the rocker, miming to her not to give him away.

Time was running out, Dino thought. He needed to create better luck for himself. Banger's offer might come to nothing, but the old man gave the impression of having clout. Very well, he'd go but it would be his very last throw of the dice.

'Hello, are you still there?' Maggy was beginning to wonder if the line had gone dead.

'Yes, I am 'ere.'

'I really owe you a treat after deserting you.'

'Then I will come. If it will give you pleasure.'

'Lovely! That smart jacket of yours… white shirt and so on?'

'Of course.'

'How about I pick you up at the corner of Shandwick Place at 2.30?' Maggy said. 'You'll have to be there on time as I won't be able to park. Okay?'

'I look forward to it,' Dino said.

A plan was forming in his mind.

'Super. See you there then. Bye.'

'Addio.'

Banger sat back, relieved, as he saw the way things were going. He hoped he'd managed to cheer Maggy up. She looked tired but had brightened up since they'd started chatting. He crunched on his last bit of shortbread.

Being of the old school, Banger knew how, in polite Edinburgh society, a second cup plus ten minutes was the 'done thing' before drawing an unannounced visit to a close. When the appointed time had passed, he glanced at his watch and, with a courteous, 'Gosh, is that the time!', arose and made his way to the front door.

'I'll pop the invites in the post, First Class.'

⊰⊱

TWENTY-FIVE

Sunday Afternoon

ૐ ✑

REPLETE with Lorna's smoked salmon pâté followed by roast beef, signature roast potatoes and all the trimmings, her guests were released to let their first two courses digest for twenty minutes before the onslaught of a calorie-intensive sweet.

Jamie, who'd been in wonderland looking at Lorna's eclectic art collection, was now assisting her wash up in the kitchen whilst Ally, sitting next to Ewan on the sofa, excitedly turned over the pages of his portfolio.

She'd immediately taken to both men. Knowing they were in the process of becoming a couple also negated much of the discomfort she nowadays felt on finding herself at close quarters to any males, especially those of her own generation.

Sharing with Lorna the full account of her rape had helped Ally dispel the lingering distress of that disastrous afternoon at the Balfour. To everyone's delight, she was once again conversing with some confidence, hesitating only occasionally. The young woman who'd defied expectation by moving to the capital and creating a new life for herself, was made of sterner stuff than even she herself had appreciated.

After Lorna had phoned Ewan, she'd sent him Ally's current draft of *Jock*. Ewan had responded the next day, saying how enchanted he was by it. He'd completed his portrait of Jamie in record time and produced the trial illustrations now on her lap awaiting, hopefully, her approval.

The images presented Jock much as Ally envisaged, transforming him into a reality of sorts and giving depth to his personality. They made her want to hurry back to her laptop and flesh out her descriptions. On the internet Ewan had discovered photos of the flat, spacious, Benbecula landscape, with its waterways backed by mournful mountains. These, he suggested, would provide context and local colour for the larger illustrations.

One picture evocatively suggested Flora playing with Jock with the minimum of wavy lines. The characters' energy jumped off the cartridge paper.

'I can see you've based her outfit on the Allan Ramsay portrait?' Ally said.

Ewan nodded.

'I think it should be less formal,' Ally said, 'more a... working dress? No flowers...' she put her hand on her own cleavage '... here? Ewan followed the hand and looked at her as if he found something vulnerable and appealing about her. To her discomfort, Ally saw it was the look of a man, not an illustrator. What had she done, she thought, to provoke that? They'd only met a couple of hours ago. Hadn't Lorna warned him how fragile she was? Her sudden apprehension must have conveyed itself to Ewan. He hastily pointed out that the drawing was only a first attempt.

Ally became very business-like and pretended she hadn't noticed what, after all, had only been a brief admiring look – was she just imagining the suggestion of something else behind it? She quickly moved on to discuss her, largely positive, response to the rest of his sketches.

But that look had thrown her off-kilter.

Another woman might have been flattered but Ally was unable to reciprocate. Sweet as Ewan seemed, even pre-Dundee he wouldn't have been the kind of man she was drawn to. It was disappointing. His sketches were inspirational and she really wanted to work with him – but any emotional pressure would make professional collaboration impossible.

Swallowing hard, Ally was on the point of suggesting where some adjustments might be made to Charlie in his 'Betty' costume, when the sound of someone entering the room dragged them back from the Hebrides to Edinburgh.

Ally turned and caught Jamie's look of discomfort. Of course, he would have seen their two heads poring over the drawings. To make matters worse, Ewan looked round, embarrassed.

'Ready for your just desserts?' was all Jamie said.

Within a few minutes everyone was back in the kitchen, purring over Nigella's *pêches melba*.

The conversation turned to Ally's book. Everyone discussed past holidays in the Western Isles. Lorna casually mentioned how she'd recently got to know Ally's friend Senga, who'd been brought up on Arran – some distance from the Outer Hebrides, but still in that corner of the map.

Jamie noticed that mention of Senga made Ally look uneasy, but he quickly picked up the thread of the conversation and talked about his own recollections of happy breaks in Orkney and its wildlife.

After three-quarters of an hour's nostalgia, Ewan, Ally and Jamie re-adjourned to the living room. Lorna soon reappeared with a tray stacked with mugs, a huge cafetière of freshly ground coffee, and truffles.

Reminiscences tend to meander. It was soon Lorna's turn to relive happy holidays spent in Pitlochry and the surrounding countryside, photographing red squirrels and unusual birds. 'I've some photograph albums somewhere which might entertain Jamie and Ally,' she said, moving across the room and hunting in a cupboard beneath the bookshelves.

'Strange how we've all moved on to relying on our computers for storing photographs, isn't it?' Ewan said. 'When was the last time you ever pasted a photograph in a book, Jamie?'

'Must be several years,' Jamie said. 'I put an album together after my mother's sixtieth birthday – what, four years ago? Increasingly I use my phone and transfer them to my computer for storage.'

'Ah, here we are!' Lorna was now clutching several books. She handed them around. 'There's about ten years between Ewan and me. We didn't socialise a great deal when we were younger, but our families teamed up with us for occasional jaunts and gatherings. You should find us in one of these, if you're interested. Another truffle for whoever who finds us first!'

Lorna passed two of the books round and handed Ally the third. Jamie was soon chuckling over images of Ewan as a toddler, clowning around and knocking down his sandcastle. Ewan sat on the arm of his chair pretending to be embarrassed.

As Lorna went around replenishing everyone's coffee cups, Ally suddenly emitted a strangled moan.

Everyone looked up.

'It's….'

Lorna put down the cafetière with a thud.

'… *her*!' Ally put her head in her hands.

The album slipped, still open, off her lap and onto the floor.

Lorna retrieved it, saw the open pages and then froze as a familiar face looked up at her: that of a woman poured into an expensive green evening dress glaring tight-lipped at the photographer.

Ewan moved up to Lorna and looked over her shoulder at the album. 'That's Mum's sixtieth three years ago,' he said. Then, raising a questioning eyebrow at his cousin. 'I don't understand?'

Lorna identified the people in the picture. 'My parents obviously. You, me and … Paige.'

Ewan's eyes widened as he too began to catch on. 'So it was...'

'Yes!' Ally yelped.

'*Paige?*'

'Are you sure?' Lorna said.

'*Yes.*'

'Then her lover must be … Cal.'

'The manager of the café-bar?' Ewan said.

Ally nodded frantically.

'Monsieur Tissot!'

'*Who?*' Lorna said looking mystified.

'I'll tell you later.'

'You're quite sure that was the woman you saw with Cal?' Lorna asked Ally.

But Ally's face was in her hands.

Jamie, who didn't know the rules of this game, looked on, totally bemused.

Ewan turned to Ally. 'I should explain. The woman in green is my ex-partner. I discovered she was seeing someone else. I never knew who it was. Until now. He was sitting with us on the same table at a dinner party around Christmas.'

Ally, her cheeks pink, looked up at him, upset and deeply disappointed. After an awkward pause, she said 'It's not your fault.' Then, without total conviction, 'I mean… how could it be? You weren't to know.'

Everyone breathed with some relief.

'I hope this doesn't make any difference to our collaboration?' Ewan said.

Throughout this hiatus, Ally had been thinking, quickly. Despite the shocks of the day, she recognised Ewan's talent. She really wanted to try and borrow that if she could. He might be emotionally capricious but, Lorna was right, he was unthreatening. And he had such a nice partner. She must have been imagining things.

Lorna began tidying up the coffee table.

'Drink up everyone!' she commanded. 'It's a glorious afternoon. Maybe a wee stroll to work off our lunch?'

❧⬥❧

TWENTY-SIX

High Society

❧ ❦

MAGGY twisted left, then right as she appraised herself in the cheval mirror. The light navy fabric still hung well, the swaying skirt pleats, lined in the same shade of raspberry as the up-turned sleeves of the short matching jacket, giving verve to the *tout ensemble*. She twirled around. A smart, timeless ensemble, she thought.

She'd lost some weight since Grace's wedding. Could it really be five years ago? The outfit, which she'd spotted in a couture boutique in Thistle Street, had been put away far too long. A bit like herself, she thought. It had needed a tiny tuck at the hips and a wee freshen up with a carefully controlled iron but had come up like new. A pity never to wear it again.

The *pièce de résistance* was her Alex Muir hat. A charming and, on occasions, deliciously waspish man, Alex had been leading milliner to the Scottish gentry for more years than he was prepared to admit. She recalled the delightful afternoon she'd spent in his salon in Pittenweem on the Fife coast. A grand day out for her and, if the estimate had initially caught her breath, the ultimate confection was worth every tenner.

Alex had managed to dye the straw the exact blue of the rest of the outfit, magically transforming it into something distinctive with the addition of three cunningly worked pieces of raspberry taffeta, clustered together on a striped ribbon and stitched around the crown. Maggy recalled his infinite patience when working out the precise angle the hat should be worn to best effect.

'*Not* on the back of the head, Maggy!' he'd appealed to her better sense of style. 'A wee bitty forward. Not so far as to throw shadow over your eyes; tipped very slightly to one side to highlight the cluster and pick up the colour in the cuffs.'

She smiled at herself as she clicked her one good set of pearls behind her neck. Picking up her bag, Maggy stood back for one final glance. Yes. She could hold her head high with any grand folk Primrose Bank might throw at her.

Another lovely afternoon. Though the laddie on the car radio warned it could break later. Maggy switched on the engine and chuntered off to collect Dino. It crossed her mind he might have chickened out at the last minute, so felt guilty when she caught sight of him at the agreed spot.

It was good to see him again, though he could have done with a hair-cut. Maggy got out of the car and exchanged chaste salutations before handing him the keys and getting into the passenger seat beside him. 'Glad you were on time,' she said, 'the local traffic control mafia can be a real pain.'

Why did that make him look uncomfortable?

As soon as they were beyond the built-up area, the Audi hummed along the motorway.

Forty minutes later, Primrose Bank's ornate wrought iron gates loomed into view.

A neglected yet once-gracious stone mansion – 'pared down Palladian,' Mhairi Barker always called it – the young Barkers, then plain Mr and Mrs, had been drawn to the place one Sunday afternoon in 1974 and spotted its potential. Buying it on impulse, they had restored it to its former glory. A new wing had been attached with an Italianate orangery for live performances, whilst a garden wizard had re-landscaped the extensive grounds. No rival to the Villa Capra, Primrose Bank – strangely they'd never changed the name – still lent this often-chilly corner of East Lothian a *soupçon* of Romantic charm.

Having raised a family before handing over the reins of their business to their eldest son, the Barkers now spent the cocktail hour of their lives organising charity events: music recitals in winter, theatrical evenings in summer; with fêtes and occasional gigs by 'golden' pop and cross-over operatic stars in between. The gigs provided work for the artists concerned who, comparatively cheap to engage, still delighted their contemporaries who'd once canoodled to their LPs.

As Maggy took the invitations out of her handbag, she was momentarily distracted by Dino struggling with the English signs and asking for directions to the car park. From force of habit, Maggy slipped her bag under her car seat. Their teas were already paid for and she had an emergency tenner tucked in her pocket. It wasn't as if she really needed her bag and it would be safe enough once Dino zapped the lock.

They made their way through the gateway, giving their names to an eccentric lady in diamanté-framed spectacles at the window of a Gothic hut.

Wandering along the pathway to the lawns, Maggy and Dino were soon greeted by the cheerful cacophony of voices and, turning the corner, a sizeable gathering of guests. In the minority were the few patriots sweating in full traditional Scottish dress – having mistakenly assumed, with Referendum politics in mind, that tartans would be de rigueur. Inevitably there was also a sprinkling of folk who always favoured heather tweeds whatever the season. The rest of the guests, like Maggy herself, had rifled their spare room wardrobes for festive attire.

Indeed, the glorious early summer afternoon had all too conspicuously brought out people's giddy side. Quite a few, if not exactly dressed to kill, appeared hell-bent on competing for the Loudest Ensemble trophy. Abandoned florals, polka dots, mixed-width stripes and ethnic prints rubbed shoulders with retro-sixties psychedelia and Joan Collins rejects. And that was just the men, Maggy joked to Dino. In her own tasteful outfit, she felt almost subdued against such extroversion.

Was that Maisie Albright over there, true to form in A&E-defying heels, tottering like a woman possessed towards the champagne bar, buttermilk trousers flapping and an excess of jangling gold bling? Always a risky business, very pale colours on the over-sixties, she reflected – especially for bottle blondes with dodgy roots. Though who was she to say? Maggy was the first person to support a woman's right to be noticed as, like herself, she slowly dwindled into silvery anonymity.

She spotted a highly animated Banger by a pergola of scarlet roses, resplendent in a pale grey suit and the pinkest shirt she'd ever seen. He was talking to a trio of men in couture T-shirts emblazoned with witty slogans, and pressed jeans a size too small; self-consciously flaunting cuddly paunches above the belt and, as they imagined, virile protuberances below. She guessed one of them was the Quentin he was always talking about – probably the animated guy in the Three-Men-in-a-Boat blazer. Banger saw Maggy, and they exchanged kisses in the air. She'd catch up with him later. For now, she must give Dino a quick tour of the estate.

They meandered around chattering, occasionally pausing to admire the rose tubs and flower beds, concentric circles of vibrant pansies and antirrhinums crowding around mock-classical statuary. Occasionally Maggy paused to comment with acquaintances on the horticulture and introduce her protégé.

'He was only *so high* when I last saw him. Imagine!'

From a huge marquee at the end of the garden came the tinkle of tea crockery and cutlery, underscored with the noisy flight of gulls heading back to the coast. Their squalls would soon be drowned out by Scottish folk melodies from loudspeakers in the trees.

Maggy caught sight of Fiona Anderson, Don's cousin, with her husband Josh and waved. Fiona beamed back and frantically beckoned her to join them. Maggy hadn't spoken to the Andersons since the funeral. What on earth were they doing here? It was the last place she expected to see them. She doubted if either of them ever used a PC, let alone Facebook – but then, the most unlikely people could surprise you with their computer literacy.

Maggy embraced them. 'How are you?' she said a little too brightly.

'I was given the tickets as a birthday present,' Fiona explained. 'A novel idea, for after all, who needs things at our age? Most of our Christmas presents go on to *Cats' Protection* as it is. Not really our style, the high life. But och well, it's a lovely day and a chance to get out our glad rags. She nodded towards her husband who was feeling sticky and self-conscious in his heavy jacket and kilt.

Reading his mind, Maggy said 'You're looking very smart, Josh. Such a pity more men don't go to the trouble of adopting their national dress on such occasions.' Josh smiled with gratitude and felt less foolish. 'And, you'll not have met my Italian friend, Maria's son from Milan.' The line now slipped off her tongue without a trace of self-consciousness.

Maggy turned around, expecting Dino to be his usual pace-or-so behind her. But no. 'Dearie me, where can he be? I'm so sorry.' She shaded her eyes with her hand. Giving a panoramic sweep of the lawn with her eyes, she spotted Dino, hurrying over to join Banger and his cronies. He'd be in safe, if over-exuberant, company. At that moment, a group of people walked in front of him, obscuring her view. When they'd moved on, Dino had vanished. Where was he? Well, he mustn't be far away and couldn't come to much harm.

Could he?

Maggy continued catching up with Fiona and Josh. Nice, reliable people despite being a trifle dull. She must have them over for dinner whilst the garden was still fresh and, weather permitting, maybe entertain on the patio. Looking at the glasses of Perrier in their hands, she remembered they didn't drink. She'd have to exhume Granny's homemade lemonade recipe.

When half an hour passed and there was still no sign of her escort

Maggy felt she must make a move. 'If you'll excuse me, I'll go and hunt for Dino. He'll be ready for his tea.'

'Of course,' Josh said, 'we'll no doubt be joining you in a few minutes. I must just look at that gorgeous apricot rose over there. Quite spectacular! I never have any luck with them. It's all about the right position…'

As she moved away, Maggy saw Banger surveying the scene from the end of the tea queue. His friends, always on the lookout for people to notice and be noticed by, must have moved on to enchant other guests with their camp prattle.

'Come and join me!' he mouthed. 'Very glad you could make it,' he said when she reached him, hugging her. 'You're looking lovely – if I may say so.'

'Likewise,' she said. 'Any idea what's happened to our mutual friend? I saw him heading in your direction with his portfolio. She noted that Banger was clutching the A4 brown envelope Dino was carrying earlier.

'We spoke briefly, but I think he found Quentin & Co a tad intimidating and soon made his excuses. Talented lad that. Be busy philandering no doubt. His last chance to pull a cute wee lassie before he leaves.'

'*Leaves*?' Maggy felt decidedly uncomfortable. Had the pair of them got to know each other better than they were letting on? Was Dino keeping something from her? If so, why?

Banger saw he'd made a *faux pas* and looked embarrassed. 'You knew he was planning to return to Italy sooner or later?'

'Yes. But he's never said precisely when. What did he tell you?'

Banger looked flustered. 'I really shouldn't worry. Maybe he was hungry and forged ahead of the rest of us tea-wise.'

'Not like him to be rude.'

'It's certainly rather strange,' Banger said.

Indeed, she thought, Dino was usually so courteous and, being their guest, unlikely to have wandered into tea without them. But they'd all be inside the marquee in a few minutes. She didn't want to risk people thinking she was jumping the queue – not in this hat. They'd either find him, or…

Calm down, Maggy told herself. Dino's a big boy, he can take care of himself and, like a cat, re-materialise when he's good and ready. She'd give herself just the length of time it would take to demolish a cup of Earl Grey, a couple of egg and cress sandwiches – and one of those filo pastry slices oozing with confectioner's custard. Then she'd seriously start worrying.

They moved on to share their expectations of this year's Festival, now only six weeks away. As Maggy scooped up the last delicious mouthful of sticky pastry with as much delicacy as finger-food convention would allow, an amplified 'Good afternoon, everybody,' drew their attention to Sir John, standing on a small podium at the end of the marquee.

With the ancient Tannoy system making him sound as if he was talking whilst crunching crisps, Maggy could barely make out '... thank you all for supporting our *Wildlife Campaign*,' and edged closer to the platform.

In that moment, she caught sight of a familiar but sinister figure in sunglasses, seemingly taking advantage of everyone's eyes turned on Sir John, to have a good recce. Being so wrapped up in herself over the past fortnight, she'd hardly given a thought to Beige Man and was hit by a sudden sense of foreboding.

Did this mean more trouble? The memory of Dino, dishevelled and bloodied at North Berwick, made her partially-digested vanilla slice churn in her stomach.

Under the layers of self-deceit, Maggy knew she'd been in denial. Maybe the time had come to finally accept the extent to which her interest in the young man had prevented her from facing up to reality.

Like a paper kite fluttering irresponsibly high, a gust of cold wind was bound to call Time and shatter the magic eventually.

Probably now.

As she was wondering if she should alert any officials she could find to her concerns for Dino's safety, Banger appeared by her side again. 'About our discussions last week...' Maggy's heart sank, having forgotten all about it and not in the mood to pursue the matter at that moment.

'Forgive me, but I don't have your email address. Any chance you could jot it down before you go this afternoon? I'll make sure you get all the bumf when it's available,'

'Nae bother,' Maggy said. 'I may even have an old card with it on in my...'

Where was her handbag? Where were her... *keys*!

Dino had them.

Excusing herself as graciously as she could, Maggy headed for the wine tent.

No sign of him there. Panic-stricken, she turned back towards the car park.

Where the Audi had been was now an empty space.

She tore across to the gothic hut and asked the ticket lady if she could borrow a phone and order herself a cab. Thank God! Her regular firm's number was etched on her brain. By chance they had a car in the vicinity. It would arrive within fifteen minutes.

Next, Maggy scribbled her email address on a piece of scrap paper and retuned to Banger, now deep in conversation with a Ewan McGregor lookalike. Giving him a knowing wink, she slipped him the note and went to wait for the cab at the main gate.

On the way home, Maggy asked the driver to break her journey at The Sheraton and The Caledonian. It was a shot in the dark. At different times, she'd picked Dino up within the vicinity of both hotels. He might just be hanging around one of them. Unsurprisingly, neither of the receptionists had any recollection of anyone fitting his description.

Mercifully, Maggy always left a spare key under a stone hedgehog in the little rockery by the front door. She paid the driver from emergency funds stored in a Toby jug on the kitchen shelf, symbolically removed her hat and picked up her mail from the doormat.

Amongst some dreary mail from the Inland Revenue was a shiny coloured postcard of an idyllic beach: Sandy Lane, Barbados.

Curious, she picked it up. It couldn't be Una. Then who?

To her surprise:

> *Taking a wee break.*
> *Having a marvellous time.*
> *The girls don't want to go home!*
> *Love, Grace, Duncan, Lyndsay & Kara x*

It was in Duncan's handwriting. Grace never did kisses – or even postcards for that matter. It was dated ten days earlier. They'd be home and have settled back into their usual routine. What was that all about? Ah, well, she'd enough to worry about right now. At least they'd made contact.

Once she'd taken off her hat and jacket and exchanged her shoes for something comfier, Maggy poured herself a stiff whisky and flopped on to the sofa in the living room. Over the mantelpiece, the portrait of Don she had had commissioned as a fiftieth birthday present, stared down at her.

Was it her guilty conscience, or did he have a malicious look in his eye?

'Don't look at me like that,' she almost yelled at the canvas. 'I know I've been a stupid lassie,' but he carried on grinning in that *I told you so* way he'd assumed whenever she'd made a fool of herself.

Common sense should have advised Maggy to contact the police and cancel all her debit and credit cards immediately as a precautionary measure, but she was in the grip of a strange sense of denial. 'There'll be a ring' any minute now,' she told herself. 'Just you wait and see!'

A couple of hours passed with only one phone call: Banger to make sure she'd got home safely. Before he got into his stride, she quickly manufactured some story about Dino having borrowed the car for quarter of an hour to buy some pastilles for an incipient sore throat. When he'd returned, they'd decided to call it a day.

She wasn't to know that Banger knew she was acting and, having had his car radio playing during the journey home, was up-to-date with local news headlines. He made sympathetic noises and promised to check on her first thing in the morning.

Maggy replaced the receiver and switched off the answerphone. Let it ring. She didn't want to be bothered with anyone else that evening.

It wasn't until the clock struck ten that Maggy idly switched on the television. She was half listening, mindlessly flicking through *Radio Times* for spoilers, when the regional round-up began with a newsreader she hadn't seen before.

Terrible hair, Maggy thought. Had to be a wig.

Alex Salmond and Nicola Sturgeon appeared, acknowledging cheers at a meeting in Glasgow with soundbites from people happy to announce their voting intentions. No, she needed a little escapism. Looking up the night's TV schedules, Maggy was about to channel hop to a nostalgic repeat of *Dad's Army*, when The Wig returned and she heard her saying 'Dino Manzoni, one of the heirs to the Piedi Bei shoe dynasty, is today on his way back to Rome...' Maggy pricked up her ears, '...where he's wanted by the Italian authorities for suspected money-laundering.'

The *Radio Times* slid on to the Axminster.

The Wig continued, 'Manzoni was picked up earlier today by the police at Edinburgh Airport. After lengthy questioning, he was escorted to a plane back to Italy. Our reporter at the scene...'

There followed a clip of Dino, tired and tousled in a corridor, guarded by an airport official and what she took to be a policeman, yelling 'It is lies! It is not me!'

In the background – was she imagining it or was he also under escort…? Och, she'd know those shades anywhere and that jacket... 'My, oh my!' she muttered to herself.

Dino was now being led towards a departure gate, Beige Man, cufflinked to someone burly, following in the rear.

The Wig turned her chair to introduce an expert in a smart suit on a screen behind her, presumably in Milan, with the evening traffic silently moving, some distance behind him.

'Since the recession,' the man said, 'the mafia has been buying up legitimate businesses and properties through which to illegally process vast earnings from multimillion-euro cocaine and extortion rackets.'

Maggy had not been entirely serious when it had crossed her mind drugs could be involved in Dino's story, and even in her wildest dreams, not at this level.

'The authorities believe local politicians may also be involved. People who refuse to go along with the deals can be threatened with violence. They are so intimidated that only a handful of the many victims have appeared in court – although if they did, they'd be entitled to compensation. Their job is made easier if they can create a smoke screen by persuading people to borrow money from them to rent leases at cheap rates. Middlemen get a commission on any loan they sell. The companies targeted range from respectable commercial businesses to construction firms, fast-food restaurants – and even Milan's prized fashion industry…'

How had Dino got involved in this scam – and why had he been obliged to flee to Edinburgh?

Poor suggestible Dino.

Even now, Maggy was giving him the benefit of the doubt.

Concluding the interview, the man said, 'The Italian police are asking other victims to come forward and help them. The public need to get involved – but are often too frightened.'

Maggy, whose knowledge of the mafia was largely based on *The Godfather* and *Some Like It Hot*, not forgetting the abusive treatment meted out to poor Doris Day by James Cagney in – one of her mother's favourite desert island videos – *Love Me or Leave Me*, was appalled to realise such practices continued to this day and age. Even in Italy.

The Wig re-materialised, smiled sweetly and moved on to inform her audience of an egg price scandal in Aberdeen, with the same degree of gravity she might have used for announcing Obama's sanctions against Russia.

Bedtime at last. Maggy couldn't concentrate on her book. Sometimes even E L James's deathless prose failed to invoke Hypnos. Sleep came patchily. She kept thinking about Dino.

Where was he – and what would happen to him?

Eventually she dozed off again, only to be re-awoken an hour later by irrational fears. The cycle repeated itself throughout the night.

The next morning, her head a little clearer, the word 'bank' flickered into it like an irritating screen prompt. She'd been so stupid, it was the first thing she should have checked. What on earth had she been thinking about? Was it that the thought of Dino, now languishing in a gloomy cell, had evoked pity and temporarily obscured her reason?

Mercifully, Maggy had only put one card into her 'smart' bag. She scurried into the den and logged in to her online account. Surprise, surprise, a single amount that, she guessed, would have just about covered the cost of a single cheap plane ticket, showed up on her statement. Had someone once said something about fresh air?

Common sense finally prevailed. She rang to cancel the card and order a new one.

She had no sooner put down her phone when it vibrated again. As he'd promised, it was the faithful Banger. This time, Maggy poured her heart out to him. Of all her friends, he was the one person she instinctively knew would understand. Whilst recognising there were things going on in Dino's life that didn't bear investigation, she also sensed that Banger, too, was reluctant to think badly of him. 'Keep an open mind for the time being,' was his concluding advice.

It wasn't until late afternoon that the doorbell rang. Maggy opened it to find a tall, good-looking young policeman with neat, hay-coloured hair, on the step.

'Mrs Galbraith?'

It went through Maggy's mind, even in her current downbeat state, that if she was to be arrested, now was the time.

The man, who was accompanied by a woman support officer, introduced himself and his colleague. There's nothing to worry about,' he said, smiling, 'we're just returning…' Here they stepped aside, to reveal the Audi on the road below, all in one piece.

'You've found it!'

'We tried to leave a message but couldn't. Normally, we'd ask you to come and collect the car yourself, but as we were both on our way home and neither of us lives far away, we decided to drop it off. It's been given a thorough going-over for finger prints and so on. I hope the boys haven't disturbed things too much. You'll be pleased to see it again.'

'Erm… yes.' To be truthful, Maggy wasn't so sure. Despite its second-hand market value, a small part of her had dared to hope she was finally rid of the cumbersome vehicle. Also, it now held bitter-sweet memories of the recent past.

'And, of course, there's this…'

Maggy was just thinking how dark blue uniforms really suited so many women, when the young woman held up her lost handbag. That she *was* pleased to have returned. Handing it to her the PCSO said reassuringly, 'I don't think much has been taken, but only you would know.'

Maggy had only put in a few essentials: keys, diary, make-up purse, comb, handkerchief, a wallet containing a few notes, and the debit card – which, of course, was missing. Everything else was there as far as she could remember. It was then that she remembered that, although she had committed it to memory, she always pencilled in her current password in the back of her diary. She wouldn't make that mistake again.

'There are one or two other things we'd like to check with you too,' the young constable said taking a small notebook out of his pocket. 'And we need to get you to sign a routine form. I don't suppose we could…?'

Maggy suddenly remembered her manners. 'Coffee?'

'A quick one would be most welcome.'

Over steaming mugs of Nescafé, the well-meaning duo attempted to put Maggy's mind at rest but emphasised the need for her to talk to her bank. She smiled gratefully though kept her own counsel, simply saying 'At this stage, I've no intention of pressing charges.'

'But if …'

'Of course. If. And *if* it was a large amount. Well then, yes...' Though she doubted it, she thought. Maggy asked them if they had any information on Dino, but they weren't involved in the case and had simply volunteered to return her possessions. 'You could try ringing the airport police later,' the young woman said, scribbling some names and numbers on the back of a card for her.

The afternoon's diversion seemed to be going well until the man casually threw in: 'Oh, and there's the little matter of the motor insurance…'

Maggy's heart skipped a beat. 'Yes?' She opened her eyes wide.

'We wanted to put to rest one final matter,' he said. 'I mean, you *are* the sole insured, aren't you?'

'Oh, of course,' Maggy said, flashing her Felicity Kendal smile.

'Then that clears that up,' he said, ticking the point off in his notebook.

Phew! Although she later fretted that her response might not have helped Dino's case.

Once the police had left, Maggy continued unscrambling her confused feelings about the Italian. She was, and would remain for some time, haunted by questions she couldn't yet answer. Would she ever see or hear from Dino again?

Did she want to?

She'd do as the support officer suggested.

Later.

In the meantime, a small voice told her to keep faith.

Que sera, sera.

∽๑๑๛

TWENTY-SEVEN

The Road to Oz

ೋ ೊ

'I'M glad you came back. I wondered what had happened to you,' Casey said.

'I've been in a very bad place.'

'Again?'

'Yes. I thought with your help I'd almost kicked it, but...' Grace shrugged.

She hadn't slept properly in Barbados. Not because of the heat. It was one of the best hotels on the island and had excellent air conditioning. She'd tossed and turned, dragged down by guilt and helplessness.

Nothing could wipe out the regret that gnawed away at her for involving a total stranger in her silly, impromptu scheme and going through with it. Silently harbouring negative emotions was one thing; lashing out so publicly had been vicious and undignified. Grace saw that now. In doing so, she'd lost any moral high ground she might have once had. Also, despite – or possibly due to – pussyfooting around whilst they were away, neither Grace nor her husband had found the courage to get into the open the sensitive matters that badly needed discussion.

She wasn't friendly with any of Duncan's colleagues, or their wives – at least, not well enough to enjoy exchanges on Facebook. And he only used LinkedIn, saying he never had time to indulge himself on social sites. For the moment, she knew he was unaware of her recent posting. Yet inevitably, sooner or later he'd find out. She was terrified at the thought of his reactions when that happened, and how it might damage his respect for her. Continued anxiety had obliged Grace, reluctantly, to visit Casey again.

'Still, Barbados sounds lovely,' Casey said.

'It was,' said Grace. 'I've never seen the girls so happy.'

'Was it your idea?'

'No, Duncan's,' Grace said. 'He's been amazing.'

Casey blinked with surprise.

'So... and did it work?'

'What?'

'The letter.'

'Ah. In the end I… didn't send it.'

'Sorry?'

'I did something awful before I could,' Grace said. 'It was in a fit of blind rage. 'So unlike me too. At the time I thought I could handle the fallout. But I can't. And as I said, Duncan's been a saint. He probably guesses I've done something I regret but knows me well enough not to challenge me. Which is part of the problem.'

'Last time, I sensed you were still in pain and had hoped it was residual, but it seems there's still a block there,' Casey said. 'Do you think your discomfort simply gets worse the longer you keep putting off apologising for… whatever it was? I mean, this *something awful*, would you like to tell me about it?'

Grace took a deep breath. She tried hard to make the events of that afternoon sound as if sharing a video on social media of your sixty-plus mother flirting with her toy-boy in a public place was regular sport for most people, but not herself. It wasn't as if she used Facebook often she explained. But it was a way of keeping up with all her college friends and, more recently, colleagues whom she no longer had time to see. And yes, she occasionally shared pictures of the twins with members of her own and Duncan's families.

When she'd finished, the look Casey gave Grace indicated she wasn't totally persuaded by her story. Grace went on 'You see, I'm confused. Sometimes I wonder why I should feel so badly about my mother. At other times, her continued behaviour seems totally unacceptable. As on that afternoon.'

'You said *seems*,' Casey said. 'How do you know that what she was doing that day *was* unacceptable?'

'Which, I suppose, is why I'm in such a muddle,' Grace said. 'Tackling her face-to-face would make me sound self-justifying, and her feel smug. Besides, cosy daughter-mother unburdening sessions aren't something we do. Correction, *can* do. There's… something, well… lacking in me.'

If there was an almost imperceptible smile of triumph on Casey's normally Sphinx-like face, Grace didn't notice. Like most people who considered themselves serious-minded, Grace believed being tough on herself was a virtue.

'You may be right. It could all have been a storm in a teacup,' Grace said, 'and I may be imagining Mum has taken it worse than I ever quite intended her to. On the other hand, it's possible she never even saw the clip.'

'Have you any idea at all what Duncan thinks of this on-going stand-off with your mother?' Casey said.

'Only that I should find a way of clearing the air.'

'And could you?'

As his wife struggled to make peace with herself in Cumberland Street, in The Amorous Prawn, a new fish restaurant off Hanover Street, Duncan tucked into his seafood cocktail.

It had been a surprise when his boss, Sam, emailed inviting him out for a late lunch. What's going on here, he'd wondered? Could it possibly mean promotion? Then, remembering how, a few days before, he'd been rather surly to Sam's overbearingly efficient PA, a seemingly ridiculous but nonetheless horrible thought had struck him. Supposing his bad manners had led to… gardening leave? Muttering 'silly cow' under his breath as he'd stormed off hadn't, possibly, helped forward his career; but could it have, remotely, been considered… harassment? He wouldn't put it past the woman to go down that route. Stupid b…

No. He was becoming paranoid. Then, what was this all about?

'I've been meaning to make time for a leisurely catch-up with you, for some time,' Sam said after some introductory small-talk, offering him a plate of wafer-thin brown bread and butter slices. 'Glad you were free.'

'It makes a nice change,' Duncan said, carefully negotiating a slice of the fragile bread, to prevent grease getting on the silk tie he'd put on especially for what was now confirmed as a business meeting. 'Things have been piling up a bit. It's good to relax for an hour.' Though given the way his heart was quietly pumping, how could he?

'I've noticed how hard you've been working recently and,' Sam paused significantly, 'if I'm not mistaken, looking as if things have been getting a bit on top of you, eh?'

'Actually…'

'That's not a criticism, I hasten to add. You've been turning in excellent work, as always, but…'

So not redundancy, Duncan thought. A 'but' however.

Sam must have sensed Duncan's tension. He hurried on '… increasingly furrowed brows etcetera. Know what I mean? I'd hoped your holiday might help, but it doesn't look as if it has. Has it?'

Duncan took a large swallow of chilled Chablis. 'Sorry,' he said. 'We've had some family issues. I've tried hard not to bring my problems to work.'

'And I've no remit to poke my nose in where it's not wanted, either. Whatever it is, it's your own affair. You're a great asset to the department, as you know. It is simply part of my job to ensure everyone is ticking over nicely and, should they be having any problems, it's not because we're piling on too much pressure. If so – or if, say, there are health matters – we'll try and see if we can support you in any way.'

'That's very considerate.'

Sam wasn't far off retirement. Overweight, balding but expensively suited and a focused yet pragmatic director, he was a survivor from a more paternalistic era. Duncan could loosen up a little now, knowing his job wasn't on the line, yet he sensed there must be more to this summons, however affable it appeared. Sam held too much responsibility to spend a couple of hours wining and dining a younger colleague – unless he had something up his sleeve.

'And my PA's noticed too…'

Of course she had.

Sam gave him a knowing wink.

'Nothing that won't sort itself out,' Duncan threw off, trying to dismiss the matter as brightly as he could, whilst crossing his fingers under the table.

'Good.' Sam didn't sound convinced but wanted to move on to the main item. 'Because I'd like to share something which may or may not grab you.' Here he spooned up and appreciatively chewed his last piece of crayfish, then wiped his mouth with finality and sat back. '

This was it.

'Adelaide,' Sam simply said.

Duncan looked puzzled. 'Australia?'

'No, Tristan da Cunha.'

Duncan gave a polite, amused grunt.

'Seriously, have you ever been there?'

'Tristan da Cunha no, but I once visited friends in Tasmania. And my wife's uncle and his family live in Sydney. Not that we're in contact much.'

'Then at least you know a bit about Oz and have people there. Good start. Quite a distance from one city to the other, but…'

'Sorry?'

'I wanted to see if you'd be interested in working there?'

Duncan was taken aback. 'For a couple of weeks, a month…?'

'Six months. If things of mutual benefit develop, maybe a year. Or even longer.'

'Oh.' Not a proper 'oh' so much as an involuntary glottal stop as his brain attempted to take in this information.

'A swap.' Sam continued. 'Initially. One of their people would sit in your desk here and vice versa. Simple as that. A representative from one of their highly regarded city construction companies came over whilst you were away to see... well, me. I considered bringing you in on it then, but decided to look into the feasibility of the idea before...'

'Surprising me?'

Sam smiled indulgently and went on: 'They do a lot of work for the city's Planning & Development department. Sharing ideas on neighbourhood re-thinking, infrastructure, architectural restoration and so on. If I'm a bit vague, it's because the final details are yet to be agreed. But it occurred to me that it was right up your street, so to speak...' Here he chortled at the professional chestnut. Duncan grinned somewhat apprehensively back. 'I wanted to give you first refusal. It is important for us – both companies – to broaden our global vision. Awareness raising... interaction and all that. Pinch some of their ideas if they are good ones – with permission of course – and vice versa. All above board. Get it?'

Duncan was taken aback but interested all the same.

'Your salary would be suitably adjusted to ensure you weren't out of pocket, and my diligent assistant...' – was that another knowing look Sam gave him? – '... has been surfing like a woman possessed, investigating pleasant suburban areas where you could rent somewhere for the duration. Even better, you and – Bob, I think his name is – might even consider swapping houses? Depends on how many rooms each of you needs.'

Something clicked.

'*Bob*? You mean we've both already been selected?'

'Only if you both fancy it. Your job here is quite safe. But...' This is where the thumb screws get ever-so-gently applied, Duncan thought. '...It wouldn't do your career any harm – and think what a great experience it would be for the family?'

If the first part of that last sentence was the kind of comment his father might have made, the second rang a louder bell. 'How long have I got to decide?

'End of the week okay?'

Duncan gulped.

All that money, Grace thought, and in the end, Casey's thrown the ball back entirely in my court. Well, what did she expect? At least she'd acted as a helpful sounding board.

As she opened the front door, Grace heard first Vicky's voice, then Duncan's. They greeted one another and he explained how he'd been out to lunch with Sam, and then been encouraged to take the rest of the afternoon off.

'You had a good time?'

'Actually …'

'It's like that then.'

Vicky had obviously picked up on Duncan's body language. 'My cue to depart,' she said, easing on her coat.

Grace uneasily removed her own and saw her friend to the front door. 'Thank you, Vicky. You've been such a good friend over the past few weeks. Don't know how I'd have got through them without you.' As she wandered down the path, Vicky hugged herself. Grace rarely dispensed that degree of open-heartedness.

Back in the living room, the girls settled for the time being, Duncan patted the spare seat cushion on the sofa.

'Grace,' he began, 'we really need to talk.'

At last.

A large brown envelope from the BBC arrived for Maggy.

Banger had been as good as his word. What with one thing and another, their chat had completely slipped her mind.

The auditions were scheduled for the end of September. Normally such matters would have been initiated and dealt with by an agent, but Maggy's short-lived acting career had never necessitated one. She would have been flattered to know the strings that had been pulled to generate the invitation. More needy actors would have killed for such an opportunity.

Maggy cast her eye over the letter, then pinned it to the noticeboard in the kitchen where it was soon buried beneath: the refuse collection schedule, postcards from assorted holiday destinations – and a small print of Edward Henry Potthast's *On the Beach* from the Brooklyn Museum. The latter had not long arrived from Una, who was currently staying with a niece in New York. The rest of the envelope's contents – the synopsis and extracts from three of Mrs Gordon's scenes – were placed on the second step of the staircase to be placed, later, for safekeeping in her desk upstairs.

✧✦✧

TWENTY-EIGHT

Designs for Living

৯ৈ ৎ৵

'GET ready!' one of the guards commanded, as his friend chained Flora's wrists and led her outside 'You're off to the Tower of London, young lady.'

Trotting after his mistress, Jock was about to leap into the cart with her, when the other man bent down and grabbed him by the rough collar they had forced him to wear.

'Whoa! Where d'ya ken you're goin'?' he said.

'Is he no' goin' with us or are we keepin' him here?' asked the other.

'He's no use here any longer and will only be a nuisance o' the journey. Will you shoot the varmint, or shall I?'

Jock barked and wriggled, desperately trying to free himself, but the man only increased his vice-like grip on the collar, almost strangling him.

Flora started crying.

'Ya dinnae want her greetin' all the way to London,' the softer spoken of the two men intervened. 'Imagine ten days o' that?'

Had he been spared? It appeared so, for five minutes later he found himself sitting at Flora's feet in the cart, keeping a wary eye on the burly man guarding them.

He didn't trust him either. Not one little bit.

They were sunbathing on a grassy spot on Calton Hill. It was Saturday. With the sun beating down, the hill was a hot spot for young tourists. Its panoramic views overlooked the length of Princes Street to the right, the sweep of the Firth of Forth behind them, whilst the velvety heights of Salisbury Crags and Arthur's Seat provided a dramatic backdrop beyond the valley ahead.

The Festival was getting into its stride. A heightened atmosphere pervaded the city. Student types wandered past, exposing enticing expanses of flesh, unselfconsciously lending sensual promise to the hazy afternoon.

Ewan was finessing a drawing of Jock looking up at Flora. She was stroking him as best she could with her chained hand. Suggesting the swaying cart had been a challenge. He mustn't overdo the background. Ewan was working out how he could frame one side of the illustration with a shaded silhouette of one of the guards; maybe with the barrel of a pistol directly aligned to Jock's terrified eyes – or would that be going over the top?

Local gossip had been responsible for Flora's arrest following Charlie's escape. After being held in Dunstaffnage Castle, she – and, in Ally's version of the events, Jock – were taken to London and imprisoned until the Act of Indemnity was passed the following year.

Ewan was fascinated to discover the long distances people travelled in the days before the introduction of the railway. Flora's life, after her marriage in 1750 to her kinsman Allan MacDonald, continued to be packed with danger and drama. They had gone on to spend an eventful period in North America, before finally sailing home. And found time to raise five sons and two daughters as well.

With Ewan's help, Ally had sent a sample chapter, synopsis, and illustrations to several publishers. Although she'd been told it would take weeks, even months, before they got any feedback, she'd received a quick response from one small company which specialised in children's fiction. The editor found the submission 'promising' whilst regretting 'we've enough historically-themed books on our list right now; but keep submitting, we won't forget you!'

A non-committal acknowledgement from another firm advised 'we use our own illustrators.'

'Tough', Ally said, '*Jock* is a joint effort. They take both or neither of us.'

Inevitably, as their collaboration developed, Ewan and Ally were seeing more of each other. A charming portfolio of sketches was accumulating for what was now called *Jacobite Jock*.

The impact of Paige and Cal's behaviour, not only on Ewan's own life but most recently on Ally's recovery, had helped encourage the bond between them. It was something else they shared. They were both victims of other people's poor behaviour. Unfortunately, Ally's vulnerability had added to her attraction for Ewan. Like Jamie, Ally was very different from Paige and, especially with her hair now cut very short, looked quite boyish. Ewan had a nagging feeling he needed to test the new ground further, to see if his growing affection for Ally was any more than the upsurge of shared creative juices. It hadn't dawned on him that his liberation might lead him to behave, if not very badly, at least thoughtlessly.

Like many people who regain their freedom after a time in the wilderness, Ewan wasn't yet at the stage where he could clearly think through self-created cause and effects. He was a child again, with a large box of chocolates, wanting to try all the different centres before deciding on his favourite – but in danger of making himself sick.

Despite all he knew about Ally, he'd ignored all the warning signals.

The previous evening things had come to a head.

Ewan was at Lorna's flat watching Ally type at the desk. Moved by the combination of prettiness and industriousness, he'd moved quietly up to the back of her chair and lightly placed his hands on the sides of her shoulders.

'No!' Ally said, startled. 'Please... Don't be silly!'

'Sorry?' Ewan said disingenuously.

'That's inappropriate.'

'I only touched you; very gently!'

'Well, don't!'

'I'm growing to like you Ally. You must realise that.'

'Yes, but...'

'But...?'

'Firstly, you're with Jamie,' she said.

'So...'

'You're an item! Do you think – even if I *was* drawn to you in that way – I'm the sort of person who'd behave like that with someone who's already in a relationship? Especially when I'm friendly with both people?'

'Well...'

'I'm growing fond of you, of course...' Ally chose her next words carefully. '...but in a... sisterly way. I'll get angry if you carry on behaving idiotically. Don't try to compromise what we already have. It's important to me as it is: a very amicable... business arrangement.'

Ewan flinched at the word 'business'.

'And secondly...,' Ally said, 'since I was... attacked,' her tone softened, 'the idea of physical contact is very difficult. With anyone.'

'That was... three years ago?' Ewan said.

'Nevertheless. She swallowed. 'How can I explain... I... I still get an oppressive, suffocating sensation when anyone gets too close to me. I'm learning to control it better, but...'

'It won't last for ever. Will it?'

'The doctor hopes I'll grow out of it eventually. And I'm making considerable progress. When I think what I was like when I arrived in Edinburgh fifteen months ago, needing my laptop and notepad to fall back on; whilst now I can even conduct a tricky conversation – like this – without help. That's largely due to Lorna...and you, too.' She gave him a wry smile. '...When you have a stroke, a part of you is killed off. I suppose it's something like that with me. I've not lost my need of friends. I need them more than ever. I just can't cope with…'

'Physical intimacy at any level?' Ewan prompted. 'Not even to show affection?'

Ally nodded and looked sad. 'Perhaps I'll get over it… some day. I don't know. I really appreciate what we have. But it must be totally, I mean *totally* platonic.'

'I… think I understand,' Ewan said.

'I hope so. I'd hate to lose you.'

'You won't. I'm sorry, I'll behave in future. I've been a fool.'

'Yes. But a kind and… talented fool. Look, Jamie's a really lovely guy, and a far better bet than me for…' struggling to find the right words, Ally let her sentence trail meaningfully away. 'Don't mess things up by being…'

'Greedy?'

She smiled again as if she hoped he'd got the message.

Afterwards, when he'd had a chance to think over their conversation, Ewan realised how meeting Ally had side-tracked him just as he'd begun to refocus his life after his split with Paige. Strangely, this emotional hiccup and his talk with her about it had helped clear his mind and get him back on track.

Jamie had read Ewan's thoughts. 'Hello, there! he said, waving a hand in front of Ewan's face. 'I'd like to talk, when you've a moment.'

Ewan held up his drawing. 'What d'you reckon?'

'Lovely, Mr Shepard.'

'I wish.'

'Now. Where do things stand between us?' Jamie said

Ewan took his time packing away his sketching materials. In an Alan Bennett voice, he said, 'Mm, I wonder what Piglet is doing?'

'*Ewan!*'

'Right,' Ewan fastened the buckle on his small canvas bag. 'I'm all yours.'

'If only.'

'Ah, so that's it. Funny, as well…'

'Hilarious.'

'I meant funny, because, well… I'd been thinking around that too,' Ewan continued.

'Was it a good or bad think?'

Ewan looked uncomfortable.

'I'd just like to be reassured,' Jamie continued, 'that you and

Ally…'

'Cliché alert! – we're just good friends. Honestly.'

'Then you still intend to move into my… *our* flat? You've no… other plans. I mean, it really is just us from now on, or…?'

'I've told you…'

But Jamie's concerns were irreversibly tumbling out. 'Sorry. I don't want to pressurise you with all this, but I'm feeling a wee bitty insecure.'

'You don't have to worry, I promise you.'

Although Jamie thought he had worked out Ewan's dilemma, he knew it was still early days for them both. Whilst they'd initially grown close quite rapidly, they still had a lot to know about each other. Ewan's post-Paige fragility and, more recently, his exploration of, possibly, another relationship running in tandem with their own, had pulled him up sharply. Jamie couldn't compete with a woman. Also, he was concerned that Ewan might become like other men he knew who wanted their love-life both ways, and put concurrent relationships into distinct compartments: Men and Women – unable to see how, by doing so, they risked devaluing the coinage of both.

'Of course, I love her *too* – but that's an entirely different matter,' they'd say.

How *different*? Discuss.

After Ewan had recounted his conversation with Ally, suitably edited, the men sat in contemplative silence for some minutes. Then Ewan said, 'If you're prepared to continue putting up with me, I'd like us to carry on as we are. It wasn't as if Ally had usurped you. It was that…'

'You wanted your haggis and deep-fried pizza as well?'

'That's sort of what she said, but not as poetically. She's on your side, you know. But, if you don't object and she still wants me as an illustrator, I'd like to see the *Jock* project through?'

'Of course.' Jamie replied, hiding the discomfort generated by the inference that he may have won the game, but only because the other contestant had withdrawn from the field.

'Knowing me has also lumbered you with socialising with Lorna from time to time,' Ewan went on. 'And then there's Senga. Although that situation may still be a bit awkward for Ally.'

'You underestimate my capacity for friendship,' Jamie said, aware that in trying to be magnanimous he was sounding pompous. His face then eased into a grin. 'Don't worry, I feel really at home with Lorna. And Ally's a smart – and brave – lass. I don't know Senga well yet, but I'm sure we'll all get along.' He'd only met Senga once and, as it happened, found her rather intense, but then she had a lot to cope with at present.

'Goodness knows, you took to my mates quickly enough. And even if we like some people more than others well, we cannae be bessies with everyone. Let's face it, other people's friends *can* be a problem. But look how you and dour Ian get along – and he's impossible sometimes!' Jamie's voice modulated. 'Just so long as…'

'What?'

'You won't be hurt if…'

Ewan wondered what was coming.

'I think you already know this, but…'

'Go on.'

'…if I'm … mildly gregarious in my own way too … just occasionally?' Jamie said, with a pointed smile.

Ewan was half-prepared for this. So far, they'd been faithful to each other, but he'd seen the way Jamie looked at other men when they were out and about – and how they returned his gaze. At the same time, he could appreciate that, until he'd really sorted himself out, Jamie needed to flag up a fall-back position.

'If I do occasionally chat up other guys,' Jamie elaborated, 'it doesn't mean I care about you any the less. It's the way I am. Sociable. The way many of us are. Probably you too – or will be when you finally come to terms with yourself. You know I'd never do anything to put you at risk – or threaten what we have. I'd always tell you too – and promise not to be a drama queen if I caught you snogging a pretty lassie, in a dark corner, either. And if we one day decided to take things further… well, we'd both agree on the ramifications of that too.'

Ewan smiled back. It was good that they could be so open with each other. In some ways, what Jamie said took some of the pressure off them both – for now – whilst holding out the promise of something more binding if, finally, they decided to stay together.

It was a bizarre new world Ewan had entered; one of strange bargains, codes of behaviour – and sometimes short, emotional shelf-lives. Yet sometimes, if he had read what Jamie had said correctly, as couples acquired greater respect for each other, a deeper sense of commitment might follow.

∽∻

TWENTY-NINE

Disentangling

ॐ ॐ

A few days later, Ewan met Paige in a coffee shop.
Cal was planning to move in with her soon after the Festival; but this was dependent on Ewan agreeing to accept an arrangement whereby she would hand over to him a chunk of her savings, in recognition of his past contribution to the flat and its contents. Cal's decision – if he hadn't had it made for him – allowed Ewan to turn his back on Great King Street for ever. He was sad, though, to be leaving behind his statue of Persephone. Maybe his mother could find her a home?

Ewan was also aware he had let Paige off lightly, but if things didn't work out longer-term with Jamie, the money would help with a deposit on a small place of his own. But he'd worry about that should it happen. He was beginning to regret his foolish behaviour with Ally, but trying to make things right with Jamie had at least brought him to his senses.

When Paige first heard Ewan was living with a man, the thought it might be anything but a business arrangement hadn't crossed her mind. Then bitchy Barnie had swanned into the office one Monday morning and astounded her with: 'Could that possibly have been your ex-hubby I saw starry-eyed and nursing a highball in The Claremont on Saturday night with an... mmm… rather *exotic* creature?'

The reactions of Snow White's stepmother to the mirror's heresy couldn't have compared with Paige's outrage when she'd twigged. Notwithstanding it was she who had driven *him* away, she saw Ewan's moving in with another man as the ultimate insult.

Paige coped with her mortification by telling everyone she'd guessed all along. Ewan's turning out to be that-way-inclined was the only explanation for his rejection of her. It was a mercy she'd found an Alpha male to appreciate her as she deserved. For the time being.

She was already discovering that the size of Cal's brain was, sadly, disproportionate to the more immediately useful parts of his body, but she needed a lodger: her salary wouldn't cover the expenses of the flat, her social life and the AGA cooker she had her eye on. She was also starting to miss Ewan's ability to hold an intelligent conversation – despite having rarely agreed with him.

Browsing Sainsbury's freezer cabinets for items that might tickle her mother's taste buds, Senga thought how strange it was that you cruised calmly down the river for ages, then all at once several powerful vessels came along and chopped up the waters around you.

At any other time, juggling her various responsibilities would have been tricky. As things had turned out – not that she'd have wished her mother's current predicament upon her – in strange ways they had proved fortuitous. Converting her currently confused feelings into positive energy fuelled Senga's work as Nora's carer. Washing, cooking and helping her mother in and out of baths and bed was tiring, but earned Nora's gratitude, giving her a sense of achievement that enabled her to sleep soundly.

By now both Senga and Cal were reconciled to giving up management of the Balfour and finding alternative employment. There was a good chance the owners might be able to help them, but they required jobs in separate establishments, and would most probably have to work as assistants to other people. Cal expected to serve notice on their old quarters elsewhere in Stockbridge, and move in with Paige within weeks.

In her head, Senga had come around to accepting that Cal's infatuation with Paige was more serious than any of his previous extra-marital liaisons, but her heart was still in denial. Even without her commitment to the promise she'd made to Aileen, the thought of continual separation created an aching void.

Some nights she dreamt Cal was simply away on a course, or that she'd sent him away for a period of atonement. He'd come back to her soon and they'd carry on their lives together as if nothing had happened. Then she awoke to the harsh reality. Whether the Paige bug – she thought of the woman as a rare virus – lasted or not, she must face up to their no longer being a couple – at least in the short term.

Lorna, always outspoken, had touched on Senga's thoughts about a possible divorce. Senga imagined it must be rather like the loss of a loved one. Theoretically, you accepted the finality whilst staring helplessly into a huge, dark pit. Something, possibly forever beyond reach, remained trapped there never to go away. Whilst she had sworn never to break her promise to watch over Cal, Senga knew the matter could be taken out of her hands. Paige, she understood, had ways of getting whatever she wanted.

For as long as she wanted it, anyway.

Senga reflected on the moral choices people made and the bounds of loyalty – or was that *bonds*? Were they like the tensile strength of metals that eventually snapped if overheated or frozen? At what point did they disintegrate and how compatible were her self-imposed obligations with her personal concepts of duty? Would she ever permit herself to irretrievably let go of Cal?

As with Ewan and Ally, Senga was grateful for the companionship of the people who had recently appeared in her life and were helping her build a bridge from her old routine to an uncertain future. In some ways, the fact that they were all new to each other meant that none of them came to the friendships with pre-conceived views and expectations. They could concentrate on the things they had in common.

Senga shared Lorna and Ally's love of literature. Not as academic in her choice of fiction as the professional librarian, but less sentimental than the would-be children's novelist, for many years her taste in reading matter had been governed by the limitations of Arran Library. Unlike her friends, fiction had been, if not exactly a guilty secret, her primary means of escape.

Whilst most of her old neighbours and friends on Arran were well-educated and intelligent, they were fundamentally practical, outdoorsy people, the local economy being based on tourism, farming and forestry. They read, of course, but for most of them fiction didn't provide the same degree of mental protein it did for Ally, Lorna and herself.

Senga had recently been making connections between her current situation and that of some of her heroes. Jane Eyre had held out through one vicissitude after another to ultimately claim her, by then, handicapped suitor. And Pierre – as portrayed in the old, maligned but, so far, only Hollywood version of *War and Peace*, which she'd first been introduced to during a Russian Studies course in the Fifth form – had gone through hell and high water to win Natasha.

The character she most closely identified with was Thackeray's Captain Dobbin who, after having his patience and passion tested almost beyond endurance for eight hundred pages by *Vanity Fair*'s vacuous Amelia Sedley, was finally united with his *tender little parasite.*

Empty-headedness was probably all Cal and Miss Sedley had in common, but Senga, like Dobbin, had a deep-rooted sense of duty. Yet the point at which love ended and duty began was often fuzzy. Cal would tire of Paige eventually – or maybe it would be the other way around. After which he would become terribly needy. Wouldn't he?

On the other hand, did she want to be Dobbin for ever?

Senga was growing closer to Lorna and, from little things that had slipped out, sensed Lorna's disappointment that Ally couldn't be as much to her as she would have liked. Sooner or later Ally would probably be secure enough both psychologically and financially to want her independence again. She and Ally had not seen each other since the incident in the Balfour and had yet to meet up and, hopefully, reignite their friendship. Maybe an opportunity would arise before too long. Senga had always liked Ally.

It had recently crossed her mind that, if all else failed, she might one day end up sharing her life with another woman. Although, like Ally, she'd welcome the companionship, but probably not require anything more. But would that be fair? Oh, why was life so complex? For now, certainly all Senga desired was sisterly support.

Time must untangle this…

Maggy was taking back more of the reins of her life. Una had joined her at an obscure European play early in the Festival. Over pre-show drinks, Maggy had finally opened up to her about her Dino escapade and how, for a while, he'd brought some zest back into her life.

'So, that explains that Facebook thingy,' Una said. 'I've been dying to know about it – but you've been as closed as a clam!'

Maggy was glad to get the episode off her chest and was amused that Una was not only sympathetic but positively envious. Why hadn't she told her friend earlier?

And why was she still resisting the grip of some higher authority, some final restraint from which her mind was unwilling to release her? It wasn't that, in life, Don had ever been noticeably managing. Her husband, highly intelligent, usually more laidback than herself, had been far too subtle for that. Indeed, it was she whom friends accused of being the control freak. But there had always been a special understanding a bond between them which, despite his passing, remained. And although that was now easing and she was aware of a greater sense of independence, there was still some way to go.

Glancing at a particularly dreary planter Fiona and Josh had once given her, now supporting sunflowers out on the patio, Maggy was reminded of her promise to invite the Andersons for lunch. Maggy always kept her promises. Thinking of how amiable but predictable conversation with them would be, it occurred to her that this was the excuse she was looking for.

It would be short notice, but she might try to extend her hospitality and make the occasion her official 'coming back' party, another step in her journey towards rehabilitation. It was high time she hosted an occasion to bring people together. Ewan and Lorna had made new friends. What better way to meet them?

Back in the day, the Galbraiths' Festival patio parties were renowned. Why not risk the unreliable Scottish weather and go for a barbecue?

After checking dates with Fiona, Maggy ran the idea past Ewan, without whose support such an event would be difficult. He reminded her that Josh always took charge of maintaining the grill at his own home. Perfect! Then the men could work together and she could don her golden-granny hostess routine and let everyone else appear to be doing all the work.

If Maggy had initially been considerably taken aback by Ewan's admission concerning his new living arrangements, she also knew, deep down, that the pairing didn't come as a total surprise. There had, however, followed some stern talking to herself and mental readjustment – and, in some way she'd felt glad that Don had no longer been around when it happened. Not that Don had ever been remotely homophobic, but whilst he had long grown to accept Lorna's way of life, he might have unnecessarily fretted that the Ewan/Jamie development was, in some way, due to his own inadequacies as a parent. She looked forward to meeting Jamie and deciding for herself how successful the relationship was likely to be.

Both men were delighted to be invited. Ewan always got on well with Fiona and Josh. Yet, when Maggy told him her next port of call was Lorna and, hopefully, Ally who she also wanted to meet, Ewan had swallowed hard. Although he'd sent Ally several new sketches recently, he hadn't met her face-to-face since their embarrassing conversation and was uncertain how the land lay. Also, he was aware that Jamie and Ally had yet to get to know each other better. Maybe this was a chance for them all to move on. If anyone could make a party swing, it was his mother.

Lorna asked if she could invite Senga. As a professional caterer, she was bound to fit in, explaining that although Senga could occasionally be dour and secretive, she also combined a strong sense of decency with a good sense of humour. Lorna thought Senga would welcome a few hours away from her mother, who was a nice enough woman but becoming somewhat demanding of Senga's time. It was high time she sorted things out with Ally too – and vice-versa.

All it needed now was for the weather to be kind.

⊷⊶

THIRTY

Social Whirl

⊰⊱

THE day turned out warm and sunny. Weekends during the Festival usually were – as Maggy always, knowingly, informed guests.

Wee Ian from next door – actually, he was six feet four – had helped her get the garden back into shape after a summer of virtual neglect. It took a couple of days, but the shrubs were now pruned and stalwart dahlias and late roses provided focus colour, augmented by newly-trimmed beds stuffed with salvias and penstemons she'd rescued from the cut-price trestles in the Garden Centre. Tubs of hanging-in-there geraniums kept company with the burgeoning sunflowers on the patio and, not to be outdone, clumps of budding white chrysanthemums and early Michaelmas daisies kept watch in the background.

After a good wipe-down, the garden furniture looked as smart as when given to them by Archie and Doris on their silver wedding anniversary. Could it really have been fifteen years ago? The chairs with their pink and blue striped canvas seats always gave the rear garden a festive, but tasteful, air.

'You get what you pay for in this world,' Doris had said. Maggy was obliged to admit she'd been right.

Having the furthest to travel, the Andersons arrived early. Fuelled by their first few swigs of granny's special lemonade, Maggy let Fiona settle conversationally into the swing seat and gave Josh time to consider how best to get the barbecue going on the paving outside the French window.

The lads arrived ten minutes later. Maggy took to Jamie immediately. Ewan greeted Josh warmly and offered to help him with the grill. Not long after, Ally and Senga turned up. Knowing something of their backstories, Maggy guessed they might be harder work.

Ally was only too aware that, partly due to her conduct – as she had convinced herself – on that fateful afternoon in the Balfour, Senga was now estranged from Cal. When she'd discovered Cal's involvement in Ewan and Paige's break-up too, she'd felt even more uncomfortable. Of course, she wasn't really responsible for either split but, nonetheless, being Ally, she imagined an unspoken tension between herself and Senga. Although Lorna had by now come clean about having – as she put it – 'bumped into' Senga – they'd not discussed how a rapprochement might be achieved.

It therefore said a lot about both women that, when Senga contacted Ally suggesting they travelled to Illyria together, they soon found their original affection for each other transcended the impasse. After greeting each other at the bus stop with tactical rather than necessary apologies, Cal's name had been declared off limits and the old camaraderie quickly renewed.

For three-quarters of an hour, over nibbles and the choice of either Maggy's powerful Festival punch or lemonade, everyone got chatting. Once the food was ready, Jamie happily relayed the slightly burnt offerings on paper plates to the other guests.

Maggy artfully arranged for the people who didn't know each other to carry out tasks that would help break the ice. Thus, Fiona and Senga handed round the trays of pre-prepared salads and baked potatoes, whilst Maggy took Ally under her wing and delegated her to ensure everyone's drinks were kept topped-up.

Some minutes later in the kitchen, Lorna, who'd been given responsibility for dispensing cutlery and paper napkins, quickly updated Maggy on Ally's progress, and the Ewan-Ally situation. Indeed, she'd observed that Ewan and Ally greeted each other with a slight caginess. Fortunately, it turned out that Fiona's best friend lived in St Andrews, and probably knew her parents, which they could see made Ally feel more at home.

Good food and drink having lowered everyone's guard, by the time people were contemplating second helpings, the facile introductory chatter had developed into earnest discussion.

Maggy was adept at getting to know people without appearing to interrogate them. It was simple: she was fascinated by them. That communicated itself and, usually, encouraged them to open up. She discussed the food and beverage industry with Senga and won Ally over by wanting to learn more about Flora MacDonald. Ally was warm but tentative – like a faulty sports car currently only up to shop runs. But as Lorna had warned her of Ally's appalling experiences. Maggy tried to see through the reserve to the person she once was.

Her first impression of Senga was of someone who was serious-minded and probably very reliable.

And Jamie?

With the fruit pavlovas finally reduced to a few white crumbs and creamy red and purple scrapings, the guests split into two conversational groups. Jamie and Ewan were sitting on their own on a bench close to a small round table. Jamie was making friends with a floppy Garibaldi, whilst Ewan looked on, amused. Maggy poured boiling water into a small cafetière before joining them with her tray of drinks, pulling up a seat by their table.

Ewan had told Maggy the bare facts about Jamie but it was still a shock to see him in the flesh and accept the full nature of their relationship. Personality-wise, he was so very different from Paige – and not just because he was a man. In an instant, Maggy's perception of her son changed. She hadn't, of course, let this show when she'd warmly embraced Jamie on arrival. Or thought she hadn't. But Ewan had watched his mother, struggling with her composure, as she too, fell under Jamie's spell.

'So, have you always lived in Edinburgh?' Maggy asked him.

'Yes. My parents were both law students. They met at a boozy uni party in the early Eighties. Dad was supported by the Jamaican government at college, but after he got his degree, was obliged to return home. It was either that or having to find the colossal sum to reimburse it, which was beyond his means.'

'Your poor mother!' Maggy said.

'I suppose he could have married her and taken her back with him to Montego Bay, but...' Jamie paused and gave Maggy a wry look.

'Between ourselves,' Jamie went on, 'whilst my arrival wasn't due to a one-night stand, neither had my parents ever been, well, exactly inseparable. I think Dad quietly sighed with relief.'

Maggy could see the idea of leaving Scotland and bringing up a small child on a Caribbean island with a man with whom she'd only had a brief affair might not be on the woman's agenda either.

'Do you ever see him?'

'They kept in touch, in the early days. Finances permitting, we enjoyed occasional visits in both directions. I remember a wonderful holiday with Dad the summer I turned six. He was such a cheerful person...'

'That's who you get it from,' Ewan interrupted.

'We had a lot of fun and both got on very well. Not long after, he married again and I acquired three half-brothers and two half-sisters in fairly quick succession. So no, sadly, I've yet to see them, but have promised myself a holiday in Jamaica one of these days.'

'I've offered to go with him,' Ewan interjected.

Jamie smiled, and – as he thought – unobtrusively placed his hand on top of Ewan's.

Trying not to notice over the low table, Maggy looked casually away as if at a passing butterfly, catching the eye of Ally who was sitting at a table opposite the others, who were now deep in discussion. Falconry didn't especially interest Ally and allowed her to take advantage of her direct view of Ewan and Jamie. Maggy saw that she, too, had observed this spontaneous display of affection.

The women exchanged knowing smiles, before Maggy returned to the men. 'Go on,' she said.

'It wasn't Dad's fault the connection almost got lost,' Jamie said. 'When I was eighteen, Mum met a lecturer in Mechanical Engineering, and decided on a clean break. Hal had a good job in North Sea Oil. They settled in Aberdeen, and still live there – although the industry is shrinking now.'

'Fairly convenient to get to, anyway?' Maggy suggested.

'It would be, if… Well, let's just say I enjoy a courteous relationship with my stepfather, and rub along passably enough with Steve, my half-brother. But it's an ultra-macho world up there. I don't have much in common with any of them.'

What Jamie omitted to say was that Hal always gave off more than a whiff of homophobia and racism. Sadly, he had transferred this to Steve.

Later, when everyone had left and she'd finished tidying up, Maggy collapsed on to the sofa, tired but warmed by the after-glow of what she thought had been a successful afternoon. It had felt good being in charge again and reassuming a sort of matriarchal role, if not quite at the Lady Bracknell level. Here an image of Doris, in full sail on a Beardsley-inspired set, nostalgically slipped into her head. She laughed out loud. On the opposite corner of the sofa, Garibaldi glanced at her questioningly. He'd certainly enjoyed the party.

What a stimulating group of new people had joined the fringe of her life! Only the presence of Grace, Duncan and the twins would have made the day, and her peace of mind, complete.

Oh, that it could have been possible.

What would Don have made of Jamie, Ally and Senga, Maggy wondered? In days gone by, an event like that would have been followed by a frank post-mortem as they snacked on leftovers, fuelled by the contents of near-empty bottles of red. How she missed Don to share it with. Lorna would be no doubt on the phone tomorrow for a blow-by-blow analysis, but she trod more carefully with her niece these days. Lorna was sorting out her life too.

Prompted partly by his mother's efforts, the following weekend Ewan finally got around to inviting Gus and Jan over for a light supper. Jan, something of a dabbler in art herself, responded quickly to Jamie and his paintings. The three of them enjoyed exchanging anecdotes about local artists.

Maybe it was because he felt somewhat left out but, whilst Gus was very courteous to Jamie, he also came across as a little guarded. Despite Gus's initial problems adjusting to Jamie's new domestic set-up, the evening went off well enough for a return match to be mooted, although Ewan was still uncertain if his old friend had tumbled to the fact they were more than flatmates.

'*She* knew,' Jamie said later, as they washed up the glasses, 'and was happy for you. And if he hadn't guessed already, he'd certainly have found out before the car pulled into their driveway.'

Which left Ewan and, he suspected, Gus fearing there was work to be done on their relationship. Sometimes, of course, you had to let go of once-best friends when one of you moved into territory the other found uncongenial. But both were patient men. Hopefully they would work things out, especially as their partners had got on well.

A few days later, Lorna thoughtfully nibbled her sandwich in the library. It was unusually quiet. She enjoyed her working lunches alone in her office, catching up on her private emails – and contemplating. Through the glass partition she could make out Ally, perched on a stepladder, returning several large books to a shelf headed Biographies: Eighteenth Century.

Lorna watched Ally find a gap for what, she recognised from its cover, was a book about Scottish politicians during The Enlightenment. The approaching Referendum had made many Scots more curious about their history. Short-term, that might have a beneficial impact on the public library service, but sadly, the role of this facility was, increasingly, becoming a struggle to justify. Would she still have a job in a few years' time?

As for Lorna's personal life, she'd initially surprised her normally even-handed self by feeling piqued when Ewan had muscled in on her friendship with Ally – despite having introduced them. But after a shaky start, a certain equilibrium had, hopefully, been established between them all.

Much as the quality of her day-to-day life had improved with Ally's arrival, Lorna was increasingly learning to value Senga too. That friendship would be a slow-burner, yet, once fully given, she sensed Senga's loyalty would be irreversible.

Lorna reflected on how Ewan, Ally, Senga and even herself, in different ways, were all on journeys. Life, after all, was a voyage of self-discovery. It was simply that, over these past few months, the discoveries had been more intense than usual. Lorna considered they had individually navigated their routes with some success.

The new friends were slowly sailing towards a harbour where they might companionably dock for a while. Sooner or later one or two might drift off in other directions but, for now, they needed each other.

৵৵

THIRTY-ONE

Major Breakthrough

MOPPING out a shower room at the Milan Clinic gave Dino plenty of time to reflect on his switchback fortunes.

Thanks to his father's intervention and the help of an expensive lawyer, Dino had been cleared of criminal activity at the investigatory stage of the money-laundering case. It turned out that he'd accidentally stumbled into a large web of corruption and helped the authorities throw a net over a team they'd been investigating for a long while. For years to come the leaders of the notorious group would practise their manipulative skills only within the federal constraints of San Vittore.

With Maggy not pressing charges in Scotland, it hadn't taken much to persuade the judge that Dino had been a foolish victim of his own naiveté – but not a felon. Sadly though, the unintentional help he'd given the police initially failed to turn him into a hero either.

The family kept telling him how he had besmirched the good name of Piedi Bei, his father demanding he complete two weeks' voluntary community service to demonstrate the company's integrity to the outside world.

Dino's real punishment was being condemned to remain at home, working for the family firm until he'd substantially repaid his defence costs. That would take for ever. He'd be old and grey before he could finally escape his parents' clutches.

Mercifully, Dino's story provided the local press with short-lived fodder. The story was soon toppled from the headlines by a lurid bedroom scandal in high political circles. When it comes to popular journalism, prurience can sometimes be more profitable than racketeering.

Dino wasn't the first, and certainly wouldn't be the last, dupe of the mafia's machinations, although it had been uncomfortable learning that Marcello, a not-so innocent suspect, was to be tried at a higher level of justice. At least it would keep him out of mischief – and Stefania's bed – for a considerable time.

As for Beige Man, since arriving back on Italian tarmac he'd vanished off the face of the earth. Maybe literally. Was he lying very low – possibly under another bituminous surface – who knew? Dino wasn't motivated to investigate. Strange were the ways of organised crime in Italy, leaving the state, with one arm pinned behind its back unable, or unwilling, to discourage it.

Then, just when Dino was at his lowest ebb, his luck changed. One afternoon whilst helping the nurses serve bowls of clam pasta to patients, an orderly had appeared, excitedly clutching the latest edition of *Oggi* open at a double-spread feature of Dino's recent shoe designs. Having, over the past month, been too busy avoiding a jail sentence to give much time to marketing his own work, Dino could only guess as to how the material had fallen into the editor's hands.

The family were quick to pounce on this piece of luck which helped counteract the embarrassment of the earlier revelations. More importantly for Dino, it finally recognised the extent of his talent. But, although *Oggi* had given him a head start, if the exquisite shoes featured in the article were to strut onto any spring catwalks, they'd have to be produced post-haste by the firm's battalion of skilled craftspeople.

The odour surrounding Dino at family mealtimes evaporated even quicker when an up-and-coming starlet happened to cross her shapely black-booted legs on an early evening chat-show.

Interest in the footwear soared.

Dino's father even allowed him to brand himself *Dino a Piedi Bei.*

Thanks to an excellent marketing team, the power of television, Twitter, and the subtle seasoning a dash of notoriety can give to self-publicity, boots with a hint of early nineteenth-century elegance became one of the season's must-have fashion accessories amongst the well-to-do, arty set.

The hours Dino had spent in the Scottish galleries and surfing in Starbucks on the Lothian Road were finally paying off.

The flat was due to be boarded up any day now. Paolo was packing away the last of his belongings in preparation for moving out, when he received a cheering text from Dino with a photograph attached.

It was doubtful if even Paolo's magpie brain embraced a sufficiently good working knowledge of Scottish period portraiture to discern a stylistic connection between Dino's shiny boots and those worn by Major James Lee Harvey in Sir Henry Raeburn's painting.

But he knew someone who'd adore them.

Due to move the next day into the flat of an attractive redhead he'd met at an Italian folk dancing event, Paolo couldn't afford such a costly thankyou for taking pity on him.

Maybe, though, bearing in mind the weeks of hospitality he'd given his old friend Dino, a little subtle encouragement might persuade him to send her a pair?

∞∂∞

THIRTY-TWO

Referendum

∽๛∾

THE masks, bells and drums were packed away; the performers had trundled off.

The atmosphere in the city, electric throughout the Festival, had mellowed with the fading applause as the cooler evenings announced the tail-end of summer.

Early September usually brought consolation with crisp, gilded mornings and the promise of a serene autumn – the gentlest and prettiest season of the Scottish calendar. Serenity, however, was an optimistic dream that year. The amiability and creativity of a month's artistic endeavour – this year with a strong vein of political comment – may have receded, but left behind an edginess as the country geared itself up for voting day on Thursday 18th.

Feelings ran highest in Glasgow where, early polls suggested, there was the greatest number of people wishing to break away from the rest of the UK. Even so, everyone was aware of some tension in the predominantly Remain capital.

Courteous and civilised as most people still appeared on the outside, you could never be sure if your next-door neighbour, the person sitting opposite you on the bus – or even members of your own family – were on the same political wavelength as yourself. Before, this wouldn't have much mattered. Suddenly, it did.

Everyone was taking sides like children at an inter-house match. As the campaigning increased and the polls, which had once indicated *it will never happen* were now hinting *maybe it could*, the result had ceased being just an interesting topic to discuss half-jokingly over Americanos in Hendersons. Opinions were now more divisive and feelings running high.

The romantic in Maggy had often led her to fantasise about being married to a soldier at the time of *Gone with the Wind*. Or was she simply drawn to the uniforms and crinolines? This, though, wasn't quite civil war – was it? That period of hostility had become decidedly bloody. Nevertheless, she'd been shaken to hear how two of Jamie's friends in Fife had come home to find their car window smashed in for having an *In* – or was it an *Out*? – sticker advertising their preference over that of many locals. Latterly, too, there had been physical skirmishes and noisy demonstrations.

Gordon Brown had spoken passionately of how a *Yes* vote could leave Scotland a poorer and more unequal country. The United Kingdom had *'proved to be the most successful partnership in history.'* Nice man, Gordon, if somewhat dour – like many decent, uncharismatic politicians, destined to have 'Meant Well' invisibly carved on their memorial plaques.

A perennial fence-sitter, even if Maggy didn't agree with all the SNP's policies, she couldn't believe the world would come to an end if, or when, independence was declared. It might make it an even better one. Who knew?

In the heady air of expectancy and change, there was a sense that, even if the Remainers won, life after The Referendum would never be *quite* the same. It wouldn't be a once-and-for-all battle. This was simply Round One. Blood of a sort had been spilt. The impetus towards independence would persist, with SNP troops waiting impatiently for the next opportunity to rally their forces.

Maybe the mood of the country was symptomatic of a general sense of unrest, not just in Scotland, but heralding a new order in Western politics. If Scotland, as seemed a serious possibility, elected to leave the UK, what next? For a while there had been rumblings down in Westminster about breaking away from Europe.

Surely that could never happen?

The restless atmosphere had begun to affect Maggy as much as everyone else. It would soon be eighteen months since Don's death. What did they say: it took two years to get over the loss of a loved one? Maggy recognised her recent flight into unreality had, nonetheless, provided a bridge to greater self-awareness. Now on the brink of her own Referendum, she knew that once the national votes had been counted, she must make some difficult decisions about her future.

And draw up her own manifesto.

Health issues pushed Maggy further towards the self-negotiating table when an MRI scan revealed mild osteoarthritis. At least she'd been spared the crippling form of the disease her mother had endured. At present, it was only in her feet, but would need therapy and regular exercise to discourage more serious trouble.

The best reason for staying in the large house was to keep herself active. Cleaning and gardening with the implied bending, reaching, climbing, and pushing-and-pulling, all helped keep her trim and mobile. But was that a strong enough consideration? Maggy attended a Pilates class and was thinking of re-joining her dance class, too. She had even persuaded Una to go swimming with her – when she wasn't swanning around foreign parts.

Maggy's health, however, was only one aspect of the wider picture. Don was gone. Ewan and Grace had been away from home for many years. Did she really need to keep rattling around in this large house with all its rooms? She could employ a cleaner of course, someone to chat and have a cuppa with twice a week. But, shouldn't she accept the time had now come to sell up and let some other family enjoy Illyria's homely magic? Sadly, it was less a home any more; simply – as the song went – a *house*.

Wouldn't it make sense to trade in Illyria for a cosy, easy-to-maintain mews flat? It would allow her to release what was left over of his money and divide it up 40-40-20 between Ewan, Grace, and Lorna. She'd retain a selection of the furniture, pictures, and ornaments for her new home, and let the rest of them take what they wanted from what was left.

The more Maggy thought about it, the more a change of environment seemed a sensible plan. Only reproachful vibes from the grassy plot across the way discouraged her from contacting an estate agent. She simply needed the courage to do something about it.

After weeks of accelerating hysteria, the outcome of the Referendum created a sense of anti-climax. Whether or not one rejoiced or despaired on the morning of Friday 19th September when the bubble burst, it left behind a soggy mess.

Maggy decided it was time to tackle some outstanding tasks at home. Although they'd long since moved away, Ewan and Grace's residual clutter – not to mention the steady accumulation of her own cast-offs and unwanted presents – still sat forgotten in disused cupboards and drawers.

Maggy had yet to rationalise Don's intimate possessions too. When he died only his clothes had been sent to charity.

There was a mahogany filing cabinet containing his private papers and mementos in the den. A dreary piece of old office furniture, it gave the room the shabby look of a Raymond Chandler detective agency. She half-expected a tweedy bespectacled secretary to bustle in clutching hand-typed papers fastened with treasury tags.

After a frustrating search, Maggy finally located a ring of what looked like luggage keys hidden in a drawer amongst old penknives and discarded cracker gifts. One was sure to fit.

One did.

Turning the key in the resistant hole, the three heavy drawers, slightly swollen after many years standing next to the window, gave way to her persistent pulling.

The dividers had been removed from inside. The first drawer mainly contained old photograph albums. A set of studio-posed pictures, showed Doris and Archie and their families outside the kirk at their wedding in the harsh winter of 1947, sunny smiles barely concealing the shivers beneath austerity finery.

There were books of monochrome snaps: seaside holidays in Skye, Elie and Portpatrick with people she didn't recognise – and later ones, in colour, some of whom she did. Then, Don in his school uniform, in fancy dress; camping, sailing; holding aloft a badminton trophy.

The second drawer held battered ring files, too tired now to fully grip Don's essays from the Sixth Form through to his BSc days. Golf club minutes, conference papers and published contributions to professional journals slid out of brittle plastic folders.

Maggy was so engrossed in an article entitled *How to Sell to the Uninitiated*, never having fully appreciated Don's flair with words, it was only as the grandfather downstairs chimed noon she realised how the time was drifting away – and there was still the bottom drawer to go. She scooped up several bundles of letters, the once-elastic bands disintegrating in her fingers as she separated them.

Don had saved all her correspondence from the *Cold Turkey* period. That touched her. There were also years of postcards Maggy assumed had been thrown away after their allotted time on the kitchen noticeboard. Fancy him saving them. It was odd finding out many, often trivial things, about the person with whom you'd shared your life.

And not so trivial, as she was about to discover.

Finally, two clumps of correspondence remained: letters Doris and Archie had sent Don over the three years he was at St Andrews and, lurking in a corner of the drawer, a handful of pale coloured envelopes with complementary tissue paper linings, addressed in a small but round, childish hand with an Edinburgh postmark. The date stamps, where she could decipher them, began in late October 1993 and ended early in February 1994.

Almost five months.

With some apprehension, Maggy prised the first notelet from its pink envelope moorings. The letter inside had a cute marmalade kitten in the top left corner and the address *Mon Repos, Golden Boughs* on the right.

Sunday

Darling Don

Thank you for ringing the other evening before you left work. I know how difficult it must have been for you finding a quiet moment when no one was around, and you had to be quick. Not a problem you usually have, eh?

Icy prickles bullied Maggy's flesh.

I'll always treasure those few days we had together in London. When I'm low – which is quite often when I get back here after a day at the office, seeing you but unable to get close enough even to squeeze your arm – at least I have those wonderful memories. Memories of us, tucked-up, feeling your soft chest hair in my fingers. Yours greedily searching for my...

On the word 'greedily', Maggy felt nauseous. She looked again. The letter was signed:

Your always loving, Jennie

Jennie McPherson: the butcher's girl. The one he'd dismissed with a guffaw. They'd both laughed over her pathetic infatuation.

Another notelet penned a few weeks later, thanked him:

... for arranging my transfer to Mr Baldwin. Lucky he was on the lookout for someone reliable. Just as well he doesn't know <u>how</u> reliable, tee-hee! Anyway, it's safer not being together, and will let me concentrate better on my work. And I've this lovely feeling knowing you're not far away...

Clive Baldwin had been Don's finance director in the adjoining office. Jennie would have been able to see Don through the glass partitions that separated the two rooms.

So, he'd lied about 'sending her packing' too.

The bastard.

Why had Jennie felt the need to send these letters when she and Don saw each other each day? She pictured the girl curled up on a candlewick bedspread in her single bedroom, sucking the end of her biro and wondering what to write.

So, Jennie had been badly smitten. But could she not have found other ways of meeting men? Had living at home with Mum and Dad precluded such opportunities?

One letter recounted her literary tastes and the heady delights of *Love on Prescription* by Sharon Opal, 'a health centre receptionist's thwarted affair with a married GP.' Jennie equated it with her own star-crossed romance.

Silly woman.

Another epistle spilled over on to a sheet of A4. Recurring references included the poignancy of the current plots in *Brookside*. Jennie, apparently, never missed an episode.

Maggy knew who she'd have buried under the patio – preferably alive.

Had Don reciprocated, Maggy wondered? Was there a stack of replies mouldering away in an old chocolate box somewhere, tied up with ribbon?

Red ribbon? Blue ribbon? *Yellow…*

No, *no*, *NO!*

That was their colour. That was sacred. Or was it now? The letters fell from her hands and scattered over the floor.

Hurrying downstairs with a sodden handkerchief in her hand, Maggy poured herself a large drink and fell into a chair, where she remained staring into space for almost an hour, her thoughts and feelings fermenting. Had her whole marriage been a masquerade – or was she being melodramatic? Had drama been the problem? Not that she was temperamental but had Don sometimes found her, once outgoing, personality too much to deal with and turned to other, less exhausting, women for stillness and solace?

Most wives, she supposed, must wonder how they would behave on discovering their husbands were unfaithful. She too, hadn't been so naïve as, when occasionally catching Don surreptitiously eyeing up an attractive woman, not to have rehearsed her own reactions to just such a situation.

'What would you do if you discovered Ben was seeing someone else?' she'd once asked Una.

'Och, scream the place down, banish him to his club, change the locks, cut up his suits, abuse the joint credit card. The usual cliché things.'

'And, after putting him, yourself and the kids through hell for a week?'

'Wear a martyred air, keep him on tenterhooks. Grudgingly, have a long talk. Ultimately divorce proceedings if it was serious.''

'But if it was just a seventeen-year itch?'

'Settle for SALT.'

'Sorry?'

'Strategic arms limitation.'

Twenty years. And she'd never had any idea of this betrayal. What really hurt was the way Don had referred to Jennie as a joke. Was that the truth? Had he simply taken advantage of her because he'd been desperate for release? A one-off coupling that had started with too many glasses of wine and ended up with 'Christ, is that the time?'

Maggy recalled she was forty-four that winter. Her body had been playing up. Aware that an early menopause might be on the cards, her GP had allayed her fears and given her an iron deficiency tonic. She had gradually recovered. Sure, she'd been off-colour and not as demonstrative as usual. But enough to trigger infidelity? Or, had they at that point in their marriage, sometimes not made enough time for each other?

Had she made the fatal mistake of taking Don for granted?

Maggy was reminded how many happy times had played out since this… intrigue… glitch? … whatever, had passed her by.

Another nasty thought occurred to her. How had Don portrayed her to Jennie? As some control freak or jokey music hall harridan?

An ageing Paige sprang to mind.

She shuddered.

What bothered Maggy most was Don's reasons for holding on to the letters at all. The cabinet was private and kept locked. Had he intended her to one day come across them as a nasty post-grave slap, wanting to posthumously reveal that their marriage hadn't always been as perfect as she liked to think? Scouring her memory, Maggy couldn't remember a time Don had ever been spiteful. Surely it couldn't be that.

Alas, now he was no longer around for her to interrogate, vent her anger on or even laugh about it all over again. Nor could anyone else put her mind at rest. Maggy had always got on well with the Baldwins, but they were some years older and had long since retired to the Dordogne. What good would it have done, anyway? Supposing they'd simply looked terribly embarrassed. How would she have coped?

Maybe, Maggy thought, Don had regretted his behaviour almost as soon as it had started, found Jennie hard to fob off and fed her a sanitised version of the episode to put her off the scent?

Her compelling need to make some sense of it all drove Maggy fruitlessly on. Gripped by the notelets' gruesome fascination, she re-read them one more time, searching for the smallest clue as to the absurdity of the episode, trying to believe that Jennie was a fantasist.

For all her lurid prose, it had been short and one-sided. Hadn't it?

She would never know.

Maggy had to hit the bottom of the pit before she could allow herself to climb back up. Only after three days of jumbled, largely negative emotions did she finally start to see Jennie, not as an unbridled femme fatale, but as lonely and not overly bright, clutching at foolish, romantic straws.

But as much sinned against as sinning?

What had Jennie taken away from her trysts? Tawdry memories of nights in anonymous hotels with unreliable men, already in long-term relationships? Stolen kisses at the office when everyone had gone home; furtive fellatio crouched over a swivel chair with the blinds down on the Friday evenings he was supposedly going to the late-night barber's or 'having a drink with the boys'?

Ugh!

Most likely Don had simply dropped the ridiculous correspondence into the drawer as being safer than a wastepaper basket or dustbin, intending to stuff them in with rubbish awaiting collection somewhere. The fact that he'd, hopefully, forgotten all about it was proof of that. Wasn't it?

She clung to that.

Something soft brushed Maggy's leg. She looked down and stroked Garibaldi's head. He purred. She usually spoilt him with something around this time of day. Someone still needed her for something.

Treats.

She wished.

It was only half a sleeping tablet but it did the trick.

Now, Maggy was relaxing in the country with Ewan and Grace. It must have been almost thirty years earlier. They were still children, playing catch a few yards away, with Don and herself happily propped up against a sturdy oak trunk. In between sips of wine they discussed what new interests the children might develop as adolescence beckoned.

An inquisitive lamb strayed from its mother and wandered to within a few feet of the picnic rug, and the remains of their lunch. Ewan and Grace noticed, interrupted their game and tiptoed cautiously towards the creature, gently persuading it to reverse direction.

The lamb ignored them and carried on. Bleating excitedly, it headed straight for the Tupperware and the last few lettuce leaves.

A very loud baa was followed by the heavy thud of hooves on plastic.

Cutlery, crockery, and glassware scattered.

Grace shouted '*No!*'

Maggy awoke with a giggle on her lips, totally at peace with the world. Then she remembered Jennie and Don and her body tensed up, awaiting the inevitable harsh descent.

Strangely, it failed to arrive.

Certainly, as the light and sounds of a new day pulled her fully back to consciousness, any levity lingering from her nostalgic dream disappeared; yet her black dog, even if he was still busying himself not far away, was no longer padding around the bed demanding attention either. When ten minutes had elapsed, heading for the shower, she still found herself, if not at peace with the world, feeling less negative. She accepted that her brain had at least created a temporary healing patch.

Over the next few days her mental attitude grew stronger. Naturally, there were lapses when her emotions kept switching gear between calmness, annoyance – and even self-reproach. She wondered if she was being shallow when she heard herself debating whether she should allow Don the benefit of the doubt, and carried on with her everyday routine, assuming her usual bright smile for neighbours and shopkeepers.

As she'd once told her father, 'it's called acting.'

The days passed. Maggy's brightness became less and less forced as, increasingly, the good memories reasserted themselves over the bad. Reason smoothed over the uglier cracks of her doubt like an indulgent aunt calming a wayward child. There were unanswered questions in any life, she told herself.

So, Don hadn't been a plaster saint. In a perverse way that let her off the hook for her own infidelities – even if hers had been imagined and indulged when he was no longer around. Did it, though, make them any the less potent? Whatever. She'd been trying for eighteen months now to release his control on her and now, from beyond the grave, he'd done the job himself.

Finally, in the late dusk of the seventh day, Maggy impulsively decided to dead-head the last of the roses in the back garden before the light completely went. Outside was clear and fine. Pausing to survey the familiar view, she gazed beyond the well-maintained back lawn to the now tired rose arch and herb garden beyond. She collected her trug and secateurs from the shed and set to.

When Maggy looked up, a vivacious girl of around twenty caught her eye. She was sitting arrogantly cross-legged on the white wrought iron bench a few feet away: smart yet nonconformist in faded blue jeans, one embroidered rear pocket peeked up to reveal the side of a spotted red toadstool. A light brown suede jacket hung around her shoulders over a black roll-necked jumper.

Staring intently at Maggy for a few moments, the girl smiled mischievously and raised a knowing eyebrow.

'*Screw you Sven!*' she said. *I've a life to lead. I'll be fine on my own. It's not as if you've been around much recently anyway, strung out high on that cloud of yours where no one can reach you.*'

Then.

Light years.

Now.

The first sharp breeze of autumn caught Maggy's cheek. A cloud momentarily passed over the emerging moon, draining any lingering light from the sky.

The girl vanished.

Maggy threw the dead rose heads onto the compost heap, put away her gardening equipment and took a final look over the now fast-darkening garden. Lights from neighbouring homes flirted with her through the swaying boughs.

The clocks would soon be going back. There would be Christmas to plan. Maybe this year would be jollier than last, and she could invite everyone over. And if she got a move on and rang that estate agent, it could even be a house-warming party. What was stopping her?

And where was that letter from the BBC?

Half an hour later Maggy was buttering a couple of Ryvitas when her mobile rang.

'Mum?'

'Grace!'

'I'm sorry to bother you, but…'

Taken off guard, Maggy immediately picked up the strained tone in her daughter's voice.

'It's what I'm here for.'

'…I'm so worried.'

'Oh, Grace,' she said. 'Tell me.'

'It's Kara. She's been running a terribly high temperature all evening and is very distressed. Lyndsay doesn't understand and wants to help her and can't, and...'

'The doctor?'

'The surgery's shut, or I wouldn't have disturbed you. And Duncan's in Adelaide...'

'*Adelaide*?'

'...I'll explain later... Vicky's in the Canaries, and...' Grace paused as supressed tears pushed through her anxiety. 'I... I haven't a clue what to do. You were the only person I could think of.'

In any other situation, Maggy would have panicked, but Grace's scared voice acted on her like balm. She'd never wanted to be a last resort so much as now.

'I'll be there as soon as I can.'

The Audi having been sold, she rang her old cab firm. She now had ten minutes to tidy herself up before the man arrived. She grabbed a dated paperback *Childcare: The First Five Years* to consult on the journey.

When Grace opened the door twenty minutes later, Maggy saw from her rumpled hair and haggard face how concerned she was. Tiredness highlighted incipient signs of middle-age. Why wasn't Duncan there? It occurred to her that Grace was only a few years away from the age she had been when Jennie McPherson had, unknowingly, entered their lives. Maggy shivered and told herself not to go there. Giving her daughter a quick kiss, she followed Grace upstairs.

'Hello, Grannie,' Lyndsay called out from her bunk through the open door of the girls' bedroom.

'Hello Lyndsay.'

'Is Kara going to die?'

'Of course not. Give me five minutes and I'll come and tuck you in.'

Kara was lying flushed but drowsy on the spare room bed. Grace said, 'I think it's starting to ease off a bit.'

'Her temperature?'

'102 when it started. I flipped, I'm afraid.'

'I'd have done the same.'

'I checked on the NHS site and, fortunately, we had some children's paracetamol in the cupboard. I gave her the recommended dose.'

'Has she been drinking plenty of water?'

'As much as I could persuade her to.'

'Good. Let's try with the thermometer again.'

Kara's temperature seemed to have miraculously dropped. It

wasn't normal yet but getting there.

'It happens, I'm afraid,' Maggy said. 'They scare the living daylights out of you, then the fever seems to leave them almost as quickly as it arrived.'

'That's more or less what the website said.'

'What have they been doing today?'

'I took them for their vaccinations.'

'That's the culprit no doubt. I'm surprised they didn't warn you and tell you what to do.'

'Fridays are manic,' Grace said. 'you know what it's like in health centres. They'd have assumed I knew.'

Maggy was aware this was no time to remonstrate.

After a soothing chat, cuddling a favourite toy penguin and her Gruffalo duvet drawn around her, sleep finally overwhelmed Kara.

'You pop in and keep your promise to Lyndsay, whilst I put the kettle on,' Grace said. 'Or I've half a bottle of Pinot Grigio cooling in the fridge?'

'A glass of the house white sounds a plan right now!' Maggy needed a boost. 'It's strange Lyndsay wasn't affected in the same way.'

'She was a little warm earlier, but not nearly as much as Kara.'

Maggy reassured Lyndsay that her sister was on the mend, sharing with her the picture-book tale of a friendly alien – star-shaped eyes – who had adventures with his girlfriend – petal-shaped eyes – on a forgotten planet. It wasn't long before all the excitement caught up with the other twin, who also drifted off.

The two women were now alone. Sitting silently and sipping the wine, Maggy, having abandoned her Ryvitas at home, was grateful for the nuts and crisps Grace produced. Munching gave them a few moments to collect their thoughts. The crisis over, the two women were at last obliged to turn the conversation to other matters.

As usual it was left for Maggy to initiate things. 'Adelaide then?'

'Yes. we've been meaning to tell you. Although, as Duncan pointed out, it's really my job…'

The whole story came out: Grace's initial shock when Duncan had told her about Sam's proposal, and how, after careful consideration and much discussion, she'd seen the upside to creating distance between the miserable time they had been through recently – not 'she', Maggy noted, but 'they'. She hoped that several months or even longer, spent somewhere very different from Edinburgh, might recharge all their batteries.

In as matter-of-fact way as possible, Grace explained to Maggy how they were swapping homes with Bob and his family. He and his wife had a boy and two girls a few years older than the twins. Bob and Amy and co would be squeezing into their home whilst they'd be taking over the house in Medindie, a suburb of Adelaide.

'Would it be all right if we gave them your number in case they need any advice on living in Edinburgh?'

'Of course.' My, Maggy thought, that was a turn-up for the books.

Grace told her how Duncan had gone on ahead to get everything ready, the plan being for them to join him in a couple of weeks' time.

Maggy gasped. 'So soon?'

'All this… today,' Grace vaguely indicated a couple of dolls on a chair, 'it completely freaked me out.'

'I understand.'

'The weekend will be spent sorting things out and deciding what to take with us.'

Maggy tried desperately not to show how hurt she was at being informed about this, potentially, life-changing move so late in the day. If there hadn't been the crisis over Kara, the family might have vanished without her ever knowing. She may not see much of them now – but Australia! When Grace added, 'And if we like it out there and find Duncan's eligible to apply for any suitable vacancies…' her heart skipped a beat and a lump came into her throat.

'Something's not been right for some time,' Grace continued, seemingly unaware of her mother's anguish. 'It sounds the perfect place to bring up the girls.'

'Uncle Fraser and his family, of course, live in Sydney.'

'Yes. Except that's about as far from Adelaide as John O'Groats is from Lands End.'

'I can believe. But it's a contact for you at any rate, should you feel the need… And hopefully you'll get a chance to travel.'

'Hopefully,' Grace echoed crisply.

As always, it was no use persuading Grace to pursue anything she didn't want to. It had to be her idea. For Grace, the connection with her uncle was remote and not a matter of much interest.

Maggy downed her wine faster than she'd intended. Grace offered to top it up, but she was already starting to feel light-headed and confused. They continued chatting about the practicalities of the exchange, treading warily around the outsize elephant in the room.

When they'd run out of obvious things to say, all that had been side-stepped still hanging over them, Maggy wearily rang for her cab. She reckoned there was a maximum of twenty minutes before it arrived. To kill time, Grace showed Maggy photographs of their temporary home in Medindie, and some of Duncan and the girls that she'd taken on recent summer outings. They looked like a normal, happy family getting on with their lives.

After ten minutes and, by now, pressed for time but heartbreakingly conscious that these could be their last moments together – possibly for a very long time – Maggy jumped in and concisely summed up her own plans: her intention to sell the house and sort out some of the financial muddle Don had left behind. She said that, if truth be told, his will had made quite good sense at the time, but he'd never left any accompanying note explaining his thinking for Ewan and herself, which she regretted.

Grace appeared to accept the information without comment and even managed the flicker of an enigmatic smile.

As the seconds ticked by, Maggy realised that what was probably their last chance to resolve the Dino/Facebook episode was slipping away. She had spent the past half hour toying with the idea of coming out with 'is there anything you'd like to say whilst I'm here?' but the memory of the blouse incident all those years ago held her back.

She sensed there were similar thoughts in Grace's mind too, but both knew that they'd probably gone as far as they could, chatting pleasantly together and allowing each other to accept the subtext. Maybe the events of the last hour had been a way of enabling her daughter to go off into the blue feeling somewhat better about herself. It was the way things were between them. Meaningful discussion could only lead to anger and that would ruin whatever small degree of openness had been achieved.

Chimes announced the arrival of her cab. Grace fetched Maggy's coat, helped her in to it and briefly embraced her. Not a long, lingering, loving squeeze, but a hug all the same.

'Thank you for dropping everything and coming over. It helped a lot,' she said.

'Glad to. You'll always be my daughter,' Maggy said. We don't always get on, but I care a lot about you, you know.'

'Yes, I know.' Grace replied, in a measured way, with that awkward grin again.

Maggy had to be content with that.

Grace watched her mother walk down the path and get into the car. Maggy waved to her through the window – a wave briskly returned – as the engine revved up and the cab moved off.

As she looked through the car window, Maggy saw Grace firmly shut the front door without looking back. Then she glimpsed the corner of a curtain on the first floor drawn back, a pudgy hand frantically waving.

Maggy returned Lyndsay's farewell until the car rounded the corner and sped away. Would she ever see the house and her granddaughters again?

Arriving back at Illyria, Maggy poured herself a very small glass of Johnny Walker, despatched her long-delayed cheese and biscuits and put on her favourite Seventies compilation.

She sat back on the sofa, overcome by a mixture of sadness and reluctant acceptance.

The jaunty strains of Tie a Yellow Ribbon kicked in. The Scotch made friends with the Pinot Grigio. Instead of skipping the track, she found herself listening with cynical amusement. The lyric now resonated with a strange irony.

She let it play on.

Foot Note

❧❧

SITTING on the sofa some weeks later, deciding whether to précis a Helen Dunmore in preparation for the next book group discussion or, after her successful audition, study her script for *Restless Weegies*, Maggy's concentration was broken by an insistent knocking on the front door.

She glanced at her watch. If that was the young couple who'd put in an offer for Illyria, they were an hour early.

Hurrying down the hall, she saw, through the stained-glass panel, the outline of someone clutching something bulky. Maggy wasn't expecting a delivery. What could it be? She opened the door. A jolly young woman stood on the mat outside with a large parcel. Exchanging pleasantries, Maggy signed for it and carried it into the kitchen.

Cutting open the outer wrapping she discovered a large box containing another longish one, beautifully gift-wrapped in white and gold tissue paper along with something heavy but smaller in plain brown paper swathed, she guessed, in layers of bubble-wrap.

She tackled this first. A thick glass jar rolled out with a folded manufacturer's note wrapped around it.

Italian Heather Honey
Gathered from the pollens of heather in Montalcino.
Good for blood circulation and the liver.

It was now well over three months since the garden party at Primrose Bank. Maggy hadn't forgotten Dino. In fact, she'd Googled and scoured the newspapers in the library regularly for the first few weeks, to see if anything more about him had been reported. There was some mention of a trial, but little she didn't already know or had, correctly, guessed.

Whenever she bumped into Banger, he continued to show an almost unhealthy curiosity as to whether Dino had been in touch. 'You're almost as bad about him as I was,' she'd snorted on the last occasion. Although new projects had taken over her life, most days part bitter-sweet, part enchanted memories of the times spent in his company floated to the surface of her mind.

She was recovering from the pleasant shock the arrival of the gift had given her, and was wondering what the box held, when the landline rang. It was Lorna.

'How are things?'

The old mantra kicked in. 'Busy, busy. You know me.' She was holding some cards close to her chest.

After the usual exchange of pleasantries about each other's health, Lorna enquired about Grace and Duncan, now acclimatising themselves to life in Medindie. That didn't take long, as all she'd so far received was a brief email from Duncan saying the family had now joined him safely and liked the house. Maggy wanted to know how things were on the north side of Edinburgh.

'Ally's down in London today to meet an educational publisher.' Ewan's keeping her company. It seems they might be interested in *Jock*.'

'I'm so glad she's getting serious bites, maybe this one will turn into a definite offer,' Maggy said. 'And what about Ewan's contribution?' He rang for chats occasionally, but rarely talked in detail about himself.

'Ally says he's philosophical about whether they use his illustrations or not,' Lorna said, 'although she's still adamant the matter's non-negotiable. We'll see. If they've at least helped catch a publisher's eye they'll have served a useful purpose. I'm sure it'll work out. You've heard that Ewan and Jamie are off to Montego Bay for two weeks at Christmas?

'Then it's definite?'

'Seems so.'

'I'm glad that relationship's bedding down.'

'That's the phrase, I believe.'

'Jamie's so good for Ewan.'

'Indeed. I'm probably speaking out of turn, but you may need to ring your milliner friend Alex Muir before long. There are whispers in the steamie of a possible wedding or whatever. Maybe in the New Year? Oh, and they've been investigating surrogacy too.'

Maggy swallowed hard. Ewan and Jamie had only known each other six months. Was Ewan quite ready for that degree of commitment? Certainly, he'd always been very good with children. Who knew?

'And you?'

There was a moment or two's silence when Maggy wondered if the line had gone dead,

Then Lorna said, 'I'm negotiating to take a sabbatical. Hopefully in a year's time. I'd like to do a PhD.'

'In Edinburgh?'

'New York. Columbia.' As if anticipating the sharp intake of breath that followed, Lorna added 'Don't worry. I can get home in under ten hours for high days and holidays. Ally will look after the flat. I've not been extravagant, and with the rent I get from her, I should just about manage. If it all works out, it would put me in line for a more challenging job. Hopefully, back here.'

'I'm delighted for you.' Maggy said. 'Truly.' Seven months ago, her heart would have hit rock bottom at the thought of yet someone else she cared about leaving her. But she was toughening up ready to move on herself, if not to a different continent – although, she joked to herself, she might soon be spending a lot of time in Glasgow.

Indeed, she was already making new acquaintances and getting back into the swing of rehearsals. She hadn't touched the Scotch bottle for several weeks.

'Have you decided on a theme?'

'I've a year to firm up. So far, my pitch has been *The Effects of Digitalisation on Reading Habits and Retrieval Systems,*' Lorna said.' Whither public libraries etcetera?'

Words like 'digital' and 'retrieval' intimidated Maggy, who was at her happiest curled up with a good old-fashioned paperback. Nonetheless, she said, 'Well done you! Come over for supper one evening next week and we'll have a proper natter. And how's Senga?'

'Nora's swapping the bungalow for a downstairs studio flat. She hopes to be in a position to give Senga some money towards the deposit on a café of her own very soon. One's just become vacant in the Grassmarket. Ally's promised to go in with her. She's bored at the library; without professional qualifications she's stymied from progressing to more challenging jobs and doesn't want to go back to legal work. In the café they'll be their own bosses. The unknown quantity is Cal. His liaison with Paige seems to be floundering somewhat. He's working as a cook at one of those hotels in Princes Street, so at least he's keeping himself.'

'I'm delighted you're all sorting yourselves out.'

Did that sound rather patronising? She didn't mean it to be.

Lorna moved the conversation to a close, jokily enquiring with strange intuition, 'And I've been meaning to ask you, Maggy. Did you ever try that honey I recommended?'

'Yes, Lorna, I did.'

'Did it work?'

'Uh-uh,' she said, 'it worked.'

'You're being enigmatic again.'

'Tell you some time.'

'It's like that, is it?'

'Mm. Have a nice day, hen.'

'You too. Be in touch.'

Click.

One of the things Maggy had kept from Lorna was her own projected move. If truth be known, having finally made up her mind, she'd surprised herself by springing so quickly into action. Now she needed time to reconcile herself to it.

Yes, she thought again, it was the right time to let go of Illyria. At least the house. Once the name of a wild region of the Balkan Peninsula, Shakespeare had purloined it and re-invented it as an idyllic island in the Mediterranean where his characters indulged their mercurial, romantic natures.

For forty years, the imaginary island's namesake had been the bedrock of their family life: the one constant, the safe place they always returned to make love, laugh – and be… mercurial. But it was the laughter one always remembered. Of course, they had all, from time to time, experienced anger, disappointments, periods of self-absorption – and deceit, as her recent excavations had made clear.

Yet, Maggy didn't need a building to remind her of the predominantly good things behind her. Illyria would always be with her, wherever she went. Illyria was also Edinburgh itself, especially around Festival time, when people's imaginations took flight, often coming to rest in unusual places.

Illyria was a state of mind.

She was ready for a new Act; a new set and costumes – maybe even some new cast members.

The box was still sitting on the table. Maggy's eagerness of a few minutes ago to open it had dissolved in the flood of unsettling news and the reverie that had followed.

First, a cuppa.

As she sipped her tea, the October sun smiled through the window and lit up the table. She picked up the package. The smart gold logos on the tissue paper turned out, on closer inspection, to comprise the repeated entwined letters *D, P* and *B*.

Heart in mouth, Maggy unwrapped the paper and, taking off the lid, drew out a pair of the most exquisite navy leather shoes she'd ever seen. Trying them on, the right shoe fitted perfectly, but an incipient bunion on the side of her left foot slightly grazed the side of the other.

They were gorgeous, but…

Och. Would it be awfully rude if…? Could she, dare she send them back to Piedi Bei with a grateful note.

Request half a size larger?

What was she like?

Still…

THE END

⊷⊶

Acknowledgements

I shall always be grateful to Donald Bailey
for suggesting my monologue
Maggy would make a good story.
My sincere thanks also to my partner John Oakenfull and:
Patrick Armstrong, Caroline Auckland, Nicola Beauman, Nicola
Coldstream, Sue Feehan, Lydia Fellgett, Michael Harvey, Lu
Madden, Greg Mosse, Kate Mosse, Di Proctor, Cedric Pulford, Liz
Robins, Barbara Rowlands, David Slattery-Christy,
Joyce Troughton and Sally Wood
for all their help and encouragement.

Cultural References

George Bernard Shaw: *Major Barbara* (1907)
Germaine Greer: *The Female Eunuch (1970)*
Simone de Beauvoir: *The Second Sex (1949)*
Tie a Yellow Ribbon Round the Old Oak Tree by Irwin Levine and L.
Russell Brown *(1973)*
Cole Porter: *Just One of Those Things (1936)*
Gordon Brown: *Pre-Scottish Referendum speech (2014)*
Sir Harold Boulton: *The Skye Boat Song (1870s)*